BLOOD
Of
A FALLEN
GOD

By: Joshua Cook

Published by Joshua Cook

Email us at joshc@adminshift.com

First published in 2019 / First printed in 2019

Dedicated to my family, both my immediate one, and all the far-flung parts that make up my clan. Love to all.

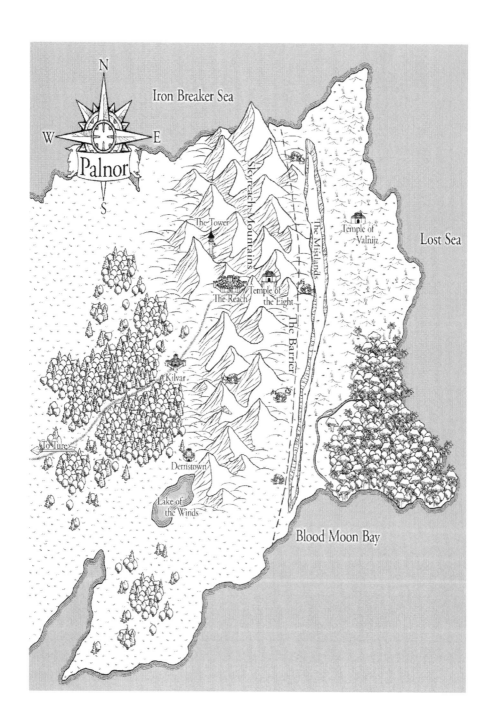

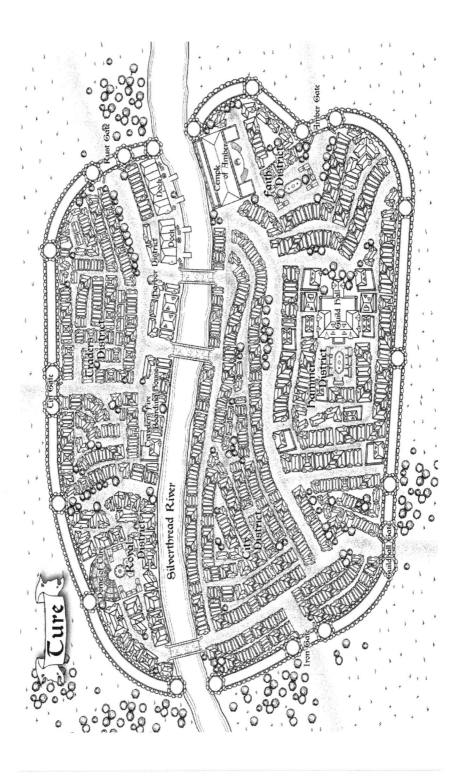

Cure

Let the blacksmith wear the chains he has himself made.

Decimius Magnus Ausonius

Books by Joshua C. Cook

The Echo Worlds

Bridgefinders
Bridgebreaker

Other Books

Project: Perception
Canitus

1.

William Reis hated running. Loose gravel slipped under Will's feet as he scrambled toward the Reach. He wasn't sure if the Valni were still after him, but he wasn't about to stop and look. *Hammer-bound fool,* he repeated to himself with every heavy footfall he took. He'd ventured into the Mistlands for one reason, to take a crystal shard. And he'd succeeded!

The Mistlands held dangers, the deadliest being the Valni. Humans once, people like Will, who, corrupted by the mist that gave the area its name, changed into something else. Now they lived for blood, and flesh. Monsters all, no trace of who they were before remained. Will tripped over a rock and fell forward, only able to stay upright with a huge running step forward, boots hitting hard.

His labored breathing and the stich in his side weren't making this easy. Will's body wasn't made for running. Give him a hammer, an anvil, and a length of steel, and he'd spend hours hammering it into any shape according to his will. Running? No.

Will forced his legs to keep going, and he was sure of the scrambling of the Valni behind him. A hint of a growl or was it a moan carried through the air. Sparks burn it, Duncan was the runner, not him! Duncan had outrun the Valni more than once in his hunt for trinkets and treasures from the ruins that dotted the Skyreach beyond the barrier. The force of each step flew up Will's legs. He winced at the growing pain in his side, and the future pain of his calves and back, assuming he made it to the barrier and lived long enough to feel the effects of this run when it was over.

Ancient wardstones, laid out in a line after the threat of the Valni appeared, would stop the things. They couldn't cross it. Make it to the line. Just that far, he told himself. Make it to the line and he would rest, he could then *breathe*. His breath caught as the cramp in his side moved up his back. His foot slipped on a patch of loose rocks, forcing his movement to slow, and the sound of his pursuers now became clear. The scrabbling of hands and feet on rock. The Valni ran on all fours most of the time, either uncaring or unfeeling the stone cutting into hands and bare feet. William once saw a person caught by the things. They'd stripped the woman of her flesh while she was still alive. Her screams had lasted for a lifetime. Will's own screams took longer to stop that day.

He would not meet her fate, he wasn't that far from the line, he had to make it. With a huge breath, he pushed himself to move faster, holding the small crystal in his hand, saying a silent prayer to a dead god to give him strength.

A wardstone came into view, not even ten cart-lengths ahead. The Valni in the lead howled, sounding far nearer than Will wanted. Nine cart-lengths; eight. Will's skin prickled cold as something touched the back of his leg. A hand! A yell born of fear and loathing erupted from Will as he half ran, half stumbled forward. Seven cart-lengths; six; five. The hand was back again, the breath of the thing behind him, its footfalls, and the smell of it too. Even while running away from the thing, a fetid stink of sweat and rot filled his nostrils, brought by the wind blowing against his back.

The hand tried again for his ankle but slipped off his boot once more. Will was almost there. *I must keep going,* he thought. His breath was fast now, his body was moving as much as he could push it, but a cold knot of fear worried his greatest effort wouldn't be enough. Four cart-lengths; three; two. A body hit him from behind as the creatures tried to stop him from crossing. Will felt the sickening lurch as feet lost their grip, his arms reached out to catch himself, his hand reached out, scraping against a rock's edge.

Falling forward, and somehow landing on the other side of the line, he stopped trying to hold it together. He could stop running, his face tight as he tried to breathe through the cramp. A scream and a howl filled his ears. Will covered them in an involuntary reaction, pulling himself into a ball, a move that brought more pain. Not yet able to stand, he rolled himself farther away from the line, farther into safety. The scream came again, the scream of a predator denied its prey. He could hear the Valni scrambling back and forth at the line, wanting to cross, but the ancient magic, born of faith, held firm. Will raised himself up enough to look.

A dozen of them, moving like beasts, their movements not matching their human shapes. Right on the line, in front, the one that had grabbed his leg stared at him, biting the air, its teeth broken. The creature wore rags, a final remnant of its humanity. Sunken eyes stared back, full of hate and madness, mad with bloodlust, pulsing with hunger and rage. It sniffed the air and picked up a rock, sniffing it again like the ripest fruit, and licked it.

The pain in Will's hand told him why the beast licked the rock—blood. Will could see the dark red line, his blood on the rock. When he fell, at the last, his hand, the scrape must have been worse than he thought. The Valni had licked his blood off the rock! Will shuddered in disgust. The knot of fear returned, with a flush of cold sweat. He knew what the stories said about the Valni tasting someone's blood. He pushed those away. Will was safe, he was on this side of the line, and he'd never cross over again.

He stood, and everything hurt. The pain in his side burned, his feet felt like he'd been beating the soles of them with his smithing hammer, and the cut on his hand still bled. Eyes blinking the drops of sweat away, he hurt everywhere. He was alive, though. Alive, and he'd succeeded in his task. Succeeded in the one thing that would—if the legends and stories were true—guarantee his admission to the smithing guild. He rubbed the crystal in his hand, taking it at a slow walk as he headed away from the line. A final plaintive scream came from behind him, but he ignored it.

The small crystal glowed, a soft white glow, matching the milky color of the stone itself. Soothing warmth enveloped his hands as he held it, warmer than his skin.

Better the slight pains he would recover from than the death the Valni brought. He'd been foolish to recover the crystal shard. Foolish and desperate. But this would do it ... this would get him where he had dreamed of.

Being a Guild smith had been his father's dream to start, though to hear his Da say it, it was the dream of generations of Reis's. That dream had passed on to Will. He had to be a guild smith. He had to do it for his father. Palnor guild smiths were known all over Alos. They commanded the highest prices, created the finest works, and given honors reserved for the nobility. Will remembered his Da's voice, telling him of the wonders that only those who trained within the Guild could produce.

Weapons that never needed sharpening, gears that never stripped, armor that couldn't be pierced by anything other than a guild-made blade. No one knew how they did it. Will had heard the legends over the years of times long past when a guild smith would be kidnapped. The kidnappers would try to force the methods the guild used from their prisoner. All that ever happened in those cases was a massive manhunt and the abductors killed. No one had bothered the guild or its Masters in a very long time.

His father attempted the test for being accepted to the guild three times. Each time he made a piece, each one finer and more perfect than the last. And each time they passed him over. No one from the Reach ever got chosen. Many in the Reach wondered why, but openly questioning the Guild would be foolish. When the time for the choosing came, a Master Smith would come, look over the applicants' work, and then leave. His Da must have been crushed by his failures. He had been a proud man, strong, at least before that day.

Will would be chosen. He had studied and practiced for almost two years, waiting until he was old enough to try. He had sworn Duncan to secrecy about his attempt and built a small forge workspace out in the mountains, about an hour from town. The crystal was the final piece of the puzzle. This would give him the edge he needed.

He imagined his Da's face, proud and worn. His Mother's face beaming at him. Duncan giving his normal half smile, happy for him but not understanding what the big deal was. He wanted to remember them that way, happy. Will stopped and sat on a rock, rubbing his sore calf, his eyes drawn to the road, back toward the Valni, toward the barrier.

His mother's screams. She'd been so close that day to making it. She had left him at home, trying to stop his cousin from crossing the barrier looking for treasure. She'd found some maps he had saved up for and bought, maps showing ruins and locations on the Mistlands side. Even then Duncan had a wild streak. Will had followed, he'd hoped Duncan would get caught, and maybe listen for once. She had crossed the barrier, not far over, but far enough. Some foolish merchant had tried to take a shortcut and drawn in the Valni.

The Valni were feasting on the remnants of one guard and the horse when they think his Mother saw the creatures, and the Valni had spotted her. Will remembered her running toward the barrier, he had hidden, hoping to see her dragging Duncan back home.

Will clasped his eyes closed tight at the memory. When he opened them again, he blinked, feeling the wetness on the edges of his vision. His father and Duncan's father had been in the mines that day. Duncan had gone with them, and they had failed to mention that he was with them. Just a simple miscommunication, one that happens all the time. But this time, in this case, it led to the death of Will's mother, and slowly, his father, and Duncan's' father.

Will's Da had been inconsolable, he blamed himself, he spent his days at work, mining, smithing. He was a Reis, and Reis's had a good reputation around the Reach. One of the oldest families, good, strong, reputable.

With the death of his wife, the elder Reis wasted away. He wouldn't sleep, he would only nibble at food. He didn't turn to strong drink, but worse things. Will's Da just sat and stared at the mountains. He said nothing for almost a month, and in that month he transformed. Gaunt, an unrecognizable figure from the one he'd been before. Will remembered people whispering about how his Da was wasting away from grief and loss. That was only part of the truth. Duncan's father Will's uncle had taken it hard to, though his grieving was different. Oh, he'd mourned the loss of Will's mother, but now he mourned the slow death of his brother. One day, a little over a month after that horrible day, Will's Da vanished in the night.

Will could remember his Uncle pacing, unsure of what to do. Finally, he'd sat Will and Duncan down, told them he would find Will's Da, and he'd be back before nightfall. He'd smiled gave both a hair ruffle and a smile. He had leaned down and given Duncan a small hug and walked out the door.

Duncan and Will stood there and watched him go, silent. They waited in silence all day, watching the day end and the night fall. They watched the glow stones in the street go out and saw the light of the new day break the sky over the mountains, but no parents ever returned. That was nine long years ago. Will and Duncan had been the only family the other had ever since.

Will winced as he stood. His calf still hurt, and now his shins hurt. He would feel that even more in the morning. Holding the crystal tight one last time he slipped it into a pocket and began the rest of the walk home.

Coming over a rise he took in the sight of the Reach. The town had no other name, nor did it need one. The town got its name from the mountains, the Skyreach Mountains. The Reach had been here for who knew how long. It had been the center of mining for all Alos longer than the written word could record. It was far grander once, before the Fall of Amder. Amder. Will's hand slipped to the crystal in his pocket.

Amder had named the Reach his blessed city, his home on Alos. The God of craft and creation blessed the Reach and made it the most powerful and wealthiest city in Palnor. But then came the Godsfall, and the Reach fell with the God. Now, more and more of the city turned to Grimnor, the god of the mountains for blessings. But not always. Reacher's still remembered Amder, one of the last places in Palnor that did.

The Reach spread out in this valley, parts of the city lit by torchlight, others by the older and now rarer glow stones. The cold air of the mountains pushed away the smoke and haze that sometimes hovered over the city of mining. In those moments the true beauty of the Reach appeared. Homes decorated with fine metalwork shone in both daylight and moonlight. And if the conditions were perfect, the city would sparkle like gemstone.

Will headed down the road, nodding to a few people he passed as he got closer to town. No walls enclosed the Reach, though there were the occasional patrol by the local sheriff group. With the barrier protecting them from the Valni, the largest trouble the Reach came across was some bandits and brigands. While never a huge town, it was respectable. It took a hardy sort to live here. Though over the years the older parts of town had more and more abandoned homes, as families left, or lines died out.

Will headed towards the Gemdust district, where the Reis family home stood. It was glow stone lit, and one of the oldest if not the original district in the Reach. They made the homes here of rock and carved with representations of life in the Reach. Sometimes they were inlaid with other rocks or even dust from Gem cutting operations, hence the name. Some of the carvings were newer, it had come into fashion to resurface homes, and do new carvings. Others had a thousand different smaller carvings, some so old and weathered no one could tell what they had ever been.

Will smiled as the house came into view. The Reis house was different and stood out even today. Only one carving was on the house, the only one that mattered. A huge carving of Amder covered the whole front, and part of each side. A carving filled with a mix of goldlace dust and Drendel steel. It was a family secret lost to time what the exact ratio was. But it shone bright in the soft light of the glow stones, a monument to a different time.

Will's hand slipped once more to the crystal in his pocket, "Welcome home." he whispered to the night as he opened the door and walked into the warm firelight.

2

"Will, where in the blood of the mountains have you been?" Duncan stood facing the fire, his back to Will. Taller and far lither than Will, he didn't even look like Will except for cast of his features. When he turned around the resemblance was clear, the same Blue-green eyes, and the same pronounced sharp nose.

"Nice to see you too Duncan." Will closed the door behind him and made his way to a chair at the large table that dominated the center of the room. He more collapsed than sat, happy that the chair could hold his weight now instead of his legs.

"You're hurt? Where have you been?" Duncan's voice rose in worry. Duncan didn't worry about anything except for Will. He was overprotective of his cousin even though they were of the same age.

"I had to do something." Will settled back into the chair, trying to relax. While the small stabs of pain still bothered him, he was safe. His dream was within his grasp, he knew it.

"That's not an answer." Duncan's voice lowered. "Sparks above Will, tell me."

Will reached into his pocket. He'd have to tell him, though he knew Duncan wouldn't understand. The small crystal gave his fingers a slight tingle, a thrill that distracted him from the aches he'd been feeling. "I had to go work on my practice piece, you know, for the guild trials. They're only a week away"

"Forget the Guild! Your life is here, in the Reach. Not chasing after something that no Reacher has any chance of being." Duncan waved his arms as he spoke, his frustration boiling over.

Will gritted his teeth but remained sitting, his legs still throbbed, and he didn't want to let Duncan see any weakness. "It's been my choice Duncan since we were little, it was my father's dream, and his father's as well!" This was an old argument of theirs. Duncan wanted nothing more in life than the Reach. And he wanted it for both of them.

"That dream was and is foolish, and why would you ever want anything to do with a dream from the man who left you alone? A man who wasted away, a man who gave up." Duncan hands made fists for a moment but released them.

"Stop right there Duncan!" Will rose now, ignoring the pain. "If you'd made sure my mother knew where you were, she wouldn't have died, and none of the other things wouldn't have happened!"

Duncan's face turned to stone. Will expected him to lash out and steeled himself. Duncan gave Will a long hard look, turned again to the fire and said nothing.

Will sat again, tension leaving his body. Old arguments. Duncan had always been the one to take care of them both. He had stepped into that dominant role when they were orphaned, and Will had let him.

Silence ruled the room, the sound of the crackling fire, and the occasional sound of a horseshoe on the cobblestones outside broke the quiet. Duncan at last turned back to him, and Will could see the sadness now. Will knew how much his wanting to leave bothered his cousin.

"I... I'm sorry." Duncan muttered sitting down in a chair at the table, rubbing his face. "I just, I don't like the idea of you leaving the Reach. You're the only family I've got left now. We are it, the last two of the Family Reis."

Will nodded. "Dunc, I know you're not fond of the guild, and even less like me joining it, but it's my dream. I need to do this. Joining the guild will be my gift to my Da's spirit, wherever it is. I have to do this."

Duncan looked at him and shook his head, a slight smile on his face. "Glad my father didn't fill my head with guild nonsense. All that stuff about the guild, honoring Amder, a dead god, long gone. You can make a good living here Will. You're good. Reacher's don't care if you're guild or not. Here you're a Reis! This house is far too big for the two of us. One day we'll have families, the Reis line will continue here in the Reach."

Will nodded. "I know, Duncan. I could be like Da and stay. And I still might, but I must try. I have to do everything I can to make that dream come true." Will's gaze looked away from his cousin, looking at the fireplace as his fingers found the crystal again.

"What did you do, Will? You're not saying something. When you try to evade answers, you look into the distance."

Duncan snapped his fingers, drawing Will's attention back to him. "The fireplace isn't that interesting."

Will looked around, the door was closed, and the windows weren't open. Will looked at Duncan and paused again. "I increased my chances in the guild trial."

Duncan rolled his eyes. "Just tell me! By the eight gods say it."

Will reached into his pocket and placed the crystal on the table. Its faucets caught the firelight enhancing its soft white glow. "I had to." Will whispered.

Silence fell once more, and Will watched Duncan's face. First his eyes widened, then narrowed as he looked at Will. A brief scowl crossed his face replaced by what, a smile?

"You did it. You know how much trouble you'd be in if anyone else saw that?" Duncan pointed to the crystal, Will's hope to change his future. "If you hadn't put that on the table, I'd have never believed you could have done such a thing. You, William Reis, the upstanding one, took a crystal from the Mistlands!"

"I know. But I had to. With this, well you know the stories." Will touched the crystal with a single finger, hunkering down to look at it eye level.

"Will, that thing means you went into the valley." Duncan started at the crystal for a moment. "I travel closer than anyone else I know in the Reach, but to go into the valley? What about the mist? What about the Valni?"

"I've been watching the weather for the last week Duncan, checking to see what the wind shifts and what direction. I had to hope that the wind would push the mist back far enough for me to grab a crystal, even a small one like this." Will smiled at the memory of this morning.

"The trip out was fine, quiet even. Saw some Berog tracks but they were old, few days past. Not a Valni in sight though unlike you I didn't go digging around in any of the ruins I passed." Duncan opened his mouth to ask a question, but Will stopped him. "I'll tell you about the ruins I saw later." Duncan gave him a grin and waved him to continue.

"Once I got to the valley, I saw it Duncan. Have you ever investigated the valley? Seen the mist, the blood red death of it, swirling around these?" Will picked up the crystal feeling the slight tingle and warmth it gave off. "This was a tiny one, at places in the mist you could see huge ones, and other things as the mist shifted and swirled. Dark things."

"The road down was old but serviceable, nothing grows there anyway. And I was right, the wind was blowing the mist away from me, but I wasn't sure how long it would be. I stood there for a long while watching it. Almost turned around and came back, promising myself I'd never speak or think of this ever again. But I didn't, I stood there and waited." Will blew out a long breath and placed the crystal back on the table.

"It was stupid to wait; I should have grabbed the first crystal I saw and got out of there. Finally, I moved, I don't know why, it was like my arms, my legs were being controlled by someone else. I held my breath, ran up and grabbed this one and got away as fast as I could." Will shuddered at the memory of being that close to the mist. "I swear the mist *reached* for me Duncan, against the wind, a tendril reached out, I swear it. Color of blood, the mist was. It moved like a living thing."

Duncan looked pale; they both knew what the mist touching you meant. What happened to you, what you became. "That was stupid. Brave I guess, but stupid."

Will shrugged. "I know. I ran away from the mist and I kept running. Ran all the way till I hit the barrier. Barely escaped."

Duncan nodded. "Damn lucky. What if the Valni had found you?"

Will looked down. "They did."

"What?" Duncan stood voice raised. "You don't leave something like that out Will!"

Will shrugged. "They didn't catch me. But it was close. I'll never cross that barrier again. Never. Not for anything."

Will's voice gave Duncan pause. "What do you mean?"

Will looked at the floor. "My blood, one of them tasted it."

"Will! *How?*" Duncan knew what it meant. After a Valni tastes your blood, they will seek you out, no tracker, no dog, no magic could track better than a Valni after its tasted blood. And Valni never traveled alone.

"I tripped and fell crossing the barrier Dunc. When I say I barely escaped, I meant it. The one in the lead, the one who tasted my blood, he had grabbed me by my ankle. I was close enough that when I fell, I fell over the barrier. My hand had gotten cut up some from the rocks when I'd tripped earlier." Will held up his hands, the cut still visible. "Blood fell on the wrong side of the barrier. It was fresh blood. He tasted it, and he smiled at me Duncan. I didn't even know the things could smile."

Duncan sat in a seat next to Will. "You are marked now Will. Can't cross that barrier ever again. If you do that Valni and more will come for you straight for you. You're sparks blessed lucky the things didn't catch you."

"I know. I know." Will sighed. "But it was still worth it. With this, I'll do it, I'll get into the Guild. I'll do it for my father, for your father, for every Reis, male or female who tried and didn't get in."

They both looked at the crystal. They both knew what it was. It was the blood of a dead god, the blood of Amder, the God of Craft.

3

A hooded figure picked its way through the rocks, wrapping the dark red cloak they wore tight. The cold didn't feel right, the lands where they normally walked were far warmer. These mountains were where some nests of Valni laired yet, so the figure had to come. The barrier was closer here, but more prey was as well, and the Valni lived to hunt.

The figure stopped and listened to the wind, holding up a long staff and moving it slowly and following it's moving end. Dark and old, the staff was black with blood in its wood. Blood spilled in the service of the true one, Valnijz the Blood God. Some given of their own free will, other times taken, the blood was bound to the wood by the will of a God, the true God.

The figure held the staff with a light touch. Using it was intoxicating. To command such power, even now, after all these long centuries, was near rapture. And even this power wasn't enough to meet the goal of centuries of work. More was needed. Another part, and then, the blood.

A scrambling sound echoed through the rocks, and the figure stood straighter. "Valni!" a soft whisper came from somewhere in the enveloping hood. Closer again the sound came, and the figure moved forward towards the ruins that they had seen earlier in the climb. Regardless of which side of the great valley you came from, the Valni congregated in ruins.

Some Underpriests said it was a remnant of who they had been before the great one blessed them with his power and blood. Other's thought it might be jealousy of what had been their own, once. It didn't matter, they were the harbingers of the great one, the mighty god of blood and rage, the bringer of destruction.

His time was coming again. All those years ago he would have completed his great work, the scourging of the lands, and the end of all. But the thrice hated Amder, the so-called god of craft had stopped him. But even in the death of his physical form, Valnijz had sowed the seeds of his return. The blood mist, formed from the holy spilled blood of the great one, had made the Valni, mortal men and women, blessed by the spirit of the god. Hunters, destroyers all.

Over the years their numbers had grown, and the time had come. The hooded figure paused once more and let the cloak and its hood fall. The cold air bit into her skin, but she stood unflinching. She stood still and raised the staff, reverently holding it in the air. A quiet stream of words spilled out of the figure as she chanted the blood oath, the oath that all the Priests of the true faith knew.

The staff, once dark, now glistened in the light, wet and red. One tendril of red mist waved off the staff, then another, more came, spilling out, searching. Reaching through cracks in the rock, flowing into the hidden places, drawn to the Valni. Shapes came out of the darkness, broken forms, each a twisted remnant of the person they had once been.

Faces torn into a rictus of a smile, dirty with grime and unknown things, the Valni formed a circle around the woman. Not attacking, they sat, waiting, starting to rock in the rhythm of her words. The woman's chant grew, its harsh words echoed off the cold stone. The Valni began to growl, and mouths frothed as the chant drew them to her, to her control. The staff raised high, the mist whirled around the assembled creatures one final time before rushing back into the wood, and silence held sway.

Her chant finished, the figure smiled, eyes wide. "Blood calls blood." She spoke into the night. One by one the Valni crept away. They were bound to her now, for she was the High Priest, and the one who would bring their God back to finish his great work, the end of all life.

***

Duncan shook his head "This is madness. Those stories, you can't believe them, can you? I mean, I know what they say, but this is, well, you know." He shifted in his seat, uncomfortable and not wanting to look at the crystal in front of them.

Will studied Duncan for a moment, surprised at his reaction. Dunc had never been one for faith or religion. In fact, Will couldn't remember the last time Dunc had even stepped foot in the Temple of the Eight here in the Reach. "You mean that it's forbidden?" Will asked. "I know, but why? I mean you know what Da told us, and his father before him. A crystal of the blood of

Amder, placed in a forge will give the next thing made in that forge a blessing."

Duncan shuddered. "Messing with the Gods. I don't like them dead or alive. I don't even think Haltim would be happy with this, and he likes you!"

Duncan was right on that count at least, old Haltim was the priest here in the Reach, an anointed priest of all the gods at least in name. Haltim had explained to him once that it didn't cover Valnijz, that dead god had no followers here in Palnor, or any civilized lands. One of the early lessons that Haltim impressed upon the youth of the Reach was to never go to the Mistlands.

One, because of the danger the blood mist gave it, two because of the Valni, and three because moving, taking, or even touching the crystal blood of Amder was forbidden. Will's Da had explained it as ancient superstition, but never had gone beyond that. At least Will thought with a small smile, Amder's blood didn't turn you into a blood craving, raw flesh-eating monster.

"Don't smile, this is serious. You can't let anyone know you did this; I don't even know what the penalty is for what you've done." Duncan's eyes moved between Will and the crystal. "You should get rid of it and forget this."

"I won't. This will get me out of the Reach and where I want to be." Will spoke without thinking and knew as soon as he had spoken, he'd said the wrong thing.

Duncan frowned. "Nice Will. You want to get away from the only family you have left. I thought we were friends, best friends even. Now this…" with a wave of his hand he stood and walked towards his room, the echoes of his boots filling the empty spaces.

"Look, that's not what I meant!" Will raised his voice. For all his wandering, outrunning the Valni or whatever else inhabits the ruins of the mountains, Duncan had no interest in going anywhere else.

The footsteps paused for a second, and Will listened, hoping for his cousin to say something, but they resumed, fading off into the darkness. Will sat in the dying light of the fire for a long time, hoping to hear his cousin return. Late in the evening Will walked off to his own bedroom and tried to sleep off the melancholy that surrounded him.

Regin yawned as the cart rolled down the trader's road through the Skyreach Mountains. "Why do we have to come here? No one from Reach ever gets in. We could skip the place, head down to the western foothills, and spend a few more days in Kilvar." Jaste looked at him with amusement. "Kilvar, huh? And why there? Could it be that girl you met last year? You know she's married or gone by now."

"She'd never do that." Regin blurted. "And if she is, well I'm sure there are other girls." he trailed off on a hopeful note. Jaste almost laughed. Regin was a decent looking young man but considered himself a great lover of women. He'd been refused many times on this trip already, even slapped once back at an inn.

Jaste shook his head "No Journeyman, we must go through Skyreach. It's where almost all the metal we work this comes from. It pays to be on good terms with the miners there."

"We have to go make friends with a bunch of rock grubbers. The metal is nice, but—"

Jaste cut him off, "Regin, never say that again. Without the miners in the Reach do you think we'd ever see Sliverflake again? Drendel Steel? Gold? We need the miners. Without the ores they provide, we couldn't do half of what we do."

Regin rolled his eyes "I was—"

"You were saying what half the Masters say," said Jaste, interrupted again, "I know. But that doesn't make it right."

Regin said nothing and stared down the road. He guided the wagon up the winding road, riding in silence. Jaste knew that Regin had picked up the habits of some younger Master smiths, who craved the status and power of a guild smith, and had little use for anyone who wasn't a noble or another Guildmaster, or a Priest of course. Jaste enjoyed working the metal, and was good at it, very good. He also had a knack for seeing talent, he enjoyed the testing trips.

The other Masters were more than happy to see Jaste go on recruiting trips. One, because they didn't have to listen to him lecture them, and two, because traveling to the far reaches of the country to judge the work of bumbling, not even Potential level work, was dull. Jaste enjoyed it, and this year he got to judge the

Reach. Master Hix had injured his eyes in a quenching accident, and Jaste had offered as soon as he had heard.

The Reach was home to the best miners in the country, if not all Alos, outside the reclusive Gorom. Most were also good with making simple tools, and even rough decorations. No Reacher's were in the guild, but the trip to the Reach would allow him to contact his usual metal suppliers, check stocks, and see what they could buy.

The testing would only take a day or two, and it wasn't difficult. A bunch of hopefuls would come in with their work pieces. Each example of metalwork gone over with care, and a few questions asked. If anything passed muster, they'd leave with Jaste and Regin, and have their final test at the Guildhall.

Jaste's thoughts jerked back to the present by Regin's loud and overdone sigh. "Master, can we stop soon, this road is about to shake something loose." Regin was still only a Journeyman and thus was still a student. Jaste decided he needed to remind the Senior Journeyman he wasn't Master yet.

"Since you need to take your mind off things, Journeyman..." Jaste glanced around and spotted a large boulder off to one side. "Ah there, Regin, that boulder... Based on sight alone tell me the three most common metals that kind of rock is found with, and the specific temperatures those metals need for forging." Regin sighed but began to recite the requested knowledge.

Jaste kept up the questioning until near nightfall. When at last, they crested a bend in the road to see Reach spread out before them. Rock houses, well lit, glowed out in front of them like a firefly parade. Jaste guided the wagon through the streets to the largest inn here, the Golden Chisel. There weren't many people out on the streets this time of evening, the Reach was not known for its nightlife. The occasional merchant closing for the evening, a few miners here and there walking home, the inns were open but not particularly loud or crowded. Jaste smiled, a hotbed of gossip, intrigue and power it was not.

Regin and Jaste both stretched muscles tight with sitting as they dismounted the wagon. Jaste paid the stable boy, grabbed a few important bags from the back of the wagon and went inside the Inn, Regin close behind. A comfortable glow surrounded them as they entered the main room. Good clean stone floors, several well-made fireplaces and sturdy wooden furniture greeted them. Nothing fancy, the Inn catered to their primary patrons, professional miners and the merchants that did business with them.

"Did I tell you about the show I saw at the Crimson Forge back in Ture? Before we left, they had these Acrobats, six of them..." Regin launched into a detailed description that Jaste didn't even listen to.

"Innkeeper, I need two rooms, two flagons and a meal." Jaste walked to the bar counter, looking for the innkeeper in question. "That will be 2 silver bits, and a half copper each" replied the inn keep, not even looking up from cleaning the large ale taps on the wall. Jaste cleared his throat, tapping his finger on the bar. The barkeep stopped, squinted at the finger, noting the calluses, looked up and blanched. "Oh, sorry Master Smith! No charge, best table in the house is yours!" He looked semi frantic. No one wanted to get on the bad side of the smiths, even less the barkeep at the main inn that miners and merchants met at.

Jaste smiled. "No sir, give me the real price." Some haggling later, they agreed on a silver and a half each, and a table by the side fireplace.

Regin sank into his chair with a groan. "It's not the capital, but it's decent," he said.

Jaste cooked on the road, and according to his traveling companion he cooked the food as if he was smelting it. It was always burned or overcooked. Jaste and Regin each nursed a good brown ale that a lad deposited on their table as soon as they sat. As they sipped, they looked around the room and relaxed. It was quiet for a weeknight. Few tables taken up with business meetings, people discussing trade, and the profits of whatever they had done. Some tables held couples, upper middle-class merchant families.

The delivery of the food broke Jaste's thoughts. Fresh bread, butter, and two different types of Klah, that garlicky spread popular in these parts. Roasted deer, root vegetables, mushrooms cooked in wine, and even dessert, a slab of what looked to be shortbread topped with caramel and honey. Simple, but delicious he was sure.

The pair ate with gusto, and near silence. Jaste wanted peace and quiet, Regin only wanted to eat. Jaste broke the silence first "In the morning go put up the signs and I'll help you put up the tent. We will get the judging done next week and leave the morning after. No need to rush it."

"But Master Jaste, Kilvar?" Regin sighed. "I know she might not be there, but..."

Jaste ignored him. "If we find someone worthy, they will come with us."

Regin snorted "Waste of time." Jaste let it slide this time, antagonizing Regin wasn't going to make the trip a good one. Jaste said goodnight to Regin after finishing his last bite of the Shortbread. A bath would be ready in his room by now, and a soft bed would be a welcome respite.

***

Will awoke to light streaming in his window, and he blinked in its brightness. Light? Light in the window meant it was far later than it should be! Will sat up, he had promised to help some miners, they'd be waiting for him. His body had other ideas, as he stood his jaw clenched as the aches and pains from yesterday were magnified by the sleep he had gotten. Fingers scrambled for the edge of the bed frame to steady himself, and Will fought to not fall over.

Gritting his teeth, Will took one step at a time as sore muscles and tendons complained in alternate rhythm with each step he took. He had made it to the kitchen when Duncan appeared with a grin on his face. "Wondered if you would ever get up! And I see your little run yesterday didn't agree with you."

Will scowled at him, the pain and stiffness in his legs and back overcoming his normal good humor. "Morning to you too. Could have gotten me up you know, now I'm late to help in that mine!" Will gingerly tried to sit. His legs were better, but his back was worse. And involuntary intake of breath came with sitting.

Duncan chuckled at Will's obvious discomfort. "Don't worry, I already explained your absence. They understand and hope you feel better soon!" Duncan turned his back to Will, and continued feeding the fire, to warm the cold main room of the house.

"What did you tell them?" Will asked. With Duncan it could be anything, and if they asked, he wanted to know what lie or half-truth they might ask him about later.

"That you'd gone out beyond the barrier, looking for ore to use for your guild attempt, and had run into some Valni. You'd escaped but were tired and sore from the flight." Duncan always did lie well.

Will corrected his thought, not lie, but not say everything. Will had always struggled with that.

"Thanks Duncan. I owe you." Will stood, taking his time to do so, walked over and clasped Duncan's arm. "I mean it."

"I know you do Will. It's only because you mean it that I cover for you." Duncan flashed him a smile. "Now, since you're up, I will head out. You rest, and I'll go make us some money, since you aren't going to be able to." Duncan waved a hand at Will's legs. "How are those tree trunks doing this morning anyway?"

"Painful." Will answered. "Be careful, going scaving?"

Duncan nodded in response but wasn't forthcoming with any details. "Dunc, be careful. I don't think I've ever been as damn scared in my life as yesterday."

Duncan waved him off. "I'm faster than you, and better at this thing."

Will sighed but gave up. Duncan's need to test the limits of what he could get away with from the ruins past the barrier were another long-standing issue between the two of them. He had to trust that Duncan wouldn't do anything stupid.

"Going to rest?" Duncan asked, changing the subject.

"Maybe. I could go visit Haltim. Not sure." Will answered eyes narrowing as he sat back down.

It was Duncan's turn to sigh, but he didn't make a comment. Will watched him prepare, checking his pack, rope, knife, a crowbar. "Will, don't mention the crystal to Haltim. Ok?"

Will nodded. "Wasn't planning on it, cousin. Be careful out there."

Duncan nodded and left. Will watched him go, feeling more trepidation than normal. It was because of yesterday, that Valni, the memories of that day... her screams. Will shook at the memory again and forced it away.

Several hours and one hot bath later, Will made his way out of the house, using a walking stick he'd grabbed. Will was not shy, but today he kept his eyes on the ground, not wanting to make eye contact. If he did, they'd ask about the walking stick, and he'd had to tell that half-truth that Duncan had already let out.

5

Jaste walked down the stone pavers heading toward the largest of three markets here in the Reach. Regin was still in bed and refused to get breakfast and go talk to miners. More signs that Regin had fallen into the entitled crowd within the guild. He could have ordered the Journeyman to come with him, it was within his power. Doing so could cause more issues though, as he was not sure Regin wouldn't make a scene and damage the relationships Jaste had built over the years.

Jaste liked to work with the miner's one on one. Guild smiths knew how to work the metals, and even could, if they studied it, recognize rocks and ores associated with them. But the miners here could find the best veins and were damn near masters themselves in getting the more fragile and rare metals out and in a usable form.

Taking a deep breath Jaste smiled. On top of everything else, he liked the Reach. When the wind blew east the smoke and smells of forging and smelting blew towards the Mistlands, clearing the air. With clean mountain air, calm hard-working people, the Reach was a nice place. Cooler at least than Ture.

His first meeting went well, as the head of the Broke Stone Mine showed him the latest finds and they worked out a good deal on the ore prices. They were finishing up when a young man walked in, using a walking stick as he limped long.

"Will!" The miner exclaimed and clasped the young man's arm. "I heard what happened, glad to know those bastard Valni didn't get you."

The young man nodded "Sorry about not making it into the mine today, my legs and back are near locked up. Running like that isn't for me." The miner, a man named Korac, laughed. The one he called Will smiled, caught sight of the guild smith, his expression changed. Jaste watched as the poor lad turned as white as the snow.

"Got to go Korac. Give me three days and I'll be in the mine first thing; we need to make sure that vein of Silverlace is true." The words spilled out as this Will walked out of the stall, limping away.

"Good lad that one," Korac said to Jaste as he looked at the figure walking away. "Whole family is, even that cousin of his."

"Who is he? What did you mean about the Valni?" Jaste asked, his interest piqued. He'd never seen a Valni but had no desire to.

"Oh... he went out yesterday doing some prospecting work, looking for better ore. For you all, he's doing the guild trial next week." Korac sighed. "Reacher's don't get picked, but he's a damn good smith, and miner. He crossed the barrier in his hunt, and the Valni almost caught him."

"Who is he? You said his name was Will?" Jaste asked as he took out paper and charcoal to jot down the agreed contract. A more permanent one would come in a month, but this was the preliminary one.

"Yeah, William Reis. Been a Reis here in the Reach forever. Good family, too bad that he and Duncan are the only two left." Korac started putting samples away and didn't notice Jaste looked up at the mention of Williams's last name.

"Reis? Did you say Reis?" Jaste asked trying to keep his voice normal.

"Yeah. He and that cousin of his Duncan." Korac finished putting away the samples. "Why?"

"Oh, hadn't heard that last name before," Jaste lied, unsure what to say. "What happened to the rest of his family? You said they were the only two left?"

"When Will and Duncan were young lads, Will's mother got killed by the Valni, right by the barrier too. Will saw it happen. His father lost the drive to live after that, vanished one night into the mountains, and his brother, Duncan's father went after him, and vanished also. Korac wiped his hands on his apron and sighed. "So those two are the last ones left."

Jaste nodded and smiled. A Reis would try the guild trials. This was unexpected.

***

Will shuffled away through the market, giving nods and smiles to other Reachers only if he had to. *A guild smith.* Sitting right there at Korac's place. The same one who would judge the trials next week. He should have introduced himself and been friendly. Now the smith would take one look at him next week and pass right over him, he knew it.

Still lost in his self-blame, Will almost walked right past the Church of the Eight. Made of rock, someone had carved it out of the side of a mountain. The workmanship was unlike any other building in the Reach. The whole thing had been made that way, one solid piece. Sunrise showed the true beauty of the place. As the sun rose, it glinted off the veins of metal that had been left in the walls. Silver, gold, reddish copper, and more. Haltim! Maybe the Priest would have time to talk, he needed guidance.

His steps echoed through the entry chamber as he made his way inside. The tip of the walking stick made tap, tap, tap noises to go along with the steps. Hammer motifs and anvils made up most of the original stone decoration here. As the outside showed the natural beauty of the Reach, the inside showed what that beauty could made into, in the hands of Masters.

Once, long ago, this building had only been dedicated to Amder. The Reach had been the heart of Amder's power, and so the church was here. Those days were long past, but the glory lived on, if faded. After the Godsfall, the Church had moved its base to Ture, the capital. And so, this place had been rededicated to worship all the gods of Alos.

Will's mouth twitched up, well, worship of six. Amder was mentioned but not worshiped, and Valnijz was ignored at best, though there was a bust of the God of Destruction in the main hall. The bust, covered with a black cloth and stuck as far in the corner as it could be, away from everyone.

Will had once, as all the Reach kids do, snuck in and looked under the cloth. The face of evil he'd thought, teeth and claw, all rage and death. Will had fled and run right into Haltim. True to form, Haltim had not yelled at him, though he had made Will dust and polish every bust of every god that wasn't covered.

Will loved to come here. His father had taken him here as a child and told him of the fall of Amder. How the Horde of Valnijz had come to Palnor, and the country rose to fight them off. The horde had been on the edge of defeat, when the bloody one himself, Valnijz came on to the field of battle. This was forbidden to the gods, but Valnijz did it anyway. Amder, forced to come into the world as well, sacrificing his leader, the Forgemaster to do it.

Most didn't pay attention to the story these days, though the Mistlands were a constant reminder. Will did, and he often would sit here, and relax in the presence of Amder. He acknowledged the other gods, but none spoke to him like Amder did. Gods of Forest and of the Sea? What business would a Reacher have with them?

"Will! Good to see you! Heard you ran into some trouble yesterday." Haltim appeared around the corner. Haltim had been the priest here for longer than Will had been alive. He'd even been the priest here when his father was young. Old, grey, and wrinkled, Haltim kept living.

The church was far too large for a single priest, but this was now considered a backwater Will gathered. Haltim had told him that even he'd fought against being sent here. He'd been young and wanted to be in the thick of things in Ture. But he'd made a choice and been sent to the Reach as a punishment, and to his shock discovered he loved the place.

Will asked once what the mistake had been, but Haltim had only shook his head with a grin and never answered the question. "Yeah, I had some Valni after me, but I'm fine. Feeling beat up." Will felt his mood improving.

"Be careful my boy. What could you ever want out towards the Mistlands? The barrier is there for a reason. You're not like that damn fool of a cousin of yours, scaving the ruins, are you?" Haltims face betrayed his concern.

"No. I was looking for better ore traces for my guild trial piece. The testing is next week." Will's eyes darted around the main foyer. "Do you think we could go sit? My legs still hurt."

Haltim gave a laugh that was oddly forced. "Sorry, I should have offered."

The taps and steps echoed into the large open chamber of the church, its more Amder specific motifs hidden behind drapes and well-arranged wall hangings. Will felt himself relax and his mood improve, being in here always did. Sitting down he gave out an involuntary sigh.

"I know that sigh." Haltim sat next to Will "Though you're young for it. Let me guess, legs?"

"You got it. Sore as if I'd been hammering stone all day." Will smiled.

Haltim paused for a second, closing his eyes and his face going serious. His eyes flicked open and locked Will's gaze. "Will. I don't think you should do this guild trial. I'm aware your father did it, and the fact he failed weighed on him for years. Reachers don't get picked."

Will's lips tightened into a thin line. Was everyone against him now? "I expected that from Duncan, but not you. You know this has been my dream for years, but now you say this? You know what this means to me. You know why I need to do this, and when I'm on the cusp, you try to talk me out of it?"

"I didn't expect you to, well... Try." Haltim's head swiveled to look at a mosaic of the Hammer of Amder, done in various ores. "Will I thought, and forgive me, that you'd let this foolish dream go once you got older. I didn't know you would try, and now? You're too young."

Will's annoyance grew. "I'm twenty-one Haltim. Of legal age to try."

The old priest closed his eyes and nodded; the frown obvious on his face. "This isn't a good idea Will. I don't want to see you disappointed."

Will stood, his anger overcoming his desire to sit. "I thought I was coming to visit a friend, and to ask that friend to bless my practice piece for the choosing. But I guess instead I came to see someone who shows a distinct lack of faith or trust in me and my skills. Talk about disappointment."

Will walked out, his walking stick hammering the stone floor.

"Will! Wait... I will bless the piece." Haltims voice came from behind him, almost regretful. Will didn't turn around, but gave a slow nod and left the church, his steps leaving Haltim in a dark silence.

***

Haltim sat still, his heart racing and his mind a blur of worry and decisions to be made. William Reis would try for the guild. He had hoped this day wouldn't come, that Will would outgrow the dream. The records say it had happened before, that a Reis wouldn't try sometimes, and the Priest assigned to the Reach would celebrate. He should have known that Will wouldn't give up though. His father had been as stubborn.

Will was more talented than his father, and if skill alone could get a Reacher in, it would be him. But skill alone wasn't the reason. If he told the High Priest of this, what would happen? Could he do that? Betray the love he had for the Reis family, for the oath he swore when he came here?

Haltim wished Will was more like that ridiculous cousin of his. Duncan Reis had no interest in smithing, though he had some talent. Will though, was born to the forge. Haltim needed to get a message to the High Priest of Amder. There had to be something he could do to fix this, he had to, he had sworn it, although that didn't help the sour taste in his mouth that came with the decision.

6.

Will's mood did not improve as he made his way back home. Haltim had agreed to bless the work, but the reaction that Haltim had given him plain hurt. The old man was the closest thing to a father that Will had now. He had always relied on Duncan's skepticism and Haltim's calm advice. Now both didn't want him to follow his dream.

Will wasn't having a very good day. His legs still hurt, he'd run away from the Master Smith, and everyone he cared about kept telling him to give up. Maybe he wasn't good enough, he couldn't make this happen. His thoughts increasing darker he ignored any attempts to talk to him by those he passed.

The house was cold when he entered, cold and hard. He had been a fool. If both Duncan and Haltim thought it was a waste of time, why should he even try? "I'll throw the crystal away. Throw it away and give up." Will's words echoed in the space, a reminder of how alone he and Duncan were. They should have sold this place years ago, ghosts of memory echoed here. Will made his way to his room and grabbed the small bag hidden under the mattress.

"I could have died, or worse turned into one of the Valni. For what? A foolish childhood dream." Bag in hand, he made his way to the forge in the backyard. The family forge, it had been part of the house for generations. Old and used, it had an anvil, and hammers. "I'll break this damn thing, crush it to dust. Bury the leftovers and forget it all."

The forge was large, reflecting once more how large the family must have been once. Will had loved coming here as a child when his father and Uncle worked. Under all the old soot and char there were decorations of Amder. He'd loved them then, now they were final reminders of his sad and foolish dream.

His hand found a well-worn hammer, its weight giving him no comfort. Will approached the largest anvil in the place. Twice the size of normal, and for all its age, untarnished. Face set with a frown he ripped the bag open and grabbed the small crystal. The white glow off the crystal illuminated the forge more than he'd thought it would, throwing carvings into far sharper relief than he'd ever seen.

He placed the crystal on the anvil, lifted the hammer high...

The sound of horns echoed through the mountains, the clash of mail on rocks as marching steps walked. A hooded man, large and clad in ornate armor stood facing a valley. He lifted a hammer, shining with a golden sheen, the face of Amder made out in silver and Blue Drendel Steel.

Will shook his head, what in the sparks of creation had that been? He steadied himself and raised the hammer again.

A cry went up from the assembled host, a mighty army, flying the banners of Palnor, it roared with each shake of the large man's hammer. The sun shone down, and the man's cloak once masked sprang into view, a golden hammer over a silver anvil.

Will shook his head, the hammer in his hand lowered. A Forgemaster! Once the avatar of Amder made flesh, they had died at the battle that had formed the Mistlands, where Amder had fallen. Why was he seeing this?

The crystal's glow was still bright, and Will found his wish to crush it quenched. "Oh Amder, why would I do this?" Will could feel some of his doubt fade. "Is this a sign? What does this mean?"

Confusion filled him, followed by a chill. Could Amder be telling him something? Him? Amder was dead! Duncan would look at him like he'd lost his mind if he said something to him, and Haltim...Well, he couldn't tell Haltim the truth. Will stood in the white glow, unsure. The hammer went back to the rack, the crystal back in the bag, and Will made his way back inside the house.

Will made a fire, needing the warmth and time to think, the warmth not removing the chill that had settled onto him. It had been a vision; he was sure of it. A vision of what though? It had been a Forgemaster, he was sure. But why see a Forgemaster? Amder's chosen, master at the craft. They said the great crucible here in the Reach was made by a Forgemaster. It was ancient, but never cracked, never got worn out. It could hold more melted material than three more crucibles combined, sit on the fire for days, and the outside would still be able to be touched with bare hands.

But they were gone. The Forgemaster had died. Dead for a thousand years or more. So why a vision of one? Will's eyes adjusted to the glow as he opened the bag to examine at the crystal again. "It is the blood of a god." Will muttered.

"Yeah, so what?" Duncan's voice came from behind him.

"Dunc!" Will's voice rose, and he stood. "Glad to see you made it back alive."

"Please some Valni will catch me? You, yes. Me? No." Duncan laughed, an easy laugh.

"How'd the scaving go?" Will asked, closing the bag up. Will wasn't sure what he would say about the vision, so better let Duncan talk about his favorite thing, himself. Duncan wouldn't believe him anyway.

"Good. Hit that old manor house on the old east trade trial." Duncan talked as he put stuff down, bags appeared from his pack, several making a heavy thunk as they hit the table.

Concern clouded Wills thoughts. "That is close to the Mistlands. Like really close."

Duncan waved his hand in dismissal. "I was fine. Didn't see any Valni. Which was unexpected. Usually I see them at a distance, but it was like they were all gone, not a one." Taking the last bag out of his pack, he hefted it a few times and threw it to Will. "Which is why I found this."

Will caught the bag, its weight surprising. Curious he opened the bag. Metal. Not any metal, but ingots. Small, silvery ingots. Removing one his breath caught and looked at Duncan.

"Yes. They are what you think they are. Found them in a broken chest, under a fallen wall. Never would have seen them most days." Duncan took one out of the bag, examining the silvery smooth metal. "Interesting chest. Found a ring of this stuff in their too." He put the metal back into the bag, careful not to bang it together with the others.

Will took one in his hand, its surface slick and almost oily. Wight Iron. Smooth as glass, and rare. So rare that Will had only even seen Wight Iron ore twice. And only in small amounts. What was in the bag was more valuable than anything else they owned.

"Use it for your practice piece." Duncan started pulling other things out of bags. Gold and Silverlace jewelry, a blue and black stained goblet, and more.

"This is too much. You can sell it and not even have to scave for money for years." Will felt the weight of the bag in his hand. To work Wight Iron would be incredible, but no, this was Duncan's and while it was a fine gift, finer than anything Will could have gotten him, he couldn't accept it.

Duncan waved him off. Pausing with his counting of his finds for the day, Duncan looked at the table for a moment before answering. "You're the only family I have left... I need to be there to help you even if I don't want to. So, take it. Use it. Get into the guild. Show them all how a Reis does it. I'm sorry about yesterday."

Will knew that this hadn't come easy for Duncan. Talking about family and the like Duncan would throw a joke and change the subject. "Thanks Dunc." Will wanted to say more, but it was better not to.

"So, what did you get up to today?" Duncan changed the subject as he grabbed a brush and a bowl of water to clean his finds of dirt and dust.

"Wandered around a bit, went to see Haltim and ran into a Master Smith in town. Might be the one for the judging." Will sat back into his chair. "Over at Korac's. Dropped in to apologize in person, and the Master Smith had to be there."

Duncan snorted, choking back a laugh. "Sorry Will. I'm sure you handled it with your usual tact and wit?"

"Ha. Didn't even talk to him and got out of there as fast as I could." Will's stomach dropped at the memory. "I should have introduced myself; shouldn't I have? I didn't know what to do when I realized who it was with Korac."

"Yes." Duncan replied, the humor in his voice choked back. "Will, you know that Korac has a connection with the guild, you should have expected the Guild judge to see him while they are here."

"Yeah, I'm aware, I didn't know they were here yet." Will replied. He held the crystal of Amder in a bag in one hand, and a bag of Wight Iron in the other. It wasn't real. With these two things he'd make the most incredible audition piece for the guild, ever. The rising excitement he felt wore away at his anger at Haltim and the confusion over the Forgemaster vision.

"How was seeing the old dusty man?" Duncan asked. "Something happened, right? You give me a small lecture about going to see the Eight, and so on. But now you mention Haltim, and nothing else."

"He was... fine." Will struggled with the right words. "He doesn't want me to apply to the guild either. He said he thought I'd outgrow that dream. What made me more irritated was that he wouldn't say why."

"*What?*" Duncan stopped his cleaning. "Haltim said for you to not try for the guild?"

"Yeah, said he'd told my father the same thing." Will waved his hand in dismissal. "Don't worry about it. Between the crystal and your generous gift, I'll craft something that will make them take a Reacher."

Duncan grinned. "Now that's what I want to hear! Confidence Will."

Will watched Duncan get back to work. He could see the fleeting of sadness on his cousin's face. Will knew he was saying it to bring him up and he was thankful for it, though he'd had enough of people telling him he couldn't do something, at least for today. And the gift of the Wight Iron, he could never repay him for that.

Duncan soon went to bed, tired from a day of scaving, as Will sat facing the fireplace. Weighing the two bags in his hands, and dreaming of what he could be, what might be.

***

Haltim paced around the knave of the Temple of the Eight, somewhat nauseous. He hadn't slept at all last night after talking with Will during the day. For the first time in years he was torn between a Reacher, those he'd sworn to help and be there for, and his order itself. William Reis caused it all of course. He'd known on some level that this day might come, he had hoped it wouldn't, that he wouldn't have to take this step.

They had given Haltim one order when he'd been sent to the Reach, just one. "Watch anyone with the last name of Reis. Do not let them leave the Reach, keep them away from the Smith Guild." He'd asked questions. Who were these people that they had to be singled out? The ban hadn't been explained, but not too long after Haltim had arrived, and met William's father, Nathan Reis, Haltim had spent several days going through the oldest records searching for the name, Reis.

He'd found it on the second day, and he knew then why the Church of the Eight didn't want a Reis anywhere near the Smithing Guild. He didn't agree though, if what the old scrap of parchment had said was true, the only real reason for keeping a Reis out of the Guild was political. A loss of power, influence. All because William Reis, was in fact of the bloodline of Simon Reis, the final Forgemaster of Amder.

"Excuse me, are you the Priest here?" A voice Haltim didn't recognize drew his attention though the sight of the man standing at the entrance. A cold sweat pricked on his forehead. His eyes flicked to the cover stone bust of Amder.

"Hello?" The man waved to him. "Are you the Priest here?"

"Yes, I am. And you must be the Guild Smith here for the testing?" Haltim tried to speak calmly and clear, to banish any uncertainty from his voice.

"Yes, Jaste Naom. But please, call me Jaste." Jaste sat down on a long bench looking around the church. "You know I've been in the Reach before, and I'd never set foot in here, this place is amazing!"

Haltim smiled. "It's an ancient building. First built as the Main Temple of Amder, a hundred years after the fall they consecrated it to all Eight. Well... All seven."

Jaste nodded and looked around as Haltim wondered why he was here. Haltim broke the silence. "Can I help you?"

"Oh yes. Sorry. Do you know a young man named William? William Reis?"

The chill brought out goosebumps at those words. This couldn't be chance, something more was going on. "Yes, I do." Haltim took another side glance at Amder's bust, not wanting to look the Guild Master Smith in the eyes.

"Good. Well this is a strange question, but I sort of ran into him earlier, and the name struck me. Reis at least." Jaste pursed his lips and fidgeted with his fingers as Haltim paced. "Reis is the family name of the last Forgemaster of Amder, wasn't it?"

Haltim stopped dead. Hands ice cold, he forced himself to stand still, a swirl of thoughts overcame him. "I am not sure." Haltim felt the lie slip from his lips with an internal wince.

"Oh... I hoped you would. I think I'm right, and imagine, a Reis in the guild! That would be something." Jaste stood giving the large space one last look. "Don't want to bother you anymore, hoped you'd know. I can always check when I get back to the capital and the Guild Hall. Just for curiosity's sake."

Haltim said nothing. He nodded in response and walked away. He needed to do two things, one take a very strong drink, and two, find out everything he could about this Master Smith, this Jaste Naom person.

7

Jaste walked out of the church in thought. His suspicions had been correct, William Reis was of the line of the Forgemasters. The old priest had been in a near panic when he'd asked, regardless of what his words were. The main question was why? Why the lie?

Jaste had never paid much attention to guild politics. He didn't care about currying favor or using power to get what he wanted. Jaste loved to create things of strength and beauty, to craft with skill and knowledge. Jaste wished he had paid more attention, why would the guild not want a Reis?

He couldn't mention this to Regin, the man would use it as a bargaining chip for more power. He wasn't sure what he would do, but if the piece that William Reis made was good, he would get him into the Guild.

Jaste made his way back to the inn, greeting various merchants, miners and others as he walked. Reachers were a friendly folk and being a member of the Smith guild got him that much more attention. It took him longer than he'd wanted to get back to the Inn, but the extra time had allowed him to come up with a plan for Regin.

"Jaste! There you are." Regin looked up from the table where he was eating breakfast, a late breakfast by Jaste's standards. Regin shoved a slice of Klah covered bread into his mouth and waved him over.

Jaste smiled, time to put his plan into motion. The sooner he got Regin down the road the better. "Morning Regin. Bit of a late morning, is it?" Jaste sat down, grabbing a small sausage off the tray on the table.

"Master Jaste! It was the long trip and with the endless quizzing, it exhausted me." Regin swallowed a large gulp of water and smiled.

"Nothing to do with that girl I saw you talking to last night?" Jaste took a bite of his pilfered snack amused by the panicked look on Regin's face. "Don't think about it Regin, I won't tell her father, the one who owns the inn." Regin turned a paler shade as he opened his mouth and then closed it again.

"But, for your safety, and for political reasons it may be better for you to go ahead, to Kilvar, remember?" Jaste nodded his head toward the innkeep.

"That's a good idea, Master Jaste." Regin stood and nodded to Jaste, not making eye contact with the owner who was wiping down the tables.

Jaste laughed to himself. The girl wasn't the owner's daughter, he didn't know who she was in fact. But Regin had a certain reputation, and he could use it to his advantage. Besides, Regin would spend the rest of the stop here in the Reach eating and trying to pick up more girls. Better to send him on his way and get things setup in Kilvar, at least he'd do some work there.

Jaste ate more off the tray before waving the Innkeep over. "My companion will check out today early, he's heading to our next stop." Jaste waved off the innkeepers offer to give him back some of the coin. What he needed to do was come up with a plan for this William Reis.

***

Will awoke with a start, still sitting in the chair before the now cold fireplace. Back stiff, but feeling more human than he had yesterday, Will stretched, hearing the audible pop as he moved joints stiff from sitting upright all night. Stretching again, his fingertips brushed against two bags on the floor. Today was the day.

"Morning Will. Interesting place to sleep." Duncan raised a glass to him as Will groaned.

"Thanks for waking me up Dunc, appreciate it." Will stood. "Could have gotten me up sooner."

"Hey, how am I supposed to know that would be what you wanted?" A quick grin broke out on Duncan's face.

"Yeah, I sleep in a chair in front of the fireplace." Will grumbled. "At least I feel more normal."

Will hefted the bags, one light, one heavy, but both the keys to fulfilling a lifelong dream.

"Dunc, thanks again." Will didn't look up. "I'm getting started today."

Silence blanketed the room for a minute as Duncan didn't respond. Will glanced up to see Duncan looking at him with a resigned expression.

"What?" Will shot at his cousin.

"Last chance, Will. You can back out of this, and we can sell that Wight iron, hide the crystal, and continue on here, in the Reach." His voice betrayed a bit of hope.

Will sighed. "Duncan, I risked my life for this. I will not back out now."

Duncan nodded. "I figured. Well then, where are we going?" Duncan stood and cleaned up from his breakfast.

"We?" Will asked confused.

"Hey, I may not understand the dream, but no cousin of mine will do this alone." Duncan attempted to smile.

"I need to eat, then we head to the forge I put together, out of town. And I'd be more than happy to have you help Dunc, I mean that." He was glad that Duncan was offering. Truth was, he hadn't figured out how he would balance all the background tasks of heat control and all the other bits while he was working the Wight iron. Having another pair of hands was great.

"No problem Will. Tell me what you need me to do." Duncan waved him off to get ready.

In short order they left the house, the blood of Amder and the Wight Iron stored next his skin, inside his heavy leather jerkin. He didn't want to take chances with either of them. Too valuable, each one.

***

Haltim sat in the inner office of the temple, trying to calm himself. He thought back many years ago to his childhood, growing up on a farm out in the Western plains. Haltim had been only six or seven when a neighbor had bet him, he couldn't ride in a cart pushed down the only hill in miles. The remembered flying feeling as the cart gathered speed and drop in his stomach as it threw him out of the cart, unconnected to everything. The pain of landing, and trying to breathe, trying to get his lungs working after the impact pushed everything out Nothing else had scared him as much since. Until now.

This situation was far worse than that. Haltim felt like everything he was trying to control was fraying away in his hand, and flying away, faster and faster.

Years of work, befriending the Reis family, was now in danger of being wasted. And if he admitted it to himself, what had started out as part of his job, had become something of an actual thing. He liked William Reis, even that questionable cousin of his, Duncan Reis, had charm. But a Reis must never become a Guild Smith. Never.

That truism had been in place for hundreds of years before he had taken this position. Now, a Guild Smith is asking questions, William Reis would do his test, and there was not a thing Haltim Goin, Priest of the Eight, could do about it.

A ping sound interrupted his thoughts, as if a piece of metal heated up was expanding. His mood became darker still with the sound. Haltim's superiors wanted to talk to him.

***

Jaste waved to Regin as he watched the Journeyman start the cart heading towards Kilvar, with a sense of satisfaction. Regin was a good man, underneath it all, Jaste was sure of that. But, if Jaste broke the rules, the last person he wanted around was Regin.

He needed to find out more about this William Reis person, and if he was lucky, talk to the lad before he could run away. Finding out more about William Reis turned out to be the easy part as everyone in the Reach knew who he was. They all told the same story about the young man.

Dependable, talented, trustworthy. The same words repeatedly. He didn't find anyone who didn't agree on those three things. One woman spent a long time wondering about how growing up without parents affected him, with no family except his cousin, whose name Jaste learned was Duncan.

As admired as Will was, Duncan was not. No one said anything bad about this cousin, a lot of, "kind of lazy", "doesn't use his gifts", and several said they'd not let Duncan Reis anywhere near their daughters.

The Reis brothers lived in the oldest part of the Reach. Jaste got lost trying to find the place, the older parts of the Reach were fitted stone, and the contours of the roads matched the natural terrain of the land, meaning lots of small rises and dips, double backs, and sharp turns.

Jaste turned a corner to find a large home in front of him, so large it dwarfed other houses on the street. He knew it had to be the place he'd been looking for at once, as it had the huge visage of Amder on the side. One person he had spoken to mentioned that William Reis was a devout believer in Amder.

His knock brought nothing, no one appeared to be home. Jaste waited a while, pacing back and forth in front of the place, waiting to see if either of the Reis lads appeared.

"They left this morning, not sure where they went, but they did head out of town, deeper into the mountains." A woman yelled at him as she swept in front of a house across the street.

"Ah, thank you. Can you not mention me stopping by to them, it's supposed to be a bit of a surprise." Jaste didn't want William to know because he didn't want to arouse any panic. He looked again at the Amder carving on the house. It fit the idea that William Reis and his cousin were of the line of the Forgemasters.

Jaste's trip back to the inn was uneventful, his thoughts more on trying to remember what he could about the Forgemasters. They were more myth and legend these days than something that was studied. At least that's what he remembered from his days as an Apprentice.

Gone and dead. But why? A thought occurred to him that gave him a chill up his back. The priesthood of Amder had long ago placed the ban on Reachers ever being a guild smith. This wasn't common knowledge, one had to be a Master to even have access to that level of information. You didn't cross the Priesthood, even if Amder *was* dead, they wielded power and influence on levels above that of Governments.

The reason had always been a subject of some curiosity, though not one worth fighting over. The Guild and the Priesthood had an intertwined relationship, one that was lucrative. If the priesthood didn't want a Reacher to be in the Guild, why make them mad?

But what if the reason, the real reason, was because they, the Priests, didn't want a Reis getting guild trained? Could the Priesthood be trying to stop a Forgemaster from appearing? The

Priesthood of Amder had power and wealth. Odd for a dead god's faith, but the wealth they had accumulated outstripped that of most small kingdoms. How they did it was unknown, but they had a way for 'blessing' forged items that made them special. And they charged fees that were astronomical. Jaste's thoughts, chaotic and mixed, were all on trying to have this idea make sense.

8

Will, wherein the stone halls of Gunnar did you build this forge of yours?" Duncan laughed as they walked, picking their steps with some care. Will had guided them off the main trail an hour ago, and onto a stone and gravel strewn path that could loosely be called one.

"You will see. You're not the only one who goes looking for places Dunc!" Will smiled at his cousin in jest. "Not far."

Duncan shrugged. He'd done some scaving out here, but most of the good finds were the other directions towards the Mistlands. Deeper into the mountains was the domain of animals and bandits, neither of which did Duncan enjoy finding. No profit in it. The steep side canyon walls were near vertical, funneling debris, water, and whatever else fell here onto this path.

A few minutes later Will vanished from Duncan's sight, surprising him.

"Will!" Duncan yelled, the echoes bouncing around off the bare rock walls of this narrow canyon.

"No need to yell Dunc, look!" Will popped up on the other side of a large boulder that merged with the walls, being the same color of stone.

Duncan followed Will and turned the corner to find, to his surprise, a tower. A stone tower, unlike any he'd seen. It was old, Duncan could tell that right off, the surface of the building weathered and moss grew in more than one spot. Yet the rocks were tight, well laid. The clearing they were in was a surprise too. Grassy almost, though evidence was here and there of rocks being moved.

"What is this place?" Duncan asked. His thoughts turned to scaving without realizing it. Wonder if there's anything valuable here, buried?

"No idea." Wills answer was quick and sure. "Found it two weeks ago. I was searching the valley we walked down to get here for ore traces and followed it to the end and found this. I figured this was the perfect place to build my forge, private, shaded, and off the beaten path."

Will waved around the clearing. "I cleaned up the place and used a lot of the stone on the ground to build the forge, which is in the tower. Didn't want it outside in case it rained, with these steep walls you know how a bad a rainstorm can be."

Duncan nodded. A bad rainstorm meant a flash flood. He eyed the tower in thought. It made this place even more of a puzzle. It should have washed a tower like this away years ago. But here it stood, whole and strong.

"Well let's see this forge then." Duncan wanted to see the inside of the tower more than the forge, despite his promise to help Will with the work.

Will led the way, entering the tower through what had been a doorway, though the door was long gone. Will had set up a simple forge. Bags of coal stacked in the corner, a small bellows, several hammers of various sizes, tongs. No anvil to speak of, though Will had found a flat piece of rock iron to work on.

"Quaint." Duncan remarked with a grin. His attention however was more taken by the inside of the tower. Smooth inside walls, almost glass like. Remnants of a stone stairway hung above them, the bottom half missing. Duncan could feel the almost irresistible urge to find a way up those stairs. Let Will obsess about the Guild and Smithing, Duncan wanted to explore!

***

Haltim waited in front of the fire, waiting the sending from the High Priest of Amder. He did not think this would be an enjoyable conversation. The rule was a strict one, and while he hadn't broken it, his failure to guide Will off this path was one he was sure he'd hear about. He hadn't spoken to anyone at the Temple of Amder in over a decade, not since Will and Duncan's fathers had vanished.

A face appeared in the fire, wreathed in smoke.

"Haltim?" The face of the High Priest Bracin asked, his face set in a scowl.

Haltim hated this man. Bracin's predecessor had been a hard man, but fair. Bracin was only hard. Fat, corrupt, and hard.

"I appear to have been unsuccessful at steering William Reis away from the Guild trials. More so, I was unaware that the Master Smith sent this year is someone who does not know the information about the Reis family. He's asking questions, pointed ones." Haltim felt his stomach flip at all this.

"If you'd done your job, it wouldn't matter who the Guild had sent. You're too old Haltim. Too old and too close to the Reis boys to make the hard choices. Mining and Blacksmithing can be dangerous work. That William Reis still lives or at least has all his limbs intact proves you can't do what needs to be done." Bracin's jowls flexed in a smug grin. "And based on your reports, the other one should have gone out one day, and just never returned."

Haltim could not breathe as he heard the words. The High Priest of Amder, suggesting that Will and Duncan be maimed or killed was so far out of what he had expected he didn't know what to say. "I'm sure you don't mean that." Haltim said, his voice low and struggling to speak.

"Why wouldn't I mean it? I have yet to understand why we even let the bloodline survive. You had the perfect opportunity when the boy's mother, father and uncle were killed by the Valni. Yet you let the boys, both, live and grow. And now, one of them is trying again to get into the Guild. It's stupidity beyond words." Bracin paused and sighed.

"Now it may be too late. This Guild Smith, what is his name? I'll go have a talk with the leadership of the Smithing guild." Bracin's face grew foul, as if talking to the Guild was something he had no desire to do.

"Jaste Noam." Haltim replied. "He is well... different." Haltim watched to see if the name sparked something on the face of the High Priest.

"Jaste Noam? I've heard the name, nothing good." Bracin replied but didn't react either way.

"So, what do I do? The trial is next week, William wants me to bless his work before the trial." Haltim asked not sure if he wanted to hear the answer this man, his superior would say.

"Fake a blessing, and nothing else. I'll do *your* job and make sure he's rejected by the guild. Once the guild has moved on, it will be time to talk about your retirement Haltim. Things should have never gotten to this state. We will end the Reis line, and never will that family cause us problems again." Bracin's face spat to the side, Haltim watched a glowing spark shoot out of the projection and land on the stone floor, still hot.

"Yes, High Priest." Haltim replied, trying hard to keep his face calm and set. Before Bracin could say anything else Haltim put out the fire with sand from a nearby bucket.

"I can't do this." Haltim said out loud to the empty room, and he began to rock as despair overcame him. How had it come to this? He had to choose, between the faith he had lived his whole life, and the lives to two innocent young men, who he knew and respected. How had it come to this?

9

"Duncan, focus!" Will said, watching Duncan's eyes focus back on him.

"Sorry Will, was only thinking." Duncan glanced upwards at the ruined stairs.

"I know what you're thinking, Dunc." Will replied with a shake of his head. "Look, help me get this done and I'll help you explore this place, ok?"

Duncan considered for a moment and nodded. He never would have found this place without Will. There was something valuable here, he knew it.

Together the cousins made short work of getting setup, even Duncan who wasn't much into forge work knew what to do. The fire was burning, and the bellows worked to make the coals hot enough from good metal work.

"What are you going to make anyways Will? A brooch? A dagger?" Duncan asked, working the small bellows to keep the fire burning.

"No, a hammer." Will answered weighing the two bags again in his hands. "Should be enough Wight iron to make one."

Duncan snorted. "A hammer? You're using that priceless Wight iron, to make a hammer? Not to mention a forbidden shard of a god's blood. To make a hammer?"

Will nodded. "I know how to make them. I don't know how to make jewelry, nor do I have the right tools." Will waved to what he had around him. "And a hammer feels right."

Duncan looked around. "Answer me another question. Why have we come here, out in the middle of nowhere, to a mysterious tower on a makeshift forge, to make a hammer? We have a well-appointed forge back home. All the tools you could need."

"Tradition." Will watched the coals. "All guild trial pieces are supposed to be done like this. I would assume you'd know this."

Duncan only reply at first was a snort. "Stupid tradition, and why would I know? I never had this dream."

Will shrugged. "I guess it's to test your abilities with the best tools not available."

"Still a stupid tradition," Duncan replied, but kept working the forge.

Will put down the bag of Wight iron, and opened the bag with the small crystal, the soft white light it gave off streaming out of the bag.

"So how do you use the thing anyways?" Duncan asked. "I mean do we toss it at the fire and see what happens?"

Will didn't answer at first, his attention glued to the small glowing shard.

"I don't know." Will answered still not looking up. "The story says you bury it in the coals and then forge and it's supposed to *DO* something."

"Great. Watch it explode and kill us both." Duncan smirked and shrugged. Will clenched his teeth for a second before answering back.

"Shut up Dunc." Will glanced up at his cousin, away from watching the forge. "Really. This isn't your thing. I know you're not a follower of Amder. I know you think this is all a waste of time. I appreciate you helping me all the same, but please. This is special. This is sacred."

Duncan opened his mouth to speak but closed it. He shook his head but said nothing.

"Coals are ready." Duncan said, grabbing the bellows and giving Will a nod.

Will nodded, and in one motion upended the bag into his palm. He watched the small white light fall, as if time was slowing down falling into his palm, he felt it touch.

The groans of men echoed around him, as they brought the wounded back from the front lines. Horrible wounds covered some of them, as the bloodsworn of Valnijz used jagged blades to great effect. A tall man, the Forgemaster walked around them, touching them, talking to them, and comforting them. The Forgemasters cloak once bright was muddy and dark at the bottom now, and the day was dark and gray. The Forgemasters face could not be seen, but the figure stood upright, his hand hefted the large hammer onto his shoulder, fingers tightened around the handle.

Will gasped for a second. He turned to Duncan "Duncan!"

A scream rent the air, unlike any heard before. Men went down, clutching heads in pain. The Forgemaster did not fall, though his grip on the hammer faltered as it slipped to the muddy ground. The scream came again, and panic set in. Men yelling, running away, a man ran by crying tears of blood, screaming "Valnijz has come! Doom to us all!"

"Will!" Duncan's voice cleared the vision from Wills head. His cousin looked concerned, almost.

"You ok there? What happened? You were still like a stone for a few minutes. That thing..." Duncan pointed the crystal in Will's palm. "That thing hasn't done something to you has it?"

Will considered for a second what to say. "Sort of. I saw a vision. Of the day of the death of Amder and the making of the Mistlands." There, said and out there.

"What? A vision?" Duncan stopped working the bellows to look at Will in the eye for a long few seconds. "This isn't the first time it's happened, is it? You're too calm for that."

"No. Yesterday. After meeting with Haltim, I almost gave up. I went to break the crystal at home in the forge and I had one then to." Will looked at the crystal. "I saw a Forgemaster, Duncan. The final Forgemaster."

Duncan spat. "Made up junk for fools and idiots. Forgemasters were made up, to keep us Smiths and Miners feeling important."

Will shook his head. Duncan would never understand. "I saw him Duncan. It's tied to the Crystal, it's part of Amder."

Duncan held up a hand. "Let's end this here Will. We both know where we stand on this, and we came here to get your forging done. Put the crystal in the fire, let's get this over with." Duncan's face was impassive as he turned back to the forge, the red light of the coals lighting his face from below.

Will nodded, there wasn't much point in going over it again. With a small inner prayer, Will made place in the coals near the bottom for the crystal and with a pair of tongs, placed the crystal in the forge.

Will placed the heap of coals over the crystal and waited. Duncan worked the bellows a few times as they both stared at the forge. Will held his breath, unsure of what was going to happen. *Would this even work?*

The change was subtle at first as the once red and black forge, transitioned. Flames and coals turned whitish grey, and the blacked coke and clink faded into a blueish grey. Will looked up to see a look of astonishment on Duncan's face.

"Believe me now?" Will asked his cousin, but he knew Duncan wouldn't answer.

Will reached down and grabbed a small crucible and upended the bag of Wight Iron ingots into the vessel, hearing the telltale moaning sound the metal made as it hit the sides and bottom. Setting the crucible in the forge, Will could feel excitement building. He would do it; he could make something worthy of being a Guild Smith.

***

"Zalkiniv," the huge man said as he bowed to the woman seated on the litter. She could feel his skin prickle from here, hear the blood rushing thorough his veins. Her mouth watered at the thought, but she pushed such desires away. Golmor had his uses still.

"Golmor. Have they have fed the host?" Zalkiniv needed her God's chosen children to be at full strength and power when the time came for his rebirth. There were only three things needed and she already had one. Her eyes fell to the staff in her lap. No staff was it, but a spear haft. The spear haft of a God.

"Yes, Oh High Priest." Golmor prostrated himself to the ground as was the custom. Zalkiniv licked her lips at the sight, she could see a large vein popping out. "Good Golmor. I have gathered enough of the Valni, it is time to make the move for the second item needed, the blade."

The blade of the spear of Valnijz. Then, the blood sacrifice. And she knew who her God demanded be that person. There was one known, through the Valni, and through her visions. His blood would be the guide for the Destroyer to return.

"Yes, Zalkiniv. We shall be the living spear; direct us and we shall make it so for the Glory of Valnijz!" Golmor kept his face down as he spoke, not daring to look the High Priest in the face.

Zalkiniv laughed. "It will come to us, not us to it. It is somewhere beyond the barrier. Stand Golmor. Your fear and the sound of your blood rushing to your head is making me hungry."

She watched as Golmor stood, unable to look her in the face. Golmor missed who she had been before, what she had been before. Once she had been his sister, Aredor, and blood ties were sacred here. Chosen to be the vessel of the High Priest. Blood had been drained and replaced with his. His blood, his mind, his power flowed through her now. She was no longer Aredor, she was now Zalkiniv, the ancient High Priest of Valnijz.

The time of waiting was almost over, the return of Valnijz was almost upon the world. No other God would stand against Valnijz now. Amder was gone, dead, and the others would not dare test their power against the Blood God anymore.

"I must prepare for the ceremony Golmor. We will summon the Blade to us, whatever the cost." Zalkiniv sat back in the litter, closing her eyes. She could taste the rich iron tang in the air, the smell of blood, the smell of power.

10.

Will watched the ingots melt, their silvery color intensified by the white light of the Amder-touched forge. He could have forge welded the ingots together. But he wanted seamless, he wanted it to be as perfect as his skills could make it. Therefore, the melt, and repour into the sand molded blocks that Duncan had made for him. One long and rectangular, one squatter and thicker for the head.

"Still don't get the hammer, Will." Duncan cleaned the sand, making it as smooth and compacted as he could. "And a metal haft? Heavy, and useless."

"It's to show my skill, Dunc. That's all." Will eyed the crucible. Was the metal ready? It was hard to tell in this light. The forge had already shown them one surprising side effect, since placing the crystal, they didn't need to work the bellows anymore. The forge, somehow, stayed the right exact temperature for working the Wight Iron.

Will grabbed a set of tongs and grasped the small crucible to pour the two new ingots for the hammer. The molten Wight Iron gave off its name sake low sound as it poured. The pour went well, and soon enough both new ingots were cooling, filling the tower space with heart.

"While those cool, want to see what's up there?" Duncan's attention once again looking up at the stone stairs, just out of reach.

Will laughed, Duncan had a one-track mind about scaving. It would take the ingots a while to cool, so they had the time, and it was the least he could do to pay back the help, and the company. Will himself found this tower a little unnerving. He always felt like something was at the corner of his vision, something warning him away. It was perfect for the forge, but he wasn't sure it was a place he'd want to be afterwards.

"Well then boost me up. I need to see what's up there." Duncan pointed to the stairs edge. "I can pull myself up with a boost."

"Fine but be careful." Will made a stirrup for Duncan to step into with his hands, bracing himself against the tower wall.

"I'll be careful; I do this all the time!" Duncan replied as he grabbed the edge of the stone stairway. "Why didn't you explore this place?"

"Why would I? It's on this side of the barrier, and I'm not about to go climbing up a broken stone staircase on my own. I wouldn't even be able to get up there by myself." Will flinched as a small stone cracked off the stair edge with Duncan's weight and hit his foot. No pain came but it underscored the chances Duncan took regularly. "Just be careful. I don't want you to somehow take down the stairs on my head, burying me under a pile of stones for a thousand years, waiting for some poor prospector to find my bleached and crushed bones."

"Not a chance cousin. Not a chance." Duncan replied. "Stairs look complete up here, surprised the bottom level is missing. There's another level! Floor looks solid from the bottom; I'm going to look."

"Ok, I'll wait here, but be careful." Will called back up the tower. He could hear the steps of Duncan on the steps, then silence. He shouldn't worry, Duncan knew what he was doing. Nothing bad ever seemed to happen to Duncan.

***

Duncan could not believe this tower that Will had found. He considered himself an expert on the ruins in the area. Even getting to where he could tell which era and wave of history each ruin was from, and what he might find there.

But this tower was unlike anything he'd ever seen. No ornamentation at all, but the set stones, the mirror smooth polish on the walls, all spoke to high skill. Even the stairs themselves after the rough edge at the bottom were in perfect shape.

What treasures could I find here? Duncan wondered. The thrill of experiencing something new coursed through him. It also helped him clear his head of the sight of the white light coming out of the forge. That situation was one he didn't want to think about, Gods and legends, nothing he ever wanted to get mixed up in.

He walked up the steps, measuring each step ready to step back if he felt any give in the next move forward and up. The opening to the next level, an open square of blackness stood in front of Duncan, the light from the forge below dim at this level.

Reaching into a pocket, Duncan took up a bit of cloth, soaked in beeswax and coal dust. A small item of his own making, he could light it and throw it into the room to give light for a good quarter hour, at least enough time to check it out.

He lit it with flint and steel from his other pocket, he always carried it with him, as a force of habit. Valni didn't like fire, and if you wanted to live while you were scaving you had to be ready.

The small cloth flared to life as Duncan threw it into the room above him, seeing the orange glow fill the space, he stepped up into the round room.

The walls glittered, and the floor danced in pinpoints of reflected light. It took a moment for Duncan's eyes to adjust, the small light he had created was being thrown back to him in a million different tiny ways. A large cube in the room's middle dominated the room, a tomb maybe. *Treasures indeed.*

As his eyes adjusted, he could see the walls were rough here, but a quick touch told him why. Every stone was carved and polished to look like gemstone. *Someone or some people spent a great deal of effort here.* The floor on this side was a rich marbled green and black, a stone that Duncan had never seen.

He caught his breath while looking at the cube more closely, it was a tomb! Jet black, and embossed with goldlace figures of men fighting, the artistry was amazing. This could be the biggest haul of his scaving life!

He paused, looking back at the opening down. There were two problems as he saw it. One, he didn't have a lot of time. Will would be waiting and wanting to work on the hammer, not take the time to open a tomb.

And, Will wouldn't help him do it. Duncan didn't understand the reticence. They were dead, who cares if he took what was there? But to Will and some others, scaving was fine, but tomb scaving was wrong. Evil, even. Duncan didn't understand the difference, but there was some in the minds of others.

Duncan would have to come back here alone. Without Will, and with the right tools, and do this himself. His light was burning out, so he'd better head back down. Duncan went down the stairs to rejoin Will, glancing back at the tomb.

"Soon," Duncan muttered, and headed down the stairs, leaving the light to sputter once, twice, and then go out, leaving it once more to darkness.

***

Will paced, Duncan had been gone longer than Will liked, and the ingots would be ready soon. He wanted to at least get the haft drawn out today, and the head shaped as well if there was enough time. Relief flooded through him at the sound of footsteps coming back down above him.

"Curiosity fulfilled?" Will called.

"Yep, just more space, pretty, but empty." Duncan answered, his footsteps echoing down the stairway. Duncan peered down over the broken stair edge. "Jumping down."

Will went to help, but Duncan already had jumped, landing on the mossy floor of the tower with a light thud.

"Strange place you've found here Will." Duncan looked around, shaking his head.

"Strange how?" Will asked, his attention was elsewhere. He tapped each of the new castings, hearing the low tone again. Perfect. He was doing this!

"Different." Duncan answered, but his tone drew Will back to him.

Duncan was staring back up the stairs, his thoughts obviously on what he had seen. *He's not telling me something.* Will wondered if he should push and see if Duncan would change his story about what he had seen. *No, it would only make him mad.*

"Ok these are ready, let's get these drawn out into the handle and the head." Will stood taking up a pair of gloves he had stuffed through his belt. Barnark skin, flexible and easy to wear, but heat resistant. Will glanced at the still white flamed forge, questioning for a second if the gloves could stand up to those flames.

Will steeled himself. He hoped he was doing the right thing, but it was too late to back out now. He removed the longer of the two castings from the sand, brushing off the few grains attached to it.

With a nod to Duncan, who stood nearby, Will took the piece that would be the handle with a tong and placed it in the forge's middle. To close to the bottom would be too hot, and to near the top impurities in the fuel could darken or stain the metal. At least with a normal forge fire, who knew with this one?

Will and Duncan watched in silence as the metal heated, the only sound the occasional turning of the long rectangular cube in the forge. Will judged it hot enough at last and drew it out. The rod was glowing yellow white as he placed it on the large flat slab of ironrock. He wished he had a proper anvil but moving one out here would be a long hard task.

Duncan's arm came into his field of vision, holding his largest hammer. Will took it with a smile and nod, his eyes gazing down at the crude carving on the handle of a man at work, forging. With a silent prayer to a dead god, Will raised the hammer and struck, starting the work of shaping and lengthening the metal into the haft.

Sparks, white hot and strong flew off the Wight Iron with each hammer stroke. Duncan jumped back a few times in response, much to Will's amusement. He had never used Wight Iron before, he wasn't sure if that was normal, but he couldn't stop it.

The other surprise was the sound. Working metal, you got the distinct clink and clunk sounds with each hammer blow on hot metal. Will had expected the stuff he was working with to give off its normal moaning sound as something struck it. But the sound he was getting was neither. Each hammer blow brought forth a rumble, as if a distant thunderstorm was working its way over the Skyreach, and the echoes were bouncing around the valleys and mountainsides.

"Will, should it make that sound?" Duncan asked and backed away from the forge, closer to the opening in the wall where a door had once stood.

"I don't know, but it seems to still be fine to work." Will couldn't stop now. Working this metal was a dream. Each hammer blow fell in place, the metal stayed hot, the perfect temperature to shape. Reheating the work in progress also took less time than he had expected. Far faster than he had planned, the basic shape and form came together.

Duncan handed him a small hammer and chisel for detail work, and Will began the final steps of decoration. A small hammer blow here and there to make the surface as smooth as he could. Grabbing a small chisel, he hammered a basic shape, the hammer and anvil of Amder onto the main part of the shaft.

Looking up and grinning, Will locked eyes with Duncan who was watching Will work. Duncan nodded but added no commentary for once. Will looked back down at the work, the joy of it filled him. *Joy of Creation* his Da had called it. He'd felt it before, but never on this scale.

"Quenching time almost here. Duncan, there's a jug of oil behind that rock, can you pour it in the crucible? Going to use that as a vessel, didn't want to move yet another thing up here." Will's concentration was fixed to the work, he had to heat it one last time, keeping the balance of heat and the metal itself.

Silence greeted his request. Will looked up to find Duncan looking up again, back where he had explored before.

"Duncan?" Will said louder.

"Huh? Oh right... oil." Duncan filled the crucible slowly making sure not to spill any.

Will rotated the first half of the work in the fire while he waited for the quench to be ready. He reveled in this moment. The smell of the hot metal, the feel of the forge on his face, how his arm felt after hammering it into place, the sight of the glowing hot metal reshaped to his desire.

"Oil ready!" Duncan stepped back from the vessel on the floor.

Will stepped forward and lowered the haft into the thick liquid. Smoke flew out, heavy and greyish white. A few flashes of flame shone through the haze, vanishing as the heat leached out into the oil. Will looked at Duncan after a minute and held his breath. This was the moment, to see if this all was worth it.

Will drew forth the haft and released his breath. The haft was perfect. The surface shone with a mirror like shine, shimmering in the sunlight that came through the ruined doorway. The light of the forge showed a different color, and the flowing ebbs and swirls of the metal itself, locked into stasis.

"That is something." Duncan spoke, breaking his silence. "I know the value of metalwork, and that? That is incredible."

Will grinned. It was. The surface was flawlessly smooth, except for the small hammer struck pattern of marks that had symbolized a smith at a forge. He couldn't have imagined a better start. It was the best work he had ever done.

Placing the haft to the side to rest, Will stuck his head outside to check the sun. The breeze ran over his skin, cooling him, and reminding him how sweaty he was. Will motioned Duncan to come outside for a moment to rest and catch their breath.

"Thanks Duncan. Thanks for helping. Thanks for everything." Will looked up at the tower.

"Just an empty room up there? Disappointing for you." Will rested with his back to a large outcropping, feeling the air and enjoying the smell of the trees nearby.

"Yep, an empty room. Whatever was there is long gone." Duncan replied while he scanned the ground for rocks to toss against a stone wall.

"Too bad, interesting place." Duncan continued. "Might come back sometime and see if can find anything buried around here." Duncan pitched rocks at his target, each one making a drawn-out ping noise as they flew off after impact.

Will wondered what had been up those stairs. He knew quite well Duncan didn't go back to places unless he was sure something was there. Will glanced up at the tower again, the uneasy feeling he had earlier gone. It was a pretty spot, and he wondered who had built it, at least for a second.

"Ready to get back to it?" Will asked as Duncan pitched the last rock. "Need to get the head of the hammer made. I know what I want to do."

Duncan sighed. "Do I need to be here for this? I mean, with the way the forge is now."

"Please Dunc? You said you'd help, so help. At least stay and talk." Will looked at the tower one last time. "Besides, this place makes me uneasy, sometimes."

"How? This isn't near the barrier and Valni territory, no sign of nearby predators. Not even signs that bandits visit here. And you found it!" Duncan shifted his weight from side to side fidgeting.

"I don't know, there is something here. I didn't feel it when I found it, but ever since the crystal shard got put in that forge, something feels ... unusual." Will looked back toward forge, its glowing white light filling the bottom of the tower.

"Well, doing things with the blood of a dead god would make you feel different. I mean, it was giving you visions. I'll be glad when that thing is out of your life, and by extension, mine." A large sigh escaped Duncan as he looked up. "All right, let's get this done."

Will felt his shoulders relax as Duncan agreed to stay, tension receding. Had he been that much on edge? Entering the tower again, Will's eyes fell to the haft they had created. Any passing worry about the blood shard vanished as he did so. The thing was a work of art, and he couldn't believe he had been the one who made it.

"Will?" Duncan held up a hammer. "Will?"

Will's head jerked up. "Oh yes, sorry. In thought. Ok, let's get to work."

Taking the other casting of Wight Iron, Will weighed it in his hand. Good weight. He couldn't detect any telltale signs that any impurities had snuck in. He had seen no off gassing either during the cooling on these castings, so he wasn't worried about any trapped bubbles either.

Letting out a long breath, Will readied himself. He placed the ingot in the forge fire again, feeling the heat off it, turning the metal to make sure it was all heating evenly, the routine work pushing away any fears or doubts. Judging it was hot enough, he drew out the metal and placed it on the iron rock anvil. With a quick look and nod at Duncan, he raised his hammer and began to work.

As before sparks flew, fat and white hot. Each hammer strike came with that new thunder sound which didn't startle them as much now. Will lost himself to the work, the hammer blows became one with his heartbeat, hitting true each time. His concentration was all on this one job, this work.

The hammer head took shape once again faster than Will could have ever imagined. Without a thought he pointed to the chisel, it was time to make the whole for the shaft to go through. Squaring his shoulders, Will struck harder, punching the tool deep into the hammer head, forcing it in. The low rumble that the earlier hammer strikes had made now became like the crack of thunder at the height of the storm. Will heard them but ignored it. Everything was the work, the metal, the hammer. Joy filled him for the work, and resolve. Resolve to prove to Duncan and Haltim that he wasn't wasting time on a foolish dream.

Will paused again and pointed to a different chisel. A small part of him wondered why the metal hadn't cooled off yet, how long had it been since he had heated it. Sweat ran down his face, dripped into his eyes, the sting making him blink.

It didn't matter though. He was connected to the forge, to the work, the hammer, the chisel. Each blow he made was in time with his breath, his pulse. Each chisel mark, laying out the face of Amder on the hammer side was perfect, no bounce, and no mistakes.

Hammer held high, Will paused, one last strike, and it would be done. His masterpiece, his dream. Letting out a long breath he pushed the hammer down, the force of it pushing the edge of the carving chisel, the last line of Amder's face appearing in perfect patterning.

Tongs in hand Duncan passed them to Will who grabbed the work and quenched it in the oil. As the hot metal hit it smoked as before, and Will felt exhaustion creep into his bones.

"That was something." Duncan remarked leaning back against the wall. "You ok?"

Will tried to read what Duncan was getting at but failed. "Meaning?"

"You don't know?" Duncan pointed at the anvil. "I swear Will, you didn't feel that?"

Will looked down, something had cracked the Iron Rock Anvil. Cracked in four places in fact. "How long was I working?"

"That's the other thing. You worked that piece for an hour, without stopping. I even tried to stop you twice, but you couldn't even hear me." Duncan walked towards his cousin; his eyes drawn up in concern. "You've got to be tired."

Will could feel a tremble in his arms and shoulders. "Yeah, an hour? Everything stopped, slowed down, I don't know. All me, all my concentration, everything was there. It was strange."

Neither of them said anything for a few minutes. Will was too tired, and Duncan by the look of him was worried or scared.

"Well let's see what you have made with all that work." Duncan motioned for Will to continue.

Will nodded, trying to push back the exhaustion that now crept over him. He pulled out the second half of the hammer. Bent up breath escaped him. "Perfect."

And it was. The shape was better than he could have ever thought, the surface smooth, glasslike, with a slight swirl to the sheen of the Wight Iron. The carving of Amder stared through Will, and he closed his eyes, giving a quick prayer of thanks to the dead god.

Duncan and took up the hammer shaft handing it to Will. "Well? Let's see if all this strangeness was worth it for you."

"Moment of truth Dunc." Will grinned as he looked at this piece, his audition. He would stun the guild smith away with this. He would be the first Reacher ever to be accepted. He had to be with this, how could they say no?

The head and the hilt slid together with an almost silent click. For a second Will could swear it had glowed, but that must have just been the interaction of the forge light at the sheen of the metal. Right? Will blinked as a bead of sweat once again hit his eyes.

Duncan gave off a low whistle. "Guild Smith or not, that's ... One hell of a hammer."

Will couldn't help grin. "Thanks Dunc. If this doesn't get me in, nothing will." He examined the connection between the head and haft and found it hard to find. They fit together perfectly, and while he had taken no steps to join them, they were joined together as if they had been forged as one unit. He gave a few practice swings with the hammer, feeling its weight. Well balanced, even for the metal haft. "Would need a good leather wrapping for real work." Will spoke as he examined his creation.

Duncan snorted. "Anyone who uses that for real work would be a damn fool. That thing is worth a lot of coin." He paused for a second and a look of concern passed over his face. "For argument's sake, if you get in, what happens to that hammer? And if you don't what happens to it? I mean, that is Wight Iron. And forged well, whatever you want to say in terms of how it was made." Duncan waved a hand at the still white glowing forge.

Will nodded. "If I get in, the hammer goes with me. I don't know after that."

"And if you don't get picked?" Duncan asked. "Hear me out. I know that's not what you want to think about, but if you don't, that hammer could set us up for a long, long time."

Will didn't want to think about that. His thoughts were on making it past the testing. "I guess I get to keep it." The words came unwillingly.

Duncan nodded, saying nothing. Will felt its weight in his hand. He knew right then, tossing it up and down, he never wanted to part with it. It was a part of him, somehow. If somehow, he didn't get into the Guild, he couldn't sell it. Ever.

Duncan and Will make short work of cleaning up and packing up tools. Will tossed the broken anvil stone out the door as Duncan hefted a pack heavy with hammers. Duncan faced the forge, and just pointed at it. "I have no clue how to put that out." Will admitted. "Normally I'd cap it off."

"But this is a forge powered by a shard of a dead god's blood, and we don't know what to do with that." Duncan finished the thought of for him.

"I could remove the crystal. If there's anything left that is. The legends never really say." Will reached for a pair of tongs. "Finding it in this might be easier said than done."

Duncan nodded. "Worth a try, I guess. We can't leave it like this."

The tongs slid into the forge as Will moved the coals, white and hissing out of the way, searching for the shard. The heat of the forge hadn't changed since the moment it had gone white, and the tongs got white hot as he searched.

"Careful Will." Duncan pointed to the rising glowing in the metal.

"I will be. Not finding anything anyway." Will sighed as he pushed around more. "Like trying to see a snow hare in a blizzard."

A slight something caught his eye. "Is that it?" Will muttered. The tongs touched something and flared white, and Will sprung back in surprise, the tongs clattering to the ground.

"Found it!" Will exclaimed as he removed his gloves and wiped his now sweaty hands on his pants.

"I see that." Duncan had jumped back as well and was as far away from the forge as he could be and still be in the tower.

Gloves back on Will grabbed the tongs off the floor and was surprised by the lack of heat he felt from them. He wiped glove across his forehead wetting it with sweat and touched that to what should be the hottest part of the metal.

No sizzle greeted his test as Will and Duncan exchanged glances. Will took the tongs to the forge again, he could see the crystal, now that he knew what to look for. With a long breath he grabbed the crystal with the tongs.

Once again, the flare of light came, but Will was ready for it, though he felt his breath catch for a second. He pulled the tongs out of the forge and examined the crystal.

What had once been a milky glowing thing, was dark now, and grey. Small cracks covered its surface. Will dropped it into the oil filled crucible, only to find it didn't smoke at all, it simply dropped into the oil, and not even a sizzle came out.

The light around Will dimmed, and he looked up expecting to find the cause be clouds gathering outside. Weather could change fast in the Skyreach, but the sunlight looked the same. The forge! Will turned towards it surprised at the already fading glow. The once bright light was less now. Will had expected the coals to turn red again, but something even more surprising was happening. The coals were breaking down as the light faded. Falling into a light dusty ash!

"Well, I will wait outside." Duncan's eyes were wide as Will glanced at him. Unease? Will would have guessed unease, knowing how Duncan felt about religion. "Get what you need and tomorrow we will come back to move anything left."

Will smiled as he watched his cousin leave the tower. "Thanks Duncan!" He gathered a few things up that would be easy to carry now and placing the hammer he'd spent so much of his hopes and dreams on in a leather wrapping and putting that inside his shirt. He would not drop that!

Will's eyes hit on the oil and the crystal inside it. Unlike the forge or even the tongs, the oil had remained dark, and still. Will guessed whatever had powered the small shard was gone now, leaving just an ordinary dull crystal behind.

Still, it's something to remember this. Wills thoughts turned to the future, keeping the small crystal and showing it to his children and children's children, after they had been sworn to secrecy.

He grabbed the tongs and fished out the small thing, dropping it into his upturned palm.

The Forgemaster stood in front of the large glowing pool of metal. Glowing white, it shimmered in the gloom. Screams and horns filled the air as the Forgemaster walked up the steps to the edge of the pool. The figure let out a small sob and stepped onto the surface of the strange liquid. For the first time Will could see the face of the man, as he closed his eyes and dropped all the way into the pool, the face... was Will's own.

Will shuddered as he returned to the tower. The crystal remained dark and cracked in his palm, the oil that clung to it making his hand slippery. Will took a deep breath and let it out. Something remained here, some small part of Amder.

"Will, let's go!" Duncan's voice came from outside. "I'm hungry, thirsty, and want to bathe."

Will put the crystal in his pocket, patting it. He had done it, now it was up to the Gods.

11

Duncan stretched feeling the stiffness fade away as he did so. The last two days he had helped Will get all the rest of the tools and supplies out of the tower. He didn't mind helping he admitted if only because he got to make sure he knew the way there and back. The hardest part was not showing his constant and growing interest in the tomb there.

The tomb he couldn't tell Will about, or anyone about. Today was the day, Will was supposed to help in some mine, and he'd told Will he'd be out scaving. Which wasn't a lie, he hadn't said where of course. Will never wanted to know. The cold floor woke him up more as he got ready smoothed with age, but like walking on ice. A splash of water in the face, and fast shave, and Duncan felt aware, and ready.

The sun was up, but only barely as he made his way downstairs, hearing Will before seeing him. Will was about as nimble as that hammer he'd made. Duncan watched his cousin with some amusement as Will banged around in the kitchen.

"Morning Will. What's there to eat? Hungry today, all that moving gear and going out scaving, need food." Duncan sat down at the table, smelling breakfast getting ready.

"Morning Duncan. Got sausages and bread from down in Copperblown." Will replied drinking a hot cup of tea and closing his eyes. "Be ready in a few."

Duncan made himself a cup of tea as well and sat down, forcing himself to calm down, to banish the growing excitement about today. "Good stuff. Copperblown has some good vendors. Nasmira's?" Duncan took a sniff of the air. "Yeah got to be."

Will nodded, still enjoying the hot beverage on this cold morning. "Good guess. Figured since you spent the last two days helping me, was the least I could do." Standing, Will checked on their breakfast. With a grunt of acknowledgement, he plated up three sausages and two pieces of toasted oatmeal bread for each of them.

"Thank you, cousin," Duncan said as he was handed his plate. A quick sniff and that smile got bigger. Sage and pork, his favorite.

Duncan tore into his, as both Will and Duncan ate in silence. Once the meal and cleanup were done, Will left, giving Duncan a quick wave as he headed towards the center of town. "Got to go, want to catch the wagons to the mine, faster than walking!"

Duncan nodded and waited a few minutes to make sure Will didn't come back for anything. He needed to grab some extra tools for this day's work, and Will would ask questions about that. As the minutes ticked past Duncan took another long sip of his tea.

Crowbar, he would need a crowbar. Rope he always had, but a good set of spikes and a mallet he rarely carried around. He also would need a better and longer lasting light source, one of the miner lamps should work.

Satisfied that Will wasn't returning, Duncan packed up the extra tools, holding the crowbar over his back. One last sip of tea and Duncan stepped out to see what he would find in that tomb. The streets were mostly empty now that the miners had headed out for the day.

Duncan found it amusing how many people loved his cousin but were only tolerant of him. But Will was respectable. Doing a Reacher's work, the Reacher's way. He'd heard it many times about Will, and it was the truth. Outside of his obsession with the Smithing Guild and now Amder, Will was a solid, respectable and rather boring member of the Reach. He'd given up years ago trying to get Will to do anything interesting. Will was Will, a great person, but still, dull.

Duncan wasn't, and he knew it. He lived for treasure finding, searching ruins, exploring, and if need be, running away from Valni, bandits and whatever else he found. Most Reachers sort of tolerated him, more for the family name, he was sure. He didn't care much; he found their reactions funnier than insulting.

"Heading out early today Mr. Duncan?" The old guard Camwell asked as he passed by the outer limits of the Reach.

"Yes Camwell, be back later." Duncan replied as he paused for a moment. The Guards knew him well, and he considered it a time investment worth the effort to keep up a relationship with them.

"Anything new Camwell?" Duncan asked, leaning on the crowbar as a makeshift cane.

"No Mr. Duncan, nothing new to see. Though about an hour ago heard a distant roar, like someone injured a beast. Saw nothing, though," Camwell said back, his lined and weathered face looking back at Duncan.

"No worries. I'll be careful." Duncan nodded to the old man and walked on.

A beast? Always good to know. That was one reason he cultivated those relationships; he never knew what information he'd get. He didn't expect to run into anything on this trip. The tower was far enough off the beaten path to be hard to find. Predators were always a worry, but he found it hard to believe that in the few days since he had been there last a wild Narmor or Berog would have taken residence there.

Soon Duncan was making his way through the narrow canyon that led to the tower's clearing. The fact that Will had found this place still stuck in his craw. Will, the over cautious had found a ruin unlike any other. As he made his way his practiced eye could see what he'd not realized before. Most of these rocks he was climbing over resulted from a rock fall, but every so often, a clear spot would be visible, below the rocks, and you would see a weathered but carved piece of stone slab walkway.

This place had once been important, very important. How it had been lost to time, or who it had been built for, he didn't know, nor did he care outside some minor curiosity. The walk was not too bad, though he kept some awareness open for any animal spoor or signs, just in case that roar Camwell had heard did mean something.

Seeing the now familiar large boulder that marked the switchback entrance to the clearing, Duncan could feel his heart beat faster. Almost there, and he would get to see what was in that tomb!

***

Zalkiniv stood at the altar, chanting in the harsh language of the desert. All was in readiness for the ceremony. The people lined up before her were ready. Ready to die, ready to give their blood to the cause. Some were willing volunteers, the true believers. Some were slaves, too worn out to work anymore, but trading their blood to get the release of a relative or friend. She would answer their wishes, though anyone released would first be converted to the faith of Valnijz, the blood god did not let people walk away. And a few were criminals and had chosen this as the method of execution.

It didn't matter to Valnijz, all blood was equal in his eyes. All was needed and wanted. Only the diseased, the sick would not be taken, for they were unclean. Zalkiniv raised her hands, holding the Spear shaft in one hand and a long thin knife in the other. Her chant ended as she crossed the items in front of her, and over the deep and empty well.

Her eyes snapped to the creatures surrounding this area, the Valni. Growling and sniffing, these blessed creatures of the Blood god would get more restless as the day went on. The smell of blood would fill the air, driving them to near insanity. But she was in control, and it was good to show all who gathered that she, the High Priest could control even these wild things, such was the power she had been granted.

With the shaft and soon to be blade both in her possession, she only would need one more thing to allow her God to return to this world. Blood. The blood of one person.

She had communed with the Spirit of her God and had been instructed. They would need the blood of the Foragemaster's line. She had tried before, capturing one of that cursed group off and on over the centuries. But without the shaft, every one of them had either died to the Valni or died waiting for her to be able to move forward. Just a decade ago, the Valni had caught one.

The Valni had succumbed to their hunger, and the man had died screaming, and she had lost her prize. There was only one left now. If the barrier hadn't been in the way, she could grab him without much effort, now that she had the Shaft. But the barrier was in the way, so other plans would have to be made, but first, the Blade.

***

Duncan drove the last spike into the edge of the stairs, sweat dripping down his face. He had tried many times to drive an anchor spike into the walls, but regardless of angle or force of his blows the spikes could find no purchase on the glass like polished walls.

Using the spikes as anchor points, he attached the ropes he had brought building a serviceable and makeshift rope ladder. Grabbing the crowbar, a hammer, and the miner's light he ascended the ladder to the stairs proper. Firing up the lamp, he again made his way up the stone steps, his long experience in scaving telling him that because something had been safe a few days ago, didn't mean it was safe today. Ruins were tricky things, and Duncan had no intention of dying.

Each step was fine, and he approached the opening with a sense of excitement. He'd only found a tomb twice before, a falling wall had crushed one, leaving part of it unable to be searched. The other had already been looted sometime in the past, though they hadn't found everything. But this tomb was untouched. Visions of goldlace, or even more Wight iron drifted through his mind. Gemstones too, or even Drendel Steel weapons. Any of it would reward him for his time.

The room was as he left it, round walls, and the large cube like tomb. The room glittered even more fiercely in the greater light of the miner's lamp he had brought. And there, the tomb. He walked around it, the carvings of a battle, embellished with goldlace, and even bloodstone! He hadn't seen that in the dimmer light before. Even the outside of this thing was a masterpiece.

Who could be buried in a place like this? Some ancient General or warrior? Duncan couldn't remember any historical battles taking place around here other than the one that formed the Mistlands. But that had been over a thousand years ago, and this place couldn't be *that* old.

Duncan took a deep breath and searched for the seam that marked the lid of the cube. The stonework was smooth to the touch and finding it would be no easy task.

***

Zalkiniv stood blood covered and panting in excitement. Over two hundred had died at her hand today, and the blood sang out to her, the final moments of terror and sadness of each person was the finest ambrosia. The Valni were whipped into a frenzy, clawing at themselves unable to feast on the bodies and blood below them. Her control over them was absolute, and it was a display of power to quell any Underpriests with ideas of promotion. She knew they had doubted her before, they did so no longer.

It would not be the first time they had done so. The Blood Gods hierarchy was full of Priests with ambition, who often needed displays to show them just how far below her they were. Let them kill each other, she was past them and always would be.

It was time, the blade must come to her now. Taking the shaft in both hands, she lowered it into the vat of blood until the part she held was above the surface. Forcing her throat to make the sounds of the ancient tongue, she called to the blade, called to the ender of so many lives, the ender of a god.

12.

Duncan felt the edge finally, a tiny hairline offset, it caught on the edge of his fingernail. Taking the crowbar, he placed it on the edge and struck hard, with the hammer. A tiny shift happened, he struck again, moving it more. More hammer blows and the lid started, finally, moving. A hammer blow pushed the lid past the inner edge of the opening. Duncan leaped back covering his face. He had heard stories of opening a tomb and getting a face of spores or dust tainted with some horrible disease, and he had no interest in finding out if they were true.

Nothing emerged, and silence filled the room apart from his heavy breathing. The air had changed around him. Not threatening, but different, as if something wasn't supposed to be here. That feeling grew, and Duncan wondered if he had made the right choice.

Shaking his head at the foolish thought, he took up the crowbar again, and with a heave, levered the lid up and over, careful to not push it too far as to make it crash down. The thick stone lid falling onto the floor was not a thought he liked.

There, the opening was large enough. Duncan paused and then bent over to look inside his prize.

***

Zalkiniv stopped the chant, cursing the day they had put the barrier in place. Followers of the dirty god, the soot stained fool, Amder. Zalkiniv needed more power, and more slave blood wouldn't do it. She needed blood that carried emotion, blood that came from an unwilling victim and she needed it now.

Her eyes swept the small group who watched her, each one a study in either fear or hate, depending on their relationship. Then she spied him, face impassive. She knew how he felt, and how she could use that.

"Golmor. Attend me," she ordered the giant of a man to her side.

Golmor came forward, his face unchanged. She could sense the uncertainty in him, feel his hate and love for her. Hate for the person who had claimed her, love for who she had been before. "Yes Zalkiniv?" he said, his voice a whisper.

Zalkiniv paused, and then smiled, and in the voice of his long-gone sister spoke to him. "Golmor, I miss you. Why did you let him take me? Why did you let me become this?" A single tear released tracing down her blood-covered visage.

The facade of impassive nothing fell from Golmor's face. "Sister? You still exist?" the large man's face gave away his joy at hearing the voice of his long gone relative. "I am sorry, sorrier than I will ever be able to say. I should have hidden you; I should have run."

"I forgive you Golmor." The quiet voice of his sister brought joy to the man's face; the smile grew wider.

"Truly?" the plaintive tone mixed with wonder and joy filled the voice of the man.

"No," Zalkiniv said as she drove her finger topped with a spiked nail cover into his neck, tearing open a main artery. The sadness, despair, anger that tainted his blood was ecstasy. Watching the slight light of hope fade out as he died was a pure joy.

"Now," Zalkiniv whispered and chanted one more time, full of the power granted to her by her master.

***

Duncan's felt disappointed. Inside the tomb were only two things. One a hammer shape, wrapped in cloth. The other a black-looking blade of something, a spearhead? A very large one if so. And why was it black? The tomb otherwise stood empty, dashing his hopes of riches.

A long sigh came out of Duncan, scaving was like that sometimes. He had gotten his hopes up, and what does he get? A hammer and something shaped like a sword. His thoughts turned to the outside of the tomb, and he wondered if that goldlace could be peeled off, and the bloodstones. He could melt it down and sell it off, at least make money off this excursion.

The sound of metal hitting stone broke the silence. Duncan looked around, dropping down to the floor. What had made that noise? The sound came again, coming from inside the tomb not outside. Thoughts fired fast. Maybe opening the tomb up had changed the temperature of the metal, and it was expanding. The noise was very much coming from inside the tomb, and louder each time.

Taking a breath, Duncan peered back inside the tomb. The hammer thing was still where it had been, but the spearhead looking thing, it was ... vibrating? Duncan reached down towards it; it drew him in. His fingers touched the surface, and he jerked back, the spell broken. He fell backwards a few steps, stumbling. His fingers had something black on them, black sticky and one sniff told him, rotten. Blood. It was blood.

How could it be blood? How could it even still be sticky after all this time? The sound came again, even louder than before. He approached the tomb again, more careful of his steps and the feeling of his heart beating strong, and reaching down, intending to grab the hammer and leave the vibrating thing alone. With the miners' lamp in his other hand he looked back into the tomb.

It was a spearhead; he could see it now in the light he had brought. As soon as that thought came to him, the spearhead shot out the tomb, flying! It flew towards the opening to the lower level, fast. Pain climbed up his arm as the feeling made him look down at its source. The Blade had cut a gash down his left hand as it left. Not deep, but long from the bottom of his palm, upwards and across the pad of his thumb. Blood welled forth, shiny and red, a few drops fell to the floor, catching the light.

"Sparks of the Forge!" Duncan yelled, his skin going ice cold and his breath catching at the sight. The spearhead was gone, he was bleeding, and whatever had been on that blade was in his wound! He had a first aid kit downstairs in his bag, and he needed to get to it, fast.

He reached into the tomb and grabbed the hammer shaped wrapped object, he could look at it downstairs, he needed to clean this up, and fast. He made his way downstairs, feeling his head get light, and the throbbing in his hand was far worse than the wound should be. "Great, I've got some disease or poison. Way to be a smart scaver Duncan, getting cut by the blood covered vibrating metal!" He berated himself hoping that he would be ok.

Pain grew in his hand as he made his way down the ropes to the floor below. Reaching the bottom, he could feel the fire of the wound almost overwhelm him. Blackness crept into the edges of his vision as the pain grew. He dumped the hammer bundle and tore open his pack, searching for his first aid kit. He always kept it stocked at least. Tearing the bag open with his uninjured hand and his teeth, he poured the contents onto the ground. There! Powered white root! A good strong wound treatment, but not good for poisons. He grabbed it and resumed searching, his face sweating now as he felt his arm erupt in pain.

Finally, the small blue vial appeared, it had wedged itself between two rocks left over from Will's forge build when he'd poured the contents out. Narmack bile. Taking it from between the rocks, he didn't want to break it, Duncan got it and tore out the seal with his teeth. Steadying himself and poured the contents down his throat, trying not to have to taste it.

Revulsion filled him as the thick blue green liquid hit his mouth, and his gag reflex kicked in strong. He forced his mouth closed, he had to swallow. Forcing himself to swallow the almost gummy liquid down, he was faced with the pain it brought in turn. A spasm of coughs erupted from him and the bile burned his throat all the way down.

Using his teeth again to tear open the white root powder he steeled himself. He wasn't sure he wanted to even look at his hand. He had keeping it under his good arm, pushing down, trying to stem the poison or whatever it was from spreading to fast. The wound on his hand which had a few minutes before been a line of red blood, was already black on the edges, and wider than it had been. Holding his breath, he dusted the wound with the white root.

Pain grew and moved up his arm, pain and a feeling of anger? Rage? Duncan wanted to kill something, someone. Tear it apart with his bare hands, feeling the blood spurting, the flesh tear. To hear the screams as it died.

Duncan screamed, trying to clear his head, stop the madness. The feeling faded, the anger dribbled away, the rage left him. And the wound, the blackness to reduce, a thin black edge existed now. The white root clotted the blood fast, leaving him with a painful scab. He shook his hand, testing its range of motion.

Pain grabbed him again, but nothing like it had been. Duncan swore and kicked a rock nearby. This would not be a fast heal, and without both hands, scaving was off the table, at least for a while. With frustration, he sat down on a rock, holding his head in his good hand. He was tired, exhausted, and injured. None of this had been a good day. And all he had to show for it was what? His eyes slipped to the wrapped hammer, still laying where he had dropped it.

***

Zalkiniv screamed with joy, the blade was coming! She had felt it tear free from whatever had trapped it beyond the barrier and had felt the blood call to her. Raising the shaft high, the blood of her sacrifices joining the stains of old, she waited, feeling it draw closer. The barrier itself proved no major hindrance; it was keyed to living beings.

There! The blade was near, and in the space of a breath, came to rest in front of her, vibrating and shaking with the power of her call. Wisps of smoke curled off the blade, evidence of the barrier passage, but it would take more than that to damage this item. A sound went up from the Valni surrounding the area, a roar of rage, a roar of pain, pleasure, anger. Zalkiniv blinked, surprised, but recovered before anyone noticed. Taking the blade in one hand she looked at it, stained with black blood like the shaft, and red?

Fresh blood! The blade had already tasted blood! Reaching out she felt through the new blood, who had been blessed to be touched by the blade? Who had the honor to be the first victim of the return of the Blood God? The answer stunned even her. She knew this blood! The scaled one moved the world, this was proof. She summoned the blood bond that linked her to the Valni, and the Valni that had tasted the blood of the Reis from before. It was different, but the similar.

Another Reis! There were two! Smiling Zalkiniv fell to her knees to prostrate herself in honor of the Blood God. This was his doing, there were two of the hated line, one or the other, or even both would be used to seal the spear, to bring back Valnijz into this world. No one would stop the Scaled One now.

13

Duncan stood, arching his back to work out the kinks. Rocks weren't very comfortable to sit on for long, and the exhaustion brought on by his near death and use of two medicines that had been strong. This whole damn scaving exercise better be worth something, and the only way to find out was to unwrap this hammer and see what he had.

Grabbing it off the ground, Duncan noticed that the lingering pain in his hand and arm was muted, distant. This was all because Will couldn't just be happy in the Reach. All this messing around with dead gods and things he didn't understand had led to his injury. Maybe it was time to teach Will a lesson about who was in charge.

Mysterious blood covered blades, shards of a dead god's blood, and now this weird hammer, were a bit too far out of his comfort zone. His irritation grew, and he felt like throwing the damn hammer away and going home to rest. He raised his arm to throw it again, arm cocked, and paused. This was the only thing he had to show for today. *At least unwrap the stupid thing it might be worth something.*

The wrappings covering the hammer were odd. Odd and old by the look of them. He carried it out into the afternoon light to look at them, and his eyes widened a bit. The cloth shimmered with the light of day, shimmered with a rainbow of colors and intensity. He felt like he was looking at something that had a rainbow woven into cloth. He'd never seen anything like it. Rubbing his fingers over it he realized, it was woven metal.

"Got to keep that, worth something. And if that's being used as a cover, what it's covering?" He wondered as he worked to find a way to unwrap without damaging the cloth. He'd expect cloth like this to be brittle, the threads fragile and broken down. But this, was as strong as if it had just been made. The only hint to its age was the smell.

Old things smell. The smell of dust, stale air, of the passage of time. The cloth was strong with it, overwhelmed with it in fact, regardless of its beauty. The smell would fade in time, given air. Finding a folded and tucked corner, he began to unwrap the hammer. The cloth was stunning as he unwrapped it. The edges had been woven and embroidered with metals, fine threads of common and rare metals formed a flame like pattern. Some Duncan couldn't even figure out what metals they were.

The glimpse of shimmering metal underneath the cloth stopped him for a second, and he threw the rest of the cloth off the hammer unable to speak. That shimmer, the silvery light, the smooth touch, the inner glow; it was like the hammer Will had made! But it was even grander. The hammer's handle had a ring of gems inlaid, each one different, but each the color of fire and flame. The hammer's head had a bas relief carving of Amder's visage, fine in detail, and impeccably balanced. Work such as this was almost impossible to get right, it unbalanced the final tool. But not this work, it was perfect.

Amder's face peered out, Duncan felt a chill cross his spine, it was looking at him, into him, and finding him wanting. "I don't believe in dead gods" Duncan whispered.

He couldn't tell what the hammer was made of, but it was beautiful, and would be worth a lot of money to the right buyer. It tickled his memory, some familiarity. Outside of its resemblance to Will's work, it was almost as if he'd seen this before, this very hammer.

Duncan pondered the hammer for a good long time before he shook himself and looked at the position of the sun. He needed to get back to the Reach. The Barrier might protect him from the Valni, but it wouldn't do anything about wild animals, rockslides, or him breaking a leg in the dark.

Taking the cloth, he folded it and placed it in his pack. That he could sell fast, he was sure of it. Traders came through the Reach often, and he could see someone from the North, near the coastline loving it. They liked all those crazy colors there, he'd seen enough outfits the traders wore.

The hammer was too big for his pack, he'd have to carry it. Throwing on his pack, Will, without thinking, reached down, taking the hammer with his injured hand. Fire. Pain like fire ran across his hand as if he'd had a burning coal land on it. He tried to let go of the hammer, but his hand wouldn't move. If anything, his fist gripped it tighter, drawing forth a scream that he couldn't stop.

As fast as lighting a lamp, the grip relaxed and the hammer fell to the ground, giving a soft chime as it hit the rocky ground.

Duncan whipped his hand to his face to see... nothing. The injury was gone. No trace remained. Not even a scar. Making a fist and relaxing it, nothing. No pain, no tightness, not even a slight pull.

What in the sparks of the forge had he found? Duncan's touched the hammer again, a fingertip touch with what had been his uninjured hand. Nothing. Not even a tingle. Why hadn't that happened before? He'd been holding the hammer when he unwrapped the cloth. He'd left the hammer on the cloth and his hand had been on the other side.

Taking a deep breath, he picked up the hammer again, again with the hand that never had been hurt. Nothing. Just a beautiful, crafted Hammer. He hated to, but he had to show this to Haltim. He was messing with things he didn't want to deal with or know about. Gods, magical hammers, strange black blood covered spearhead too much for him. Squaring his shoulders, he started the walk home.

***

Will took the hammer he'd made out again, still delighted with his work. Perfectly balanced, he could toss it and catch it every time, he could feel it move like a living thing. He never dreamed he'd ever be able to make such a thing. He kept wanting to use it as an actual hammer. He fought the urge at least for now, this was to be judged, and this had to get him into the Guild. It had to.

He'd take it to Haltim in the morning to be blessed. He couldn't wait to see the old Priest's face. Haltim would see that he'd been wrong, William was more than ready for the Guild.

Duncan stepped into the main room, and Will turned his attention to his cousin.

"Dunc! How was the scaving today?" Will paused, something was off with his cousin. One hand was clenched in a fist, and his jaw was tight, Will could see the tendons in his neck work as his cousin came closer.

Duncan paused, and closed the door behind him. "I'm not sure. I found this." Duncan pulled from behind his back a large hammer.

Will felt his breath freeze up, that was a near replica of his hammer! A closer look revealed that if anything it was even more fine, the gemstones, the carving, all excellently done.

"Where did you get that!" Will asked. He also couldn't ignore the feeling the hammer gave him. The moment he'd looked at it, he had the sense of timelessness, of something waiting.

Sitting down with a sigh, Duncan poured himself a glass of water from the pitcher they always kept on the table. He took a long drink and poured a bit on his hands and rubbed his face with it.

"You're not going to be happy when I tell you." Duncan looked down at the ground as he talked.

Will knew what that meant, Duncan had never been able to look anyone in the eye when he felt guilty about something. Thing was, he almost never did feel guilty about anything, so the fact that he did now, meant something.

"Well?" Will asked. "What kind of trouble did you get yourself into?"

"I lied to you. The other day in that tower." Duncan held up a hand. "Let me finish."

"There was something in the room upstairs. A large stone box, cube. I went back there today and opened it. This hammer was in there, and something else. I didn't tell you about the thing that day because…" Duncan trailed off.

Will felt his anger rise. He knew why Duncan had not said anything that day. He'd thought it was a tomb, and he knew how Will felt about grave robbing. So, he'd lied.

"By the spark Duncan. You thought it was a tomb, didn't you! You thought you'd go off and get rich grave robbing and I'd never know. You promised me Duncan. You promised me you'd not do that." Will felt his anger spill over.

Duncan's eyes opened, and Will took a step back, his eyes were raw, and the person looking at him, wasn't Dunc.

"*ME?* How dare you lecture me about lying? You went after a blood shard; you didn't tell me!" Duncan stood now, taller than Will and somehow looming over him. "*All this messing around with Dead Gods, and faith and all that nonsense.*" Duncan raised the clenched fist, skin white from the force of the grasp. "*I should have never helped you William. You won't get in, Reachers never get into the Guild!"*

Will stepped back. This wasn't Duncan. Something else was there. Something he didn't expect. "I will put an end to this foolishness!" Duncan yelled and grabbed the hammer he'd found, looking around his eyes lit onto the hammer that Will had made. "No practice piece, no guild trial!" Duncan with a scream lifted the hammer he'd found and before Will could stop him hit the practice piece, the work of Will's life.

Light. That's all Will could see. White and strong the light blinded him, then came the sound. A thrumming noise, but loud, so loud. He could barely hear Duncan's voice saying... he couldn't make it out, the thrumming was so loud.

Light faded and the noise with it. Will blinked and rubbed his eyes, trying to regain the clarity of his vision. He could hear Duncan now, crying.

"Dunc? You ok?" Will asked, still not seeing well. Everything had this off colored glow to it as if he'd been staring at the hottest part of the forge for far too long.

"I think so." Duncan's voice whispered to him, trying to stop the tears. "I'm sorry Will, I just... I was so... I wanted to break something, the hammer. Even you. I saw you standing there, and I wanted to take the hammer and..."

"Don't Duncan. Just don't." Will interrupted him. He felt sick to his stomach. What was going on!

"No Will, I have to say it. I wanted to smash your head in. I wanted to see your blood spill. What is happening to me?" Duncan whispered.

Will blinked as the last of the glow faded and he could see, and he went to his cousin. "It's ok Duncan." He patted Duncan on the back, "Get up, and let's talk about this."

Duncan stood, "I didn't tell you what else was there."

"There were two things in the box. The hammer was one, the other... it was a blade, a spearhead. A Huge one though, massive. And it was sticky with black blood, do you get it? Sealed in a stone box for how long and it was still sticky? How is that possible? I picked it up and it flew away. It vibrated and flew off. But it cut me Will. Cut my hand."

Duncan held up his hand, but Will couldn't see anything there. "It was like my hand was rotting away in front of me, the pain was so bad. I thought I was going to die. I grabbed that hammer I showed you and it healed the wound."

Duncan sat back into a chair. Will rarely saw this part of his cousin. Always so sure. There had always been a raw edge in there, but well hidden behind bravado and sarcasm. Here it was now on full display.

He wasn't sure what to do. There was only one person in the Reach who might be able to tell them anything about this, Haltim. One more thing to talk to the priest about, when he blessed his piece. His audition!

"Oh gods." Will stood looking for his practice piece, the hammer he had made. There on the table still it sat, and it was … it was fine. In fact, you couldn't even tell it had been hit with anything. Perfect. Undamaged.

"And I broke your work Will, I'm so sorry. I had to smash something, I *HAD* to." Duncan wiped his eyes with the back of his hand.

"Duncan," Will said, holding up his hammer.

Duncan looked up, and some of his sorrow drained away. "It's ok?"

"It's fine. Untouched." Will smiled at him. He knew he had rights to be upset at Duncan for this. A small part wanted to punch him in the face, but the man was hurting.

"What about the other one?" Duncan looked around the room, finding the other hammer, the one he'd found lying on the floor.

"Fine as well." Will answered reaching down to pick it up.

Titans. A huge figure, silver metal shining in the sunlight stood towering over all the men nearby. Across the narrow valley another titan stood, scaled and muscular, its mouth blood covered and grasping a spear, a spear covered in blood as well, some fresh and red, and some black with age. The silver titan held up a hammer, huge and shining and with a roar pointed it at the scaled giant, the two Titans ran towards each other, the sunlight fading in the smoke.

"Will!" Duncan's voice came to Will.

"What?" Will blinked a few times, trying to process what he'd seen.

"You stood like a statue, like when you touched that crystal." Both the Reis men looked at each other and the hammer.

"This isn't any old hammer Duncan." Will said holding it in his hand. The thing shone with its own light, even stronger than the hammer that he'd made. "This, I think, is the Hammer of a God."

.

14.

Morning came and found Will and Duncan tired. They had sat up late into the night, each lost in their own thoughts. Will had spent most of the time considering what Duncan had found, and he was sure Duncan was thinking about what had happened last night. Will was worried about his cousin. He didn't know what Duncan had found in that tower. But the behavior last night, it scared him.

"I am sorry." Duncan broke the silence.

"It's fine. Wasn't even thinking about it anymore." Will felt himself cringe a bit at the half truth. While he hadn't been thinking about that in particular, all he could think about was what was going on.

"Come on, we need to see Haltim. He's the only one in the Reach who will be able to shine any light on this." Will cleaned up and laid out a large leather apron, thick, perfect for heavy forge work. Both hammers got wrapped up in it. Will took pains to not touch the hammer Duncan had found with his bare skin. He put on a forge glove for that particular purpose.

Duncan smiled, and appeared for a second to be able to crack a joke at Will's expense. Will rather wished he would, that he'd expect from Dunc, not this worried, scared man.

Hammers wrapped and under his arm, Will and Duncan left, with Duncan carrying his pack. Will wondered at that, there wasn't anything else they needed to bring, but he decided not to ask. The morning was cool, and foggy. Fog was common around the Reach in spring, with the cool damp air rolling down the mountain sides into the flat valley that the Reach was situated in.

Forges and smelters were only now getting moving for the day, so their smoke hadn't mixed with the fog yet. Once the afternoon winds kicked in that would get blown away, but mornings could get bad, the air so hazy you couldn't see past arm's length.

The walk to the Church of the Eight wasn't short, and Will was thankful that they didn't get stopped by a bunch of people to say morning and gossip. The closer he got to the church, the more his thoughts turned not to the hammer, but to the spear blade. In his gut Will had an idea of what it was, but he wanted to be wrong. Very wrong.

Entering the Church of the Eight, Will felt a bit of the weight on his shoulders leaving him. The air here held a stillness, a peace that helped him relax.

"You always liked this place." Duncan spoke for the first time since they had left the house. "I never got it. I'll admit this edge I've been feeling, it's less now."

Will clasped Duncan on the back "Well, let's find Haltim, he will be shocked to see you here."

Duncan did laugh at that, a short barking laugh that echoed through the ornate stone walls.

"Who in the fires of Amder is making all that racket?" Haltim said, his voice coming through the doorway that led to the main hall.

Will and Duncan nodded at each other and entered the main hall. Haltim clad as usual in a plain white robe, was dusting the altar.

"Well ... Both Reis boys? To what do I owe the honor? Will I have expected, but you Duncan?" Haltim stopped his dusting and sat on the floor in front of the altar, looking surprised.

"Well I brought my audition for you to bless, and Duncan ..." Will trailed off seeing if Duncan would tell the reason, but his cousin looked at him with a pained expression and shook his head. "And we have to tell you something that happened, something important."

"What could be so important that it brings both of you to me?" The lines on Haltim's face drew up as he smiled.

"Ha. Maybe important," Will said feeling more at ease.

"Well which first?" Haltim motioned them over to a waiting bench in front of where he was sitting. "Blessing or Story?"

Will and Duncan exchanged glances, but neither said anything. "Blessing? Blessing first." Will shrugged as he put his stuff down. He unwrapped the leather bundle and removed his own hammer.

Haltim's reaction was everything he'd hoped. The old priest's face slacked as he took in the hammer that Will had made, before a smile of pride and joy broke forth.

"William Reis! This is ... that is remarkable!" Haltim stood and reached out to take the hammer. "How on earth did you make this?"

Will handed the hammer over to Haltim with a smile of his own. "Wasn't easy. Duncan helped me find the materials and assisted in the forging."

Haltim lifted the hammer Will had made, feeling it balance, and tapped it with a finger. Hearing the low moan, his eyes lit up. "Wight Iron?"

Will nodded. "Yes. Duncan found some ingots when he was out scaving."

Haltim swung the hammer a few times, the smile on this face never leaving. "My boy, this is one of the finest pieces of metalwork I've ever seen. It's simple, but perfect."

"Will you bless it? In Amder's name?" Will asked, finding himself holding his breath. Haltim had tried to talk him out of the guild trials. While he had offered to bless it as a way of apology, Will wasn't sure if he would or not.

"Yes." Haltim nodded. "I'd be happy to and honored to."

Will watched, not saying anything as Haltim approached the Altar of the Eight. He'd only wanted a blessing in Amder's name, but he would not stop the old priest now. Glancing over at Duncan, it surprised him to see his cousin in what looked like a prayer. Duncan praying?

His wonder was short-lived as Haltim began the blessing of the hammer. Will couldn't hear what he was saying, the words ran together. Whatever he was saying did not take long, and soon Haltim stopped speaking.

Haltim had reached the end of the blessing, but stood still, his back to them for a long minute or two. Will was about to clear his throat to get the Priests attention when Haltim turned around smiling with the hammer outstretched.

"It's a remarkable piece of work Will. I wish you luck." Haltim sat down again after handing Will his audition. "Now, what was it you wanted to talk about?"

Duncan spoke up telling Haltim of the tower that Will had found, how strange it was, and how he'd found the room upstairs. Will could see Haltim start to disapprove and caught the old Priests eye long enough to shake his head. Will didn't want to start that fight, not now. Not with the mental state his cousin was in.

Duncan went on, telling how he'd gone back a few days later, and opened what he'd thought was a tomb only to find two objects in it, a hammer and a large spearhead. Will watched Haltim's face and was not surprised by what he saw there. Haltims face had turned pale, and his eyes round at the information that Duncan was sharing. Will's own stomach fell, he couldn't be right, his fears couldn't be real.

Duncan described the spearhead and how he'd gotten cut by it, how it had flown away through the air, the race to save himself from what he'd been sure had been death. Reaching down into his pack, Duncan drew out something that Will had never seen, a strange but beautiful cloth, the candles and torches here highlighting each thread, a rainbow of colors. It was stunning!

"The hammer was wrapped in this. After I unwrapped it and picked it up, it healed my hand. The wound, gone." Duncan raised his hand moving his fingers. "Like it had never happened."

Haltim was silent, face now as white as his robes. Finally, he spoke, his voice soft and broken. "Is that the other hammer? The one you found Duncan?" Haltim pointed at the leather wrappings still covering the find.

Will nodded as Duncan was lost in thought. "When I touched it with my skin, I SAW something. I didn't want to touch it again, so I wrapped it in this."

"This is very important William, what did you see?" Haltim asked his voice calm, but Will could see he was anything but. His hands were fidgeting, and his legs had a tremble to them. Was that nerves? Excitement?

Closing his eyes Will tried to picture it. "I saw two titans, giants." His voice trailed off for a second. "No, I saw Amder, and the blood god. Huge in the sky, I saw them attack each other, I saw the day of the Godsfall." Relief flooded through him at getting that out.

Haltim nodded. "Duncan can I see that cloth for a moment?"

Duncan nodded and handed it to the Priest. Haltim held it up for a second, and passed his hand over it, eyes closed.

A long sigh escaped him. "Before I get to this, something else happened with all this, didn't it, Duncan." Haltim looked right at Duncan, gaze locking eyes with him.

A slow nod was all Duncan gave at first. Then he spoke, lowering his head unable to look Haltim in the eye. "Last night, I got... I wanted..." Duncan looked up and over at Will, eyes red with suppressed tears. "I wanted to kill Will. I wanted to smash his head in, and with the blood..."

Haltim interrupted him. "Hush, its ok lad." Haltim sat in silence for a moment.

"William and Duncan Reis. How did it come to this?" Haltim sighed. "I will tell you what I can. There are some things I can't tell you. For reasons that may one day become clear."

"Will, you know what was found. I can see it written all over your face. And Duncan, you suspect, but you don't want to believe it. I will be as blunt as possible boys. The tomb you opened Duncan; it is special. I don't know how you found the place William; it's been lost for years beyond counting, but that was the resting place of the Hammer of Amder, and part of the Spear of the Scaled one." Haltim pointed to the broken bust of Valnijz.

"These are the weapons of Gods. The rage you felt last night Duncan? It will happen anytime you get angry. You're tainted by the cursed blood of a fallen God. I'm amazed that you managed fight it off last night, but it's quite possible the Hammer of Amder had something to do with that." Haltim stood and paced. "The fact that the Hammer tried to heal you, tried to fix the problem says a lot. It couldn't heal everything though. The wound itself yes, but the blood taint or curse, had already spread."

"The cloth? It's Amder touched. The inner writings of the Priesthood describe it exactly, and this matches those descriptions. So, you two, have returned the Hammer of Amder to the Church. I should do cartwheels right now if I could do them. I should jump up and down." Haltim paused his shoulders hunched for a second.

"But I can't. Because you also found the Spearhead, and it flew off. And I'll bet that it flew past the barrier, and into the lands of those that still worship the Blood God. And that boys, is bad. Very bad." Haltim faced the bust of Amder, face impassive.

Haltim sighed. "Why did it have to be the Reis family?" Sitting down he rested his face into his palms, covering it.

"What does our family have to do with anything?" Will was confused. Confused and worried. He believed in the Gods, but this was crazy. Finding the lost hammer of Amder? Duncan got cut by the weapon of the Blood God. This was all too much for him to deal with.

Haltim shook his head and didn't answer. Will glanced over at his cousin, trying to read him, read his reactions to all this. Tainted blood or no, which Will was having a hard time grasping, Duncan was his cousin, and the only family he had left.

Oddly enough Duncan didn't look shocked, only thoughtful. Will would have thought he'd be upset or sad, or even dismissive knowing how Dunc felt about all religion. But no, thoughtful was the best word for what his face looked like now.

"Haltim, I have a question." Duncan asked his voice calm, almost monotone.

"I'm sure you do, please, anything I can answer ask away." Haltim answered, watching Duncan. Will wondered what was going through Haltim's mind, what wasn't he telling them?

"Why did Amder fight Valnijz? I mean, he was the God of Craft, of Creation, making things... why fight the God of Blood and Rage?" Duncan's voice quavered as he said the name of the Blood God. "I've never understood it."

Haltim cleared his throat. "Well not the question I was expecting, I can answer it all the same." He paced back and forth again, then stopped and sat down next to Duncan.

"Amder fought because no one else would. The other Gods didn't like the Blood God, but they didn't see him as a threat to them. The Gods of the Mountains? Oceans? Forests? All these Gods are Gods of nature. We worship them, and they answer, but they, at least at the time, didn't care much about what the Blood God was doing. While they have their people, we've always been taught that they, the other Gods, considered the fight somewhat of an internal thing for humans." Haltim shrugged as he spoke.

"When Valnijz attacked, he also attacked here, the seat of Amder's faith. More than the other Gods, Amder was a god of people. Valnijz was in a way an opposite, they also called him the God of Destruction. Amder had no choice." Haltim placed a hand on Duncan's shoulder. "Does that make sense?"

Duncan nodded. "I guess."

Will waited for Duncan to ask the important question, about the tainted blood. But Dunc just sat there, looking lost. Will stepped in. "Ok, if Duncan won't ask, I will. Tainted Blood? Spear of Valnijz?"

"Yes. That is the important question isn't it?" Haltim sat back for a moment collecting thoughts. "When Amder and Valnijz fell, and their battle formed the Mistlands, their weapons, the Hammer of Amder and the Spear of Valnijz were taken from the battlefield. At least partially. The forces of Palnor, Amder's side, could recover the Hammer, but only recovered the spearhead, not the rest of Valnijz weapon. It's been long suspected that those loyal to Blood God recovered the rest."

"The High Priest of Amder hid away what they had found. During that process he cut himself on the Spearhead, and unlike Duncan here, died after he hid away the items. The location of where they were hidden was lost. I always believed that was on purpose, to hide the items away from temptation. Lost and forgotten. The Amder faith searched for them many times, but always came up empty." Haltim looked over at Will his expression unreadable.

"How do you lose the relics of fallen Gods? Sounds incredible to me." Duncan didn't wait for Haltim to answer. "Two of them most valuable artifacts ever, and you can't remember where they got put?"

"It wasn't that simple. That time was chaotic. Amder was gone, Palnor was in turmoil. In the wake of both deaths, raids went out from each side. There was no barrier yet, the first Valni were appearing, and no one had any idea what was going on." Haltim shrugged. "By the time things got under control, almost twenty years had passed, whole villages had been destroyed in the Skyreach, and the information was lost."

"I will not speculate about why they have been found now, and by you two." Haltim looked down and went silent.

"You're not telling us something Haltim, and you know it." Duncan stood, looking down at the old Priest. "You didn't answer Will's question before, about why our family is involved. There's more here than you're letting on, and we deserve to know it."

Haltim sighed but said nothing for a long time. Will glanced at Duncan and the both nodded and started to leave.

"Wait. I can't answer that question, not now. But I will say this. Duncan, you must try to stay calm. You must. The Blood taint will get worse the more often you let yourself lose control. I do not know if there is a way to fix that. The Hammer of Amder must stay here boys, and the cloth. You can take your practice piece of course Will, but I must insist that your find stays here." Haltim stood, his simple white robes shining in the sunlight streaming from a skylight far above.

"Nothing bad will happen to it here, but you must understand. I can't allow the Hammer to go." The old Priest sounded sure to Will's ears.

"It's Duncan's choice. He found it," Will said looking at his cousin. He wasn't sure what Dunc would do.

"Keep it. I want nothing to do with the Gods, now or ever again." Duncan's voice, flat and uncaring spat out the words. "I never want to see it again."

Will agreed. Believing in the Gods was one thing but getting involved in all this insanity was another. "Goodbye Haltim," Will muttered as he placed his practice piece under his arm and he and Duncan made their way out of the Church of the Eight.

15

Haltim watched the two leave. His insane situation was now impossible. How on earth had those two found the Hammer and the Spearhead? Haltim knew how, but he wasn't even close to sure what he could do about it. The Gods were moving. It was that simple. The Reis line was being pushed to ascendancy, which meant nothing good for the Church. Or at least the Church as it stood now.

Bracin and his ilk only saw things to gain power, and power meant influence and wealth, two things the church had in spades. They were parasites. Parasites on what was left of their own god. Haltim had refused to be involved, it had been one reason they had sent him here, to what they considered what the least glamourous position in the country of Palnor.

Oh, keeping an eye on the Reis line was part of it of course, but he was in a backwater. Haltim had already broken an order from his High Priest, he had blessed Williams' work. A true blessing.

That hadn't been his plan. When he and taken the Hammer to the altar, he'd planned on doing as he had been told. But the moment he placed it down, he knew. He couldn't fake it. The work was too good, it sang. Forgemaster blood indeed.

He had hidden his surprise when that hammer that Will had made had been presented to him. It was a masterwork, incredible craftsmanship and made from a very special material. Far more special that either of those two had known. It had been a delight in his hand, well balanced. How could he not bless that in the Eight's name?

His eyes flew to the hammer left behind, what appeared for all the world to the Hammer of Amder. The actual hammer used by the God himself to both create and do battle. Haltim knew what he was supposed to do. He should be downstairs right now, contacting the High Priest and revealing everything he'd heard. The Hammer found, the Spearhead found, and flying away!

But they'd take the hammer and pervert it as they had with other things, and of course, they'd hunt down Duncan Reis. Haltim had taken a terrible risk letting that boy leave. He'd only told him the least dangerous version of the old lore dealing with those kinds of injuries. Worse things by far were recorded and had scared Haltim to death when he'd read them so long ago.

He'd only let the boy go because of the Hammer. If the Hammer had cured the wound itself, maybe it had lessened the impact of the taint. And now the spearhead was gone, just like that. Gone. Flew off as Duncan had said. That worried him more than anything.

There were dark places and dark countries even where the Scaled one, the Blood God was still worshiped, and glorified. If one of those people had both the shaft and the spearhead, they could wreak havoc. The Valni could become an army under their control, an army of ravaging monsters. Unfeeling, vicious, insane, brutal army.

Haltim kept the Hammer of Amder under its leather covering. He had to hide this. He needed time to figure out what he would do. And time wasn't something he had a lot of. Something was coming, some change, and everything pointed to it being far bigger than he was ready for. He'd hide the hammer near the forge, it belonged there.

***

Jaste awoke and stretched, a smile on his face. Testing day had come at last. Regardless of the restrictions, he enjoyed testing days. He hated disappointing those who didn't make it but finding new talent for the guild was something he was good at, and something he loved to do. And this time, he had something extra to look forward to.

William Reis would try. And regardless of what the old Priest had said, Jaste knew, the Reis line was one of the Forgemasters own.

There were however a lot of questions circling here. Was the main reason no one from the Reach ever was to get picked was the fact that the Reis line continued here? But why would that be? If anything, Jaste thought the guild would use it as they used everything else. Saying a Guild Smith was a Reis would carry a lot of weight and power, at least in certain places. The Reis name wasn't as well-known as it had been centuries past, but it still had power.

The only group who could keep the Guild from using it was the Priesthood. And that made more questions still. Of all the groups in Palnor, only the Priesthood carried more weight than the Guild. And for only one reason, the Making of Amder.

No one, not even the guild knew how it worked. But for exorbitant amounts of money, or even titles and land, the Priesthood could give a special blessing to an item and they would change it. Swords would never break. Cloth would never tear; silver would never tarnish. The list went on. But no one knew how it worked. No one outside the Church hierarchy.

All anyone knew was that items that were to receive the Making, were taken into the Priests compound, stayed for a day, and then returned, with these abilities. As a result, the Priesthood had power over all; even the king did not cross them.

If the Priesthood didn't want the Reis line to be in the Guild, Jaste could see how the ban had been put in place. But it still didn't answer why.

Glancing outside at dissipating fog of morning, Jaste shook his head. All questions he could figure out the answers to later. He cared not for the politics, nor did he care much about the Priesthood. He cared about talent. And if the Reis boy was good, he would get him into the Guild, one way or another. Even if he had to lie, change the boy's name, and hide it for the rest of his life.

Breakfast was another quick affair, bread and Klah, and a mug of warmish tea. The guild tent had been put up overnight by some out of work miners he'd paid well for the job. And they did a better job than Regin could have ever done. Everything was in order, and with the hour approaching, Jaste got himself ready, changing his over shirt into his more formal guildwear, and making sure he was presentable.

The over shirt was threaded in gold and stripes of Grey and Red crossed it. The small emblem of the Cross hammer and tongs was on its breast, done in silver to show his rank. Jaste thought it was a stuffy piece of clothing, it had no practical value other than to show off. He almost never wore the thing, except for the judgings, where it was expected. The only other exception was the Day of Rank when the whole guild got together for promotions.

Other than that, it stayed folded up in his bags. If he had to wear something showing rank, he preferred his guild cloak.

The appointed hour came and with a slight flourish, Jaste opened the flaps to the guild tent, letting the group of eight youngsters in.

There he was, William Reis! The young man who had garnered so much goodwill in the Reach stood at the back. Dressed in a clean and serviceable outfit of brown leather and linen, he was also nervous. His skin was pale, and he kept fidgeting. That was not unusual, they all were nervous. They weren't all from the Reach of course Jaste knew. Some were from smaller towns nearby or had missed a closer choosing for whatever reason and had come here for this one.

One by one they placed a wrapped item on the long-padded board in front of Jaste, standing behind it and trying to look calm. Jaste remembered his own testing. He'd been sure he would black out or throw up, or both.

Jaste walked to the end of the board, the young man standing there was well dressed, and solid enough looking.

"Name?" Jaste asked, following the formula to the letter.

"Martin Darkin." the man replied, shifting his weight back and forth.

"Where are you from Martin?" Jaste asked, trying to put the young man at ease.

"Tarno sir. I missed the testing there when my father's fields got flooded and I didn't think I'd make it. It was a long trip here, and my horse threw a shoe. Nearly ran off ..." Martin trailed off, realizing he'd been blathering.

"Tarno eh? Quite a trip. Out on the other side of the Skyreach Mountains, right?" Jaste had been to Tarno once, it was near the westward end of the Skyreach Mountains near Lake Denth. The Denth was so large that Tarno had good rain, and thus farmers, but there was some good mining there, though not even close to the same level as the Reach.

"Yes sir." Martin replied, he opened his mouth to say more and closed it again, turning paler than he had been.

"Relax, Martin from Tarno." Jaste watched the young man. "Take a breath and present to me your work."

Martin blew out a long breath and removed the cover cloth off his practice piece. Jaste turned a critical eye to the offering. It was a nice piece. A decently forged decorative piece of iron work shaped like a disk with an abstract knot work pattern. It looked like the young man had blued it as well for skill purposes. Decent hammer blows, no noticeable edge strikes.

Jaste picked up the piece and examined the back side of the piece, his trained eye picking up the few flaws that stood out. Martin had used old iron, and forge welded it Jaste could tell, he'd not recast it as molten into new ingots and gone from there. The backside held a few edge strikes, places where the hammer blows had skittled off. Not a bad piece, but not great either.

Jaste put the piece back and nodded to the young man, who looked like he wanted to know what the answer was right then. Jaste yet moved on, moving down the line, a man from Kilik, a young woman from Dernstown, a Gonnoship trader's son. Some pieces were better than others, most were ornamental in nature, though the Gonnoship trader's son had made a very nice set of scales out of brass and bronze.

At last, Jaste stood in front of the one applicant he'd been waiting to talk to, William Reis.

"Name?" Jaste asked following the formula.

"William Reis, from the Reach." The young man said, adding his location without being asked. Jaste noted that Williams' eyes kept flicking to the other's work then looking down at his covered piece. Either very proud or anxious Jaste thought to himself.

"Well William Reis from the Reach." Jaste waved at the covered piece in front of him. "Present your work."

Jaste watched as Will's hand reached out, paused, made a fist, then reached out and removed the simple leather cover from his practice piece.

The intake of breath from the other applicants and from Jaste himself made the silence after it stand out. The work was a hammer. But it was stunning. The way the light struck its silver surface, it glowed on the padded bench. Jaste could not even see a single hammer mark, its surface was smooth, except for the simple but well-placed lines marking out a man at a forge.

Lifting the hammer Jaste amazed at its balance and lightness. He took a small piece of iron he kept in his pocket for things like this, and tapped the hammer, the low answering moan made him nearly drop the hammer in shock.

"Wight Iron?" Jaste asked Will, already knowing the answer.

"Yes, Master Smith." Will's face was a struggle between trying to maintain composure, and breaking into a grin, Jaste could tell.

"How on earth did you manage to get THIS much Wight Iron?" Jaste had expected something good, but this was far beyond that. The value of this much Wight Iron was almost a year's pay to a journeyman Guild Smith!

"My cousin sir. He's a Scaver, searches ruins, found a bag of Wight Iron Ingots. I smelted them back down and recast them as 2 ingots and made the hammer." Will couldn't keep the smile off his face now.

Jaste was more than impressed. Working Wight Iron was not an easy skill and working it this well? Jaste knew then he would have to move forward with his plan. William Reis had to come to the guild which meant that none of the others here could. He couldn't risk them saying something.

Jaste had been hoping that it wouldn't work out this way that none of the others would make the cut, and the choice would be simple. Not to be however, as at least two other pieces here met the level of skill needed to go to the second level of testing, though none were anywhere close to the work the Reis boy had done.

The hammer still in his hand, Jaste marveled again at its balance and almost fluid quality as he gave it a practice swing. "Have you used this to make anything? It's a standard forge hammer design." Jaste was curious about why he'd chosen a hammer to make, it wasn't a standard choice.

"No Master Smith. Tempted, but haven't tried." Williams's voice, calm now, he had gotten better control of his excitement, Jaste could tell.

"Why the hammer? With the Wight Iron you could have made a great many other things. All as good looking as this is." Jaste placed the hammer back on the bench still not quite sure how this person, this William Reis had made such an amazing piece of work. He was a Reis, true, and all that the name carried with it, but this? From an untrained lad?

"I wanted something practical Master Smith. Something useful. I have nothing against decorative pieces, but I, well, I just wanted a tool." Jaste chocked back a laugh for a second as the young man stumbled through his explanation. He'd have to get training on diplomacy, a normal training set for Apprentices in the Guild. Being able to calm a customer down or build a rapport with a Lord was something that had paid well for the Guild over the years.

Assuming he got past the second test, the anvil test. Jaste realized he already in his thoughts had put this William Reis past that point. Odd, he never did that.

"Thank you all. While I am impressed with all your work, I have some hard choices to make. This is how this will work. I will give each of you a piece of cloth, each a different color. After I have made my decision, the pennant on top of the tent will change to the color or colors of those chosen. I will expect you here, ready to go." Jaste paused smiling at the hopefuls. "It has been an honor for the Guild, and I, to see your work."

"Please take your work with you. The pennant on top of the tent will change tomorrow morning, I know you were all hoping for faster, but it's tradition." Groans had already escaped several of the applicants at the news that a choice wouldn't come till the next day.

As each applicant left, he assigned them their color, saving William Reis for last, handing him a Yellow cloth. He watched as Will studied the cloth for a moment happy to see the look on Will's face then. A look of longing and hope. Jaste knew Will was a kindred soul.

Watching the young man leave, Jaste shook his head. "One more reason to talk him into the plan."

16

Duncan had not slept well. His dreams had been full of strange and disturbing images, most involving blood. There had been an attractive woman in two, but she'd been cruel, and evil. Just his luck, dreaming of a beautiful woman, and it turned to be a nightmare. It might have been the same dream, he wasn't sure, the light of day was making the dreams fade away, leaving him with echoes.

Will had already left to go to the choosing, and Duncan found himself not wanting to be here when Will got back. Either his cousin would be despondent, or he would be happy and smug. Both extremes would annoy Duncan, so it was a good day to go scaving. The last time had been a disaster, he had found nothing other than that hammer and the spearhead. Both of which he never wanted to even think about again. But the day hadn't been a total disaster.

Duncan opened his pack to see his prize inside. With Haltim talking about the Hammer and the Spear, the cloth, the Amder touched cloth had been forgotten, and that was still in Duncan's pack. Valuable, assuming he could find the right buyer.

Traders came often but had a limited supply of gold. He could trade it for a small pile of gems, but gems weren't worth as much here, when such a supply that could be found in the Skyreach was nearby. But still it was worth a great deal. If he could find the right buyer.

Duncan's thoughts turned darker, remembering what Haltim had said about the blood taint, and how he'd never be free. Stupid old Priest. Duncan wanted nothing to do with the Gods. *NOTHING.* Slamming his hand on the table, he startled even himself, how had he got so angry that fast? Could the old priest have been right?

No. He couldn't have been, he was sleepy and on edge about Will's choosing. Putting the Gods and tainted blood out of his mind, Duncan got ready to go scaving. He pulled out an old but well-preserved map and examined it. This was his favorite map, showing the location of every ruin he knew of near the Mistlands. Which ones had he cleaned of items, which ones he was sure still held value, and even which ones he'd not searched yet. Marking out where and when he needed to go, Duncan figured that today he'd search a late Masterdon manor that was a mile and a half beyond the barrier. Masterdon period nobles and rich commoners had liked to use a lot of small individual charms and items on their clothing. Small meant easy to lose, and for him, meant good haul most of the time.

Duncan had always thought the idea of wearing all those small charms was silly though, must have made a huge racket when walking or running, and dancing. But the rich were their own people, he'd met a few, and strange was an understatement.

Packing up for the scaving, he felt himself relax into his routine. Exactly what he needed, a day in a normal ruin, doing his normal thing. He'd be careful of the Valni, search the manor, and be home by dinner. Routine sounded superb right about now.

All packed, Duncan gathered his gear and headed out, giving a wave to the few he knew. For once he didn't feel like talking to anyone, and in fact his reactions surprised him when he did pass a small group of miners coming back from a night shift. He'd felt his heart race, and this powerful feeling of avoidance gripped him.

"Not going to the choosing today Mr. Duncan?" The old guard asked, cleaning his fingernails with a sharp stone.

"No, that's Will's thing, not mine." Duncan forced himself to say the words, to stay calm.

"Ah well, sorry for the lad. He's a Reacher, and Reachers and the guild don't mix." The old guard spat on the ground and said nothing more.

Picking up the pace, Duncan made for the Mistlands road, ignoring the warning signs placed around to push would-be daredevils away. Duncan knew the risks better than most, he would not do anything stupid. He could see the barrier in the distance, the white slanted posts showing the line where the Valni couldn't cross.

Duncan lost in his own thoughts approached the line when it happened. He'd been walking and then stopped. He couldn't go forward! Duncan pushed, and felt whatever had pushed him before push back, harder. The barrier was keeping him from crossing!

He knew the reason, the blood taint. The thrice forged blood taint! He picked up a rock and threw it at the barrier as hard as he could, screaming with anger. As if to poke him further, the rock sailed through the unseen force without a hitch. Duncan felt his fury rising, the rock skittered to a stop, lying there, where he couldn't be.

Blood pumped in his ears, his anger flowing through his body, he needed to break something, or even better someone. Feel their bones break, the ripping sound of skin being torn off with his teeth …. Duncan screamed and went to his knees. This was not who he was, he would not be this! Haltim, he had to talk to Haltim, there had to be a way out of this. He had to calm down first, he couldn't, wouldn't be this person. What had he become?

***

Will smiled as he made his way back home, he'd done it! He'd managed to enter the guild trial. And the Master Smith had complemented him on his work! He felt like he was walking in the clouds, a dream for so long, fulfilled. "I'll do it Da. I'll break the disappointments, the setbacks. I will be a guild smith." Will prayed the words, his eyes on his hammer. His perfect hammer.

His stomach grumbled at him, and Will realized he hadn't eaten today. He'd been too nervous this morning to eat a bite, he'd drank tea, and that was all. Now that most of his nervousness was gone, his hunger had returned. The Chisel was nearby, and the food there was good, quite good in fact. Will wanted to treat himself to a full lunch before heading home, a nice way to celebrate.

This time of day the Chisel was busy, smelters and various forge workers on mid-day breaks. A mix of traders and merchants rounded it off. Most he knew by name, and there were a good many who waved and yelled out a greeting as he entered.

"Master William Reis! What can I do for you today?" Kinler asked as he wiped down the bar for what was the twentieth time today already.

Will liked Kinler, he was a good man. Honest, kind, and set a great table. "Lunch today. Treating myself."

Kinler laughed, the innkeeper smiled and looked around. "Master Duncan joining you today? Haven't seen him either in a while."

"No, he may be out scaving, you know how Dunc is." Will shrugged as Kinler led him over to a small table not too far from the main stairs. Will liked this spot, and Kinler had remembered. Out of the way enough not to be noisy, but Will could see anyone who came in or out.

"Ah well, tell that cousin of yours to come by, I have need of both a new necklace for my daughter, and a laugh. Duncan always had a quick wit about him." Kinler said as Will sat. "Now, normal lunch today is the Klah, brown sweet bread, a slice of cheese from Tarno, and some stewed fruit. Will that be ok? I can heat up some leftover spit roasted pork from last night."

Will's stomach grumbled at the thought of all that food. "Standard lunch is fine, but yes, please, on the pork! And water and tea to drink, not here to lose my wits."

Kinler nodded and left to get Will's food ready. Will looked over the room, watching the various people come and go, relaxing into his seat as he waited. Kinler appeared in short order with everything but the pork. "Be a minute on that pork Master Will, heating it up on the fire now, making the fat extra crispy for you."

"My thanks." Will took a deep breath; it had been too long since he'd eaten here. And if he was lucky, he'd be leaving the Reach and not have the chance to again for a long time.

Kinler left as Will tucked in. He was lost in his food when a shadow cast down on him. "William Reis!" A voice said that was familiar, but he couldn't place.

Looking up Will choked on his food. The Master Smith! By the sparks what was his name? Master James? No Jaste! Master Jaste.

"Don't choke William!" Master Jaste smiled and without asking took the seat across from him.

Will was surprised, what was the Guild Master doing? Will swallowed and took a swig of tea to clear his throat.

"Master Jaste! Sorry Master Smith, I was eating lunch. Is there something wrong? I can get another table if this one is yours." Will stumbled over his words.

"Calm down! It's fine, I'm staying at this Inn, and saw you sitting here, and wanted to say hello." Jaste leaned back in his chair.

Will studied the Master Smith. His first impressions of the man was good. There was a craftiness to him that reminded him of Duncan. The Master's eyes darted about but always came back to Will. Was he being sized up?

"Master? Is that allowed?" Will frowned. "I'm an applicant to the guild, I don't want to introduce any controversies into the choosing."

"It's fine, Will, I'm allowed to have lunch with anyone, assuming its ok I have lunch here with you?" Master Jaste asked.

"Yes of course Guild Master!" Will could not suppress his smile. Not only did he enter the Guild trial, he was having lunch with a Guild Master Smith! Will wanted to drop his fork and ask the man all the questions he had swirling in his head, but it was smarter to let the man eat and ask what he wanted to.

Kinler appeared with the reheated Pork, sizzling from the fire, basted in butter and herbs. "Here you go Master Will." Kinler startled for a second seeing the Guild Smith sitting with Will but the innkeeper that he was recovered quickly. "Ah, Guild Master! Choosing go well?"

"Yes. Well indeed," Jaste answered, but keeping his eyes on Will.

"Well then, you've met our Master William Reis here? Good man! Good family! Solid and Dependable. Even Duncan his cousin, though he's one you've got to watch." Kinler gave a half smile, his eyes darting to a teenage girl who was helping him serve lunch.

"Sort of, I met Master Reis here this morning, at the Trial." Master Jaste sat back, tapping his chin in thought. "Not met his cousin yet."

"Trial?" Kinler gave Will a look of surprise but said nothing else.

Will shook his head not answering the unspoken question. "Guild Master Jaste here is hungry Kinler, can he have the same thing I'm having?" Will steered the conversation away from where it had been going.

"Yes please. Looks fantastic!" Jaste added.

Kinler walked away though Will saw him glance back at the table where they sat a time or two.

"So Master Jaste, what do I do to deserve this honor?" Will asked as he ate.

"Wanted to talk, chat. Nothing serious." Jaste answered. Will knew there was more to it than that. The Master was up to something, but what?

The innkeeper's arrival with a second tray of food for the Master Smith interrupted his suspicions. "Here you are Guild Master." Kinler laid his food out "Be careful with the pork, it's hot!"

"So, William, tell me, what's it like living here, in the Reach? I've always liked the place myself." Jaste began to ask questions as they ate lunch, and soon they were deep in conversation about life here, mines in the area, and techniques used to recover valuable metals.

17

"Haltim!" Duncan yelled as he burst into the Church of the Eight out of breath. He'd run the whole way back from the barrier once he'd calmed down. The old priest was nowhere to be seen, so Duncan sat in the same seat he'd sat it in the day before when he found out about this curse he was now afflicted with. His hands were quivering with the remnants of the feelings that still teased his mind. Why couldn't he feel normal? Why couldn't be himself again?

The busts of the Gods shined in the light streaming from the skylights far above, lighting each one in what Duncan was sure was an attempt to make them look more blessed and holy. Each face was different, fixed in either a pleased-looking expression or a stern one. He hated them all. He would not be a puppet, something to dance and flail for their amusement.

"Duncan? Twice in two days? Will miracles never cease?" Haltim's voice echoed through the room.

"Haltim!" Duncan stood and whirled at the Priest. *Hate...kill...* the whisper of the rage he'd felt before came to him. He could smell the old man's blood flowing through him. His skin was thin, and Duncan was sure he could see the throb of a vein in his neck. One slice, and that delicious hot blood would flow. A hunger grew deep inside, kill the old man, and hear him scream.

"Is William all right? Did something happen between you to?" Haltim stepped forward into the light more, his white robe picking up the sunlight, letting off a reflective glow. Duncan blinked, and the hunger vanished.

"No, as far as I know he's fine. No, Haltim. I can't cross the barrier anymore! It won't let me!" Duncan paced around as he spoke. "I went to go scaving, get my mind off things, and try to get back to normal. I got to the barrier and it wouldn't let me cross. It was like trying to push through stone the closer I got to the other side!" Slumping into the bench again Duncan sighed.

"I got furious. I wanted to do things... hurt people. It's this curse, this tainted blood, isn't it. It's what the barrier is stopping. What do I do Haltim? This is what I am, this is what I do! It's not mining or smithing, it's what I'm good at. I scave. And now, I can't even do that." Duncan lowered his head, quiet now.

"I'm sorry Duncan. I am. I didn't think that the barrier would act like that though, thinking about, it I could see that it might. We know little about how the barrier works." Haltim sat down in front of the eight-sided altar. "I don't want to be a scold Duncan, but I told you not to get lose control. I know it must have been hard."

"It was terrifying. If I'd been with another person there, if I'd even seen another person..." Duncan whispered his eyes distant in thought. "Haltim I could feel the flesh tearing, my mouth... my mouth watered at the thought of blood."

"I am so sorry. I can't think of what else to say. You've had your one thing you were best at taken from you and now have to live knowing that if you get angry, you could kill someone without thought." Haltim stood looking around the church.

"I dedicated my life to the gods. It was all I ever wanted to do. I came here, many years ago. Sent here to be the agent of those Gods here in the Reach. I don't know what I'd do if it was taken from me the way things were lost to you." Duncan said nothing but watched Haltim walk toward the covered bust of Amder, the brilliant Gold and Silver cloth glinting on the light spilling down on it.

Haltim placed a hand on the bust, almost in a benediction and paused that way for a moment. "Duncan. You may not like it, but you are a Reis. Smithing is in your blood. Stronger than any taint, it ties you to the Reach, and to Amder. I know you aren't fond of religion. I know that in some ways you blame the Gods for your father's death, and Will's parent's deaths. But you, like Will, were born with a gift, it's time you used it."

"What? Be a smith?" Duncan trailed off for a moment. "It's so boring. There's no adventure, no risk. Metal, Hammer, Fire. Will loves it, but that's Will. That's who he is." Duncan didn't know what to do, how could he leave everything he was? Everything he wanted to be?

"Give it a chance Duncan. If only because you may find it calming." Haltim gave Duncan a smile.

Duncan forced a smile. "True, get bored, but not mad." That mollified Haltim. There had to be another way, there had to be a way to beat this. A memory tickled the back of his head. A dangerous memory.

Duncan stood to head back to the house but stopped for a moment and looked back at the old priest who was watching him go. "Thanks Halim. I take back half of what I've ever said about you." Then Duncan walked out into the bright cool day. A day that brought him no joy, or satisfaction. There was one way to control his anger, one way to make sure he never hurt anyone. Will wouldn't like it, but if it meant not killing anyone, Duncan had to try.

***

Will arrived home, surprised to see Duncan's pack by the door. Could he run fast enough if Duncan got mad? Could he escape? Will shook those thoughts off. Duncan was family, the only family he had.

He figured Dunc would be out still for a while, but he was glad to see he wasn't. Not only had he made an impression with the Master Smith with the hammer, but he'd had a long lunch with him! Will was already thinking about ways to use some tidbits of information Master Jaste had let slip about techniques that the Guild taught to its students.

"Will." Duncan's voice broke into Will's thoughts.

"Dunc! Wasn't expecting you back home already. Saw the bag though, scaving go well?" Will knew something was wrong the moment he said the words as Duncan's face flashed something before returning to an odd calm.

"No." Duncan walked over to a window that looked toward the mountains. "I don't think I'll be scaving anymore." Will could see in the dim light Duncan doing, something, but couldn't make it out.

"What?" Will could feel himself tense up. "What do you mean?"

Duncan stood at the window for a long time, looking out, saying nothing. He turned and Will's breath stopped, for the first time since they were children, he saw pain, raw pain written across Duncan's face.

"I can't. The barrier it won't let me cross it. This taint, this thrice cursed and damnable blood taint, it won't let me. When I realized it, I wanted to hurt someone. KILL someone. I wanted..." Duncan paused closing his eyes.

"It doesn't matter. I had to go see Haltim, and he confirmed it. My life as a Scaver is over." Duncan's voice moments before on the edge of tears, was flat now, and his face came to an odd calm. A calm and Will had seen before. A calm that couldn't, shouldn't be on Duncan's face.

"I have to find a new life, a new thing. Haltim suggested blacksmithing." Duncan sat in front of the fireplace, sinking into the chair there. Will discounted his thought, there would be no way Duncan would do what he feared.

"How did the testing go?" Duncan asked, watching the fire.

"Forget that. What do you mean you spoke to Haltim?" Will found this all hard to get right in his mind. Duncan would stop scaving and pick up blacksmithing?

"I'd rather not talk about it right now, how'd the testing go?" Duncan's still calm voice echoed in the room. A flat voice. A sound that brought back memories, and not good ones.

"Ah... well... Great. And then I treated myself to lunch at the Chisel, and well. I ended up having lunch with the Master Smith here for the testing!" Will felt the words rush out of him. "Duncan, some of the skills he was talking about, it was incredible!" Will went on, talking about techniques and methods of hammer strikes, alloying, and other skills.

Duncan finally turned to Will "Good, I'm glad for you. There's something else." But there was no smile, no joy on his face. Will discounted his feelings again, Duncan wouldn't, he couldn't do that.

"If you don't make it into the guild, one of us needs to move away. To leave the Reach." Duncan stopped Will from opening his mouth. "Stop before you say anything and hear me out."

"This taint, you don't know the thoughts I have now if I let it get control. What I want to do. If you stayed, and we both lived here, the chances are that one day I'd get mad about something, and I'd snap, and hurt you, even kill you. I can't do that. You're the only family I've got. I can't deal with the thought of killing you." Duncan's voice, a flat uncaring voice didn't match the words. "I've done what I can to stay calm, and I'll keep it up as long as I can. But it's for the best."

"Dunc that's crazy. I'm not leaving, and neither are you. We will find a way, we always have." Will paused thinking about Duncan's words. "What do you mean you've done what you can to stay calm?"

Duncan's expression didn't change as he stared at the empty fireplace. "I have to stay calm. Always. I've done what I can to stay that way."

"You didn't answer the question." Will shot back, now worried. "Duncan, what did you do?" His stomach fell as he already knew the answer. He knew that flatness, that lack of feeling.

Duncan turned to Will that same odd calm on his face. He reached into a pocket and pulled something out, showing it to Will.

The vial gleamed in the light from the windows, the milky liquid residue inside still visible. "Damn you Duncan. That better not be what it is." Will whispered. "Don't tell me that."

"I had to. It's the best way." Duncan's voice even sounded hollow. "I took it when I was looking out the window. I'm better now."

"You're not better! That stuff will bring you nothing good Duncan Reis." Will felt like a weight was crushing him. He'd been so damn happy about his own life and not considering Duncan's. And now Duncan had taken Cloud. *Cloud.*

"It's ok. Cloud will just make it so I don't hurt anyone." Duncan started before Will cut him off. "Cloud will turn you into a shambling wreck. It's a drug Duncan, not a cure." Will continued. "Da took that stuff when mom died, I remember him being unable to even care about anything at all. This isn't the way, Duncan. We both watched him waste away from it. This is your plan?"

"This was part of your Da's stash of Cloud. I found it years ago. Kept it, in case." Duncan's voice was a monotone now. "Uncle was a wise man. The anger? The pain? It's gone now Will, gone."

Will waved his hand away in disgust. "It's hidden, not gone. And once the stuff wears off, all that pain, anger, it will come back and come back with a vengeance, Duncan. And there's not a damn thing you can do about it."

"Then I won't let it wear off." Duncan whispered, but Will heard it.

"You must. Don't do this, Duncan. We will find a way. A better way. Haltim was right, Smithing can be very calming. It's part of you." Will walked over to Duncan crouching down to look him in the eyes. "You don't need a drug to hide from your anger."

"Haltim said something similar. 'It's in your Blood, Duncan.' It may be, but I want nothing to do with Blood, mine or anyone else's." Duncan closed his eyes and sat back, calm, flat.

Will watched Duncan for a long time. First watching Duncan fall asleep in the chair, and then when he was sure his cousin was asleep Will got to searching, he had to find that damn Cloud drug, and get rid of it, for everyone's sake. Find it and destroy it.

Will stretched, groggy. He'd finally found the drugs, hidden in his father's old room, up in the rafters of the closet. Will had taken each vial there and taken them to the family forge. He'd started a small fire and poured the contents out, one by one into the fire, covering his face from the acrid smell and fumes.

Duncan had slept all night in that chair, like Will's father had after he'd taken Cloud. Will should have recognized that look on Duncan's face right away but hadn't even considered that Duncan of all people would turn to a drug to hide away from a problem.

Will crept out and spied him still asleep. He figured Duncan would be under for a while longer, Cloud had that effect on people. He made some breakfast taking care to not wake Duncan, and took it back to his room, munching on bread. He'd been so damn happy and hadn't even considered Duncan's problem. How crazy had things become?

They'd found the Hammer of Amder! In truth he'd only found the location, Duncan had uncovered it. But Duncan had been blood tainted by that spearhead thing, and everything had gone from bad to worse. Blood taints, the Gods themselves getting involved, all this insanity. All he sparks made wanted was to get into the Smithing Guild!

Will started, the Guild!! He searched through his pockets and yesterday's clothes, finding the yellow scrap of cloth he had been given yesterday. The results were this morning, the answer was already up! Panic set in as he paced around. But what about Duncan? He couldn't walk away from his only family. And what if there was more Cloud hidden somewhere?

"Gods above, why these choices!" Will spoke out loud, sitting on the bed again.

"Go Will." Duncan stood in Will's doorway. "Go."

"Duncan!" Will stood to steady Duncan who waved him off.

"You were right. Using the Cloud was stupid. Drugging myself out of anger will not work. I couldn't take the idea of what the blood taint does to me when I do. I wanted to run, to hide." Duncan gave small smile, lopsided but still an emotion. "Me, Duncan Reis, hiding from something."

"This is your dream. Go. Find out if you've succeeded at least. I'll be ok, I swear I'll not take any more Cloud." Duncan paused and held up his hand. "I swear."

Will made his way through the morning crowds, the yellow cloth clenched in his fist. He'd not wanted to leave the house, both for Duncan's sake and if he admitted it, for his own. This was it, the culmination of all his hopes and dreams since before his Mother died. A dream passed on from one generation to the next of Reis's.

Will stopped at the corner, knowing that right around it he'd be able to see that banner at the top of the Guild Masters tent, and if he'd made it. If they had picked him. Will closed his eyes, taking a large breath and blowing it out, feeling his hands get damp and the lump in his throat get larger.

Will opened his eyes, and took the steps, there it was the Guild Smith's tent, and above it, Yellow. Bright and bold, flapping in the cool breeze of the Reach. Will had done it, he'd made it past the test.

***

Jaste fidgeted in the tent, taping his fingers against the chair arm he was sitting in, wondering what was taking William Reis so long. The testers picked would often wait for the banner to even go up and would rush in as soon as the color was shown. But Jaste had put up that banner almost two full hours ago, and still no sign of William Reis.

Jaste felt his annoyance rising, where was the man? The lunch yesterday had confirmed what he already thought, that William Reis was a talented smart youngster. If he went along with the ruse that Jaste had come up with, he had a future in the Guild. "Excuse me? Master Jaste?"

Jaste looked at the youngster. Will looked tired, but excited. Jaste figured he'd not slept well, thinking about the test, and what might be. Jaste had seen that over and over for years on the faces of other applicants.

"William! I was thinking that you weren't coming." Jaste smiled and clasped Will on the shoulder. "Congratulations! Your work was amazing, and I have given you the honor of coming with me to the Guild Hall to go through the Anvil test, and then if you pass, then into the Guild itself."

"Anvil test?" Will's face fell. "There's another test?"

"A small one. Yes. I will explain more once we are at the guild hall." Jaste waved him over to sit and took a seat across from that one. "But Will before we get to that, we need to discuss something else."

Will sat down and kept his mouth shut. Jaste liked that, lad was willing to listen first, ask questions second.

"Now, Will... or do you prefer William?" Jaste wanted to get the lad relaxed some before he hit him up with the gamble.

"Will is fine, only Haltim the priest calls me William anymore." Will answered. "Master Jaste what is it?"

Jaste smiled for a second. "Well, Will, how much do you know about the Reach and the Guild?"

Will nodded for a second. "I wondered if that would come up. I know that no one from the Reach has gotten into the guild for a long time, if ever. No one knows why. But I did it!"

Jaste held up his hand to quiet Will. "Listen, I can tell you the reason, or at least what I know. The Guild has the policy because the Priesthood of Amder wants it that way."

Will's face crossed from confusion to panic in a moment.

"Hold on, let me finish." Jaste continued. "Even I'm not into the reasons why, though I have my suspicions. All I can say is that the Guild's ban of Reachers is because of you. Well not you personally, but your name, the Reis name."

"What?" Will's voice rose. "How does my name have anything to do with it?"

"I'm not sure Will. I only have suspicions. No proof ... I will not name them yet either, so don't bother asking. I need more information first. You will have to trust me on this." Jaste looked up at the hole in the tent's top, looking at the clear blue sky far above.

"But Master Jaste, if that's true, that the reason no Reachers get into the guild is because of me ... because of the Reis name, how can I get into the guild now?" Will's voice was quiet, though Jaste could hear the confusion in it.

"Yes well, here's the hard part, and the reason I've sent the journeyman away who was supposed to be with me. You will join the guild, but not as William Reis. From the moment we leave town, you will use a different name, and be from somewhere else. It's that, or nothing I'm afraid." Jaste turned to look at Will watching him for a reaction to this news.

Will's face looked like he would be sick, then resolved, then sick again. "You're asking me, to lie?"

"I could try to give you a long, complicated answer that makes it look like you're being honest, but the truth is, yes, I'm asking you to lie. You don't like it, I understand that, I even admire it. But without that lie, you won't be getting in." Jaste looked Will in the eyes. "What do you say?"

"But if anyone finds out, I'll be out in a heartbeat. The priesthood would see to that." Will looked so uncomfortable Jaste wanted to buy the lad an ale and tell him to forget it.

"You wouldn't be the only one who is taking a risk here. I would as well. If they discovered this, I had done this, let you into the guild knowing your real name, I'd be stripped of my rank and cast out. I am as much a risk here as you are." Jaste let that sink in for a moment before continuing. "I'll make it easy and low risk, I'll tell you all I can about the place you will be from, enough to please the curious."

Jaste watched as Will bowed his head. Silence was the only answer before he spoke at last. "If I have to, though I do hate to lie, Master Jaste," Will said with a sigh.

"Great!" Jaste paused. "Look, if there was any other way, I'd go for it. But this is the only way I know of or could think of."

Will said nothing, Jaste was sure he was worried and confused, better to move forward and not give a lot of time to think about it.

Jaste smiled. "Good lad. Ok, I've had time to think on this, how about your name being Markin, Markin Darto, from Dernstown."

Will mouthed the name "Why that?"

"Well both are common names in the area of Dernstown. Plus, Dernstown out of the way, and I can't think of any other Guild applicants from there. Most won't be able to know much about it, so they can't challenge you on it." Jaste replied watching for William's reaction. But to his way to thinking, talent was more important that some silly rule.

"Got it, I guess. Markin Darto. Sounds, odd." Will gave a half smile, at least the lad was trying.

"Ok then it's settled. We leave tomorrow, at dawn." Jaste stood and organized things in the tent.

"Tomorrow? Dawn? That fast?" Will's asked surprised.

"Yes lad, I still have a Journeyman to pick up and two other trials to run before we get to the Guild hall. Then, we have the anvil test. Then, if all goes well, you Markin Darto ... will be too busy in classes and hands on practicum, you won't even know what day it is." Jaste smiled and waved Will out of the tent. "Go on, enjoy your last day in the Reach, the last day for quite some time if all works out."

18

Duncan had waited a few minutes to make sure William was gone and taken a sip of Cloud. Just a sip. A full vial and William would know. A sip, he might not. Just a tiny amount, to not feel this anger. A slow disassociation from everything. No anger, no fear, no sadness, but also no joy, no happiness. On a more logical level he finally understood the appeal, he wouldn't get to have to deal with any of the issues that emotions could cause. He was sure Will had spent a large part of the night searching for and getting rid of any Cloud he could find. He'd expected it.

Duncan had taken pains to make sure that Will only found what he wanted him to find. The stash of Cloud that was easy to find was a small part of the amount that was hidden in the house. Duncan had found the Cloud years ago, but had done nothing with it, either way. He'd not destroyed it, nor use it, until now.

Duncan fished another small vial of Cloud out of the main hiding place he'd discovered. It was a false panel in a bedroom that had been empty at least all of Duncan's life. The panel sat on the side of a storage chest, seamless, and hard to spot until you moved the chest out into the middle of the room. There were twenty vials there, enough Cloud to last for a month or more. Will's Da had bought a lot and hidden it everywhere.

He was thankful the Cloud didn't lose its power with age. Sealed in glass vials, the stuff could last forever. It wasn't even that hard to get for some. Healers and setters often would have some on hand, no pain meant easier treatment.

The front door slammed against a wall downstairs. Will must be back from finding the results of the testing. He wondered if he should take more Cloud now or wait until Will had left again. While his thoughts turned to whether Will had gotten into the guild, he found that he didn't care, one way or another.

"*DUNCAN!*" Will's voice carried upstairs.

Duncan secreted the small vial in an inside pocket of his pants and pushed the chest back into position. He could hear Will moving up the stairs, faster than usual. The heavy footsteps could be felt through the floor.

"*DUNCAN!*" Will yelled again.

Duncan stood facing the window, looking out at the mountains. Snowcapped and always cold. He could not put any emotion to them. They just, were.

"There you are! You won't believe it! I got in! I'm going to the capital!" Will's voice carried the joy that he must be feeling.

"Oh?" Duncan said, unable to give it any feeling.

"What are you doing in here?" Will asked looking around. "This room has had no one in it for years."

"Just wandering," Duncan answered, the Cloud still masking emotions he felt.

"Ah. But did you hear? I am leaving! Tomorrow! I have to pack!" Will was joyful, Duncan could tell. Frantic almost.

"Ok." Duncan tried to feel something, there, a quiver? Sadness? Joy? But it was gone before he could understand it.

Will's hand grabbed Duncan by the shoulder and turned his around. Duncan could see Will's face now, a face full of both excitement and confusion. "Duncan?"

"It's the Cloud Will, still wearing off." Duncan felt far away, like he was talking over a long distance.

"You took more didn't you Duncan? You told me you wouldn't! I can't believe this. I can't leave you like this." Will sat on the bed. He had the chance to fulfill his dream, but how could he leave now?

"Duncan, I need to talk to you about something. Something you must swear to never repeat" Will's eyes locked on Duncan's face.

"Ok." Duncan felt it again, curiosity? But it faded off once more.

"Sit Duncan." Will waved him towards the chest to sit down.

Duncan sat, Will paced, keeping his thoughts straight as he related the information that Master Jaste had shared with Will. Duncan's thoughts were all over the place, why would the Priesthood not want a Reis in the Guild? What was going on? But these thoughts were logical ones, with no emotion behind them.

"I don't know, sounds risky." Duncan let out a breath, feeling emotions start to crowd back, a sip didn't last that long. He needed to take more Cloud, he needed to get away from this taint, but not now, not with Will here. "And you don't do well with misleading others. And this name he wants you to use, Markin Darto? Will you be able to remember that?"

"I know Dunc. I know. Then there's you, us, our family. If I leave, and go to the Capitol, and make it all the way into the Guild, I won't be back here for at least a year. I'm not sure that this is a good idea, with the Blood taint and Cloud."

"Go. You have won this much, giving up now, that's not right." Duncan could feel the Cloud really wearing off now, a pit of regret. Sadness? It was growing in his stomach. A sip did not last long enough.

Will threw his hands up in the air in clear surrender.

"You owe this to yourself. To Your Da... By the Sparks, even to my father and me!" Duncan sighed closed his eyes forcing these feelings back down. He needed Will to leave, he wanted more Cloud.

"I don't want you to leave. But, it's the best thing, both for you and me." Duncan opened his eyes, observing his cousin.

Will looked lost he thought, and unsure. "Dunc. I guess so. I feel like I need to do something."

"What? I'll do it with you. One last hurrah of the Reis cousins." Duncan attempted a smile he didn't feel.

"I guess I just want to go for a walk. Get out of town for a bit. Maybe grab dinner at the Golden Chisel. What do you say?"

"Ok. But we'd better go now. We have to get back and you have to pack, right?" Duncan stood. It would be good to at least get outside, walk around, clear his head and if that didn't work, he rested his hand on his pocket, feeling the vial of Cloud inside.

"Right!" Will grabbed the hammer he had made and shoved it into the tool loop on his belt.

"Why the hammer?" Duncan asked as they exited the house, blinking in the bright light.

"Oh. You know, I don't know. I just like having it." Will looked down and away. Duncan knew that he was hiding something, but Will was bad at hiding his true feelings. Duncan let it go though, it had something to do with the Gods or some such, nothing that Duncan wanted to know about.

The walk was uneventful. Will kept up a steady stream of chatter about forging and the Guild, and Duncan threw in the occasional nod and grunt. Checking his pocket, the small vial of

Cloud was safe. He needed it. They left the Reach, taking a trader's path that led further into the mountains, and eventually to the south. Though it was late in the season for traders to be using it, it was in good shape. Which was why when Duncan stopped to take a small rock out off the bottom of his boot, he waved Will ahead. *No dangers out here. Nothing to make him angry.*

***

"Now Youngster. Where's that cousin of yours? Our job is for both of you. Both Reis boys, both dead." The man speaking was dressed in old chain and leather. Bandits. "It's nothing personal. But you've made an enemy. A rich enemy."

Will stood still trying to understand. He'd been ahead of Duncan not wanting to talk about his belief that Amder himself had guided him to the tower. He'd turned the corner only to find these three men, well-armed, waiting for him.

"Enemy? How? How could I have an enemy?" Will felt himself stalling for time. Time for what he wasn't sure.

"I don't know, and I don't care. The amount of money we'd get for killing you and the other one is more than enough. We've been watching you most of the day as you walked." The man who had been talking smiled, thin lipped. "No one is going to hear you all out here."

"I don't get it; how did you find us?" Will blurted out, hoping that Duncan was somewhere nearby.

"We've been watching you all day boy. When you left that town of yours, we followed. That simple." The bandit pulled a sword out of its sheath. "Be calm, you'll be dead before you know it."

Will grabbed the hammer at his belt, pulling it out and swinging it around. "You don't want to do that." Will tried to make himself sound threatening, gruff.

"Don't make me laugh. Waving that hammer around won't help you. I'm trying to make this easy for you. Right lads? But I'll take it when you're dead, looks pretty. Must be worth something." The bandit who had done all the talking looked at his two companions. One nodded the other shrugged.

"Don't matter me any to me. We get paid either way." The shrugging one said. "Shouldn't the other one be along soon? Kill this one, then kill the other one."

The one Will thought of as the leader sighed. "All right have to do it the hard way I guess." The bandit stepped forward as Will jumped backward, laying about with his hammer, trying to find a way to escape.

Out of the corner of Will's eye he saw a shape move, fast. Duncan! The shape sprung upon the bandit that had shrugged and a scream unlike any other Will had ever heard came forth. Will ran toward the scream, convinced they had injured Duncan.

But it wasn't Duncan who was screaming. The bandit was, Duncan had *bit* the man! Bit him and ripped off his ear! Will watched in horror as Duncan sunk his fingers into the man's eyes, blood everywhere.

"Bloody Gods above!" Will heard the bandit leader yell and run towards Duncan's back sword raised overhead.

Will ran towards him, being closer to Duncan and determined not to let this man hurt his cousin. He raised his hammer and swung on the back of the Bandit who went down with a yell of his own. Will was no fighter, but he was strong from the forge and could swing a hammer hard.

Duncan whirled around at the noise and Will scrambled back. That was Duncan, but not Duncan. The Blood taint! It twisted Duncan's face into a rictus grin, his eyes were like slits, unseeing and maniacal. His one hand was covered with the bandit's blood, and as Will watched in horror, Duncan licked some blood and gore off his fingers.

Without a word Duncan attacked the man Will had hit in the back, arms grabbing the bandit's head. With a wrenching motion snapping his neck. Taking a rock from the ground and smashed the back of the man's head in! Blood spattered as Duncan hammered the man time and time again. Each blow brought forth a sound from what had been Duncan, a sound of animalistic rage.

The final bandit threw his sword on the ground, raising his hands in surrender. Duncan didn't even notice as he attacked him, ripping the man's throat open with his teeth. A wheezing gurgle escaped the final bandit, whose arms and hands attempted to push this thing from him. A few weak movements, and the bandit lay still.

"Duncan!" Will yelled trying to get through to the person he knew, not this blood crazed thing. "Duncan it's me. Will!"

Duncan stood and turned toward Will his face still frozen in a grin, blood covered and crazed. No words escaped his mouth, only breathing. Will could see his jaw, clenched tight. His jaw muscles bulged with the strain, distorting his face.

"Duncan!" Will yelled again, backing up. The eyes were the worst. For nothing else showed the truth, there was no Duncan anymore. His body was overtaken by hate, anger, and hunger. What was he going to do? He couldn't fight Duncan!

"Dunc, listen to me. You've got to calm down! It's the blood taint." Will kept as much distance as he could from the approaching figure that his cousin had become. "Dunc!" he yelled again in a more plaintive tone.

Saying a silent prayer to Amder Will backed up again, this time his leg touching the corpse of the first bandit, his eyeless face facing upward. Blood soaked the ground, and now his boots. It was hard to get good footing. Will choked back a wave of nausea, but then a glimmer?

A small vial, filled with a White liquid. Cloud! A vial of Cloud! Will knew that Duncan must have dropped it. A split second of anger infused him; Duncan had hidden it from him! He had promised no more of that stuff! Then he focused. He hated it, but maybe, if he could get Duncan to take it, he'd get out of this state, away from the Blood taint and be... Himself?

Will took the vial and blew out a long breath, keeping his eyes on whatever, this thing was that his cousin had become. "I'm sorry, Duncan." He whispered then charged.

Will lowered his shoulder as he ran, carrying the hammer low, in case. He only had one chance at this. He didn't know if Duncan would kill him like he'd killed the bandits, the thought was terrifying.

Will felt the impact travel down his back. Duncan went flying backwards, thankfully not knocking his skull open on a rock as he fell. Will's blow had knocked the wind out of him for a second, and Will felt the guilt flow through him as he sat on Duncan and watched him gasp for breath.

The muscles in Will's arms bulged as he struggled to keep Duncan pinned down. Whatever the blood taint did, it made Duncan stronger. He was trying to thrash around, but Will was still the stronger of the two overall, but he was tiring, and Duncan was not.

Will watched Duncan take a few real breaths, his face still warped into that tight smile, blood covered. The smell of it filled his nose. Iron tang, mixed with sweat, and Gods knew what else. He forced Duncan's hands over his head so that he could hold them with one hand. If only for a few seconds. Long enough for him to open the vial and pour the contents down Duncan's' throat.

"By the sparks! Stop struggling!" Will cursed out loud. Duncan's face quickly moved up, biting at the air, biting the air right next to Will's ear.

Will took a deep breath and gave a shout in effort as he pinned both arms down with his left hand and flicked the vial open. Duncan was still trying to bite him, so he didn't need to try, and pry open his mouth. The milky white liquid flew out of the vial, and down the throat of Duncan, who coughed and sputtered in his unknowing rage.

Cloud worked fast, and not but a few moments later Will could feel Duncan's limbs relax. Will stayed here he was, perched on Duncan's stomach, not letting his grip go yet.

"Get off." Duncan's voice came, weak, but still, a voice.

Will got off, rubbing his wrists that had bent at some painful angles to pin the blood raged Duncan down.

"Dunc... Don't look." Will glanced around the clearing, the three bodies spilling blood all over the once green grass that covered the sides of the path. This was already going be more than he wanted to remember, and once the Cloud wore off, the sight of these bodies would haunt Duncan, Will was sure.

"What Happened?" Duncan whispered. The Cloud he had been forced to take making his voice into an eerie calm.

"Bandits... well, or killers. Someone hired them to kill us! I don't know who or why... or even how they found us." Will waved his arms around. "You went, crazy."

"The Blood Taint." Duncan sat up. "Did I kill them?"

"I said not to look." Will stood and felt sick. The danger and excitement faded as he trembled. His breath came in ragged breaths at first as he forced his mind to calm.

"Cloud?" Duncan asked, head still down as he sat up.

"Yes. You dropped it. You hid that from me!" Will yelled at Duncan but stopped. "Though I guess if you hadn't, we'd not be having this conversation. I couldn't stop you Dunc. I had to calm you down, and the Cloud was the only way I could think of."

"I understand," was Duncan's only response.

The two of them sat there for a long time, the shadows gathering around them. Will stood and looked up at the sky. "We'd better get moving. Going to be dark by the time we get back to the Reach."

Duncan didn't speak but stood and without a word walked home. Will sighed and ran after him, night fell as they walked, and Will steadied Duncan with a hand a few times, but they walked in silence, each locked into their own thoughts.

19

Will sat up, blinking in the sunlight that lit his room. His room. The last morning he'd be spending here for a long time, if ever. After they had gotten home last night Duncan had retreated to his room. Will had made one attempt to talk to him last night only to be ignored, and finally exhaustion had set in, and he'd gone to bed, sleeping fitfully.

It was morning now, and his rising uncertainty over what to do about Duncan threatened to overwhelm him. His dream was within his grasp, but leaving his home, and his only family was hard enough. And now? With this blood taint thing swirling around Duncan like a waiting snake, poised to strike, could he leave the Reach?

He sat up in his bed, looking at his pack on the floor. He was ready to go. He wondered if his father would have been so worried about leaving the Reach if he had made it this far? Or any of the other Reis family? Could he do this?

Will stood, glad he was up this early. He dressed and went to knock on Duncan's door again. He needed to talk to him. Yet when he got to Duncan's room, the door was open. Duncan wasn't there, but there was on the bed, a letter addressed to Will.

Will frowned. If Duncan wasn't here now, and if he knew his cousin, would not be here at all. He had run. Unfolding the letter, Will read.

"Will. Yes, I'm not there. And I'm sure you know why. I also guess if I know you that you're having second thoughts about the Guild. About leaving the Reach, and of course, this thrice hated blood taint of mine. Don't. You're a damned good smith. And an even better person. You deserve this. Go. I don't understand why the Guild doesn't want a Reis any more than you do, but that's the reason you must do it. Not for yourself. Or your father. But for the whole damn family, going back who knows how far. Not only do you have to be in the Guild, you have to blow everyone else away. Do it for every Reacher who ever tried.

I'll miss you cousin, but you better not be home when I get back. Have a great trip and show them what a Reis can do.

--Duncan."

Will sighed. He should have figured Dunc would do something like this. Blood Taint or not he knew that the letter was Duncan's way of saying goodbye without having to answer any questions about himself. And maybe, once he made it to Guild Master, he could find a way to help Dunc, permanently.

"Always running away!" Will said, his words falling away into the quiet of the house. Will put the letter down and looked around, trying to soak in the memories. He walked around its rooms, now empty, but once full of life and people. The Reis home. Pride filled William at the thought of what he had done. He'd done something that no Reis had managed in an unknown number of years. He'd gotten into the Guild.

The house would once again, someday be filled with family. His descendants, Duncan's, their Children and children's children. Will smiled and grabbed his pack. It was time to go.

***

Will shifted in his seat, feeling each hard bounce from the wagon and wishing he'd brought something other than some clothes to sit on. Master Jaste had met him at the Golden Chisel, packed and ready to go. There weren't many people up and about even yet, which in a way had made it simpler for Will to get up on the bench seat next to Jaste and leave town.

The Guild Master had been silent leaving the Reach, but once they had gotten out of the town proper, had started a steady stream of information about Will's new name and city. "Markin Darto from Dernstown" sounded so odd to William. He almost mentioned to the Guild Master about what had happened yesterday, with the Bandits. But how did you bring that up?

"Retrieved the hammer of a dead god, got attacked by Bandits who wanted us dead, by name. Not sure why, and of course, my cousin who is afflicted with something called a Blood Taint from the Scaled God of Blood and Rage, tore those same bandits apart with his bare hands. I drugged him with Cloud to get him to stop. How was your day?" Will could picture the Guild Master pushing him out of the wagon and leaving him by the side of the road for that.

As it was, he listened to the information about Dernstown. Not a mining or smelting hotbed, but a little of both went on. Dernstown was a town specializing in Marble quarries. Boring.

Jaste stopped the wagon and looked around. "Ok, Will. A few things. One, from this point on I'll only call you Markin, you need to get used to answering. Two, there's a bag in the back of the wagon, a blue one. Put all the clothes you have in that bag and take the ones out of that bag and put them in your pack and pick a set to get changed into."

"What's wrong with my clothes?" Will asked, unsure. He was wearing normal Reacher garb.

"Nothing, but you look like a Reacher. You can smell the forge and the stone on you. It's also way too thick for someone from Dernstown. Get changed, Makin." Jaste winked at Will and turned away to give him privacy.

Will grabbed his bag and did as Jaste had asked. The clothes that were something at Dernstowner would wear were odd to him. No leather, No thick wool and canvas. Everything far brighter colored as well, Blue shades and some greens. Will changed out of his Reacher garb and felt like some exotic bird.

Jaste nodded his approval when Will rejoined him in the wagon's front. "Good, you at least look the part now Markin. So, let's see what you remember so far... we have two days to cram everything I can into your head about Dernstown before we get to Kilvar and Regin. What is the most common food in Dernstown?"

Will sighed, this would be a long two days.

***

Duncan took his time, picking his way across the rocks. He was wandering, unsure of where he was going. Mentally he was doing the same. By now Will had left and was on his way to a new life.

Duncan had no issues walking away, he never got to close to things, or people. William was an exception to the rule. He'd wanted to stay, but with all the recent things, old habits had taken over. Run away. He hated thinking of it that way, but it was the truth. He was hiding. Hiding from saying goodbye, hiding from the truth by taking Cloud, hiding from himself.

He hated this new life he'd found himself in. He wanted to be out there, scaving, braving danger, feeling excitement. Now he was being a coward, not even wanting to admit that his life had collapsed. Duncan sat on a flat piece of stone, feeling the sun beat down as he closed his eyes.

He knew what he needed to do. He didn't want to do it. There had to be another way. But there was no one to talk to about it, to try to figure it out. William knew, but he was gone. The only other person was Haltim, but Duncan wasn't sure he liked the Priest, even now. Haltim had been at least helpful before, but all that stuff about a Reis not getting into the Guild, Haltim had kept that from them.

Duncan sat for a long time, trying to come up with answers, but getting nowhere. Finally standing, spat on the ground and sighed. He'd gone over it a thousand times, he had to talk Haltim, if the old priest had answers.

The walk back to the Reach was slow, but Duncan had no problems finding his way back. He picked his way around the Reach to get to the Church of the Eight. It would be faster to go through town, but he'd didn't feel like dealing with people today. He knew he'd get asked about scaving finds, where Will was, and he didn't feel like answering those questions, at least not right now.

It was almost dark when he came within sight of the Church, and the view made him stop. There was a group of wagons in front of the Church, large ones. And armed men? Duncan squinted to get a better look, not trusting his eyes. Yes, armed men, wearing the livery of the Church itself.

Duncan would have walked down and asked, but Haltim's recent conversations still clung to his memory. He was a Reis, and the Church had something against them. Not Haltim, at least not that he could tell, but the Church itself. That thought gave him pause as he watched the armed guards light torches and place them around, lighting a large area around the entrance to the church.

Duncan watched as a hooded figure exited one wagon, the only covered one and entered the church. The armed men stood around, talking, but their words couldn't be heard from where Duncan was. Nothing else was happening, and after a while Duncan was about to go down and see what was going on when a flurry of activity erupted. Haltim came running out of the church, looking disheveled and yelling something.

The hooded figure from before came after him, carrying a large pack which he threw to Haltim and then he went back inside, followed by the guards. Haltim was being kicked out! Duncan frowned. He needed to talk to Haltim, and he needed to do it now.

Haltim was still standing by the door, looking lost when Duncan approached him. "Haltim, what is going on?" Duncan asked, keeping his eyes on the door of the church.

"Who?" Haltim spun around. "Duncan! Oh, thank the Gods. But you shouldn't be here, go!" Haltim glanced back at the Church. "If you being here is discovered..."

"I have questions Haltim, things I need to know." Duncan grabbed the Priests robe to get his attention. "What by the Sparks is going on?"

Haltim pulled his robe from Duncan's grasp, and looked back at the church again, as if he hoped the door would open. "Fine. Let's get out of here." Haltim grabbed the pack that had been thrown out of the church after him. "But not the main road."

Duncan nodded. "Let's get out of here. But where? Not the house, at least our house. Maybe one of the old homes?" The Reach had several older abandoned homes, especially in the Gemdust district.

Haltim paused for a moment. "It should be safe, at least for now. But we need to stop anyone from seeing us. I'll explain when we are inside and out of view."

Duncan knew something was wrong here, but he needed answers. Motioning Haltim to follow, Duncan and the priest picked their way in the gathering night through a path, one of those that generations of Reach kids had made as shortcuts. With the night came the cold, even now in spring. Duncan could feel it, he hadn't planned on being out this late, and hadn't dressed for a cold night, and if he could feel the chill, he was sure Haltim could.

"Be back home soon." Duncan whispered. "Get warm, some food, and then answers." Haltim appeared to nod in the gloom and followed.

Finally, the shortcut ended, a few blocks from the Reis house. Lights lined the streets though no one was in sight.

"Hold Duncan." Haltim's voice was quiet. 'Let me get my breath, and get something out of this pack, at least I hope it's there."

Haltim dug into the pack and pulled out a hood, which he put on. "There. Now people at least won't know for sure it was me."

Duncan nodded and led Haltim down two windy side streets, and finally into an empty house. The family that had lived here had left four or five years ago so the place wasn't fully falling down. Duncan waited until Haltim was inside and barred the door with an old chair.

"Ok Haltim, we are inside, hopefully safe. What exactly was that?" Duncan asked sitting down on the floor and motioning Haltim to do the same. "Let me make a little light." Duncan risked a small fire in the fireplace, thankful that the people who had left the house hadn't taken everything with them.

"Duncan my lad, I've been ... replaced." Haltim looked at door. "The Head of my order, the High Priest, he replaced me. I didn't think he was serious when he said it."

Duncan sat back, watching the priest. Duncan wasn't William, he didn't trust people to tell him the truth, at least not all of it. Over the years he'd gotten good at reading people. Traders had tried for years to pull one over on him when it came to sell his scaving finds, and those same skills were screaming at him that Haltim was leaving something out, something big.

"Haltim. You're not telling me everything. Why were you so relieved to see me? You didn't ask where Will was. Be honest with me, or out on the street you go." Duncan demanded, keeping himself under control as best he could.

The old priest looked at the fire for a long time without speaking. "I'll tell you. I was relieved to see you because if the High Priest sent someone to replace me, it meant he sent someone to kill you. You and William."

"Kill me! Kill Will!" Duncan stood, his anger rising. He could feel the rage in his blood growing. "You knew about that? You knew someone wanted to kill us and said nothing?"

Haltim held up a hand. "Duncan! *KEEP CALM.*" The words escaped him in a hiss.

Duncan took a deep breath, rage infusing the edges of his vision, the desire for blood rose up in him, wanting to hear the screams of pain. *NO!* he yelled to himself, closing his eyes, and trying to force away the anger and rage.

"I knew. I didn't believe it. I should have said something. They tried, didn't they?" Haltim's voice came to him quietly, barely audible over the cracking of the wood in the fireplace.

"They tried. I killed them, Haltim. I tore them apart. Will had to drug me with Cloud." Duncan tried to think about other things, not wanting to remember. Duncan opened his eyes. "Why?"

"I'm so sorry lad." Haltim voice was low as he investigated the fire. "They have replaced me because I didn't stop Will from trying for the Guild. The High Priest has decided to end the Reis line. The ones before him were willing to let the line continue as long as none of you ended up in the Guild."

Rubbing his hands in front of the fire Haltim looked at Duncan again. "I refused to be a part. So, they replaced me. Kicked me out. And not only out of the Church here, I've been defrocked." Haltim lowered his head. "I've been a Priest for almost all my life Duncan. To not be one anymore, is a strange and frightening thing."

Duncan started. "Haltim! The Hammer!"

Haltim held up a hand to silence Duncan. "It's hidden. I had told no one about it. As far as I know there's only three people who know about the Hammer of Amder being found. And two of them are right here."

"Haltim I need to know everything. What in the sparks is going on?" Duncan sat back against a wall. "Everything."

Haltim investigated the fire. To Duncan's eyes, he looked all his years. Old, tired, resigned. "I can tell you Duncan Reis, but it may be hard to hear." Haltim gave a great sigh.

Haltim took another sip and put the cup down. "Last time we spoke in the Church, with William there, we touched on the fight between Amder and Valnijz. What we didn't get into was how things got to that point during the battle. You've heard of the Forgemaster?"

Duncan sighed. "Of course. If for no other reason that William is obsessed with them. Some super priest of Amder, right?"

Haltim's face winced at that, then he shook his head. "No, not a Priest. The Forgemaster was a special person, a man or woman given special gifts by Amder himself. A small part of his divine power, and they used those powers to the betterment of all. A Forgemaster was as likely to help a peasant fix a wagon axle that never would snap again, as much as he would make a spear for a king. The Priesthood existed to provide a structure for the worship of Amder, but the Forgemasters were how Amder was loved."

Haltim looked at Duncan, and Duncan felt the Priests gaze lock him in. "This caused friction with the Priesthood. The people loved the Forgemasters in ways the Priesthood could only dream of. This friction caused the Priesthood to resent the Forgemaster. People get jealous. I don't think the Gods understand us sometimes, I don't think Amder understood the resentment that was growing."

"At the battle, when Valnijz took the field in physical form, Amder had to respond. But to respond he had to draw back all the power he had given to his Forgemaster. He had to strip him of his power, and the last Forgemaster had to give his life to be the template for Amder's physical form. This wiped out the Forgemasters. Only Amder can make one, and with the fall, no more were ever named." Haltim took another long silence before he continued.

"When the fight was over, and both Amder and Valnijz were dead, they searched the field. The Hammer of Amder and the Blade of Valnijz were found and hidden, but something else was as well. The Heart of Amder. A crystal, like the ones that dot the mistlands, but rose colored with streaks of silver. At least according to the legends. The priesthood took that heart and realized after some time; they could use it to give them powers like the Forgemasters. In the chaos that came with Amder's fall, those in the Priesthood who had resented the power of the Forgemasters cemented their power. They learned how to use the Heart, and they used that advantage to the fullest. The priest blessing. That the Priesthood uses now to enrich themselves? To give them power. That's from the Heart of Amder." Haltim shook his head. "By telling you that, I've broken nearly a dozen church laws you aren't supposed to know, that no one is. Even most normal Priests don't even know. I only know because of my past."

Duncan nodded that made sense he guessed. "Nice story, but what does that have to do with Will and me?"

Haltim nodded. "I know, I was getting to that. The reason the Church made the edict, the reason for watching the Reis family and for keeping anyone in the Reis line and to be safe anyone from the Reach from ever being a Guild Smith? Because the last of the Forgemasters, the one that gave Amder his form, was a Reis. He was Simon Reis. He was and is, your and William's direct ancestor."

Duncan laughed, unable to contain himself. "You're joking! Who cares who an ancestor was?"

Haltim didn't even crack a smile. "Duncan, it's important. The Reis line still carries power in it. Skill. If a Reis were to be trained by the Guild? Training that takes a Smith to the highest level of skill. That could give that Reis the skills and knowledge to bring Amder back to life!"

Duncan's face lost its smile. "Are you serious? Bring a God back to life?"

"Yes. And if Amder were to come back, the Priesthood would have to pay for what it did, for what it's done for a thousand years. They'd lose power, money, and privilege. Not to mention whatever punishment Amder gave out. They kept the bloodline around, in case. But the current High Priest, a vile man named Bracin, he wants the threat gone, anything that threatens his power is something he wants gone and gone fast. That's why the killers were sent, that's why you're in danger. And that's why Will is in danger as well." Haltim shook his head. "How far my order has fallen."

"I'm complicit Duncan. I knew all this for years, decades. I kept my mouth shut. Only now with this change of wanting to kill you and Will have I done anything about it. With the finding of the Hammer? Something is moving to bring Amder back. But the finding of the Blade says Valnijz may try to return as well. The horrors that would come if the Scaled one returns, and not Amder, is something that chills me to the core." Haltim slumped where he sat, silent.

Duncan said nothing for a long time, if Haltim was right, William was in far more dangerous waters than he'd known. And that Master Smith, did he know the truth of all this? Was he part of some plot to kill William? "Haltim, why didn't you say this before? Will is gone, he could be dead right now for all we know!" Duncan stood and paced, trying to control his emotions, which were changing from confusion and disbelief to anger.

"Hold Duncan. You need to tell me everything as well. Where is William?" Haltim grabbed Duncan's arm as Duncan paced. "It's important Duncan. I need to know."

Duncan shook off the Old priest's hand, starting into the fire. "He's gone to join the guild."

Haltim stood, his mouth open in surprise. "How? No Reis can!"

Duncan waved him off in dismissal. "That Master Smith that was here, he hatched a plan. He wanted William in the guild, so he gave him an assumed name, and would get him enough background on it so he'd be able to make do. But now I question if it wasn't some plot to get rid of the one Reis who wants to be a blacksmith."

Haltim nodded and sat back down. "I don't think you need to worry about that at least. I talked to that Master, Jaste? He came into the Church a few days back, asking questions about you two, and Will in particular. From what I gather, because I looked into it after that conversation, he's a bit of a problem in the Guild. At least to those who are powerful in the guild."

Duncan whirled on the Priest. "What do you mean he came asking about us? Why didn't you say that to start with?"

Throwing up his hands Haltim let some irritation show. "Am I supposed to mention every time I hear your surname? I don't think the Master Smith is involved in any plot to get rid of William. Yet, if he's taking him to the Guild, he's in a great deal of danger. More than I like to think about."

Haltim stood and put a hand on Duncan's shoulder, turning him to look at him, eye to eye. "As are you? You more than William. If he's traveling under an assumed name, he might be able to vanish. But Duncan Reis? You're a target. With the Blood Taint and its dangers, the possibility that the Scaled one may try to return to this world, you my boy are treading dangerous ground."

Duncan knew Haltim was right but hated it. "Ok fine, I'm in danger. Big scary danger. So what? William is the one that wants to be a smith. Not me. If either one of us is of the bloodline of this Forgemaster you talked about, William is more the heir to that, not me."

"True. But you still carry Reis blood. And from what little I know of the dark rituals the Scaled God followers use, that blood carries great power." Haltim sighed. "We need to leave the Reach and find them."

The old priest was right. Duncan didn't like the idea, but this had spun out of his control, or his own abilities to deal with. "Fine. But how do we find them? He left, but he only told me the assumed name. Getting to the capitol isn't a huge chore, but finding him in that many people, impossible."

Haltim nodded as Duncan spoke. "True, but we know he will be going to the Guild. Assuming we can get to him before he enters the Guildhall, we should be ok."

"Why? What happens after he enters the Guildhall?" Duncan quizzed the old Priest noting the downward cast of Haltim's eyes as he answered.

"My boy, once he passes through those doors, he won't come out for a year. The guildhall is a self-contained miniature city. And first year Apprentices cannot leave. Ever." Haltim sighed.

"By the sparks." Duncan mumbled as sat down. "So, if we don't find him before then, we are stuck?"

"Don't fret Duncan, we can find him, we leave in the morning?" Haltim sighed and stretched. "We need to sleep. Both of us. We have a long day tomorrow."

Duncan nodded saying nothing. His thoughts on the possibility of missing Will and having to wait a year to warn him were grim. That's assuming he ever came out again. If the people, no, if the Priesthood is behind this, and they had as much power as Haltim had let on, William would be long dead before that year passed.

If he ever got his hands on anyone who hurt Will, no amount of Cloud would stop him. "We will need supplies, I can get gear from my house, enough for both of us, and some money. Assuming no one is there to stop us, that is. I'll go now." Duncan stood, brushing dust off his legs. "We can sleep here tonight. I'll get bedrolls as well. Stay here."

Haltim started to say something, but just nodded in response. Duncan pulled his hood back up, and slowly opened the door, peering out to the side streets. The fire they had made was small, and it wasn't totally unusual for kids to hide out in some of these houses, so he didn't think the small fire would arouse too many questions.

Slipping out into the street, it didn't take him long to get back to his home. He didn't see anyone around. That didn't mean much, but at least there wasn't an armed man waiting for him outside his door. He approached the house and his heart fell. Someone had been here; the doors lock had been broken.

"Don't know who they were, but they left already." The voice came from behind him. A familiar voice. Falkirk Darrew. Duncan turned around.

"I'm not going to ask what's going on, or why armed men wearing Church of Amder clothing was searching your house. I didn't know them, and the Priest with them wasn't Haltim. But they left." Falkirk shrugged. "And I don't think I'll remember seeing you tonight. But if I were you, I'd get what I could and go elsewhere for the night."

"I will Mr. Darrew, thank you." Duncan nodded at the man.

"No need to thank me. You're a Reacher." Falkirk waved a hand. "Go on, I'll keep watch."

Duncan slipped inside his home. Those church guards hadn't wreaked the place, but they certainly had been searching it. It didn't matter, he needed his gear, and the spare set he kept as well for Haltim to use. He also grabbed a sack and took as much food that would keep as he could fit in it.

He slipped back out to see Mr. Darrew standing with his back to the wall, smoking his pipe and looking for all the world like a man just out and enjoying the cool night air. He said nothing but nodded to Duncan, then walked a few doors down to his own house and sat on his doorstep, ignoring Duncan.

Keeping his hood up, Duncan made his way back to the place where Haltim was, finding him still sitting there, watching the flames. "Here, use this." Duncan handed the Priest his spare set of gear and a bedroll. "The house had been searched, but no one was there."

Haltim shook his head. "Get some sleep my boy, rest will help," He said, and setup his bedroll, laying down facing away from the fire.

Duncan sat down and stared into the fire, wishing he'd never gone to that damn tower in the first place.

20

William kept his mouth shut. He figured it was safer that way, now they were about to meet up with Jaste's Journeyman who he'd sent ahead so he could hatch this fake name plan. Will still felt uncomfortable with it, pretending to be someone else, from somewhere else. He hated it in fact.

Yet, it should work, Dernstown wasn't that different from the Reach, though they dressed different. There wasn't any real accent difference which William was happy about. Jaste had explained that everyone who lived near the Skyreach Mountains sounded the same to most people. When Will had pushed on it, asking about if someone recognized a Reach accent, Jaste had sighed and said to tell them his mother was from the Reach.

It was all neat and well thought out. But he still hated doing it. This was the first real test, this Regin character was on his final Journeyman trip before accepting his Master sash and promotion. Master Jaste had explained that while Regin wasn't a bad person, he just loved the internal politics of the Guild. He was a good, if not great Blacksmith, but loved creature comforts even more.

Kilvar was near, and that at least was interesting. He'd never traveled outside the Reach much, only once as a child before his Da had died. And then over to an unnamed Hamlet farther into the mountains for some business deal his Da had been involved in. Kilvar was a proper town, not as large as the Reach was, but far more people. As they devoted the Reach to mining, smelting, and smithing, Kilvar was based around goats and sheep. It was still to rocky here for cattle, but the smaller herding animals did well.

"Kilvar is a good town, though, if you don't mind the smell!" Jaste laughed as they drove closer.

Will was going to ask what he meant when the wind shifted. Then he knew what Jaste meant and lost what little he had eaten that day. Large number of foraging animals in pens for harvesting wool, milk, skins and meat meant lots of waste. The overpowering smell of animal droppings turned his stomach and his face too by Master Jaste's laughter.

"Come now Markin! The smell of the stockyards isn't that bad this time a year though I'm sure it's different from Dernstown." Master Jaste said and threw William a wink.

"Yes, Master Jaste." William replied. Markin Darto. He still thought of himself as William Reis, but from now on he'd have to be Markin Darto.

Jaste smiled and drove on, approaching the gates of Kilvar, which at least distracted Will from the smell. The Reach had no need of walls, there wasn't any point to them with the barrier on one side and the mountains themselves protecting the other. But Kilvar lacked those protections and that brought the wall. Fifteen spans high they had made it of thick heavy logs and stone. Solid granite and quartzite rocks from the look of the rock. The cart stopping drew his attention back to in front, Master Jaste had stopped and the guard post.

"Good morning or is it afternoon? I'm Master Jaste Naom, of the Smithing Guild." Jaste brought forth a scroll from somewhere and presented it to a bored looking guard.

The guard took the scroll and yawned as he opened it, looking bored and unimpressed yet halfway through reading the scroll he snapped much more upright and handed it back to Master Jaste with a snap.

"Yes, Master Smith. How can I help you?" the Guard spoke with a hint of an accent that Will hadn't heard before.

"Here for the testing. I sent my Journeyman ahead a week ago." Jaste replied. Will noted that Jaste always spoke to people the same way, combing the power of his office with a friendly tone. It got results.

"I heard a Journeyman smith was staying downtown, at the Silver Bell," the guard answered, then turned his gaze to Will. "Who is this then if your Journeyman is already here?"

"Ah, a promising recruit from Dernstown. Markin Darto." Jaste answered and lowered his eyes, giving Will a look as he answered.

"My pleasure sir," Will said, unsure what Jaste wanted him to say.

"Well, if that is all, I'll be heading to the Silver Bell," Jaste said, more statement than question, cutting off the guard who was about to ask something else.

"Oh, yes Sir, Have a good testing Master Smith." The Guard waved them through.

Will let out his breath, not even realizing that he had been holding it in.

"Calm Markin, nothing to think much about." Jaste said, trying to calm Will's fears. He wondered if he'd ever get used to this, this deception.

"Not worried Master, not used to this." Will paused for a moment and gave a soft laugh. "My cousin would be better."

"Yes well, he's not the one who has the gift though is he?" Master Jaste kept his eyes on the road ahead. Kilvar felt far more active than the Reach, because it was smaller. People walked here and there, small herds of sheep were being moved at times making the cart lurch to a stop, and street merchants hawked wares left and right. Mostly items dealing with sheep and goats from the look of them.

"He never tried smithing much. When he did, he could do good work, but he found it boring, never found the joy of the forge. He craved excitement, and scaving gave that to him." Will watched the people as they passed by, wondering at the oddness of it all.

"Well, he's not here, and you are," Master Jaste said, and dropped his voice even lower, "and I'd not mention scaving again, since that's a word only used in the Reach area."

Will had only been Markin Darto for a short time, and he'd already slipped up. "Sorry Master Jaste," he said, his voice a mumble, then shut his mouth. He'd never make it in the Guild. He knew it. This plan wasn't going to work.

Master Jaste glanced at him and frowned for a second, then stopped the cart. "Stay here Markin."

"Are we there Master Jaste?" Will asked, but Jaste was already out of earshot, though Will could see him head toward a Merchant nearby, buying two items, though Will couldn't see what they were.

Jaste returned and handed a small wrapped package to Will. "Here, open these and give your opinion."

Will frowned but did so, surprised to find a pair of shears and a bell. "I'm not clear, Master, on what you want me to do?"

"Markin, as a Guild Smith, when you are a journeyman, you will help people like that Merchant. Making tools, helping commoners." Jaste pointed at the shears and bell. "What's wrong and what's right with them?"

Will frowned but picked up the shears first, examining them with a practiced eye.

"Master, the shears, whoever made these...The metal is average quality, though the steel used wasn't heat treated enough, especially in the blades. They won't last that long, and any edge you give them will have to be redone, often. There's also some trace hammer marks here and here: that's fine on work tools, but when those marks are on the blades and the interior side, there's potential for sticking." Will wasn't sure what the point of this was but continued.

"No makers mark either, so whoever made these did so without a master involved."

Jaste smiled and nodded. "What about the bell?"

Will picked up the bell and winced. "Cheap." Master Jaste laughed then, a loud chuckle. "More than that, Markin."

"Poorly folded metal, some sharp edges on the seam and bottom edge. The clapper inside is untreated iron, and low quality. Rust will be a problem. I'd guess that this was made to fall apart, so that whoever bought it would need to buy a replacement soon." Will shook the bell, hearing the dull clang it gave off. "And it doesn't even sound very good."

"Good, now, what do those two items tell you?" Master Jaste asked. "What do they tell you about who made them?"

Will paused studying the two items in his lap. "That while they had some skill, they either weren't careful, or made these tools to fail." Will paused gathering his thoughts. "That's it, isn't it, someone made them to fail?"

Jaste smiled and nodded. "Excellent Markin. Yes, they were, do you know why?"

Will shrugged "Because they want people to buy again?"

"Exactly. That exact reason is why sending Journeyman smiths out is so important. It not only teaches the Journeyman what the people need and use, it allows the people, common people, to get and see true skill." Jaste's smile faded. "That's how it supposed to work at least. The truth is most of the time the Journeymen charge a rate that is so high, only the richest of the commoners can afford their work."

Will nodded, he'd gathered as much from everything he'd heard. Master Jaste pulled the wagon over to the side again.

"Another test Master Jaste?" Will asked looking around for what it could be this time.

"No, we are here Markin." Jaste pointed to the large building in front, Will looked for a sign but didn't see one, but then saw the actual bell, larger than normal, shining silver in the light of day.

Master Jaste looked around and put a hand on Will's arm. "Remember who you are, remember where you come from. Journeyman Regin isn't stupid." Jaste spoke so that only the two of them could hear. "If he suspects anything is amiss, he won't let it go until he figures it out, so don't give him any reason to suspect anything."

Will swallowed and nodded, feeling the knot in his stomach grow. He hoped off the cart, and followed Master Jaste into the Silver Bell, hoping that this wasn't the end of his dream already.

***

Zalkiniv swung her blade slicing through the neck of the scout, his blood gushing onto the stone floor. "Die for your failure, but your blood will not go the Scaled one, it is worthless in our sight." Zalkiniv spat on the man's corpse as she watched his eyes betray his pain of her words, before they became lifeless.

Days. Days her human agents had been searching for this other Reis, only to face failure after failure. The scouts were few, and personally loyal to her, and not ever touched by the blood. They couldn't be, or the barrier would not let them through. But all the vaunted scouts had been able to find out was that both of the cursed blood had left the Reach, and apparently the old Priest of the Eight had vanished at the same time.

A Priest of the Eight! Zalkiniv almost laughed at the thought of someone claiming to follow all eight gods. Only Valnijz was worth following. Blood was power, blood was life. Why follow a God of the Sea or Trees? Mountains? Men weren't fish, or birds or rocks! Worse yet, they followed the cursed one, Amder, the betrayer and blighted one. Who betrayed the Scaled one, and fought the Blood God and somehow defeated him, though the betrayer fell at the same time.

And a Priest of the Eight from the Reach would be steeped in Amderite lore. And now the other Reis had fled with one!

Zalkiniv paced in her study, stepping over the cooling corpse. Her human agents were failing her. She'd use the Valni, but the barrier stopped them cold, they couldn't get past it. She groaned in the frustration, they knew of two of the bloodline of the blessed of the betrayer and both were out of reach!

She had lived for a thousand years, lived through many bodies and many lives, there must be something, some scrap of knowledge that she could use! There was a way. She needed to search her memories, to consult the blood, all the blood, regardless of cost.

"No cost is too high to return the Blood God." Zalkiniv whirled around pointing to an unmoving attendant. "Prepare the Blood memories, all of them." The attendant's eyes widened, cracking the dried blood patterns on his face before he bowed low and made his way out of the High Priests study.

There was much to prepare Zalkiniv knew, and she must rest before attempting what she had to do.

***

"I need to rest." Haltim half groaned half whimpered as he sat down on the ground panting. Duncan turned his head away and rolled his eyes for the fifth time that day. Too many rest stops and they weren't making any good progress. There should be a well-stocked traveler's cabin a day away, but at this rate they wouldn't get there till next week.

"Haltim, we have to keep moving. The cabin is only a day's travel, we will spend the night there before heading down and out of the Skyreach. But I for one don't want to be out here at night more than we have to be." Duncan leaned on his walking stick. The old priest looked grey and sick to Duncan's eyes, though he'd been spry enough this morning.

"Why the rush Duncan my lad?" Haltim spoke with his long breaths in-between the words. "We are far past the barrier now, and I haven't heard of any bandits in the area." Haltim shifted his position rubbing his legs as he spoke.

"I'm not worried about Valni or Bandits. I am however worried about the weather, and possibly animals." Duncan pointed to the westward sky. "Those are rain clouds. I'm not sure if they will get hung up on a peak between here and there, but if they don't the last thing we want is to be on the downward slope in a rain storm."

Haltim sighed and stood, Duncan watching him wince as he did so. "As true as ever, but I'm not made for this hiking around." Haltim sighed and leaned on his own walking stick.

Duncan agreed with that. They had left early in the morning from the Reach, each of them kitted out as best they could with what was in the house. The only downside was that during the packing, Haltim had seen the cloth. He'd not said a word but had taken it out of Duncan's pack and stored it in his own.

Duncan himself carried something else, fifteen double doses of Cloud were secreted and well wrapped in his pack. He knew Haltim would never approve, but as much as he and the old priest didn't get along, he still didn't want to be the one who ended the old man's life.

"Come on, let's get moving." Duncan waved Haltim forward and took off, taking measured steps to allow the far older man to keep up. Duncan kept glancing up at the clouds as they walked. His mood turning darker as the western sky continued to darken and a cold damp wind blew from that direction.

"How much farther?" Haltim's voice came to Duncan, laced with concern. Duncan sighed, the storms were moving in faster than he'd thought, and they still had some to go.

"Some. And we need to move faster." Duncan yelled back over a gust of wind that came blowing down the canyon walls. Stuck in a canyon, heading downhill when a storm was barreling down. All that water would flood down this canyon in a second, and there wasn't any way for them to escape it if it did so.

Haltim yelled something back to him but the words slipped away in the wind's noise. A huge rolling crash of thunder came, reverberating off the granite walls of the canyon. "Damned Priest, we need to move faster," Duncan yelled, not caring if Haltim could hear him or not.

Not caring to see if Haltim was keeping up, Duncan moved, being less careful about where he placed his steps around the rocks of the valley. While the trail normally was clearer, it had been a wetter spring this year, and storms had dropped many boulders on this path. Duncan regretted not taking the normal road.

The clouds grew, increasing the tension Duncan felt. Maybe the cabin was closer than he thought? He hadn't been this way in quite some time, maybe he had the distance wrong.

Haltim and he had discussed their route last night and took a lesser used path out of town. If only to throw off any pursuit by the Priesthood guards back at the Church of the Eight. They weren't sure if they would be followed, but not wanting to take the chance, they had gone this way. Now Duncan could only wonder if they would even last the first day out, washed away by a flash flood.

As the first fat cold raindrops hit his face, he saw the travel cabin, perched up out of the valley, a stone cut steps leading to the sheltered overhang. "Haltim! There it is!" Duncan pointed the way, turning around to make sure the old priest saw him.

Haltim had fallen behind again. The Priest gave him a nod and waved his walking stick in acknowledgement. Duncan moved forward again, making his way to the cabin.

Reaching the door, he opened it to find a dry, and serviceable travelers' cabin. These cabins had been set up in several places in the mountains many years before. Mostly for the use of prospectors and miners, in case they got stuck overnight out in the mountains. Travelers were welcome to use them, though based on the trail Duncan was sure no one had used this cabin in quite a while.

Throwing off his pack, Duncan turned back to the valley. Where was Haltim? An involuntary shiver went down his back as he peered out the doorway, but the old priest was nowhere in sight. As he looked another boom of thunder and a flash of lighting split the sky, and as the rain started, Duncan could see nothing else.

***

Zalkiniv stood in the Chamber of Memories, stripped down to nothing. In all the lives she had lived, all the bodies she'd gone through, she had never attempted this. To read all the memories of all the Priests since the death of the Scaled one. She had read four one time, and that had been a trying experience. This would be harder.

She shook those thoughts out of her mind, any sacrifice, any challenge was worth the return of the Blood God. Stepping into the stone bowl in the floor she sat down, crossing her legs. A small army of attendants filed in, each carrying a crystal flask, and in each flask was the blood memories. All the knowledge, all the secrets, all the skill of every priest in the last thousand years, bound to the blood contained in each flask.

Thirty-nine. Thirty-nine flasks, each flask having the blood of hundreds of Priests. A hint of doubt crept in, would she go mad trying to absorb all this, all these memories? Setting her face in a scowl, Zalkiniv held out her hand for the consecrated blade. A hooded attendant handed her the ragged edged blade, old and unclean itself.

Placing the blade against one arm, she cut, slicing up her forearm, and repeating it on the other. Blood came forth, but her skill showed as it cut no major arteries. With a grimace she repeated the cuts on her thighs, pushing harder than necessary to punish herself for her momentary doubt.

With her body prepared, and the blood flowing from her wounds, she steeled herself. "May I be a vessel for the Scaled One. May the blood of those who have given all for the God of Rage, give me the knowledge I seek. May the Blood God grant me the power I need in his stead." Zalkiniv intoned the words the clasped the blade to her chest and bowed her head.

That was the signal, and each lined up before the sitting bleeding figure and one by one starting with the oldest flask, poured a drop of the blood into the stone bowl. Zalkiniv could feel each drop mix with her blood already, blood spoke to blood. Each drop filled with the knowledge that she might need.

The memories and thoughts overwhelmed her, too many names, and too many faces. She was Gann, a warrior-priest of the Rage God, killing an Amderite in one of the final skirmishes of the God's war. She was Fenli, taking slaves and experimenting with the blood mist effects, proclaiming the new creatures the Valni, in honor of the Scaled One. She was the Silent Master, who cut out his own tongue in a vision of coming glory.

Each drop made her head swim, each drop brought her the pains and ecstasies of lives long gone. But each drop brought her secrets too. Secrets guarded; secrets never shared. Secrets that were hidden away but could never be hidden from blood.

Zalkiniv shuddered when the last drop hit the now full stone bowl, the flash of memories mixing with the thousands already rushing through her veins and mind. So hard to concentrate, so hard to stay who she was. She was the High Priest of the God of Rage and Blood. Nothing else, nothing less.

A flash of something, a scrap of a hidden secret from ... a betrayer? She felt herself dive into the remnant of a life long gone, an arm of Priesthood long gone, the Bloodfinders. She'd heard the name, and now the memories around her flooded her with information about the now destroyed order. Scouts and assassins, they had been broken up because of suspicion of heresy, and the suspicions had been right! No one had needed to access these memories until now, but in her mind flashed the knowledge, a traitor, one who turned their back on the Blood God. Disgust made her fingers curl into fists as she felt the memories of the traitor, only the fresh shock of the pain this caused made her relax her white knuckled anger.

There, a secret way, under the barrier! Given to the traitor by an agent of the false god. The Valni still couldn't pass, but a Priest could. She forced herself to take in the memories of the betrayer, she had to keep these, and she needed the information.

She pushed the other thoughts and memories away and out of her blood, one by one. By the time it was over the blood in the stone bowl had congealed and grown cold. But she had what she needed, what she had to have.

Standing, she raised her now healed arms and legs, the self-inflicted wounds already faded into scars that in time would vanish as well. She had done it, now who to send to track down the last two of the Reis blood? An Underpriest? No, to dangerous. Allowing one of her want to be rivals that much glory would be a foolish move. One of her blood enhanced guards? They would never betray her, but they weren't known for their minds, and this could need clever thinking.

An idea sprung to mind and drew a smile from her, she knew who was perfect for the job, and there was not much time to waste.

21

Haltim shuddered as the cold icy rain obliterated any light he could see. He could feel the chill pierce deep into his body, and the ice like water was rising. Already the water was rushing around his mid-calf, cold and dark in the night.

Drowned or frozen, what a sad way to go. Haltim teeth chattered as he felt the water push him forward and into a large rock. Somehow, he hauled himself onto the boulder, trying to keep his face clear enough of the rain to even breathe. He was too old, too frail. He'd felt it all day, he wasn't strong enough for this sort of thing anymore and hadn't been for a long time.

Being the Priest in the Reach had been one of quiet reflection. He'd clean the church twice a week, dusting, preside over the occasional funeral or wedding, and on an occasion counsel a Reacher in need. He'd grown soft many years before and had at one time gotten rather fat. Age had robbed him of the fat part. He rather wished he was still fat, he'd be warmer.

An involuntary shiver started in his body, and he knew it wouldn't be long before he slumped into unconsciousness. He'd either die on this rock frozen or slip into the still rising water and drown. What a sad end, and they'd only been gone from the Reach for a short time!

His hands unsteady, Haltim opened his pack enough to dig into it, and grab the Amder cloth. The cloth of woven metal that had covered the Hammer was special, blessed. He regretted taking it from Duncan now. It wouldn't be in danger of being washed away. Duncan would look for him tomorrow, and while he still had some hope for the lad, he knew Duncan was as likely to sell it as to keep it safe as a holy artifact.

He closed his eyes and said a prayer to Amder, asking for his protection and guidance as he passed from this life to the beyond. Haltim knew he'd have to pay for his wrongs, his going along with the ever-growing corruption in the Church, keeping his mouth shut. While he was a Priest of all Eight Gods, the truth was in his heart he was a Priest of Amder, and always had been.

He could feel his consciousness slipping away between words, and the sound of the rain faded, and he wasn't cold anymore. He wished he'd made it to warn William. He prayed for Williams's health and survival in whatever was to come.

"William is safe enough, for now." A voice pressed in on Haltim stopping his thought.

"Haltim Goin. Priest of Amder. What are you doing here?" the voice came again, surrounding Haltim. He found himself unable to open his eyes, but a feeling of warmth enveloped him, like warm metal on a spring day. He swore he could smell a forge fire, the odor of burning coal.

"I asked you a question Priest. Why are you here?" the voice was stronger now. Powerful.

"I was traveling," Haltim said. Did his mouth even move when those words came?

"Yes, that was obvious. But why Haltim? You left the Reach; you left the temple to that other person. You ran off with the less pious of the Reis line. Why?" The voice commanded him now. *"Speak Haltim. And do not dither."*

"To warn William Reis," Haltim said, blurting out the words.

"Exactly. You are not a bad person, and while you've made mistakes, you're at least not corrupt." The voice had a tinge of humor. Resignation?

"Amder?" Haltim asked unsure if he sound even ask.

"Yes, it is Amder! My Priesthood. I rue the day I even forged the order. For years I've been waiting, working to return. And the Priesthood, my own Priesthood, stood in the way. Only a Forgemaster can do it. They need the Heart, my Heart. And that the Priesthood will never give up." The voice of Amder trailed off, and Haltim could hear hammer blows. The distant ring of a hammer striking something, in rhythm.

"I chose one of the last two of the Reis line, and have pushed him, will all the power I can muster now, into the Smithing Guild. William could be the finest Forgemaster to ever live. But he will need help. I am at the limit of my powers now. You all must help him." The voice of Amder sounded worried now, and the Hammering sounds harder, stronger.

"Even now, my erstwhile brother, the Destroyer also works to return. And if he should manage that before I can, the world and all its works, will be swept away. The other Gods will not fight

him. They hide, they will run. They live in fear of where I am, in what I have become." Amder's voice trailed off, and Haltim could only hear the Hammering now.

"My Lord Amder, Forgive me. Forgive the Priesthood." Haltim rushed through the words. "I am dying my Lord Amder and will not live much longer. Please, watch over both the Reis boys. Duncan lives with a Blood curse now, nicked by the Spear blade of Valnijz..."

"*I know.*" Amder's voice overwhelmed him and Haltim found himself unable to speak. "*Duncan Reis has his own path, but there are chances, possibilities for him. As for you, Haltim...*" The voice halted. A burning feeling enveloped his right wrist, and Haltim opened his mouth to scream but couldn't make a sound. Was this punishment? For all he had been silent on?

"*You will not die, not here, not now. Go, open your eyes, and find Duncan, rest. This is your chance to atone Priest, to seek forgiveness for all that you have done.*" Haltim felt the cold return with a shock that made him inhale, coughing as he breathed in the rain.

"Haltim?" Duncan's voice cut through sound of water. Haltim could see the lad standing not four feet off, holding a hooded lantern aloft. Steeling himself, Haltim grabbed his pack to his chest and slid down the boulder he'd clutched, landing in ice cold water that was up to mid-thigh. Taking each step with care, he grabbed another rock jutting out from the swift moving flood.

Duncan was doing something, but he couldn't make it out in the falling rain. How was he going to get over to him? Amder himself, or some remnant of him had given him a sacred duty, atonement for his blasphemies and wrongs, he didn't want to die. Something snaked out the air in front of him and he jerked backward, almost losing his grip on the rock he was holding on to. A rope!

Haltim grabbed the line with one hand, still clutching his pack to his body with the other. He could make out Duncan pulling him closer, one hand over the other, pulling him out of the torrent that was still rising in this forlorn valley.

Gasping and cold to the bones, he threw an exhausted arm over Duncan's offered arm allowing Duncan to lead him up to the cabin. The driving rain still made it hard to see until they cut back and were under the overhang. Blinking the rainwater out of his eyes, he let go of Duncan's arm and shuffled into the cabin, his clothes wet, his skin numb. The warmth of the small fire Duncan must have made before he looked for him drew Haltim close. Warmth.

Holding his hands to the fire he could feel life returning, though shivers still traveled around his body, and his teeth chattered. He reached forward with both hands, and then froze. A different sort of chill crawled up his spine, one that his addled brain had a hard time accepting. On his wrist, there was now a bracer, a wide thick thing, multi-colored metal woven across it and emblazoned upon it was the symbol of Amder, the anvil and hammer, surrounded by the fire.

22

Will couldn't help comparing this place, with the Golden Chisel back home. Both had a lot in common, the main difference to him was the feel of the place. The Bell was far more crowded than the Chisel ever was. The Bell was also larger, its main room being half again as large as the Chisel. The place was set with finer and more expensive furnishings, catering to the wealthier drovers and ranchers. And like now, to Guild masters and their flock.

"Master Jaste!" a thin man waved a hand in greeting from behind the bar. Will tried not to stare, it was the thinnest tallest man he'd ever seen.

"Goodkeep!" Jaste greeted the man with a smile and made his way over to the man, where they shook hands. "Is Journeyman Regin around? We got in from an earlier testing up in the Skyreach Mountains."

The tall thin man looked down at Will with a confused expression but turned his attention back to Jaste. "He was earlier but haven't seen him for a few hours. He may be at the testing tent here, he set it up over in Mudmarket." Goodkeep peered at Will again. "And who is this? I don't recall you ever bringing anyone else here before."

"This is Markin Darto, from Dernstown. He came to the testing in the Reach, and made it past the first round, so he's traveling with us to the Guildhall." Jaste placed a hand on Will's shoulder and squeezed.

"Dernstown eh? Haven't seen a Dernstowner in years, but they don't cross the mountains much, if at all." The tall man reached out a hand that looked far too big for his arm. "My name is Goodkeep, Naman Goodkeep. But everyone calls me by my last name. I own this place, and any Guild member is welcome here."

Will swallowed for a second. "Thank you, sir. Markin Darto, but call me Mark, no one calls me Markin except my mother and Master Jaste here." Will felt a light flash of surprise at the words that had come out. He had lied to this man and done it without a problem.

"Mark it is." Goodkeep answered with a smile, but his eyes still held a hint of a question.

"Mudmarket you said?" Jaste spoke breaking the moment. "If you'll have someone deal with the horses, and take out things to the rooms, Markin here and I will head there now."

"Master Jaste, not a problem," Goodkeep answered and turned away to speak to a staff member.

Jaste took that as a cue and led Will back outside and out of the earshot of the innkeeper. "Mark, eh? Well, it works. Good improvisation. And with Goodkeep none the less, I was concerned about that meeting."

Will shrugged off Jaste's hand "Why would you worry? And what's the situation with that man? I've seen no one so tall and thin in my life."

"I forget that people ... from where you're from, don't see a lot of outsiders. Goodkeep is a Trinil. One of the blessed of the Forest God. And while not mind readers, they are good at sniffing out lies." Jaste smiled at Wills obvious and near instant discomfort. "I've known Goodkeep for a long time. He won't say anything to anyone other than me, assuming he says anything at all."

Will still didn't like it, he'd heard of a Trinil, but Master Jaste was right, it was rare to see anyone who wasn't human in the Reach. Very rare. He'd never really thought about it.

"Master Jaste, why is it that there aren't a lot of non-humans in the place where I am from?" Will stopped himself short of saying the Reach.

Master Jaste maneuvered past a street merchant selling some strange meat that had been balled up and grilled on skewers before he answered. "That my dear Markin, is a great mystery. They don't go there. There's not a lot of non-humans around anyway to start with. And..." Master Jaste paused and looked around to make sure no one was paying any attention to their conversation.

Jaste leaned in and whispered. "No one knows why, but no non-human will go anywhere near the Mistlands. They refuse and die if taken there by force."

Will frowned. None of that made sense. The Mistlands were dangerous, he knew that well himself. The threat of the Valni was a true one, but death for even going there?

"Ah... Mudmarket!" Master Jaste sounded almost joyful as they made their way from crowded street to the largest town square

Will had ever seen. And the smelliest. It was clear why Mudmarket had its name, the ground was being churned by the feet of goats and sheep, hundreds, if not a thousand. That many animals, that much animal waste. Will raised an arm to cover his nose, trying to not breathe.

"The smell takes some time to get used to Markin, I'll grant you." Jaste smiled at Will and Will wondered if he was enjoying his discomfort. "Journeyman Regin hates the smell, which I'm sure is why he will have several braziers going and anything else he can do to kill the odor."

Will followed Jaste as they made their way across Mudmarket square. All along the edges of the square were various merchants, but unlike the street hawkers they passed before, all these goods were of much better quality.

Jaste saw him looking and nodded. "Yes, this the real tradesman market. The stuff before was for town bound types, or the poor. The equipment here is of better quality." Will kept his face calm but was almost impressed by some metal work he saw. It wasn't up to Reach standards, but it was good.

In the distance he could see the top of the Guild tent, but differently colored than the one they had brought with them. Will wondered why, and almost asked, but got distracted by trying to not step on something he couldn't identify in the muck.

The tent's flaps were closed when they arrived, and Will couldn't hear anything from inside. Master Jaste paused for a second and looked Will in the eyes. "Be careful, Regin is no fool. Stick to what you know, but don't offer up anything he didn't ask, he won't let it go if you do." Jaste's voice was low, a whisper. "With any luck we can leave here tomorrow and by the middle of next week have you in the Apprentice class and away from Regin. He'll be ascending to Master, and hopefully he won't get picked to teach."

Will nodded. He couldn't do anything else; it was far too late to back out now.

"Journeyman Regin!" Jaste's voice boomed through the tent as Will followed him. This tent was like the one Jaste had used in the Reach inside as well, the only difference was the four small braziers burning in the corners of the space covering up the ever-prevalent odor of goat.

"Master Jaste!" A man who had been lounging in a chair scrambled up, surprised. Will didn't like the look of him right away though he couldn't say why. Regin was good looking, well built, and made Will uneasy.

"I wasn't expecting you till tomorrow Master Jaste." Regin stood still smoothing down his more formal Guild clothes. The bright red sash of final year Journeyman emblazoned across his clothes. Regin looked to say more but spied Will standing behind Master Jaste, clad in the traveling clothes that Jaste had given him.

"Who is that Master?" Regin's voice carried an edge of... Humor? Insult? Will couldn't place it, but it set his teeth on edge, and dropped Regin even lower in his opinion.

"This is Markin Darto. He came to the testing in the Reach from Dernstown and passed the first test with flying colors." Jaste motioned Will to come forward more, which he did, feeling Regin's gaze lock onto him.

"Dernstown? Why go all the way to the Reach for a testing?" Regin asked. "Well Markin? Why travel all the way to the Reach?"

"I had been sick when the testing had come closer to Dernstown Journeyman Regin. The next closest testing was in the Reach, so I went to that one." Will looked down, unwilling and not wanting to look Regin in the eye.

"Humph." Regin mumbled. "So Dernstowner..." Regin was interrupted by Master Jaste clearing his throat. "Regin don't you have other things to do than interrogating a Potential? How's the testing here?" Jaste looked around the tent.

Regin shrugged "Not horrible, there is one potential. She made a rather good torc, the piece shows good control, excellent inlay work. Here." Regin pulled the rounded shape of a torc out from a small cloth nearby. Will didn't have a lot of experience in that kind of metalwork, but even his eye could see that it was a well-made piece. Some black metal inlaid with Silverlace and small semi-precious gems. Garnets maybe? The best work was the ends, each made into the head of a fish, and the eyes were cats' eye agate. Amusing, a fish with cat eyes.

Jaste rubbed the torc, looked at his thumb. Will realized he was checking for flake off. "Nice work. Anyone else?"

Regin shook his head. "No Master Jaste. The rest were not worth my time."

Jaste turned on Regin, and Will could see his hand grip the torc tightly, the tendons of his hand snapping into stark relief. "What did you do, Regin?"

Regin shrugged again. "Applicants came in, what they brought was total junk. Not worth my time. I dismissed them as fast as they came in."

"That is *not* how it is done Regin. There is a defined method of judging, interviewing, and dealing with those who wish to join our ranks." Jaste was angry now. Will had never seen this part of Master Jaste. So far, he had always been in a good mood, and seeing anger was surprising.

"I don't have time to waste on shepherds and drovers. At least in the Reach you could talk to people who knew something about what we do even if it's a bunch of diggers. But the people here? Mud grubbing herders and drovers. The place stinks and the filth always makes me have to burn any boots I wear here." Regin's sense of superiority was on full display. "The one woman who made that torc isn't even from Kilvar, she's some innkeeper's daughter from out of town."

Master Jaste locked his jaw forward and pointed Regin to the chair. Regin sat down, not without a loud sigh. "Journeyman Regin. That is not how this works. Not now, never. Period." Jaste was as blunt as Will had ever seen.

"Master Jaste. You know it's true! These people wouldn't know good metalwork even if it came out of these animals of theirs!" Regin pointed at Will who had kept quiet and was trying hard to blend into the tent wall. "I'll wager that even that a Dernstowner could see how bad these were."

Wills head came up giving Master Jaste a look, eyes wide.

"Leave the Potential out of this Regin. We will discuss this later in private. Forget spending the night with whatever distraction you've found this trip. You are not a Master yet, and so you will spend the evening writing out a full detailed description of all the methods of clink removal and reduction during hot forge operations. And that, after we've had further discussions." Jaste pointed at the Journeyman who rolled his eyes but stayed silent. He placed the torc back where Regin had gotten it from.

Master Jaste stomped out of the tent, jerking a thumb towards Will to follow him, which Will did, if only to get away from Regin. He'd prefer the smells of the stockyards to spending more time with that entitled fool.

"Damned foolish Journeyman. I knew he wasn't fond of the testing, but that is not how it's supposed to be done," Jaste explained as they walked, far faster than they'd been going before. "Markin, remember who you are. I wasn't expecting him to find another Potential, but, based on that piece, we must take her with us. Just remember who you are."

Will said nothing but wondered if he would be able to keep this up. Yet another person to lie to. Deflated, he followed.

23

Zalkiniv rode out accompanied by a mounted escort of her sworn guards, and a roving mob of Valni. The blood memories had given her the information she needed, and she knew who to set on this task. Problematic it might be, there was only one person who she could trust, and wouldn't fail her. Herself.

Her word was law, so no advisor or under priest raised as much as a hint of concern, though she expected blood to flow once she was far enough away. It was the way; Valnijz was the God of Blood and Rage. Murder and revenge were rife in the Temple and always had been.

The memories had shown her a cave, a small cave that led under the mountains, and under the barrier. Deep enough under that a person could cross over, if one knew how. It would require her to do things that made her skin crawl. But anything for the glory of Valnijz.

Her guards, the Valni, they would stay and guard the entrance to the cave, but she would have to go alone. She had prepared. Clothes taken from travelers, food, stuffed into a pack. She'd even had to wash. Cleaning herself of the blood that marked her. She felt, naked, foreign in her own skin. She wished this method would allow her to send Valni, but they were tied to close to the Scaled One. Her guards might be able to cross, but she wasn't sure if it would draw attention if they went with her. No, it was better she went alone.

She'd not in any life, even at first, had ever crossed over into the Skyreach mountains. To see the enemy up close, to understand them, would be a good thing. When Valnijz was reborn, and the barrier shattered, she would understand her new prey, and how best to bleed them. She might even take one or two and test them now if she could find a good time to do so.

"High Priestess, we are near to the spot on the map you pointed out." The voice of her personal bodyguard rasped out, interrupting her musing if the screams of an Amderite sounded different from ones she had heard before.

Zalkiniv looked around. They were at the far southern end of the Mistlands, a dry, windy place. The blood mist rarely flowed this far south. There were none of the telltale crystals either, which suited her fine.

"High Priestess. There it is!" The rasping voice of her bodyguard drew her attention to a small overhang where a cave, almost just a crack could be seen, dark and leading deeper into the rock.

Pulling up in front of the overhang, there was nothing to give any outward sign of the importance of the cave, but then again, why should there be? Zalkiniv dismounted nodding to the guards to do the same. Without a sound they all did so, the only noise the breathing of the horses, and the sounds of the armor as they moved. Only her bodyguard could talk, she had cut out the tongues of the rest and drank in their screams and blood when they'd sworn to her service. The blood let her know none of them would ever betray her, they were hers, always.

She steadied herself and took the shaft holding it upright. She'd left the blade back at the temple, protected. The shaft she needed to command the Valni. Blood as well, but that was easy. She prepared herself, this would be the last time she'd get to work the blood in total freedom.

Holding the blood-stained shaft upright, she summoned the Valni from their ranging, their loping moving bodies betraying their true nature, regardless of how much they look human. The closer they came she could see one of them had found some kind of animal, its face and hands covered with fresh blood, the iron tang wafted through the air, arousing her.

With the Valni gathered she needed to seal them to guard this place, and that required more than a wave of the shaft. Pointing to one of her guards, she beckoned the man to her. He bowed and removed his helm his shaved and painted head gleaming in the sunlight.

He kneeled in front of her, his eyes alight with the passion and reverence he held for her and Valnijz. Drawing forth a dagger from a fold of her robe, Zalkiniv plunged the dagger into the man's right eye, blood fountained forth from the wound. A good sacrifice, a strong heart. Before the man could collapse, she touched the end of the shaft to his forehead. The dead guard's body gave a spasm, and locked itself upright blood spurting out, staining the ground.

Whispering prayers to the Scaled one, the High Priestess dipped each finger in the blood and one at a time touched the forehead of each Valni. At her touch each of the creatures lowered its head, each giving forth a guttural growl. They were sealed to the place now until she released them.

Taking water from a different guard she cleaned the blood off her hands, saying a silent prayer of atonement for removing the holy liquid from her skin. But the time for subterfuge had come, and beyond the barrier she had to abide by a different set of rules, at least for now.

Removing her robes, she dressed in a set of clothing taken from a wagon that had strayed too close to the Mistlands and fallen to the Valni. Strange clothes, leather and plain white cloth ... Boots and a simple knife, a sharp knife, completed the outfit.

For a long moment she studied the shaft of Valnijz. Bloodstained wood sticky to the touch shone in the sun's light. She wanted to take it with her, to bring this authority along. But the other Reis was traveling with a Priest, he might know what the shaft was, and that was a risk she could not take.

"Guard this with your life, all your lives." Zalkiniv held the shaft out for her bodyguard captain to take. She was wasting time, she needed to get past the barrier and into the Reach today. Each day she was in the Amderite lands was a day too many. The blood memories didn't state how long the travel through the cave would take either. Best to get started.

Without a word or a look back, she took a lit torch from a silent one and entered the cave, her mission was simple. Find and bring back a Reis, for then, her God could return, and all would know the glory and price of Valnijz.

***

Haltim and Duncan awoke to a damp sunlit mountain pass the next morning. The water was small meandering stream instead of the torrent it had been the night before. The changes the water had wrought to the landscape were awesome to Haltim, but when he brought it up to Duncan, the young man shrugged. "It's rocks." Duncan said and walked down the valley.

To Haltim the valley had become a wonder. The water had cleaned moss and vegetation off old rocks and pushed new ones down, and everything shone in the sun, glittering and shining.

"Duncan is any of this valuable?" Haltim asked.

"You don't know? How can you call yourself a Priest of the Eight? Are not Gunnar and Amder part of the Eight? The Gods of the Mountains and the God of Craft?" Duncan waited for Haltim by a blue tinted boulder that had a dramatic streak of black through it.

"I'm a Priest, not a miner!" Haltim struggled to catch up with the younger man.

"No, Haltim." Duncan waved at the boulder nearby. "That over there may have come from a deposit of silverleaf but since there's no way to know where the boulder washed away from, it's useless. Now, if we see anything worth scaving that might be worth something. But as it is? All this?" Duncan waved his hands "Rocks."

Haltim nodded. "I guess you're right. Just feels... like a waste."

Duncan didn't answer but shrugged again as they walked on in silence for a time. The sun was rising and warming the surrounding air but when they turned a corner and had to stop. The storm had pushed rock debris into a choke point, and the path was blocked.

"By the Sparks," Duncan stared at the high wall of stone rubble the storm had pushed together.

"What do we do?" Haltim asked, sitting on a nearby outcropping, breathing hard.

"I don't know, at least not yet. Might have to double back. There's another track, little more than a hunter's trail, but we'd have to go all the way back to the cabin from last night. I didn't want to do that for many reasons." Duncan sighed. "We can try to climb past this, but its loose rock, odds of breaking a leg or twisting something might be high."

"And you don't think I can do it." Haltim added.

Duncan faced Haltim. "No, I don't. Even this walk downhill has winded you, but climbing up that wall of loose rock? Where one bad step could make you fall? Break a leg? Or worse? No, I don't think you can do it."

Haltim felt his irritation rise, but the lad was right. He couldn't do this climb. The fear of making Duncan angry also played on him.

He had to admit, the lad was holding up better than he had expected. Amder's Hammer must have something to do with it. Even with that help, getting Duncan to stay calm was a task he now had to work on.

"So, the other track?" Haltim asked. He wasn't looking forward to doubling back nor going uphill, but if it was that or having to go all the way back to the Reach, it would have to do. "We have to get to William before he enters the Guild."

"I know old man. I know." Duncan spat on the ground. "Fine, let's get started." Without another word, Duncan turned around and started back to the cabin from the night before. Haltim followed, leaning forward and trying to keep his balance.

24

Zalkiniv shuddered as she crossed the barrier, feeling the touch of the ancient Amderite prayers and magic on her skin. The Blood memories had been accurate. The quick ritual to allow passage had been easy and had involved nothing more than touching the barrier in four places in the cave

The touch of the Amderite magic even now clung to her like a second skin, making her shudder in disgust and feel sick to her stomach. She wondered if even with the ritual if she'd still had the shaft or the blood on her skin if she would have been able to cross over. She doubted it.

She climbed up out of the cave, picking steps with care, stopping to take a sip of water now and then. Finally, a dim light could be seen ahead, the cold grey light of the mountains. The air was clean and cool, and for a split second she allowed herself to enjoy the feeling of being out of the oppressive walls of the cave.

She took a long breath and felt herself get almost sick again. The air... it smelled... wrong. In the lands of Valnijz, the air always carries the smell of blood, smoke, and death. Those are the ways to power. Here, in this soft land, they ignored the true power, and delved into the earth for metal and rocks.

She breathed and tamped down her disgust. She needed to find the Reis bloodline and fulfill her destiny. She was so close now, so close. To find the Reis blood, she could work a ritual, but she needed something first. She made her way down the mountainside, until she found a path, one worn and well used. She hid herself and waited.

The wait wasn't long, a man driving a donkey laden with tools ambled down the path. She had heard him coming long before she'd seen him. Some sort of miner or prospector she assumed, all alone. She doubted if anyone would miss him, and what if they did? Zalkiniv was sure people went missing in these mountains all the time.

She waited till he had passed by, but still within sight when she stood and screamed, running down the path towards him, looking over her shoulder.

"Some animal! Help!" she yelled, feeling amusement as the old man turned, shocked towards her.

"What?" he said before she was on him. She clasped him tight.

"Oh, thank you. Someone else... There's something after me, some... beast. I had gone on a walk." She made up her story as she went along. She could almost see the fool puff up, protecting a lone female out in the wilderness.

"Now girl calm down." the old miner said, but nothing else as her knife, thin and razor sharp pierced the spine at the back of his neck.

"Pathetic." Zalkiniv smirked as she watched his face, not even understanding his fate as he died.

Reaching down she sliced his major arteries, careful to not get blood on her clothes. As much as she wished to bathe in this kill, she was on a mission, one that she had to keep to. Fingers dipped down, and came back sticky, red, and hot. She drew the needed symbols on a nearby rock face, working with careful practiced technique.

She nicked her finger then, adding a drop of her blood to the mix, and concentrating, reached out through the blood to the connection she had with the Valni. Even here, on the far side of the barrier, the connection was there, though fainter than she was used to.

A Valni had tasted the blood of a Reis. It didn't matter which Reis, blood was blood. She could use that to make blood call to blood, to give her a way to track both cursed bloodlines. The blood blessed one, given the kiss of the blade was hard to track, and had been since he'd taken up with that Amderite priest. Hopefully on this side of the barrier it would be easier to find him.

She called, saying prayers to the Scaled One, forging the link. She had wanted to do this on her side of the barrier, but the ritual wouldn't work once she crossed, she had been sure. This was the only way.

There! A slight tug, a pull, not as far as she had expected, far closer in fact. She wasn't sure which one it was, but close!

Zalkiniv cleaned up the blood from her fingers, lingering over the taste. Dragging the old man's body behind a rock, she started towards the pull. She was so close now; she would not let this chance escape!

***

Duncan and Haltim paused for the fifth time in an hour. Haltim was too old and weak to do more than he was, Duncan knew, but it didn't stop him from being annoyed. Walking the line between annoyed and angry was tiring. Still to be careful, he patted the two vials of Cloud he kept on him. There was more in his pack, but he carried some always.

Halim wheezed out another long breath, as Duncan squinted in the sunlight. At least there weren't any more storms coming, he'd been surprised at the power of the storm last night. He glanced back at the Old Priest who had his hands clasped inside his robes, eyes closed as if he was praying.

Haltim's ability to survive last night had surprised Duncan. He'd been sure the old man was dead, frozen to death or crushed by the raging waters. But somehow Haltim had survived. Somehow. He could not help the thought that some connection to the Gods had helped the old man, but he banished the thought. Gods were not in the business of helping anyone.

Dumb luck. Duncan kicked a small rock, watching it glitter in the sun as it bounced down the path. "We need to get moving again. At this rate it will take all day to get back to the cabin, we will have lost a day of travel. A day lost is a day Will is closer to the Guild, and a day closer to us losing him, at least for a year." Duncan let that trail off. He wasn't about to let his only family left get killed by a bunch of old Priests or jealous guild smiths.

"I know my boy, I know." Haltim's voice was resolute. He had gotten strength back at least.

"Let us be off," Haltim said and picked his way back up the valley. Duncan watched him in surprise for a moment then shook his head in disbelief. Priests.

Duncan lost track of time, when turning past a sharp turn in the valley they were climbing back up he realized that they had made it, they were back at the cabin. The sun hung a lot lower in the sky than he'd wanted it to be, but they had made it back. The small wooden structure stood under the stone overhang, empty and quiet.

"How are you?" Duncan asked to the Priest, who now sat on the same rock Duncan had rescued him from last night in the flood. Now the ground was dry though traces of water could be seen in small hollows here and there.

"Tired my boy. Exhausted." Haltim's voice was quiet, weak. Duncan knew they would have to spend the night here again. The one thing he didn't want to do. Losing time. But Haltim couldn't navigate the other path in the dark, and exhausted? Forget it.

He considered leaving Halim here, and heading on without him. He should be safe here, and Duncan could travel far faster without the old man slowing him down. Only two things stopped him. One, Will would be furious if he found out he'd left the old Priest here alone. And two, if everything Haltim had said was true, they needed the old man.

"Tired? Well c'mon then. Let's get into the cabin and rest there." Duncan tried to sound magnanimous about it, but he was sure he'd failed.

Haltim cocked an eye at him, but nodded in response, and they entered the cabin, unaware of watching eyes and the thoughts that accompanied them.

***

Zalkiniv couldn't believe that the Scaled one could have blessed her search so already! There, the blade blessed one! She could feel the pull of the blood to her own, the tall good-looking young man. She had found the first Reis already!

Zalkiniv knew this wasn't the one the Valni had tasted though, she could still feel that one, distant and growing more distant as the day wore on. It was the other person she saw that gave her pause. The old man was awash in the power of the cursed god. She could feel it, almost taste it. Smoke and ash, stone and dust. It clung to the man like a film that could never be washed away.

The Amder Priest. There was no mistaking it, and there was something unusual about him. In former lives she'd interacted with and even sacrificed a few of his kind, but this one Priest, this weak looking old man, felt... different. There was a strength in him she could see, a blessing of his thrice cursed god that she couldn't quite pinpoint.

This would be tricky. How to separate the Reis boy from the Priest? She could wait till they were asleep, sneak in and kill the old man, work a ritual with his blood to bind the Reis child and leave. But there were a great many dangers with that plan. Whatever this power the Amderite was holding onto could prove a problem. She had every confidence in her skills, but she in any life was careful.

Zalkiniv knew she needed to know more. Where were they traveling to? Where was the other Reis? She could still 'feel' him, out there, far away. Out of the mountains she was sure. But where would that one be going? The Reis line lived in the Reach, and now the last two leave within a week of each other? Nothing like that happens by chance.

She could pull the lost girl act again; it had worked wonders on that wandering man she'd killed to work the blood link to track them down. From what she gathered it was 'honorable' to help a lost traveler on this side of the barrier. Stupid. The lost were weak, and you exploit the weak. Use them, and then if they still live, get rid of them.

Stupid it was, yet it gave a perfect opportunity to get information. She needed to make sure that the old man couldn't discover who she was. She had no doubts she could fool the younger man; he'd be easy to distract with a flash of leg and a flip of hair. And if that didn't work, she could work something to at least force a trust in her through the blood blessing he'd received.

But the old man? Tricky. There was a ritual she knew that could at least give her some time to figure out a more permanent solution, it would last a day two, that might be all she needed to figure out how best to get the Reis child and go.

Zalkiniv eyed her knife but didn't draw it. For authenticities' sake she'd need to make the wounds look more ragged, rough. Searching she found a shard of a rock, glinting in the fading sunlight sharp tipped enough to do the deed. Taking a breath, she breathed the words of hiding as she plunged the shard into her left leg, feeling the blood flow out. She gasped in the pleasure, the power. Her lips moved in an unconscious prayer, thanking the Blood god for the power. She moved her hand down, cutting the skin in a ragged gash, biting her lip to silence her scream of pleasure. The blessing of the God, to be welcomed.

Zalkiniv dropped the shard on the ground, red stained now and glittering wet. Dipping her fingers into the blood streaming down her leg she drew the symbols of misdirection on her face, her fingers moving without thought. Uttering the final words of the ritual, she gasped at the power release. Valnijz was with her! She bound her wound, only allowing it to heal a tiny bit. Her wound needed to look real and serious, otherwise her ruse could fail at the start.

She wiped the blood off her face, removing the symbols, though she added back a splatter or two on her cheek and shirt. She searched her memories for information on cities, places. She was wearing clothing from the south, she had her back story. Grasping her leg, she limped toward the cabin, wincing in actual pain with each step.

25

Duncan sat in front of the fireplace in the cabin, struggling with his feelings. He wanted nothing more than to leave Haltim here. He was sure the old man knew it too. The day had been a total waste, and it frustrated Duncan. He slipped his hand into the pocket with the Cloud. Duncan could take one now, one wouldn't hurt. He wouldn't have to deal with this irritation, and the rising feeling of resentment he had. He'd feel nothing that would be the best thing.

The last thing he expected was the single knock, not loud, on the cabin door. Duncan carefully got up, unsure of where or how a knock could happen here. Haltim was asleep still, the day's travels having exhausted him. The knock came again, a single knock. Curious, but wary, Duncan grabbed a length of firewood to use as a club. Slipping toward the door, he listened. He heard no voices, or the sound of a horse or mule. They had gone this way because it wasn't used much at all, at best an old prospector or two might use it. No trader or caravan used this route, there wasn't anything on the way between the Reach and Ture this way.

He could feel the tension in his body, and a growing pool of nervous energy. "Calm," Duncan muttered to himself.

He opened the door, cocking his arm out of sight with the firewood log.

There in front of him was a young woman, attractive even. Long dark hair, shining in the fading light. Something had torn her clothes, they were dirty, but looked like those from the Southlands, far away in the plains and forests in those lowlands, and unsuitable for the Skyreach. She was also bleeding.

Blood, thick and clotting covered her left leg, and a smear or two on her face. "Help me." Her voice was weak, tired.

Duncan didn't hesitate, he dropped the firewood, letting it fall to the stone floor with a loud thud, and reached for the woman. The moment her skin touched his, he felt a rush, a fire in his blood, a burning rush of rage and anger that was gone as soon as it came to him. Duncan gasped, unable to control the reaction.

The woman looked at him, her eyes, dark, piercing, and for a moment they were far older than the rest of her. "Let me help you inside." Duncan draped a free arm over his shoulder and took her into the cabin, helping her limp along, taking her to a bench on the wall.

"Who are you? Where did you come from?" Duncan asked once she was sitting down, examining her wound.

"I'm a trader, well... My father was. From Renivit." The woman answered her head leaning back against the wall, injured leg extended in front of her. "My name is Rache. Rache Lontree. My father let me come on this trip to the Reach. But on the way bandits hit us."

Duncan watched her face fall into sadness. "Let me guess, bandits killed him, raided the trading wagon. How did you escape?"

"They couldn't decide what to do with me. One wanted to kill me then and there, another wanted to sell me to a slaver he knew somewhere, the third..." Rache's breath caught in her throat.

"I get it. No need to say more on that." Duncan stopped her from going into the details, he could imagine well enough what a mountain bandit would want to do with an attractive woman like her far from home.

"The one who wanted to sell me won the argument. With some luck I escaped and then wandered through the mountains. I fell and cut my leg on a rock or something in the dark. I tried to bandage it but didn't do a great job. I smelled smoke and set off in the hope I could find it. Thankfully, I did." Tears ran down her face, making steaks in the dirt and dried blood.

"I understand." Duncan examined the wound, cleaning it would be the first step. He might have to wake Haltim, the man did know healing.

"So, what do we have here?" Haltim's voice came from behind Duncan.

***

Will sat in silence, not wanting to break the tension between Journeyman Regin and Master Jaste. They'd argued half the night and had not spoken to each other since. Jaste had sent the Journeyman out this morning to pack up the tent by himself, and that had earned Will a look of anger and spite from Regin. He'd wanted to say something in his defense, but kept his mouth shut remembering Jaste's earlier admonishment to stay quiet as much as he could around Regin.

The only good thing was the other new Potential, Myriam. Will had been waiting at the cart when Master Jaste, Journeyman Regin and a beaming young woman had come down the street. Will liked her instantly. She laughed a great deal and picked up on the tension between Jaste and Regin right away, or at least that was his impression, as she spent a lot of time trying to get either of the men to laugh with bad jokes and stories about life in an inn.

Their own introduction had been brief, an exchange of names and a handshake. She had given him a look or two at times, as if she expected him to talk, but Will kept silent. He would have liked to know her better, meeting another Potential would be interesting, but pretending to be Markin Darto was still new to him.

They had left Kilvar as soon as Regin had finished, leaving Will with some mixed emotions. As much as he wanted to be away from that stench, something he was sure that no one got used to, he wished he'd been able to spend more time there. Exploring the place would have been interesting. And Kilvar had only been a mid-sized town. What would the Capital, the great city of Ture, be like?

Will missed the Reach. He'd woken up today missing the smell of the forges, the cold wind blowing the smoke out across the valleys. He even missed the food; he'd had a craving for Klah that had only grown over the last few days. When he'd been in the Reach, he'd eaten Klah of course, but never thought about it one way or another. Now? It was all he could think about.

Klah and wondering how Duncan was. It worried him. Leaving his family, as frustrating as Duncan could be was bad enough. But leaving him with the Blood Taint, Will couldn't help feeling like he'd betrayed Duncan. He knew he hadn't and there was nothing he could do, but still, he hoped Haltim was watching the situation.

The cart jumped over a rut in the road, making Will wince from the impact, and bringing him back to the now. They were continuing the descent from the mountains, and the terrain had changed. Less rock and stone, more clay and dirt. The trees were different to, what trees that grew in the Skyreach mountains were always-green, needles and thorns. Down here those were still found, but more and more broad-leafed trees and greener than Will had seen up to that point.

It was also warmer. It wasn't hot, but far more temperate than the Reach ever was. Will found himself sweating and taking off his coat. Something he regretted as soon as Regin noticed.

"Are you feeling well Apprentice Markin? Sorry, *Potential* Markin" Journeyman Regin took every chance to remind him he wasn't in the Guild yet. Will knew the man was madder at Jaste, but even Regin wasn't going to make a Guild Master mad. So, William was the target.

Will nodded, wiping the sweat off his forehead again. "Then why are you sweating so much? You'd think it was high noon on a midsummer day the way it's dripping off you." Regin studied him. "You think you can handle the heat of the forge?"

"I'm sorry Journeyman Regin, I guess I'm not used to the weather here. Dernstown gets cool breezes a lot, this air feels... thicker." Will dropped his eyes not matching Regin's gaze. He struggled to do so. Everything that had happened so far on trip backed up his initial thoughts on the Journeyman. Will looked forward to never seeing man again.

"Markin, it will be warmer still in Ture. I should have reminded you of the temperature change," Master Jaste continued before Regin could chime in, "but, since we are all talking now, let's quiz our new Potentials over items while we ride. It will be a good review for you Regin, before your final review before the Master test, and for these two here, a better understanding of what kind of things they need to know for the Guild."

Journeyman Regin turned to Will with speed and threw out a question over the melting points of Silverlace versus Goldlace. Will answered back and was satisfied to see Regin give an involuntary blink in surprise.

More questions followed, on hammer techniques, best kind of tongs to use when turning metal for even heating, even fuel sources to use when creating an alloy. Will parred each question with a quick and correct answer, at least the ones that Myriam didn't answer first. She knew her craft. She was able to answer items on inlay and jewelry far better than he. He enjoyed the look of both confusion and irritation on Regin's face. *Not so high and mighty are you now?* Will couldn't help enjoying the moment.

The wagon lurched to a halt. "The driving chain is loose in the back, feels off. Markin can you help me?" Jaste hopped out of the driver's seat and went around to the back of the cart, looking under the deck and something by the back wheels. Regin sat where he was staring at Will.

Will jumped out of the back of the cart to join Master Jaste. "What in the Sparks are you *doing?*" Jaste whispered the moment Will crouched next to him. "Are you trying to get discovered before we even get there?"

Jaste grabbed the driving chain and shook it, clanging it against the axle on purpose. "I don't understand Master..." Will didn't understand Jaste's anger.

"You are Markin Darto from Dernstown... *DERNSTOWN.* Yes, you're a good smith, but you're still a Dernstowner. Yet your answering questions without even thinking about it like someone raised up in smithing and smithing at a very high level. You're answering like a *Reacher.* They will already know you have skill from your work example but tone it down on the knowledge." Jaste's voice never rose about a whisper but Will heard every word. He knew Jaste was right. He'd been so focused on making Regin look bad, he'd forgotten who he was pretending to be, who he had to be now. A pit formed in his stomach; how could he have been so blind.

"Sorry Master Jas..." Will said before Jaste held up a finger silencing him.

"Don't apologize. I know Regin can be irritating. Just don't let yourself get drawn into it." Jaste clanged the chain again for good measure. "And while we are on it, there's Myriam. You barely speak to her. All that's going to do is arouse suspicion. She's a smart girl, you talk to me, you talk to Regin, and avoid her. Don't."

Will shook his head. "But Master Jaste, if she finds out..."

"I'm not saying tell her your life story, but you're going to have to interact with other Apprentices in the Guild. No better time to practice than now." Master Jaste gave Will's shoulder a pat.

Will flushed, but before he could say anything, Jaste clanged the chain one last time. "There!" Jaste said in a much more normal volume. "Chain was stuck against the axle. Gotten rotated and wedged."

As they returned to their seats Will watched Regin give him a long look, eyebrows furrowed. The Journeyman opened his mouth to speak but closed it and said nothing. Myriam on the other hand arched an eyebrow but smiled at him. *Dangerous.*

"A few more hours and we will be in Gamel, spend the night, then two days to Ture!" Master Jaste announced, cutting off any further questioning from Regin. Will nodded and looked out over the fields and forests around them, missing the mountains, missing not having to hide who he was, and missing home.

26

"She's a lost traveler. Jumped by bandits, escaped, and saw our smoke." Duncan answered Haltim for her.

Zalkiniv smiled. Perfect. The Reis was already buying into the ruse. She hadn't been sure what to expect when he'd opened the door. He was taller than she'd expected, thinner. In her mind she had pictured him like any other smith, thick, strong, but dirty. He was an Amderite after all.

She could see, almost taste, the blessing of Valnijz on him. With every heartbeat she could feel it call to her, it made it hard to concentrate the draw was so strong. The old man that was another matter. Her skin crawled looking at him, and even more so when he spoke. He felt wrong. "Your name, miss?" The Priest asked, his eyes locked onto hers, probing.

"Rache." She answered, making her voice quiver. It wasn't hard to do, the blood blessing the younger man held was affecting her being this close to it. Desire coursed through her when he got to close.

"I'm Duncan. Duncan Reis," Duncan said, he waved to the older man, "and that's Haltim. He's a Priest."

"Not anymore Duncan. I'm retired." Haltim smiled at her, and the flickering of a many tiny lights came on the edges of her perception but vanished as fast.

"Thank you. I am sorry to impose like this, I would have never knocked, but with my leg." Zalkiniv sighed and bit her lip as she straightened her leg out, the pain nearly making her moan.

"Hush, let's see what I can do." Haltim held up a hand. "Sit there, I need to get my pack."

She could feel her mix of pain and attraction to the blood of the Scaled one. She could use that. Fooling this Haltim was not going to be easy.

"Good, stay calm." Zalkiniv would have laughed out loud if she dared. It looked like her gambit was working, and even more so that her sealing was working. She didn't know what skills this Priest had, but he didn't appear suspicious, the fool.

She felt the bile rise when the man touched her, the sour taste in her mouth drawing forth a grimace. Let him to his work, then convince them to let her sleep here tonight. She'd bind the

Reis, and with him under her control she'd have time to explore the depths of how much pain this old man could handle. She'd could even free the blessing on the Reis and let him finish the old priest, ripping him apart. Lost in her plans, she didn't even realize Haltim was done with cleaning her leg wound.

"Nasty cut that, but you will survive. Good job staying still and silent, many could not do that." Haltim stood, wiping his hands on a scrap piece of cloth. His words gave her a push, she was getting ahead of herself. *Be here, and now.*

"I was thinking of my father, wishing he was here." She improvised a quick response. Haltim nodded sadly. "I'm sorry to impose further, but can I rest here tonight? I'll leave in the morning, but I'd really like to rest."

"Of course!" Duncan replied, and made her a space near the fireplace, moving his own things farther away.

"Ah well... yes a good night's rest will do you good. I'll check that leg in the morning, see if it will be good enough to make the trip to the Reach at least." Haltim shrugged and went to clean up his medical supplies and wash.

Duncan appeared with a smattering of food, a small piece of hard cheese, a thick hard slice of bread, smeared with some awful smelling paste, and a glass of water. "It's not much, but here's some food. Travel rations. Good cheese from the Reach, travel bread with my own supply of Klah, and water."

She took a few bites of the cheese and drank some water, but didn't touch the bread, the smell of that spread revolted her. She laid down and pretended to sleep, waiting for the two men to do the same so she could put her plan in action.

"Is she asleep?" She could tell the difference in the voices. That was the blood blessed one talking.

"I think so. Even if not, I doubt she'd care about this." The Amderite Priest answered.

"We need to hurry Haltim, we wasted a whole day today. A day that Will didn't waste. If he's being targeted by the Priesthood, he will be walking into a forge fire of danger the moment he enters the Smithing guild." The Reis said.

"I'm aware my boy. Will is too honest to carry out the deception that Guild Master came up with. The moment a Master figures out a Reacher is getting guild trained that forge fire will rage. The danger of a new Forgemaster will propel the corrupt to act."

Forgemaster! Zalkiniv almost sat up in shock. The other Reis was trying to become a Forgemaster! That meant that Amder the accursed could return to this world instead of her Master. This could not be! Not even the slightest chance of that happening could be allowed.

Her brain raced, she had planned on killing the old man tonight, binding the younger Reis and leaving. But this news changed everything. If the other Reis completed training and became a Forgemaster Amder would or at least could return. There was always a chance that he wouldn't, but the risk was high.

If she moved ahead with her plan, she should get back before anything like that could happen, but the possibility worried her. In all her many lives, the Forgemasters had hung like a shadow over her thinking. Those 'blessed' men and women, living their lives in service of the false one. She needed to find the right path, but she was lying on the ground, pretending to be asleep as these two fools prattled on about this William Reis and the Guild.

"We need to get moving early tomorrow then." The Reis said. There was a long pause. "What about her?" he followed up with.

"With any luck we can sneak out, leave her some rations and I'll draw up a rough map to get her to the Reach," The old man said. "Her accent is strange you know. I've met people from that far south, and I don't remember them sounding like her, though it was a long time ago."

Zalkiniv forced herself to keep her breath steady. She could not give up the game now. She had to wait till they were both asleep, then she had to go and commune with the Blood God. For the first time in many years, even almost a century, she wasn't sure of her course of action.

***

Will tossed in the blanket they had given him, the ground felt hard under him, and it was still so hot! The heat of the forge was one thing, but this oppressive wet warmth lay on him, the air almost thick to breathe. Will was still angry about his mistake earlier too.

It had been so satisfying to see that puffed up Journeyman lose some of his pride. Still, Jaste had was right. He had to watch himself. This had been his father's dream, his dream, generations of Reachers, Reis and others dream. He'd blame himself for the rest of his life if he screwed this up now. He couldn't throw this chance away just to make Regin look bad.

Myriam was a different story. He'd be pretending to be someone else. She was a good person, at least from what he could tell. No, he'd just keep it friendly, and that was all. And yet, he found himself looking at her without even realizing he was doing it. More than once. And worse, she obviously knew it, because his gaze was often met with one of her own.

Gamel had been smaller than Will had expected, more a stop for travelers to Ture than a real town It hadn't smelled like Kilvar, for which Will was grateful. He'd smelled that animal stench on his clothes for two days after leaving.

They hadn't even stopped in Gamel, much to Regin's complaints. Master Jaste had given them time to get their clothes cleaned by a local washerwoman, eat some bland food, and get a quick bath before hitting the road again. Will guessed that Jaste wanted to get to Ture and the Guildhall as soon as he could, to limit the time that Will and Regin had to be around each other.

Since the incident every time Regin had talked to Will, Jaste had stepped in, turning the conversation away from Will. Regin had caught on to that fact, as shown by him trying to wait until Master Jaste wasn't around. Those times were few, and Will had found reasons not be be nearby.

Trying to sleep, Will closed his eyes again, imaging the Skyreach Mountains around him, the cool wind sweeping through the Reach, the faint hint of smoke and the forge that slight tang of metal that tickled the edge of the tongue.

"Markin? You awake?" Myriam's voice interrupted his dreams of home.

"I guess so." Will propped himself up on an elbow. Myriam was half sitting up in her bedroll, and her hair had fallen from the normal simple bun. It looked rather nice... Will stopped his thought. Just friends.

"So, since you've barely spoken to me, did I do something? I mean, we are traveling together, and I don't want to bother Master Jaste, and I very much don't want to deal with that fool Regin." Myriam glanced over to their traveling companions, both of which appeared to Will to be very much asleep.

"No, sorry, I just... keep to myself usually." That was another half-truth, but at least it didn't feel all the way like a lie.

"Well that's silly. You know your stuff, I'm impressed, and how'd you learn all that in Dernstown?" Myriam brushed her hair behind her ear as she spoke.

Will moved his eyes back to the sky and laid back down, *just friends*. "I always liked smithwork, I forced anyone who knew anything to teach me what they could." Another half-truth.

"Well it worked. Can you show me your audition piece? I really want to see it. Master Jaste said I had to ask you." Myriam's voice came closer to Will, but he kept his eyes on the stars he could see through the trees.

"Yeah sure. In the morning." Will heard her shift around. She WAS moving closer.

"What's it made of? I made mine out of blacked steel. If I could have found something better, I would have. I wanted to use Darkstien, but I couldn't get enough." Myriam's voice began to lull Will a bit and his eyes fell and closed. Sleep overtook him, and the last thing he remembered was the smell of rosewater that Myriam wore.

Morning came as the sun broke through the edges of the forest in the distance, the light streaming across the meadow they had camped in. Will awoke, and yawned, at least the mornings down from the mountains were tolerable. Master Jaste was awake as well and already standing. Only Regin remained in bed, he was always the last to wake.

"Ah Markin! Be a good Potential, and get the fire going, and some breakfast started. I want to get back on the road early. If all goes well, we could reach the outskirts of Ture this evening." Jaste stamped around and stretched.

"Master Jaste, if we reach the outskirts tonight why don't we head to the guildhall then?" Will asked. "It can't be that far, can it?" Will stood grabbing a small piece of tinder from the back of the wagon, doctoring the fire from the coals of the night before.

Myriam was already up and joined Will in getting the fire ready. "Go on, ask Master Jaste, I'll take care of the fire. My father's an innkeep, I can do this blind." Myriam nodded in the direction of the Master.

"Potential Markin is in for quite a shock when he sees Ture, isn't he Master Jaste?" Regin's voice came from behind Will, and Will felt himself tensing up at the tone.

"Now Journeyman Regin, Dernstown is a nice place, but in size? Nothing compared to Ture." Master Jaste stood straight and stretched again. "You have to understand, Ture is huge. It will take a full day of travel to get from the outskirts to the Guildhall. Partially that's because of distance and the size of the city."

"The other is because there's so many people there," Regin added before Jaste could finish.

"Quite so," Jaste replied, his voice calm.

"Dernstown might fit into one of the smaller quarters of Ture, maybe the Gilly district." Regin threw that in, and Will could tell by the tone that there was an insult there somewhere, though one he didn't understand.

"Regin, that's enough." Jaste held up a hand to silence the Journeyman.

"Master Jaste, can I show Myriam my audition piece?" Will pointedly ignored the Journeyman in his question. Did he really want to show the work to Regin? He did, but only to make the man shut up again.

Jaste however smiled took the hammer, still covered with a large square of leather out of the cart. "Yes! That's a fine idea."

Regin stood as well, "I want to see this great work made by a Dernstowner." His voice filled with the scorn he had for the idea.

It's a good thing Duncan wasn't here, he'd hit Regin so hard the man wouldn't be able to use that jaw for days. Will just smiled but said nothing.

Unwrapping the hammer Will smiled again at the sight of it. Morning light shone off its surface, catching the simple carving he'd done on it. The Wight Iron and its flawless surface shone silver, almost with a light of its own. The shimmer it gave moved as you looked at it, a lazy swirl of light and power.

"That's beautiful! What metal is that?" Myriam's voice rose and then she continued the words rushing out. "I've never seen a metal shine like that. And it's surface, so smooth! It's stunning! Though, your carving could use some work, you should have inlaid instead of chisel marks for the decoration. And why a hammer?"

Use some work? Will felt a flash of annoyance at that comment. It was perfect, how could she criticize his hammer? But almost as instantly he knew that she wasn't being mean. Inlay work and jewelry were her specialty. He was only slightly aware of how to do that sort of thing. He knew that she didn't mean it to insult him.

Regin's reaction made Will smile. The man stood there, looking at the hammer with a tight-lipped frown. So tight-lipped Will wondered if the cords of the man's neck were going to snap. The best part was when his lifted his head and met Will's eyes.

Regin knew what kind of skill and talent it took to work Wight Iron, and to this level of skill. And he hated the thought that Will, not even a full Apprentice, could do this. Anger, a black jealousy, filled his gaze as he looked at Will.

Will nearly took a step back and and looked away, almost. He forced himself to keep the gaze, and finally Regin looked away, not saying a word. Will waited until the man wasn't looking at him anymore and smiled, covering the hammer and handing it back to a bemused Master Jaste.

As Master Jaste put the hammer back, Myriam returned to working the fire and helping Will make breakfast. All the while asking him questions about the hammer. He tried his best to answer them all, at least without giving anything away.

The had the fire up and going in short order, and the four ate a quick breakfast. Breaking camp, everyone resumed their places on the cart heading towards Ture, and the Guildhall, and for Will, the next step in his dreams.

***

Zalkiniv laid still, breathing slowly, feigning sleep as she listened to that old fool, and the Reis she had her hands on fall asleep. She had to be careful, there was only one good way here to commune with the Scaled one, and it would not be easy. She needed blood but not any blood. The old man would be perfect for a sacrifice, but his blood wasn't going to work. Not for this.

As much as she hated to admit it, her centuries of life and memories clarified that Amderites had some power. That barrier of theirs, and other interactions, plus, there was something about him that unnerved her. Some feeling that if she moved against him, things would not go well for her, at least if she did it now. That only left this Duncan, and of course, her own blood.

She'd be weak and worthless if she used her own for a good few days, or even a week. That kind of time couldn't be wasted, too much was going on, too many plans in motion. Being stuck recovering wasn't where she wanted to be where she needed to be. That left Duncan.

The Blessing! She would have slashed her palms if she could have. This Reis had the blood blessing! The blessing of the Scaled one should make it possible to commune with less blood needed, far less.

But how to get it? Raising her head off the ground she watched them both, asleep by the banked and dying fire. She watched Duncan stir, and smiled at the growl he made in his sleep. The blood was with him in his dreams, she could feel the call of the rushing through his body, even from this far away. It drew her in.

A smile played on her lips, he was a young man, she was a young woman, or at least looked like one. It would be easy if she didn't wake the Priest. A slow stretch moved across her form as her thoughts turned to using the blood of a blessed one. It had been too long since she had used that route, far too long.

Standing she loosened her clothes in places, tightened it in others for its greatest affect. While there were no mirrors to see the results, she could imagine. This body had been one of the most attractive when she had taken it over. She could use that.

She crept over to the sleeping form of her goal, who was still in the throes of some dream. She reached down and touched his face. "Duncan?" she whispered.

His eyes shot open and locked onto hers with a ferocity and anger that made her flush with excitement. Such rage lived inside this man. More than the blood blessing, there was far more than that at work. The moment passed, and the rage faded, followed by surprise.

"Rache? Is everything ok?" Duncan sat up. "What's the matter?"

"Nothing's wrong. I wanted to thank you for saving my life." Zalkiniv leaned forward, increasing Duncan's view of what she was offering. She almost laughed out loud as she saw the emotions cross his face, embarrassment, arousal, confusion. All warring with each other.

"Well um, you're welcome." Duncan gave her a smile. "Very much so Rache."

Zalkiniv leaned forward glancing at the sleeping form of the old priest nearby. "Why don't we go outside for a moment, I can show you how thankful I am." Without waiting for an answer, she stood and gave a practiced slow walk toward the door. The pain in her leg only accentuated her walk.

She could hear Duncan stand and follow her, her smile one of victory. "You might want me to go first, could be dangerous," Duncan whispered from right behind her into her ear.

"By all means." She stepped back and let him go first. Grabbing her knife from by her bed she walked after him.

The night was clear, cold, and the stars were out in force. She still didn't like the air here, she missed that salty tang, the hint of death that she knew.

"Now Rache, what did you want to show me?" Duncan turned around towards her, his face bearing that cocky look that all men wore when they thought they were being rewarded.

"Just this." Zalkiniv stepped toward him leaning forward in a kiss. Duncan leaned forward as well their lips met, and then she struck.

She bit down hard on his lips, tasting the blood rushing into her mouth, controlling the moan of joy it brought to her. The blessing! The rage! As Duncan tried to jerk back from the pain, she placed her knife behind his right ear, the point digging in.

Duncan froze, but she could taste the rage building, the Scaled god's touch was about to explode! But she knew how to control that. Drawing on the blood in her mouth, she spat out a single word, one of control. Duncan froze, still as a corpse, but standing upright. She could have used her knife to draw the blood, but biting was so much rawer, it made her shiver.

"That will do," Zalkiniv whispered as she stepped back. She felt the cravings for his blood rise but tamped them down. She had to commune with the Scaled one, anything else was secondary. "You are a wonderful specimen Duncan Reis. I need your blood. Not all, but enough. You won't remember this when I'm done, and all you will know is you got a special thank you from me."

"Blood to blood." She intoned and closed her eyes, reaching for the Rage God, the destroyer and master of all.

27

The sounds came first, the slow heartbeat, the rush of the blood moving around her. It was hypnotic, almost a lulling sound until the screams came. One, two, a thousand. Screams of all sorts and types, each one a living soul, bound in eternity to Valnijz. Each one a sacrifice... some had been screams for longer than anyone knew. She had wondered once who the first had been, how lucky they were to be the first.

"We know... you are here... we know what you want..." the voices came now, each one alone, but together, and each one, her own. A voice from every life she'd had, male and female alike.

"Tell me Scaled One, Blood and Rage, the Destroyer and Ender of all. I can return you to life now, I can take the blood gifted descendant of the Reis and bring you back." Zalkiniv paused hearing something new in the sounds.

"WE KNOW. Blinded we are not even if we have drifted over these long years. You are wrong. You must have both. MUST!" The voices screamed back at her. *"This one has not the skill, he has some blood, but the other... the other is stronger."*

Her head rang with the screams of the voices, the Scaled one was afraid?

"NOT Afraid, but there can be no Forgemasters, the blood of that line MUST end now. They must not return my brother's life. It has been long... too...long..." The voices trailed off for a second before screaming back at her. *"End the line, you must sacrifice both. Others are working towards this goal as well, but do not know they do it in my name... Soon... soon... I will walk the world again, blood will flow... blood will..."* the voices trailed off and vanished, leaving her with the blood, and the echo of heartbeats.

Awareness filled her; the Blood God was gifting her with the knowledge of how to control this Duncan Reis. Her body taunt, the ecstasy of the mind of a God touching hers was almost too much. The blessing will give her power to use him, control him when she needed to. With it came a second bit of knowledge, how to mask who she was from that Amderite Priest for longer.

"For the Scaled one," she whispered and opened her eyes. Duncan still stood before her still frozen, eyes open but aware, she could taste the feelings flowing from him. Sharp, hot, bitter. The taste of fear.

"You know who I am then? I am not surprised; my lord likes fear mixed with blood. Terror gives life ... spice." Zalkiniv smiled and stroked Duncan's face, digging her fingernails in for a moment before restraining herself. "Don't worry, you won't remember this; you won't even dream about it. Your life is now mine to control when I want it. You will take me with you to Ture. There, we will take your cousin, this William Reis, and you will help."

"Then I will take you both back, back to the pits and altars of the Blood God and there, you will both die. He in terror and fear, and you in sorrow and despair. And the Scaled one, The God of Blood and Rage will live again." Zalkiniv smiled, a blood tinged grimace as Duncan's blood dried on her lips and chin.

"Now let's have you forget this. You will go lie back down. The only memory of this will be of you and I going outside, and me showing you how grateful I was. You will insist that I come with you tomorrow to that old man. But first, let me clean us up." Zalkiniv used a tiny bit of the blood to fix the bite she had used to draw the blood. Not all the way, she could use a remnant of the bite to give the memories something real to hold onto.

She wished they were closer to this other Reis, but the best she could do was try to slow him and whomever he was traveling with. If she had access to her Valni it would have been a simple matter to send them, but she did not. What she did have however, was the last of the blood and rage flowing though her. Blood and rage she could use.

Reaching out, she finally found something she could use. Some predator, large, hungry, and predictable. She disliked controlling animals, primitive minds and instincts. This was however a meat eater, and she could use that. She pulled the animal using the last of the power and fixed it on the echo of the Reis blood. Hurt, maim. Kill anyone else. Simple instructions for a simple creature. Sending the animal into a rage and sending it off like an arrow shot into the dark. Her control over it wasn't strong, but with any luck it would slow them down.

Satisfied that she had at least done something, Zalkiniv retired for the rest of the night, her thoughts troubled with the faint sound of a forge in the distance.

***

William yawned, frowning at the bitter tang in his mouth. His dreams last night had been dark. A woman he couldn't see, the taste of blood, rage and anger. It all made him think about Duncan, and his burden to bear, the blood taint. He wished a silent prayer to Amder that his cousin had peace and wasn't taking enough Cloud to dull himself to a point of nothing.

"Good Morning Markin." Master Jaste sat next to their small campfire making breakfast. Toast and sausages, by the smell. William's stomach grumbled in hunger, though he longed for a taste of home. "Today, we arrive in Ture!" Jaste exclaimed with a smile. Standing and stretching, William noticed Journeyman Regin wasn't around.

"He's gone ahead. I sent him a while ago," Jaste said, answering the unspoken question. "It was better that way. He was getting on my nerves." Jaste let out a small laugh. "Come, eat." William sat beside the small fire, happy to eat and break his fast.

Myriam was also up already, and she gave Will a smile. "Morning Markin. I wondered if you were ever going to wake up."

"Well, people could have woken me up." Will answered. *It would have been a respite from whatever that was last night.*

"I could have, but then your snoring wouldn't have been useful to repel large animals or robbers on the road. So loud they must have thought it was a minor earthshake." Myriam answered back and laughed.

Master Jaste walked by and gave a chuckle but didn't add anything. Myriam was quick on the banter, Will had to give her credit there. He never had been, Duncan was the one who could do that.

Myriam grabbed her pack and walked off a bit to finish getting ready, away from the two men, which gave Will some time think. Master Jaste took the time to sit by Will and poke the fire. Lowering his voice Jaste looked William in the eye. "It was also better to send him ahead because we need to talk. We need to go over the final steps to enter the guild, and more to the point, make sure your story is correct and boring."

William washed down a large bit of toast with water. "Boring?"

"Yes, boring. Your skill will draw more than enough attention. Your story should answer any questions but not make you interesting enough to warrant close examination." Master Jaste sat back and looked at William. "I don't think you quite understand the risk I've taken here. It is forbidden to let anyone from the Reach into the guild."

William nodded through another bite. "Yes, though no one wants to tell me why. I don't get it, *WHY*?"

Jaste sighed and looked down at the ground. "You deserve to know or know at least as much as I can tell you. It's because of you."

William stopped chewing. "What?" was all he could say. He gathered his thoughts before saying anything else. "How could it be because of me?"

Master Jaste looked up at the sky for a moment before answering. "I don't know all of it. I have suspicions, theories, and possibilities." Jaste shrugged "That doesn't matter."

"The reason is your name, your real name. William Reis. Reis. Like it or not, you, and that cousin of yours are the last two descendants of the final Forgemaster, Simon Reis. The one who gave up his life to allow Amder to come into the world and fight the Rage God if you believe in that sort of thing." Jaste took a long sip of whatever drink he had in his mug.

"The guild allows no one from the Reach to join because of the Reis family line. The reason the guild does this ... is the Priesthood." Master Jaste looked at William. "Do you understand?"

William had felt his stomach falling, churning as Master Jaste spoke. Those visions he'd had when he'd touched the blood crystal, the Hammer of Amder he'd seen his ancestor? He knew, somehow, that fact was the truth. But why would the Priesthood not want him in the Guild? "Only sort of." This couldn't be right, Haltim would have told him, right? Only then did his mind turn to his old mentor trying to talk him out of trying for the Guild. Haltim had known.

Master Jaste clasped him on the shoulder. "I'm not sure you do Will. You only know that old Priest in the Reach. Haltim, right? He is not representative of the current church. The guild doesn't sneeze unless the Priesthood tells them to. It's not something we broadcast, that the two groups are so connected, but it's true. The priesthood has the power to make or break the guild. If we lost their blessing, we'd be gone in a flash. No better than a talented hedge smith."

Will nodded, though he wasn't sure he understood. "Why then does the Priesthood want no one from the Reach, or really, anyone named Reis in the guild? I mean, a Forgemaster would be a good thing, right? Priesthood of Amder and a Forgemasters descendant."

Jaste shook his head. "I can't speak for all, but consider this, the Priesthood of Amder is powerful here. Powerful. Even the king bows down to the High Priest. A Reis, of the bloodline of the last Forgemaster, if he was to become guild-trained? He would be a direct challenge to the power the Priesthood holds."

"Me? A Forgemaster?" Will laughed at the insanity of what Jaste had said. "I'm trying to get Guild trained, to make a better life for me, and my family. To be the best and fulfill my father's dream. I'm not a Forgemaster, I'll never be a Forgemaster."

Jaste nodded. "I know. Always remember though, for men in power, the mere thought of a challenge to that power is enough to move them to action. The Priesthood wanted to make sure that no Reis would ever be guild trained. That no Reis would ever be a threat."

Jaste looked William in the eye. "Understand me? You are walking into a dangerous situation. One mistake, and the full fury of both the guild and the Priesthood will fall upon us both, Markin Darto."

Will noticed that Jaste referred to him as Markin. He got why, but he had one more question. "Master Jaste. If what you say is true, if the reason is to keep a Reis from becoming a Forgemaster, why help? Why give me this chance?"

Jaste smiled and gave a rueful chuckle. "Because of your skill. I have never seen someone with as much natural talent. Because you would become a Great Master, one of the revered elders of the Guild. Am I taking a huge risk? Yes, of course I am.

One that may cause my being disbarred or worse. But still, here I am."

Or worse? Did Jaste think the guild and the Priesthood would kill him? William gathered his thoughts, unsure. "Master, could I see the hammer I made?" Will asked, his feelings unsettled.

"Yes, of course." Master Jaste stood and started digging into the cart. He took out a leather wrapped bundle and handed it to William. "Can I ask why?"

William shrugged. "It ... calms me. With everything you've told me, I don't know what to say, or do, or think. But the hammer, it calls to me. That's all I can say."

Jaste answered back. "And that my boy is why I'm doing this. Only a true smith would or even could say that, understand it. Take a few minutes, we will need to pack up and head into Ture soon, but I did lay some rather surprising information on you. And oh, good job with Myriam. See, making friends isn't that hard."

Master Jaste cleaned up and packing as Will stood and walked towards the woods behind their camping spot, unwrapping the hammer as he walked.

There it was. The morning light playing over the silvery sheen of the Wight Iron, touched by the Gods blood of Amder, forged by his own two hands. His hands. Will looked at them. Flesh and blood, but the blood of the last Forgemaster? He hadn't known the final Forgemasters name was Reis. Simon Reis. Every Reacher knew of the final Forgemaster, but none knew his name.

His picked up the hammer, feeling its lightness and strength. He knew it was strong, stronger than anything else he'd ever made. The hash marks forming the symbol of Amder shone bright in the sun, as if the forge fires themselves were burning through, giving the hammer their heat. He was proud of this work, very proud.

"It's impressive Markin, very impressive. That hammer rivals the work or even surpasses the work of any Master I've seen. You've got talent." Myriam's voice came from behind Will. He spun around, seeing Myriam watching the hammer in the light. "The shine, the balance, it's incredible."

Will knew she was right though he felt a flash of guilt. What she didn't know, what no one, other than Duncan, knew was how this hammer had been made. It wasn't the skill; it wasn't the Wight iron. Those were important, true. But they had used the blood of Amder in the fire.

He wanted to tell her the truth, he wanted to make sure she understood that this hammer, was the product of more than skill and great materials. But, he couldn't. There was too much at stake, even more than Will had ever thought.

So, he said nothing, other than giving her a smile and covered the hammer back up. They walked back to the cart in silence, but a comfortable one.

"Put that up for now Markin. The cart is ready, we need to get moving." Master Jaste slipped back into Master to Potential mode, as he and Myriam appeared. Will, who was still at least mentally reeling from what Master Jaste had said earlier, just nodded.

Will handed the hammer back to Master and followed Jaste to the cart. He and Myriam climbed in the back and Master Jaste started the cart. He could feel the pressure building in him, not only now was he trying to fulfill his father's dream, he would be walking a line that could lead to his death.

The cart had only moved a fraction of the distance to the city when a roar burst from the forest to the right. The horse pulling the cart reared up in fright, leaving Master Jaste cursing and desperately trying to calm the beast.

The roar came again as to Wills shock, a fully grown Narmor burst out of the undergrowth heading straight for the cart. Waist high and muscled, the Narmor was fully grown, and very angry. Speckles of froth clung to the sides of its head, as the fangs of the beast snapped at the air.

"What is that?" Master Jaste yelled as he attempted to calm the horse.

"Narmor!' Will yelled but had no time to say anything else as the creature slammed into the cart, knocking him over and onto Myriam.

A clawed paw reached forth and tore at the cart, leaving several furrows in the wood as the creature bit at the side, trying to rip it apart.

Will didn't know much about wild animals, but he knew enough to know this wasn't usual. Narmor's were mountain hunters, and ambushed prey, they didn't attack head on, and were never found this far out of the Mountains.

The sound of splintering wood as the beast ripped a board off the side of the cart, breaking it in half as it bit down forced him to stop thinking and to act.

"Stay down." Will yelled to Myriam as he tried to get his hammer out of the bag Master Jaste had placed it in only minutes before.

"Can't do that!" Myriam yelled back and pushed past Will to his surprise. Her hammer was already in her hand. "Come on!" She yelled at the beast.

The Narmor stopped its assault of the cart for a moment, and roared again, directly at Myriam who squared her body for a moment before launching herself at the animal.

The animal leapt out of the way of the charge, backing away, a low whuffing sound of surprise escaped from it. The Narmor roared again when William finally stood up in the wagon, and the beast lowered its shoulders and charged at the cart again.

"Sparks!" Master Jaste yelled as the beast struck the cart forcing it to tip over, spilling him, William, and all their gear over the side of the road. William yelled in surprise and rolled over and struck his one shoulder hard on an exposed tree root, yelling in pain.

Myriam yelled again, charging the beast and this time swinging her hammer, upwards into the animal's muzzle, and right into its nose.

A whine of pain greeted the meaty smack as the Narmor, now dazed stumbled backwards pawing at its bleeding nose. Will stumbled up, holding his shoulder, and trying to get over to Myriam to help her, when the Narmor whuffed again, and turning, ran away, back into the woods.

Silence filled in the spaces as the three of them caught their breath. "Well Markin, what's a Narmor?" Master Jaste finally asked, standing. "And is anyone hurt?"

"I'm unhurt." Myriam shook herself, taking deep breaths. "Markin?"

"My shoulder hurts. But I think it will be fine." Will moved it carefully in a circle. "Just sore. That was incredible Myriam!"

Will pointed with his unhurt arm. "Narmor's are predators, I've never heard of anyone doing … what you did."

"I treated it like a dog." Myriam lowered her head rested her hands on her legs leaning forward. "Back at the inn, sometimes the caravans would have these mean dogs to protect them. A few times they escaped and would terrorize anyone they could find. I learned that if you charged back and could hit them in the muzzle, they usually backed off."

"But that was a Narmor, not a dog!" Will pointed out. "I've heard of Narmor attacks killing armed guards and dragging a body back to be eaten."

"It worked, right? It appeared to want you really. It ignored the rest of us, when it could." Myriam wiped some of the sweat off her forehead. "Come on, we need to right the cart and load everything up, just in case that Narmor animal of yours returns."

Will nodded. He winced a few times as he helped right the cart and loaded their baggage and supplies back into the cart. "Well, let's get going."

"Fine by me!" Master Jaste got the horse moving again, after he'd spent more than a quarter of an hour calming the animal.

Will watched as the woods faded behind them, why would a Narmor be here? It didn't make sense. His eyes lingered on the furrows still showing the new wood that the claws had cut into the wood. He was glad Myriam had been here, very glad.

28

Duncan awoke troubled. A mix of dark feelings and desire washed over him, memories of Rache, that girl he'd helped yesterday, kissing him, her hands moving over his body. But there was a vague memory, like a remembered dream, that something bad had happened, something evil.

For a moment he panicked, thinking in a moment of passion his blood taint had swelled to the surface and he'd killed the girl. That thought was interrupted by a feminine yawn coming from where she had laid down last night. Relief filled him, at least he hadn't killed an innocent, or at least if his memory of last night was any guide, a somewhat innocent.

"Good morning." Rache had sat up and gave him a smile, her beauty clear in the morning light. "Sleep well?"

Duncan smiled and nodded, not wanting to say anything else, at least not with Haltim in the room. Haltim. They were to leave today, to try to intercept William, before he entered the guildhall. They had already lost enough time that he felt like it was a fool's errand, but still they had to try.

He had prepared himself to leave Rache here, but after last night, he didn't want to. In fact, the idea of her not coming with them filled him with a sense of panic, even dread. She had to come, had to. There was no other way around it.

Standing, Duncan looked over at Haltim, who was still asleep, snoring. If anything, Haltim should be left behind, he was going to slow Duncan down. But without the Priest, he wasn't sure how he could convince Will of everything they had learned. His life being in danger wasn't something that Will would even consider. No, both had to come. And based on the light from outside, the day was already getting away from them, they had to get moving, and soon.

"Haltim." Duncan shook the man awake. "Haltim, it's morning, we need to get moving."

Haltim blinked his eyes open, pushing himself into a sitting position. "Morning Duncan." A wince crossed his face but vanished. Duncan knew Haltim was hurting, but also knew that the old man would never complain about it.

"Haltim, Rache should come with us." Duncan blurted out. A part of his mind wondered why he said that, but he continued. "She has no one in the Reach, and at least in Ture she might find a caravan or another Trader heading to her homeland." Satisfaction? Happiness? He wasn't sure of the feeling, but the moment he got the words out, he felt better. Strange.

Haltim blinked at him a few times, no words spoken before the Priest turned his face towards Rache who appeared to be trying to ignore them both but was gathering what few possessions she had with her when they had come to her rescue the night before.

"And you young lady? Do you wish to come with us to Ture? How's the leg?" Haltim didn't state his thoughts on her coming with them.

"I'm good the leg hurts of course but it will be fine. Haltim? What should I call you?" Rache replied, not turning around.

"Haltim will do." The Priest turned toward Duncan. "Are you sure?" was all he said.

Duncan looked over at Rache, and smiled a huge smile, she had to come. There was no way he would leave her behind. She had to be with them that was all. "Yes, I want her. To come with us, I mean."

He could hear the snort the old man gave behind him. Duncan packed up his gear, keeping his eyes down and off Rache. The last thing he wanted was Haltim poking at him for being after the girl. A rumble of his stomach reminded him that there was something they were forgetting. Food.

While he and Haltim had brought food supplies for the two, adding a third would cause issues. These wayside cabins, even older less used ones like this cabin, had a supply of Travelers bread. Hard and chewy, they still were edible, though tasteless.

A quick search of the cabin brought him to a sack of the stuff, along with extra rope, hooks, and gloves.

"Rache, these might be big for you, but if you're coming with us, you might need them, we will have to take the higher route, and that may mean some rough rock." Duncan handed her the items he'd claimed.

"Do we need to leave money for these?" Rache took the items but asked, her voice a whisper.

"No, part of the Travelers aid around here. Don't you do things like this in the south?" Duncan asked took a bite of a dried-up apple he'd brought.

"I don't know. My father never talked about the journeys he took, only what the trading itself was like." Rache sniffed a piece of the bread and made a face before taking a small bite. He could tell she wasn't liking it, but she ate it anyway.

"Let's eat and walk, saves some time," Haltim said behind them. He was packed and ready, and he'd already made sure the coals from last night's fire were out and cold. He waved them towards the door. "Duncan you lead, I'll come next and Rache you bring up the rear. That way if I fall you can catch me!" Haltim gave her a wink.

Rache said nothing but nodded at Haltim in response. Duncan could feel a flash of irritation at the old man, but it faded. Shaking his head, he walked out into the cool clear morning. It would be a long day, the path they were taking was a harder one. He had to get to Will though, and nothing would stand in his way.

* * *

Ture was like nothing William could have ever imagined. He had always thought the Reach was large, but it could fit in a single section of this place. And the people ... so many people! He'd always remember his first view of the city. He was sure Master Jaste had taken this road for the greatest effect. They had crested a large hill, and been able to see Ture, stretched out in front of him. Buildings of a thousand shapes and sizes, designs from plain to fantastical filled the long low sloping river valley that Ture was built on. Cutting through Ture was the mighty Silverthread River, heading toward the sea.

In the far distance, way out in the distant haze he could see the palace of the king. A palace. He shook his head. What was a Reacher doing here? The world was a crazy place.

"Myriam, put this on." Master Jaste produced an orange hooded cloak from one of the many packs in the cart as he pulled a dark blue one out for himself. "Markin, here's one for you as well." Jaste pulled out a second orange hooded cloak from a different bag.

"I will, but what is it for?" Will slipped it on, surprised at its inner softness.

"It marks you as Guild Potentials. Mine signifies my Master status. In Ture the Guild is powerful. Very. These cloaks allow us to bypass a lot of the headaches that come with dealing with guards." Jaste waved to the city below them.

"Regin is down there, somewhere, in a Red cloak and hood. Signifying his senior journeyman status. There's Orange, those in your position. When you are an Apprentice in the Guild you must wear a gray cloak, a Senior Apprentice wears a green one. A starting Journeyman wears a black cloak. At least in the city. And usually in the Guild itself, though it's not a requirement." Jaste started the wagon again towards the city gates which were still ways off.

"I thought I wasn't allowed to leave the Guild for a year once I enter." Will asked watching the city, and other roads and gates with their own traffic in the distance.

"That's true. But even in the Guild you are your rank. Just the rules." Jaste pointed at the city. "I tried to impress on you the size of this place, but I don't think you got it. What do you think now?"

Will shook his head. "It's... massive. He looked around, taking in the sights of the city walls, the other roads and ways into the city, that were vanishing from his view as they descended to the same level as everyone else.

Myriam, who had been quiet to this point, joined in. "I've been here before, but a long time ago. I thought my memories were wrong. I was little then, so everything looked big, but this, this is larger than I could have dreamed of."

"Why Master Jaste are there no other carts on this road? I'd think we'd see others this close to Ture." Will frowned as he asked the question.

"Good thinking! Well the answer is twofold. One, this road isn't used much because it's owned by the Guild. And Two, I'm one of the last who would travel back, any other recruiters would be back by now." Jaste shook his head. "I'm sure I'll hear about being late from some of the others."

Will didn't respond, his eyes taking in the sights of Ture approaching. The city walls alone were impressive, huge stone walls, grey and red, blueish and green. Rocks and minerals from the Skyreach mountains, carted all the way here. Free from plant growth, the walls stood tall, towering over even some trees.

Myriam poked Will. "Markin, what kind of rocks are those, the blue green ones? I mean you're from Dernstown, right? Do you know?"

Will felt the drop in his stomach for a second, but recovered, He knew the answer to that one. "Lanzinite. It's found more in the Northern end of the Skyreach." Will nearly thanked Amder for the luck of knowing that but stopped himself. Dead God or not, things were confusing with Amder right now in his head.

"Lanzinite. Good to know. I like it, I wonder if I could inlay that in silver." Myriam tapped her eyebrow in thought. Will smiled at that. She'd done that several times over the trip. He wasn't sure she thought about it, but it was noticeable. *Settle down, keep it friends, she probably won't even think about you once you enter the Guild.*

The gate they approached was smaller than he expected, guarded by four rather bored looking guards. They had looked rather surprised to see the Dark blue cloak that Jaste was wearing. It surprised Will when none of the guards even spoke, they only gave a small bow as they drove past. Jaste gave him a look to quiet the question he could feel coming. "Later," Jaste whispered as they entered the city proper.

The street they were on was broad and looked prosperous enough to Will's eye. He had thought the other places they had passed through had been strange, but Ture, Ture surpassed them all. Signs everywhere, people walking here and there, in clothes of a hundred different colors and designs. The smells of food wafting out of an inn, strange but interesting. Here and there a shop for things he didn't understand, a barrister? What was that? Vermin remover? Will shook his head, crazy things these lowlanders must do.

The oddest thing yet was the people themselves. It wasn't the clothes but the types. Most looked like a normal people, skin tanner, or hair shades you didn't see much in the Reach, but here at there, the non-humans would appear. Tall and thin, a Trinil would appear, like back at the Silver Bell. But they could see even more usual people. Short and draped head to toe in brown and gray robes and a hood, what could only be a Gorom walked past them, faster than you would expect on such a short body.

"Oh, a Gorom! And over there, a Dyan." She pointed to a woman who seemed to be wearing an outfit made entirely of leaves, though she hushed her voice. "We got a fair number of non-humans at my father's inn. We were off main southern trade route, lots of traffic."

"Gorom's come here to talk to the Guild sometimes, but only to the Grandmaster, no one knows why." Jaste whispered. "Sometimes they bring raw materials with them, ore rivaling anything that comes out of the Reach, and other times they leave with wrapped parcels that no Master admits knowing the contents of." The Gorom vanished out of sight in the distance.

Other faces, races could be spotted sometimes, but Will wasn't sure if what he was seeing was real or something illusionary formed by the moving of the crowd. Did that figure have sky blue scales on his face? Was that woman picking fruit off her green hair? He shook his head, and closed his eyes, opening them to see nothing but everyday humans walking by.

Riding on in silence, they pulled in front of a rich well-appointed place, named the Hammer and Tongs. "Here we spend the night. Tomorrow we will get to the Guildhall, and your final test will happen." Master Jaste waited while Will got off the cart.

"Myriam, can you reach around and grab my pack? Left it in the front." Master Jaste waited for Myriam to turn around and took Will by the shoulder and leaned in. His voice came in low tones. "We will speak more in private later, but from now until then, only talk when spoken to, and don't draw attention to yourself."

Will nodded. The guild and the Priesthood had spent hundreds of years keeping him and his family out of the guild. He was playing a dangerous game. The danger seemed not to be real to him, maybe because he couldn't quite believe it. He was just William Reis, no one important.

Myriam stretched as she got out of the cart. "I for one am looking forward to a bath, and a hot meal that Markin and I didn't have to make."

Will shrugged. "It's not so bad, if I didn't have to keep stopping you from killing us with spice."

Myriam snorted. "You like bland tasteless food. I guess I'll just have to educate you on what flavor is." She flung her pack over her shoulder and followed Master Jaste into the inn, leaving Will by himself.

Will grabbed his pack but looked around the street. He was here. Ture. The home of the Guild. He had made it this far, just a bit longer to go. He followed Master Jaste and Myriam into the Inn, his eyes lowered, but his spirit soaring.

***

Haltim watched his step, wincing for the hundredth time today as his knees gave notice that climbing over rocks at his age was not something that they liked. He'd almost slipped and fallen several times but had saved himself the embarrassment. Haltim wished he'd been more active in the Reach, taken walks. This would all be much easier if he had. He had finally let that girl Rache go in front of him, he couldn't keep pace to stay in the middle.

Reaching over to his own wrist he touched the always warm metal there, the surest sign from Amder that this was something his God wanted him to do. That along with a tiny sliver of pride kept him going. He could see Duncan in the lead, the tall young man picking over the trail with easy practiced steps. Following Duncan, the girl, Rache.

His mouth moved down into a considering frown as he watched her. She was moving well through the rocks, better than him at least. But even so, every time he looked at her there was a feeling that something was wrong, something was strange about her. Her accent for one thing. He'd met people from that far south, and they didn't sound like that. He'd said so earlier, and the longer he thought about it, the more he was sure.

But the worst was the feeling he got around her. Every time she looked at Duncan, to Haltims eyes the gaze was almost predatory, hungry. He admitted he wasn't a fool about this thing, he'd been a young man once, long ago. And this Rache girl was beautiful, exotic looking, and Duncan was a good-looking lad. But there was more to it than a two young people being attracted to each other.

"How you are keeping up old man?" Duncan's voice made him look up from his thoughts. Standing at the top of a ridge Duncan was not even looking tired, smiling in the cool wind. Haltim was happy to see him smiling. Ever since that sparks bound blood taint had happened the lad had been so controlled with his feelings, not wanting to let a hint of anger out lest he lose control and wreak violence on anyone in his way.

But now, he smiled. It could be the girl. Haltim considered that all his suspicions of her could be his grumpiness and old age getting to him. She hadn't done anything out of the normal that he knew of, she'd been polite to him, though distant. Maybe he should put his suspicions to rest.

"Haltim?" Duncan called again, louder this time.

"Oh, sorry Duncan, lost in thought. I'm doing fine ... Just fine." Haltim felt another twinge, this time in his left side, and the possibility of a cramp made him tense up. "Duncan, can we stop for lunch soon?" Haltim yelled back up. Rache had reached Duncan now, and they both stood there looking down at him. She didn't look tired at all either, strange.

Duncan looked at the sky checking the suns position. "Yes, I guess so. Get up here, well rest and get a bite. It's downhill from now until we get back to the road."

Haltim watched at the two of them got some items out of their packs and set up lunch on a larger but flatter boulder. He trudged up to them, finally arriving after everything had been setup. "Just in time I see." Haltim joked, hiding the pain shooting down his side. By the Sparks he needed to rest.

Duncan shook his head in response, and as usual Rache said nothing. She didn't even look him in the eye. They all ate in silence, their simple lunch of bread, cheese and water. Duncan smeared some Klah on his lunch, which once again made Rache wrinkle her face is disgust. Duncan offered him some as well, but Haltim waved it off. He'd never gotten into the stuff, even with all his years of living in the Reach.

"So, you mentioned the road?" Haltim asked Duncan after eating, feeling no pain for the moment.

"Yes. This path should take us downhill now and meet that road that was blocked from before. Basically, we are bypassing the problem. You've done better than I thought you would Haltim, we'll make a Reacher out of you yet." Duncan flashed him a smile and laughed.

The rest of the lunch ended in silence, and Haltim cleaned up since the other two had gotten it all ready. They traveled downhill now, easier going, though a step wrong, and you'd go slipping or worse tumbling down rocks and gravel. Near dusk they rejoined the road, making camp when darkness fell.

29

Zalkiniv fumed. She'd had to spend all day hiking, listening to the Amderite huffing and puffing behind her. She had said many prayers to the Scaled One, hoping for the old man to slip, so she could get away from the foul man. But no such blessing came. If she could have, she would have worked a real blood pact to force it to happen, but she had not the time to make that happen.

To make matters worse, her hope to slow the other Reis down had failed. Her link to the animal she had sent after him had broken, far faster than she had wanted it to. Those were the risks with dealing with instinctual animals, but the failure still stung. The Scaled one had been clear, this other Reis, this William, he could not be a Forgemaster.

What a strange idea it was anyway, to be a master of hammering metal and making of ... things? Pitiful, but what could you expect from followers of such a God? True power lay in blood, in life, in breaking the spirit of a person, feeling their despair and sadness. That was power. The anger, the rage that was the meaning of all life.

The rest of the day had passed the same way. Her leg which she wounded the day of finding this Reis threw jolts of pain, but that didn't bother her, it was a gift to her God, a clear reminder of what was at stake. At last they reached the road that Duncan had mentioned to the Amderite Haltim, and while she kept her mouth shut, Zalkiniv almost laughed at calling it a 'road'. More like an overgrown track, still strewn with rocks and boulders, though it was at least wider than the one they had used that day.

She sat back and watched the interplay between Duncan and Haltim, their banter revealing much to her. Haltim trusted Duncan, but was guarded around him, and she noticed that Haltim kept giving her side glances when he thought both she and Duncan weren't watching. The Amderite was no fool, and she'd have to keep up the blinding that kept him from being able to figure out who she was.

Duncan for his part was wary around the Priest though he respected him. From what she gathered the other Reis, William was friends with Haltim, which could present problems when the time came. But they had to get to her target, something that was less and less likely to happen in time.

Zalkiniv waited for nightfall, and her enspelling of Duncan once more. Each time she did so, he moved that much closer to being under her total control. The blood blessing gave so much power to her workings, she could do things that normally would take the blood of several slaves with only a small amount of Duncan's blood.

Still she had to be careful, at least until she was sure what would happen with this other Reis. Her lips crouched down into a thin smile at the thought of sacrificing the last two of the final Forgemaster's bloodline to her God. Amder would never return, and the Rage God, the Bloodied Lord of Chaos, the Scaled One, regardless of what name you called Valnijz ... He would return and wipe the lands clean, leaving an eternity of pain and death in his wake.

Nightfall came soon, camp made, as she had to lay there and listen to the Amderite prattle on about the stars above and the Forge fires of the betrayer. "Duncan, did you ever hear the story about the Forge of Haval? That star there, the large blueish one." Haltim's voice carried through the cool almost cold night air.

"No Haltim, but I need not know." Duncan's voice was flat, almost tense. Good, annoyance could lead to anger, making the blood easier to work. Besides anytime that he wasn't listening to the prattling of the old man, the better.

"Yes, I think you do." Haltim preached about some sad Amderite who wanted blue fire to do some other foolish thing in honor of the Forge god. In all her lives, male or female that Zalkiniv had not understood. They worshiped a servant, not a master, not a god of power, but a servant.

Thankfully the story ended, and silence fell. She reached out using her senses to feel the flow of blood in each of the men, telling when they were asleep by the beats of their hearts. When she was sure both were asleep, she rose and crept to Duncan.

"Duncan, I'm cold," Zalkiniv whispered in his ear waking him.

Duncan's eyes suddenly opened and narrowed for a second. Opening his mouth to speak, Zalkiniv bent down and kissed him, biting down once more and drawing blood. The rush! She could taste the rage again, the distant call of the blade of Valnijz, waiting for her on the other side of the barrier. Duncan yelled into her mouth in pain, trying to break free.

Zalkiniv swallowed the blood in her mouth and worked a silent freezing, silencing Duncan mid yell. "Hush my prize. You won't die tonight, nor the Amderite. I need your blood. That's all. Push a little more power in the blood blessing given by the Scaled one." Zalkiniv whispered to the frozen man.

She could feel the blood rush at her words even if he couldn't move. His limbs trembled, muscles straining to move, sweat pooling on his skin, she could smell it. "Good. Fantastic. Get angry, I want the rage." With a smile, she bent down again, sucking more blood from the bite on his lips.

Moments passed, and she stopped at last. "That's all I need for now Pet," she whispered again to Duncan.

She removed the memories of tonight from Duncan once more, giving him false ones of passionate kisses and awkward emotions. So easy to do, she released him from the paralysis and watched as he fell into slumber littered with dreams of death and rage.

She slipped back into her blankets herself, and dropped asleep, her leg wound healing as she slept, satisfied with the night's work.

***

William awoke the next morning with lingering pain in his mouth again, and a slight metallic taste, like iron.

Throwing on his clothes he left his room only to turn right around and throw on the orange hooded cloak Master Jaste had given him to wear yesterday. It felt odd to wear it in all this warmth, but then again it wasn't to protect him from the cold.

Myriam was up before him again, and he wondered how she did that. And she always looked ready for anything, he found that annoying if anything about her was annoying.

"Good morning, Markin." Myriam waited at the top of the stairs for him to approach. "Sleep well?"

"Good enough. You?" Will felt his eyes being drawn to her face, and realized he was more looking at her lips than hearing what her answer was. *Stop it! Just friends.*

"Let's get some breakfast, I'm sure Master Jaste is downstairs," Markin answered. He had no idea what she had said and hoped it didn't show.

Heads turned toward them both, slight nods and conversations lulled as they walked by. He found it an unsettling experience. If they reacted to a mere Potential this way, and not even a full Apprentice, no wonder some Masters and Journeyman had a high opinion of themselves.

Sitting against the far wall in a corner was Master Jaste, wearing his dark Blue cloak of rank, eating breakfast. He caught Will's eye and waved him over. "Good morning Markin, I trust you slept well?" Jaste's voice was conversational but carried through the room. "And you as well Myriam?"

"Yes, Master Jaste, very well. Almost forgot my cloak, though," Will waved over the nearby serving man.

"Yes, Master Jaste. Had to wait for the slow one here to wake up though. Considered going into his room to get him up but wasn't sure what I'd find." Myriam answered giving Will a wink.

"Nothing but a man happy to be sleeping in an actual bed." Will couldn't help himself and winked back. *Two can play that game.* A boy appeared from somewhere, asking for their breakfast order.

"I'll have whatever Master Jaste is having for breakfast, Thank you." Will told the boy before he could ask.

"Dark bread, two sausages, and green fire sauce, if you have it." Myriam said, adding to the order.

"Hungry?" Jaste laughed as the lad headed to the kitchen. The smell of the food made it hard to think about today. *Sparks above that smells good.*

"Very Master." Will could still feel the eyes on them. The closeness in which they watched him made him shift in his seat. He wanted to stand up and take a bow they watched so closely. "You get used to it lad, especially here," Jaste whispered to Will with a wink.

Myriam nodded as she put her hand on Will's arm. "Markin, you will get used to it."

"How come you don't feel that?" Will asked her, conscious of her hand still touching his arm.

"Back at the inn I was the innkeeper's daughter. I had more than enough men looking at me. This is kind of a relief, truthfully. They are looking at the cloak, not me. Remember that." Myriam removed her hand, but Will wished she hadn't.

Will didn't think he would ever get used to it though, regardless of what Master Jaste or Myriam said. It felt uncomfortable. The boy returned, appearing to pop up out of nowhere again, carrying a large plate of food and a steaming mug which he placed with a rather over the top flourish in front of Will.

"Eat up. This is liable to be your last meal this good for a while. Food at the guild for Apprentices leaves a bit to be desired." Master Jaste smiled and sat back in his chair, taking a sip out of his own mug.

Will dug in, and it was all as good as it smelled. Myriam did the same, though he hesitated to ask what the pungent smelling green sauce tasted like that she was enthusiastically dunking the bread into. They ate in relative silence for a few minutes before Master Jaste leaned in to talk again.

"Today we go to the Guildhall. Be careful, remember everything we discussed and practiced. Everything." Master Jaste tapped his temple with that last sentence.

The rest of the meal passed, only broken up by the occasional question from Master Jaste, quizzing them on minor smithing questions, all of which they both answered. He even managed to get a question about hardening goldlace answered before Myriam did.

"Master Jaste, you mentioned something called an anvil test before, what is that? We are here after all." Myriam asked quietly. Will had forgotten that.

Master Jaste smiled for a second before answering. "The test is tonight, get through it, and you're in. Fail it, and you go home."

Will felt his stomach once full drop like a pit. "What do you mean?" he lowered his voice trying to hide the sudden nerves. He let out a long breath, his tongue feeling thick and the sudden surge of panic he felt. "Why wait to tell us this now?"

"First off, it's tradition. We tell no Potentials until the day of the test." Master Jaste held up a hand to silence Will's coming objection. "Markin, wait." Jaste waited for Will to close this mouth, a thousand questions looming on his tongue.

"The anvil test is simple. And special. A Potential candidate, like you, brings their audition, the forged item, before a special anvil. You then take your work to the Anvil and strike it against it. The anvil will make a sound, the louder the sound the better the piece. If it makes no sound, you are out. And before you ask the anvil is a relic of Amder. It will detect if you didn't actually make the item." Jaste looked down took another large bite of his breakfast.

Will felt himself turn cold, his food no longer holding any appeal. But Myriam just shrugged. "Is it common for that to happen?"

"It happens. It's one reason we don't advertise the practice. Catches the cheaters." Master Jaste smiled. "Not that the two of you have anything to worry about." Jaste stood. "It's time we headed for the Guildhall. Coming?" Jaste headed for the door.

Will's flesh had broken out in goosebumps under the cloak and his hands were clammy. What Jaste didn't know was the one thing that could cause all of this to fall apart. The blood shard of Amder he'd used in the hammers forging. A blood shard forged hammer, hitting that anvil? What in all the gods had he gotten himself into?

30.

Duncan awoke groggy. It had been another night filled with screams of rage and dreams filled with blood. It had to be related to the blood taint, and by the sparks he hated it. The only pleasant memories he had of night now were the evenings Rache came to him. He considered talking to Haltim about it, which almost made him laugh out loud. A few months ago, even the idea of talk to Haltim about a problem he was having would have been ridiculous.

He wasn't going to do it though. Haltim wasn't quite as bad as he had always thought, not as sanctimonious as he had feared, but still. *Talking to a priest? Him? Ha.* And there was the other issue, the girl, Rache. There was a chance, slim it might be, that if he talked to Haltim about this, she might hear. And he didn't want her to know about his problem.

Both Haltim and Rache appeared to be asleep still, and the sun was only peeking over the hills, here at the end of the Skyreach Mountains. Duncan slipped a hand into his pack, feeling to the inner pocket that held small vials. Cloud.

He could take a sip, a small sip, tonight before he went to bed. A small sip, and his dreams wouldn't be filled with all that death and rage. He'd be fine in the morning; a small sip would have worn off by then. He was sure. He wished he'd brought more of the stuff from the Reach. It wasn't like he couldn't get it in Ture though. It was the capital of the country, more people using Cloud there than everyone who even lived in the Reach.

A small sip, it wouldn't hurt him. Tonight. Duncan looked forward to the oblivion of not feeling, no anger, no stress, no anything. If Rache tried to wake him up, he'd have to make sure he feigned sleep. He'd spent the last few days pretending hard to be normal. Smiling, being talkative, and trying to be his old self. It felt like a mask now, something he did to hide. The dreams were getting worse; he needed that Cloud.

A sound from Rache's bedroll made his hand shoot out of his pack, along with a feeling of guilt. Why should he feel guilty? He didn't even know this girl why should she care of he was looking in his own pack? He didn't put his hand back into it.

Haltim stirred, and Duncan turned his attention to his traveling companions. He hoped to be in Ture by tomorrow, if all went well, based on the trader's maps he had gotten back in the Reach. He'd used them to mark locations for scaving, but they still gave a good representation of the roads and how long it would take to get to Ture.

"Good morning Duncan, how'd you sleep?" Rache's voice was like a purr to him, and he felt a rush of something, not an attraction, not passion, but irritation, but in some way, he liked it? Duncan shook his head; he needed that Cloud.

"Fine. Will be glad to sleep in a bed again, hard ground and blankets is not the best way to get rest," Duncan sighed.

"Beds are nice." Rache's voice dripped with a double meaning he was sure.

"I agree, a bed would be good." Haltim's tone stopped that thought in an instant. "And a bath." Haltim added with a sniff.

"None of that will happen while we lay here." Duncan added standing and giving a stretch. "If we get moving soon, we should get to Ture tomorrow. Haltim, let's say we get to Will, what then? He will not want to walk away from his dream. Being in the guild has been his singular goal since he could have one." Duncan paused and kicked a rock as he thought.

"I know, but he deserves to be warned at least." Haltim paused looking at Rache.

"Oh, go on, it's not like she knows about what we are talking about, and she wants to get to Ture to find someone to help her get home." Duncan motioned for Haltim to continue.

"Fine. If the Priesthood ever finds out the truth about Will's true heritage, his real name. There is nothing, and I mean nothing they would not do to stop him. He needs to know that. What he does after that is his decision." Haltim touched the bracer hidden on his arm, feeling its warmth leach into him, giving him strength.

"He may stay Duncan. You know that, right?" Haltim looked at him, giving him that weighing look that teachers, priests, and well-meaning busybodies always give.

"Yes. And if he does, I know what I'll do," Duncan answered. "I'll stay as well. I must. I'll find some work in the city and stay. That way if things go south, someone will be there to help him." Duncan turned around to the priest. "Now your turn.

You've been kicked out of the Priesthood; they will not welcome you back with open arms you know."

Haltim nodded. "I know. I must stay as well. There are a few people in the Priesthood I can trust, who may be willing to help me and us get a message to Will if we are too late. They may also be willing to help us find a place to stay and even work to do. You and your cousin are now my primary job, keeping you safe."

Duncan glanced over to Rache to see how all this talk was affecting her. She wasn't even listening; she was putting her bed roll away and munching on a piece of bread she had taken from somewhere in her pack.

"Rache?" Duncan asked. "What Haltim and I were talking about, you can't repeat that ok?"

Rache looked up and locked eyes with Duncan. A feeling of a stranger came over him, and he could feel a scream reverberating in his mind, an endless stream of pain and anger. "I wasn't paying attention Duncan. I'm thankful that I met you two and not bandits in the mountains. Once we get to this Ture, I'll find a way to get home and be on my way."

Duncan broke eye contact, and the scream faded. Why was he sweaty? Why did he want to hurt someone, something? Grabbing his waterskin he splashed ice cold water on his face, and the feeling faded. That blood taint was getting worse for some reason. Cloud tonight.

***

Will could feel his stomach churning with a mix of excitement and nerves. He wanted to be excited, he wanted to shout out loud what he was about to do, that he William Reis, a Reacher, was about to enter the Guild. None of that could he say. And what's worse, it might not even be true. He hefted the leather wrapped hammer; his hands clammy with sweat.

He regretted using the blood shard now, and a bitter taste of fear tingled the edge of his senses. He had wanted every advantage, every possible trick that he could use to get into the Guild. He'd never have gone that far if he had known about this anvil test. He had the skill, and the materials, the Wight iron was second to none. His inborn talent should have been all he relied on.

But there was nothing he could do about it now. He sat in the cart with Myriam, their bright orange cloaks drawing more than a few looks, along with Master Jaste's blue one. This sense of dread made him wonder if this was what prisoners felt like when they were headed for final judgement. Nothing he could do to change his path but having to walk it all the same.

He was sure Myriam would get in. He wondered what would be on her face when he failed the test. Disgust? Sadness? Pity? Nothing he wanted to think about.

"Look upon the Guildhall, the Smithing Hall. In the old names, called Hammerwrath Hold." Jaste stopped the cart, pointing ahead of them.

The sun was over the building, and Will's thoughts faded in the sight before him. White marble and polished granite overlaid with lines of metal, every metal. Copper and tin and blued steel. Then an almost fanciful layout of gold-lace and sliver-lace, interspersed with the symbols of Amder done in Drendel Steel and even Wight iron, like his hammer.

Myriam whistled. "That work! It must have taken months, years even!"

"We aren't sure how long it took. But we know Amder himself took part." Master Jaste smiled at his Potentials. "And the Forgemaster at the time."

Everything about the facade screamed power and permanence, strength and skill. This place took metalcraft to a level that no living man could touch, Will was certain. He loved it. "It's beautiful." Will managed to say.

Myriam poked him in the ribs. "Why thank you, Markin. So, kind of you to say that."

Will looked to her totally confused as to where she was going with that. But her laugh soon showed him.

"Ah Markin. You're about three shades of red right now. I know you meant the building." Myriam smiled but rested her head for a moment on his shoulder.

Will didn't want her to move it.

Jaste smiled and made a clicking sound, getting the horse moving again. "I'm glad the two of you think so. It will be your home for a while. But you've not seen anything yet."

Will knew he was trying to be reassuring, but all that it did was return the knot of cold that had been faded. Calm down, he told himself, breathe and be calm. Fears were hard to force down, at least this one was. To get this close and then be turned away? Known that Master Jaste would be kicked out as well over this if it was discovered? And Myriam.

"Stop the cart." Will croaked as he clamored down, running for a side alley where his breakfast returned to the rest of the world.

"Nerves? Nothing to be nervous about." Jaste said as Will climbed back into the cart, his stomach making its continued displeasure well known.

Myriam nodded. "That hammer is quite the audition piece. You have nothing to fear. Me, on the other hand, I'm not so sure." She pulled the torc out and examined its inlay carefully. "I still think it would be better with different metals. I did what I could with what I had." She locked eyes with Will. "If one of us is leaving, it will be me."

"Don't say that!" Will blurted out, a bit louder than he expected. "You did really excellent work with that!" *I shouldn't care. Don't get to close.* He knew that was a losing battle though.

"You don't understand." Will paused. He couldn't say it. All this work was based on a lie. Will's stomach, now empty, was still sour, and feeling like knots. "Never mind, just nerves."

At last they pulled to the gate of the Guildhall, and Master Jaste hailed the two guards who came to greet them.

"Marcus and Chettish. They still letting you two decide who gets in and who doesn't?" Jaste grinned at the two men. Both clad in black leather with breastplates of blued steel and looked like they'd spent more time in the alehouse than the guardhouse.

"Master Jaste! And here we thought you'd driven this cart of yours off a cliff. Cutting it close this year, aren't you?" The larger of the two men, with a moustache that touched that breastplate chuckled as he spoke.

"No such luck Marcus." Master Jaste waved towards Will. "These are my newest finds, Markin Darto, Dernstown. And Myriam VolFar, and from nowhere to hear her speak."

The smaller of the two men nodded at Will. "Dernstown eh? Far afield for you Master Jaste, didn't know you headed that way this trip."

"I didn't. Markin missed the Master who did that leg, he came to the Reach to get tested." Master Jaste shrugged. "He came all that way, figured I'd let him try. His work was exemplary." Jaste paused for a second. "Don't suppose you've seen Journeyman Regin? He came on ahead a few days ago."

"Yeah, we saw the Journeyman. As pleasant as always that one." Marcus' voice betrayed his dislike of Regin, which made Will like the guard.

"Good. Well we better get moving. Anvil trials tonight, so much to do." Master Jaste clicked again as the two guards opened the main gate to let them past.

"Good luck to you both." The smaller man, Chettish, Will thought he'd heard Jaste call him, waved as he rode past, and closing the gate behind them.

"Good men and don't suffer fools," Master Jaste whispered.

The courtyard they soon came to was busy, and colorful. The cloaks of different groups stood out even more here, orange and blue, green, black, all. The courtyard was far larger than Will had expected, at least from the outside. Most of it was paved in smooth stone, stone that showed its age by the faint ruts worn into the side where other carts were sitting. There was a large tree in the corner, tall, green. *Strange, he should have seen that tree over the gate, but he hadn't noticed it.*

"Usually not this busy, but it's the day of the final test, so things are unsettled. Let's get you two set up and then I need to go and report in," Master Jaste said, answering the unspoken question on Wills' lips.

Myriam poked Will in the side and leaned in. "Can you believe we're here? This is amazing!"

Will looked around, his excitement and joy at finally, being here at this moment, battling with his unease at what was still to come. So many people, and the best of the best for metalwork,

Smithing, forging. He felt at home, almost like he was back in the Reach, and realized it was the smell.

The smell of the forges, of worked metal permeated the air here, even if there wasn't any smoke. It clung to the people as they walked by, it clung to the clothes they wore. If Will closed his eyes, and it had been much cooler out, he could imagine he was back at the Forge line in the Reach. That memory at least pushed back the fear again and made him smile for a moment.

"It's good to see you smile." Myriam rested her hand on his arm. Will struggled for a moment for what to say. He liked this girl, a lot. But he was a lie. So, he didn't answer, but he didn't move her hand away either.

"Myriam, if you would follow me?" Master Jaste waved her forward. "Markin, wait there for a moment while I get her settled." Myriam gave Will a smile and followed Jaste into an arched door across the courtyard, leaving Will to wait. He closed his eyes again and tried to relax. Reaching under his robe, his hand found the hammer he had made, and some of his nerves left him. It felt right.

He had to figure out what to do about Myriam. What could he do? He needed to talk to Jaste. He knew Jaste had told him to see what happens, but he needed to know one thing.

"Markin?" Master Jaste's voice came to him as Will opened his eyes, blinking for a moment in the sunlight.

"Follow me Markin." Jaste led him through the same door, which opened to a hallway with various alcoves and doors down its length. Jaste started walking, but Will stopped. "Master Jaste, I need to ask you a question."

Master Jaste stopped and turned toward Will. "Can it wait? We are already a bit late."

"It will be fast, Master. But it's something only you can answer." Will put a strong emphasis on the *you*.

Jaste cocked an eyebrow, but followed him into the alcove, and away from prying ears. "What is it? I wasn't joking, we are late."

"Master, will I always be Markin Darto from now on? Can I ever return to being William Reis?" Will paused, looking around. "I need to know what you think."

Jaste looked out the window here, a large window, made of true clear glass, other than the border of red and orange. "I suppose that's a question you do need the answer to. I would love to say no, that once you are done here, you can go back to your old life and name. But I do not think that will be possible. The odds are that from now on, for the rest of your life, your name is Markin Darto. I know that wasn't what you wanted to hear."

Will felt his hands clench, but then the other answer came to him. If he was Markin Darto from now on, then maybe, just maybe things would work with Myriam. Maybe.

"Come, we have to go. We can talk about this another time, when there *is* more time." Master Jaste led him to a small door, chased in copper and some green stone that Will didn't recognize.

Entering through the door they came into a large room, empty except for a single table and a single chair. The chair occupied by a blue cloaked figure, large, almost fat, and looking bored.

"Master Firgan!" Jaste called out as they entered the room.

Firgan startled at the sound of Jaste's voice for a second, but a broad smile broke out at the sight of Jaste.

"Jaste Noam! I'm very glad to see you! When that journeyman of your arrived yesterday without you, the rumors started fast. Journeyman Regin refused to talk about where you were the damned fool." Firgan stood and shook Jaste's hand.

"I'm afraid he got rather cross at me during our trip out, nothing he didn't deserve," Jaste replied. Turning to Will he waved a hand towards him "This is Markin Darto, Dernstowner. He's got the skill Firgan, wait till you see his audition."

"Dernstown, eh? Don't hardly see a Dernstowner here. Welcome Markin. I'm Master Firgan Gindolap, but call me Master Firgan. I'm the..." Firgan trailed off waving around the room.

"What he's trying to say Markin is that Master Firgan here is the coordinator of new male Apprentices. He's a good man, and a damn good smith." Master Jaste smiled for a second. "And one of the few Masters that would be happy to see me!" Master Jaste gave a short barking laugh.

"Nonsense Jaste! Take that back at once. I'm the *ONLY* Master happy to see you!" Firgan laughed back and slapped the table hard.

Will liked this large man, friendly enough, and if Master Jaste liked him, that was good enough for Will. A short bit of paperwork later, names, all long coached through by Master Jaste before they had met back up with Regin, Firgan dismissed them.

"Looking forward to seeing your audition later Markin Darto. Master Jaste here has a great eye for talent even if his political leanings are less popular." Master Fargin gave Will a wink and waved them out the door.

"He's right you know; he will be the only Master happy to see me." Master Jaste smiled as he said the words, but Will could see his eyes glance down and he knew the thought was not one that Master Jaste liked. "Anyway Markin, let's get you to the waiting area. Where you can reunite with your traveling companion." And with that Master Jaste set off down a long hall, walking at a fast pace.

Will followed behind, keeping up, though he would have liked to move slower. As they walked, they passed open rooms with brilliant displays of metalwork, rooms that Will wanted to explore. Storerooms as well, and even a room where the heat of the forges and the sound of hammers could be heard through the thick door, and the muffled sound of a cadence of someone leading a set of hammerers.

They stopped at a door unlike the others, it was colored Orange, like his cloak. Orange and with a single simple hammer done in bronze and chased in Silverlace with garnets inset sat upon the door.

"The chamber of the applicants. It's all very formal this process. Markin, you are to wait inside with the other applicants with your audition. It is to stay covered and not to be shown to anyone until the Testing of the Anvil. This means, that every applicant in the room always shows off their work as soon as they are sure no Masters or Journeymen are coming in." Master Jaste smiled for a second. "Every Master here has been in that room at one time or another. Remember that."

Master Jaste waved Will towards the door. Will's hand was on the handle when he heard Master Jaste one last time, at a whisper. "Keep in mind who you are, remember why you are here." And then without another word, Master Jaste walked off down the hall, his dark blue cloak swirling behind him.

31

The door handle was cold in his hand, as he grasped it. He took one long breath and let it out and pushed the door open. A large group of people, male and female all clad in orange cloaks were standing around, talking, and all the voices stopped at once the moment the door opened.

Closing the door behind him, Will looked around and nodded to the few who met his eyes. The room was large and held a long table along one wall. The table was appointed with food though simple fare. Bread, cheese, some fruit, and water with leaves floating in it. Chairs were all over, wherever anyone wanted to put one to sit and talk to someone else. Will's eyes searched the room for Myriam, but with half the people in the room having their hoods up, she was hard to find.

"Welcome. I'm Gerad Miltilk, From Ture itself. And you are?" A voice came from behind him as he walked, one that was friendly enough. Will turned and saw this Gerad holding out a hand in friendship.

A small man, someone slighter than Will would have expected, but his hands had the callouses of a smith, and one who didn't wear gloves often. Reddish brown hair that was slicked down and a friendly-looking smile was attached to that hand.

"Markin. Markin Darto, from Dernstown." Will grasped the man's hand and gave it a single shake before releasing it.

"Dernstown? Did you just get here? Which Master brought you for the final test?" Gerad asked, his voice still friendly. Will could see the hardness in his eyes now though. So friendly but guarded.

"Master Jaste Noam. And yes, we got here today. Spent the night in Ture at some inn and came here this morning for the anvil test," Will answered and sat down in the chair he'd spied before. The other silence in the room continued, as the others in the room, almost twenty listened and watched Will and Gerad talk. The quiet was becoming uncomfortable.

At Master Jaste's name several of the applicant's faces tightened and looked sour. Will noted their reactions with some surprise. Gerad's face didn't react though his eyes flicked to the hammer wrapped in leather still in Will's other hand.

"So Markin, going to show us your work?" Gerad asked, now looking at the bundle openly.

Will felt that familiar struggle inside him. The rules stated no showing, but Master Jaste had told him everyone did it. That twist in his gut made him scowl for a second.

"Hey Dernstowner, no need to get all mad." Gerad's voice brought Will back.

"Sorry ..." Will mumbled for a second, looking at the leather wrapped hammer. "Fine," he said and removed the leather with a single motion.

Will heard and felt the gasp that went through the room. The hammer, his hammer, almost glowed white in the faint sunlight that came into the room from the high set windows. The torchlight brought up competing red glints in the design he had made. It looked, otherworldly.

Will caught the flash of anger that vanished before it could register on Gerad's face.

"Markin!" a female voice spoke up nearby. Myriam.

"You to know each other?" Gerad moved over a bit to let Myriam into the conversation. Will could see his eyes appraise Myriam, and the way she moved to Will's side.

"We traveled together with Master Jaste, and Journeyman Regin," Myriam answered.

"That's... nice." Gerad walked away, not saying another word.

"Don't mind him. He wanted his piece to be the best one in the class, and you just showed him that would not happen." Myriam sat down, pulling Will into a seat by her. Myriam cocked her head toward a group standing together by the wall. "Those over there, all the children of Guild Masters. Tried to talk to them and they gave me a look like I'd stepped in ox manure."

"So Markin, nervous about this anvil test?" Myriam rested her head on Will as she looked through the room. "I am."

"A bit, yes." Will could feel his stomach churning again. It had almost settled, then she'd asked about the test. Or was it the fact she was close? Master Jaste had told him, he might never get to be William Reis again. Could he lie to her? Be Markin Darto? Would it be lying if that was who he became? He wasn't sure yet. It might all useless worrying anyway, if he failed this anvil test.

"You shouldn't be. That piece beats everything else I've seen around here. I mean it." Myriam unwrapped her torc, examining it closely once last time. "I knew I should have used a lighter touch here, you can clearly see a raised edge, right there." She held the torc up to Will's eyes.

"It's fine. More than fine." Will answered. He didn't see the edge she was talking about.

"You're just saying that. Be objective." Myriam sighed as she examined her piece again.

No one else spoke to them as they waited, though several nodded, and a few smiled after glancing at the hammer which was still uncovered. Will smiled back and threw the leather back over the hammer. *The fewer questions the better*, he thought.

32

Every minute that passed made him wonder what would happen when God blood forged Wight iron touched that anvil. At least everyone would be surprised when it happened, including himself and Master Jaste. It would be a true reaction, not a practiced one! He found the thought amusing and almost laughed out loud.

"What so funny?" Myriam raised her head from his shoulder.

Will opened his mouth but the doors swung open. The room went quiet. Two men, clad in the dark blue cloaks of a Master walked in. One was Master Fargin, who he had met earlier. The other was unfamiliar, but he had a hard face, all angular and smooth.

"Welcome all. Line up and follow us. No talking in line, the time for the test of the anvil has come," Master Fargin said, his voice which had been friendly and almost jovial before now carried with the weight and tradition of a Master of the Smithing Guild.

Will got into the line that formed. There was some pushing and jockeying for position near the front of the line, that Gerad person he had met earlier had gotten himself into second place, behind a woman with skin as white as new snow, but who out massed half of the people male or female in line. Will took a place wherever, he wasn't interested in trying to make himself more visible.

Myriam lined up behind him, and as she got in line, she tapped him on the shoulder and whispered a 'Good luck'. Will could feel his stomach about to be sick again, he was so nervous. He thanked Amder that he had eaten nothing here in the room, he would have lost it right now if he had.

The two Masters led the way, walking side by side down the long hall, turning at last at a set of huge bronze and steel doors. The doors swung open, balanced on hinges that didn't make a sound, they revealed a room far larger than it felt like the place should have. Will had noticed this now several times. The proportions of this place didn't make much sense being as how it was in the middle of a huge city, how was there this much space?

They all filed into the room; each orange cloaked Potential standing in a circle around the middle of the room. In that middle sat six blue cloaked masters, each one's face hidden. They sat around an anvil; three times larger than an anvil needed to be. Will wanted to whistle at the sight.

A normal anvil would be a huge slab of cold iron, smooth and strong. Or steel, even Drendel steel, though he'd only ever seen one of those. This was something else. Its metal was tinted blue and chased through the anvil were veins of gold and silver. The top surface the striking surface was as smooth as glass and reflected as much light as a mirror would have. It was the most beautiful tool he'd ever seen outside of Amder's Hammer itself.

One of the blue cloaked figures stood, their face still hidden. "Welcome potentials. We have found each of you to have the skill to join the Guild. Each of you has the talent. This is the final test. The anvil will tell the true smith from a pretender. Each of you will, one at a time, take your audition and strike it on the anvil. The anvil will test it, and you." The voice that came from the cloak was strange and made Will feel like it came from far off, it echoed around them.

"The Guild has done this test for centuries. The anvil itself was made by the Forgemaster, and Guild masters. It's like has never made since, nor will it ever again." The figure sat and waited.

Master Fargin stood and nodded to the seated blue cloaked figures. Without a word he turned to the white skinned woman who had led the group of Potentials and nodded. She stood and from under her cloak took out a dagger. It looked well made to Will's eye from here, and it used an interesting metal from the look, though he wasn't sure what it was from this distance.

Approaching the anvil, the potential bowed, and rapped the dagger once hard on the top. A tone came forth, pure and strong, that lasted far longer than it should have from such a blow. A grin broke out on the Potentials face.

"Welcome Apprentice." Master Fargin said and pointed her to the far wall to another set of chairs. She had passed the test.

Next Gerad stood, pulling out a piece of jewelry, though again from where Will sat, he couldn't tell what it was made of. He approached the anvil and rapped it with the item in his hand. Silence filled the room, and all held their breath when nothing happened. At last a low tone came forth, but not as long or as loud as the one that had come before.

"Welcome Apprentice." Master Fargin waved him over to the chairs, but Will could see the embarrassment and anger on Gerad's face.

This went one through the Potentials, until one hit their piece on the anvil and nothing. No sound at all. A quick look around the room and all said nothing. The Potential, a youthful man with reddish hair turned pale and hit the anvil again with his piece, a helm in a style of an opened mouthed bear.

No sound again, even the rap on the anvil sounded deadened, as if it hadn't been touched. The other Master that had gathered them with Fargin, who hadn't said a word yet walked toward the young man and placed his hand on his shoulder. He leaned into the young man's ear and appeared to whisper something, and the Potentials shoulders fell. They both, Master and Potential walked out of the room, into a small door that was almost completely hidden in the shadows.

No one said moved or said anything for a few minutes, then the Master who had ushered the Potential out reentered the room and nodded to Master Fargin.

Myriam's turn came, and Will found himself holding his breath. She deserved to be here, far more than he did. She always smiled, but now, in this moment, even she looked solemn. She pushed her hood back, and taking the torc she had fretted over, struck the anvil a quick blow. A pure tone sprung out almost at the same time. Not quite as loud as the dagger, but still quite loud. He even forgot his fear for a moment.

Finally, it was Will's turn.

He held his breath as he stood, the beating of his heart was the only thing he could hear. He could feel his skin getting clammy, as a layer of sweat sprang forth. His heart hammering in time to each step as he approached the anvil. At the start of all this he had marveled at its craftsmanship, and now each step his brain yelled out it would be the undoing of his dream.

Standing in front of the thing he paused and removed the leather covering from the hammer, grateful that the leather let him wipe some sweat from his palms. Will had never been this worried or scared in his life. If the ride this morning had been nerve destroying, this was worse. This was the moment. And to fail here, in front of these people, Myriam too? At least she had passed.

At the sight of the hammer he heard one of the seated figures inhale, the light catching the Wight iron in a soft white reflection. All his hopes, everything he'd ever wanted, everything his father had ever wanted, everything every Reis and Reacher had wanted, here, now, was at hand.

Will raised the hammer, watched as if from outside his body, his arm fall, the hammer striking the anvil, a simple flat blow.

A spark, tiny and red orange flew from the site of the impact, Will's eyes caught it fall, glowing bright and then … all forge fire broke loose.

The ringing from the strike never stopped, louder and louder it came, to where many of the Potentials and new Apprentices covered their ears, even a few seated Masters. Then the glow. The anvil erupted with light, orange and red, silver and gold, the light shone from the exact point of impact, as if someone had shoved the sun itself into the anvil and forced all the light of it through a small hole. Will almost dropped his hammer, his hands clammy, but managed to hold onto the handle, if barely.

Then, at last, the light faded, the noise faded, and silence filled the room. Will couldn't even hear anyone breathe; stillness filled the air.

Then as if a wave had broken over the room, the other Potentials broke decorum and a whispering and mutters broke out. Will could hear more than one voice rise in confusion. Will himself was in shock. Of all the things to have happened that was not one thought that had crossed his mind. He'd half expected the anvil to reject him, knowing his creation was born of his talent but also from the blood of Amder himself.

It was the reaction of the assembled Masters that was the biggest surprise. After the silence had come, several of the Masters had stood up so fast their chairs had fallen backward, and at least two rushed out of the room, blue cloaks flying behind them like a flag.

Master Fargin walked towards Will, his eyes wide and his face white. "Markin…" he whispered. He reached out and looked down at the hammer still in Will's hands. Will tightened his grip for a moment on the hammer, swallowed and placed his work into the Masters hands. Master Fargin almost didn't take the hammer, opening and closing his hand as if to convince himself it was the right choice.

Master Fargin held it up in the light, as several other cloaked Masters joined him in examining the hammer, heads together and whispers between them loud but unclear. The main door swung open and a rather flustered appearing Master Jaste his hood down, half ran, half walked into the room.

He looked at Will with an unreadable expression and joined the other Masters in discussion ignoring Will. At last, Master Fargin nodded to a figure on his right and took a long look at Will before handing the hammer over to Master Jaste and walking to Will who still stood right where he had been, next to the anvil.

"Markin Darto, if you will please follow me?" Master Fargin said loudly and formally. Will felt his stomach fall, they were kicking him out now! He had failed. They somehow knew of the truth, of what he'd done. His palms felt slick as they became sweaty, and the doubt he thought he'd vanquished threatened to crush him. Everything he'd ever wanted, everything his father had wanted, gone, like that. He couldn't turn to look at Myriam that would just make things worse.

His despair was overcome by confusion, as instead of leading him out the side door, the door that led out into Ture, he was led out the main doors to the room!

"Master Fargin, where are we going?" Will asked as they walked faster than Will had expected down the hall, he had to run to keep up. Master Fargin didn't answer, in fact didn't even acknowledge his presence until they arrived at a plain steel door, oiled and shiny, but otherwise unremarkable.

"Wait here please." Fargin pushed the door open to a smallish room, a single Window set high on the wall. A single chair, desk, and a small cot were in the room, and nothing else. Will swallowed, his unease returning. As soon as he stepped into the room, Master Fargin closed the door behind him and was gone, leaving Will alone with his thoughts and fears. His fears returned at the sound of the door being locked. As he sat on the edge of the cot, he battled back a few tears and tried to take a normal breath. What was he going to do?

Will sat alone in the quiet. As the rush he had felt at the sound wore off, the doubt crawled back into his mind. He tried with little success to keep his hands steady, but they trembled along with his legs. It was over, he knew it. He would get kicked out, the hammer taken from him, and he'd be alone. Left to his own devices in Ture, unsure of how to get back to the Reach.

But no, if that would have been the case, wouldn't they have taken him through the small door? The side one where all the failed Potentials go? What was he doing here, in this room? Will paced, both nervous and bored at the same time. Finally, he laid down on the small cot, closed his eyes and tried to rest. The smell of the place comforted him. The metallic tang intertwined with the fait smell of burning coal. Make it cooler, and he'd think he was taking a sevenday nap back home.

He had no way to know how much time had passed when the door opened with no warning. He hadn't even heard it being unlocked. Three figures walked into the room, all dark blue cloaked Masters. One was huge, a massive man who looked like he could wield a two-handed sledge with one arm. One was a woman, middle-aged but with laugh lines etched on her face, though she wasn't smiling now. The third was Master Jaste, looking apprehensive.

"Get out of that bed boy." The woman spoke first, she pointed to the chair. "Stand and sit there. We have questions, and no answers."

Will did as they told him, facing the three Masters who stood in front of him. Each of their faces were different in expression, and Will did not understand where the questions would lead them.

"Your name in Markin Darto, from Dernstown, correct?" The woman asked.

"Yes. Master?" Will let the question hang in the air, unsure of what to call her.

"Ah yes. Introductions. My name is Master Reinhill. You know Master Jaste of course. And this is Master Greenmar though the Apprentices call him the 'Green Mountain' still." A trace of a smile crossed her face but faded into a small frown.

"Now Markin, let's talk about what happened today with the anvil. Who made this hammer?" From some hidden pocket she pulled out the hammer he had made, its surface still glimmering white in the dim light.

"I did, Master Reinhill," Will answered. He paused for a moment and then sighed. "My cousin worked the bellows for me, Wight Iron needs to be..." He stopped talking as Master Reinhill held up her hand to stop him.

"Yes, we know about Wight Iron. So, your cousin worked the bellows you say? Any other help? No one else had anything to do with the forging of this?" Master Reinhill Asked again, her eyes locked onto Will.

"No Master. I was the only one to lift a hammer," Will answered. That was true he told himself, no one else had worked a hammer on the metal but him.

The huge man, Master Greenmar took the hammer from Reinhill and smacked it on his hand, a meaty and loud thwack. "You present an issue, Markin Darto. We have never, not once in the Anvil's history had it react the way it did today." Master Greenmar's voice could be felt in his very bones.

"The anvil was made long ago, very long ago, before the fall of Amder. Its purpose is to make sure that any piece struck against it was made by the person who does the deed. It serves as a check to make sure no one is trying to cheat their way into the Guild. The sound it gives off is also a gauge of the innate skill of the maker. The quickness and volume of the peal it gives off indicates the raw skill and talent of the maker." Master Reinhill said as she paced around the room.

"But never in any record can we find so far, and we've looked at least quickly looked, has the anvil ever had a sound that loud, and *NEVER* has it given off light. Never." Master Reinhill stopped and looked at him, her eyes locking with his again.

"Which leaves us with two possibilities. One, you're either the most talented Apprentice to ever walk through these doors by an unknown factor... Or... You've cheated the anvil in a way it can't understand so it did what it did." Master Reinhill paused. "Which is it Markin Darto?"

Did they just call me an Apprentice? Will swallowed hard. "I didn't cheat, I mean it I was the only one to lift a hammer when making that Piece."

The whisper in his head yelled liar at him again, but he ignored it.

"So... you're the most talented Apprentice we have ever seen or had, is that what you're saying?" Master Greenmar asked pointing Will's hammer at him. Will blanched. He hated this, he wanted to go home, go back to the Reach.

"I don't know if I am or not Master. I know no one else helped me make the hammer. No living person but I lifted a hammer against that metal." Will bowed his head and didn't look up. He was not lying, but he wasn't being honest, and he felt sick.

"Look up Markin." Master Jaste said his voice calm.

Will raised his head and look at Master Jaste. He felt bad enough, this made him feel worse. He knew what Jaste was thinking. He was thinking that all this was because he was a Reis. Because he was of the line of the Forgemaster. That was the reason why. Will knew he was wrong though.

"I believe you Markin." Master Jaste smiled and gave him the slightest of head nods.

"I believe you as well," Master Reinhill said, this time giving him a real smile.

"I don't know what to believe, but I see no reason to expel you." Master Greenmar shrugged. He tossed the Will's hammer from hand to hand. "It's a very nice piece. A few small mistakes." He paused and handed the hammer to Will. "But we will get to that... in class."

Will wasn't sure he heard the words. "In class Master?"

"Yes, Markin Darto, in class. Tomorrow morning, nine bells. Don't be late. I find tardiness annoying," Master Greenmar said in a grumbled tone, and with that turned on his heal and walked out of the room.

"Goodbye for now Apprentice Markin." Master Reinhill smiled and nodded at Will and followed The Green Mountain out of the room, leaving Will and Master Jaste alone.

33

Duncan awoke not tired for the first time in days. He'd taken a sip of Cloud last night, a sip to keep those dreams of anger and death away, and it had worked. He still felt foggy from the stuff, but he could feel, sort of. He didn't care. He hadn't had those nightmares.

"We will be at Ture this morning. But we will have to hurry and hurry to make the Guildhall in time." Haltim's voice came from behind him. Turning Duncan saw the Priest already up, and ready for the road.

"Haltim. What time did you wake up?" Duncan tried to concentrate on the words, trying to push the fog away.

"Haven't been up too long. I'm looking forward to being in Ture. No more camping, an actual bed to sleep in!" Haltim replied taking a sip of water from his canteen.

Duncan had to admit Haltim had impressed him. He'd been sure the old man wouldn't make it, and yet here they were outside of the Capital, and he was up and ready before Duncan was. Rache sat up, and one look told Duncan that she had not had a good night's sleep. Her face was set like stone.

"Duncan. Haltim." Rache almost spat the names out and stood, saying nothing else.

Haltim gave a look at Duncan that in his current state he couldn't make out, but it didn't matter. Nothing mattered.

"Duncan! Get up. We need to go. Will, remember?" Haltim's voice cut into the fog.

Will! Right! They had to save Will! That thought managed to cut through the Cloud induced haze and made him nod a few times. They had to go and save Will.

***

Zalkiniv could not believe it. Last night she had proceeded as always, waiting till Haltim was asleep, and then working to strengthen the ties to the blood blessing that Duncan carried. Only this time, she couldn't. Every time she tried to work the ritual; the connection faded out. She could FEEL the blood blessing in him still, but it was faint, as if being seen through cloth and far away.

She cast a glance at that old fool Haltim. Could he have somehow figured out who she was? Did he know something? But, if he did, why didn't he confront her? Duncan was only being an extension of the Blood God; she had no direct control over him yet. So no, he didn't know a thing about her true nature.

Then what? What could cause this? Zalkiniv cursed under her breath and felt her anger grow. She had to figure this out. The Glory of Valnijz depended on it!

***

Haltim watched Duncan get ready and could see the signs on him as clear as day. The boy had taken some Cloud. He'd seen the effects too many times. It didn't look like he had taken full vial if he had he'd still be deep under its influence. So, a small dose? For nighttime? He took a glance at their hanger on, Rache, who had woken up unhappy about something, and was not getting any happier.

Haltim wondered to himself. Could something have happened between the two of them in the night that cause Duncan to take Cloud? Young and hot-blooded people do stupid things at times, it wasn't out of the question.

Rache finally went off to change her traveling clothes, and Haltim made his move, straight to Duncan. "Duncan. Why?" Haltim pointed at him. "And don't play dumb. I can see it on your face. You took Cloud."

Duncan peered at him, his voice breaking the silence. "I had to. Every night Haltim these dreams come, dark dreams. Full of blood and anger. Violent dreams. The Cloud kept them away last night. I didn't want to have to do it, I couldn't take another night. It's the Blood Curse. I know it is."

Haltim sympathized with Duncan, he did, but he knew that Cloud would not fix anything, only hide it. He placed a hand on Duncan's shoulder and got in Duncan's face. The lad needed to hear him.

"I'm sorry Duncan. I am. And you're right, the odds are it is the Blood Curse. But Cloud will not fix it. It's going to mask it. You will have to take more and more of the stuff to get through the nights. This isn't the way." Haltim sighed.

"I have to Haltim. I can't take those dreams. I dreamt I ripped Wills eyes out of his head Haltim. Wills eyes. And you... I ripped your throat out with my teeth, like some kind of rabid animal. I wanted it... I wanted to feel the blood on my face and in my mouth. I wanted to rip and tear, to be rage itself." Duncan whispered, closing his eyes. Haltim watched as Duncan shuddered at the memory.

"It was horrible. I could not take it. I never want to see those things again. Ever." Duncan shook the priests hand off and turned away.

Haltim was about to answer when Rache, freshly changed appeared again.

"Well then, let's be off," Haltim announced trying to sound upbeat and cheerful. His thoughts were anything but. Cloud wasn't the answer, but he also could tell that Duncan was in true torment over his dreams, and what they meant for him. The Blood Curse was getting stronger somehow. In his sleep, it was taking him over.

***

Duncan could feel the effects of the sip of Cloud that he had taken wear off as they traveled. The traffic on the path they were on picked up once it merged with one of the larger roads heading into Ture. They even accelerated their travels when a farmer stopped his wagon near them and offered them a ride most of the way there, in deference to the robes that Haltim was wearing.

He wasn't going all the way to Ture and dropped them off a mile off. Duncan could feel himself smiling. The weather was good, he'd had a good night's rest, and he found himself even excited to see Ture. He'd never been there.

They were rounding a bend when Haltim held up his hand and gestured Duncan up a ridge. "Unless my memory has failed me Duncan, let's climb this ridge here, there's a sight to behold." Haltim waved to the Ridge on the right, formed by the road they were on that had cut some ancient hill in half.

Scaling the Hill behind Haltim, Duncan climbed to the top and found himself in awe. Stretching before him was Ture. And it was far more than anything he could have thought. A walled city that also bordered the wide and flat Silverthread River, you could take all the Reach and put it in the corner and never know it was there. Tall buildings in the distance, the Spire of Amder was there, marking the home of the High Priest of Amder. It stood out, and its Gold and Orange coloring, mimicking the flames of a forge shone in the sunlight.

Farther away from that stood the Dome of Ture, the home and Palace of the King. The Dome swirled with colors, even from this distance. Duncan had heard the Dome itself was made of all the metals in the country, forged into sheets of metal that had formed to skin the dome.

And the people! Even from here he could see several gates where people came and went, far more than he would have thought.

"Ture," Haltim said as he caught his breath. "I've been away a long time Duncan. But it's still Ture. It's a huge place. We don't have a lot of time to spare though if we will intercept William we need to hurry even more."

Duncan nodded. He wondered how in the forge fires of heaven they would find Will in all that, but he figured Haltim knew where the Guildhall was, and if nothing else they would manage to intercept him there. And then, he'd have time to explore this place, Will safe and heading back to the Reach together in a few days. All would be fine. He'd keep taking small doses of Cloud to help him sleep, and things would be almost normal, though the Priesthood would still be an issue.

Deep down Duncan still had a hard time believing the Priesthood of Amder, the same order than old Haltim was a member of, the Priesthood of the God of the Forge and Creation wanted them dead. They hadn't seen or heard of anything since they had left the Reach, had it had all blown over?

It was not long before the Gate loomed before them. Walls old and thick, and even Duncan could see they had been worked somehow. He could see here faint hammer marks and there, and the materials were stone like, but not quite stone. Haltim held up a hand and held a finger to his lips. He leaned forward to both Duncan and Rache.

"I need you both to be quiet until we are past the gate. I'm going to try something to make our journey to the Guildhall faster. I worry that we are already too late. Don't act surprised, say nothing." Haltim looked at them each and nodded.

Duncan nodded back, and Rache shrugged, glancing at all the people walking by. He wondered what her problem was, she was far from pleasant today. She had never been talkative, but he could almost feel the anger coming off her in waves.

Looking back to Haltim he watched as the Priest ducked around an outside corner, out of the view of the Guards and fished something out of a bag, and before Duncan's eyes, threw on a cloak he'd never seen before.

Black, a deep dark black, but broken up with orange and red threads in some pattern he couldn't quite make out. Where had the old man gotten that from?

Duncan heard an intake of breath from Rache that made him glance over. Her eyes locked onto the Robe. Her face changed. Eyes opened wide then fell to slits. The sharp intake of breath gave way to a long drawn out hiss. Did she recognize it?

Haltim turned around, the cloaks hood over his face and he walked, with purpose towards the guard. Duncan had been with Haltim for a while, he knew the man. The Priest had a slight shuffling walk as was expected of someone of his age. But now? He strode with strength and purpose, as if putting that cloak on had made him younger, stronger.

Duncan was more surprised by the reaction of the Guards. They took one look at the cloaked figure and blanched. Both bowed to the figure of Haltim, cloaked as he was. They stopped all traffic through the gate as Haltim waited.

Duncan moved forward a bit but could not hear what the Priest was saying to the two men, but both men looked at him, and then at Rache, faces blank. Then without a word they nodded and bowed again. Haltim said nothing, but beckoned Rache and Duncan to follow him as he walked, again with a surprising strength and purpose past the gate into the City of Ture.

Quiet, they walked right behind Haltim, though Duncan noted the reactions of those around them at the sight of Haltim. Most lowered their heads and got out of the way. Some turned white and adverted their gaze, and a few turned to stone, locked in place.

After almost ten minutes past the gate, Haltim turned into an alley, dark and shadowed. He removed the hood and took off the cloak, breathing deeply and looking pale himself.

"There. I hope I never have to wear that horrible thing ever again," Haltim said as he picked up the cloak from the ground where had dropped it and stuffed it back in his bag.

"Haltim... What in the sparks was that?" Duncan asked. "I've never seen that cloak, in all my life. And the reaction people gave you... Some looked like they would be sick seeing it!"

Haltim nodded. "I can explain. That's the cloak of an order in the Priesthood. One that I was a member of for a short while. I left the order, but never remembered to return the cloak." Haltim sighed. "I don't know why I kept it, but at least it did me some good today."

"What order?" Duncan asked. "I've never heard of the Priesthood of Amder having any orders."

"He is one of the Tempered," Rache blurted.

Duncan turned to her, her eyes were wide, and he could see how angry she was. "The Tempered?" Duncan asked, still confused.

"Yes." Haltim nodded a small frown appearing. "I'm surprised you know of it my dear Rache. How did you come by that knowledge?"

"Never mind that right now. Will one of you tell me who or what the Tempered *IS*?" Duncan snapped out. He hated being out in the dark, and right now he was.

"The Tempered is an Order. One dedicated to Testing the faith of members. Rooting out heretics and the like," Haltim said, his voice low. "At least that was what I joined for. However, I left when I realized the order was not that, but a tool for the High Priest and his friends to stifle dissent and make problems disappear."

Duncan wasn't sure of what to say. Haltim, kindly old Priest Haltim, had been what a church of Amder sanctioned ... Torturer? "What?" was all Duncan could think to say.

"The Tempered are known to me. That is all." Rache snapped the words out. Duncan saw the look she gave Haltim, one of loathing and hate. What had happened? Rache had never been all that warm to Haltim since they had met her, but there at least had been a peace of some sort between them. But this information may have changed everything.

"Haltim, how did that help us though? I mean we are still walking in a huge city to someplace only you have been to. I thought when you said it would speed us on our way you meant like horses, or a carriage or some other mode of transport," Duncan asked, still trying to process what Haltim had revealed about himself.

"My boy you must understand this." Haltim paused and looked at Rache, unsure of what to say.

"Might as well get it out Haltim," Duncan said. "She won't be around much longer anyway."

"Rache, for whatever you have against the Tempered, I have that and much more. But what I'm about to say you must swear to never reveal." Haltim locked eyes with Rache.

"Fine." Rache spat the word out, still full of whatever fury had come over her.

"Duncan, You and I are wanted by the Priesthood. You know why. If we had crossed the gate as normal, we would have been interviewed, and that information would have been in the hands of the High Priest within an hour. Every guard, and half the merchants or more in this city, plus who knows else would have been on the lookout for us." Duncan paused for a second.

"By putting back on the robes of the Tempered, our arrival will not be reported. That simple. The Tempered have status that allow for that." Haltim sighed.

Duncan nodded. That made sense, then to wear the robes. He still couldn't quite believe Haltim had been part of that, but then again, he'd gone to the Reach, not exactly the highest of honors, right? And it made sense the more the thought about it, Haltim had always been circumspect about his past before coming to the Reach.

"Come, let's walk. While I've not been in Ture for a long time, I still remember a few shortcuts," Haltim said as he walked down the alley, away from the main road.

Duncan followed, as did Rache. The buildings were close in here in this alley, old buildings, some stone, and some wood. Most had someone living in them, but he wasn't sure of the safety.

Haltim glanced back and must have seen the feeling on Duncan's face. "Don't worry my boy. These robes, my normal Priest robes, will keep all but the most foolish of robbers and thugs away."

Rache spoke up to Duncan's surprise. "Why?"

"This is Ture. The richest city in the world. Between the Priesthood of Amder and the Smithing Guild, this place is awash with coin. Guards are paid well; thieves are paid even better not to bother any Priest. If one is foolish enough to do so, either the guards get him, or his companions do. No one wants to undo a good thing."

Rache didn't respond. Duncan didn't either, he was too busy being careful where he stepped. As they moved further away from the main road, the houses got in more and more disrepair. And the ground, at first rough stone, had given way to packed dirt, and then to dry dusty ground. He was surprised at the lack of smell. He would have expected in a slum like this for the smells of inhabitation to be strong.

"Haltim. Why doesn't it stink?" He asked.

Haltim laughed. "Not what I would have expected, but I'll tell you or show you I guess." Haltim walked for a while then stopped. He took his foot at brushed dry dust off a square metal plate that Duncan hadn't noticed.

"Sewers. Even the poorest parts of Ture have a working sewer system. The story goes that at the founding of Ture, Amder had a hand in it. And part of it was a sewer system. It became an edict. There's an old rumor that if you build in Ture without hooking it up to the sewer system, within a week the building will collapse." Haltim tapped the covering with his foot.

"Come on, let's get moving faster." Haltim motioned them forward.

They turned a corner and found themselves back on a larger road. While not as crowded as the large road they had been on before, this one was still busy, and shops and business lined the street.

"Good. I remembered. Come, this way." Haltim waved them down another side street. Duncan followed trying to both take Ture in and keep an eye on Haltim. They walked for a long time in silence, at a brisk pace that surprised him. He took in the sights of Ture as they walked, passing by buildings large and small. Some brand new, and some could have even come from the Reach. The sun was low when Haltim led them down another dark alley. There in the distance, was a huge building, covered with metal shining in the sun.

"The Guildhall." Halim motioned to the building at the end of the street.

They walked as fast as they could without knocking anyone over. Duncan wanted to run, but they couldn't risk drawing attention to themselves. He hated it, and felt like he was letting Will down, but what could he do? If they got stopped because they knocked someone over that would be the end.

They stood before the doors. Duncan felt himself almost gasp at the beauty. Goldlace and Drendel steel, Iron and Copper, Silverlace and metals he wasn't even sure of blended together in pure art. It was breathtaking. Will would have loved this when he was saw it.

A large man in ornate armor approached them. "May I help you Priest?" the man asked with a bow.

"Yes, we need to see an applicant, one ... Markin Darto," Haltim answered, standing tall.

The guard got a strange look and said nothing. A second guard came out. "Who were you looking for Priest?" he asked.

"Markin Darto. We have a message for him," Haltim answered again, but Duncan could see that something was bothering the old man.

The two guards looked at each other.

"I'm sorry Priest..." The larger guard started to say.

"But the testings are done. No one may speak to an Apprentice now, not for a year." The other guard was trying to be helpful, but this news made Duncan upset. The man was keeping him from warning Will. They were too late, they had failed. Will was trapped inside, not even knowing those who wanted him dead were nearby.

Haltim turned to him and motioned him to follow, he did so Rache behind him. He could feel anger growing. They were so close! They couldn't give up now. Will was right there, behind that gate. There had to be a way! Haltim led them into a small dark alley before stopping and looking around.

"I'm sorry Duncan. This is my fault. I slowed you down too much," Haltim whispered his face fallen. "Now it's in Amder's hands."

"No. I will *NOT* give up!" Duncan yelled back, the anger growing.

"Calm Duncan," Haltim whispered.

"I will *NOT* give up!" Duncan yelled again, kicking a wall in frustration. All that travel, all that work arounds and problems, all of it. For nothing? Anger grew again, blossoming into a rage. He wanted to hurt something, hear it scream in pain, break its bones, feel its blood. Yes, the crack of bone, the sweet marrow …

"*DUNCAN.*" Haltim's voice cut into the red fog of rage and anger that enveloped Duncan, for a moment. With shaking hands, he removed the vial he had taken a sip from last night. Haltim took a step as if to stop him hand out raised.

"Back," Duncan hissed at the old Priest and forced himself to drink what was left in the vial. Hands clenched, he fought the anger, the rage inside. Teeth gritted he slid down the wall to sit, forcing the rage back. His hands stopped shaking and unclenched.

"Haltim," Duncan spoke in the monotone that comes with the drug.

"I'm sorry lad. I'm so sorry." Haltim knelt, his hand on Duncan head.

Neither saw Rache, her eyes wide, turn to narrow slits.

Haltim sighed. "I don't know what to do Duncan. We were too late."

Duncan stood. "Yes. Late. But Will is still inside." His voice flat, calm, cold.

Haltim stood as well, sighing and nodding. "Yes. And we are out here." Haltim glanced around then motioned for them to follow. "Standing in an alley will not get us anywhere. We need to have a plan. I have given some thought to what do if this happened, now we have to try it."

***

Myriam sat still, the room with the Potentials still a whirlwind of noise and chaos. Other accepted Apprentices looked at each other, and more than a few looked at her. They knew she had traveled with Markin, so of course they wondered if she knew something, anything. But she didn't. Not that anyone seemed to believe her answers.

She could barely trust her own eyes. His hammer was an incredible piece of work, she had known that the moment she had laid eyes on it. His talent, and his refusal to say he was that talented, was one of the things, the many things, she liked about him, but she did find it annoying sometimes.

But this? She had wanted to cheer when the sound started, Markin had earned the top spot, she had been sure, but the sound had grown, and then become deafening. And the light! What did that mean? And more worryingly, the Masters here had been as stunned as she was. If they didn't know, it must have never happened before. Which worried her, for Markin's sake.

He must be in the Guild. Her hands gripped the torc she had spent so long on tightly, the sweaty palms hidden by the metal. There was no way he had cheated, that would make the anvil silent, right? So, he had to be in. Had to. But what had that all meant? Markin avoided talking about his home as much as possible, and only came alive when the subject of smithing came up. She liked him though. *He must have been accepted into the Guild.*

34

Haltim led Duncan and Rache through a narrow tangle of streets once more, pausing to get his bearings from time to time. At last he led them out into a larger street and to a shopworn but clean looking boarding house.

"Let me do the talking." Haltim said to them both as he led them up onto the porch.

Duncan nodded. The effects of the Cloud, not even a full dose made him unwilling to talk to anyone anyway. Everything was foggy, far away. A small part of him knew he shouldn't have taken the Cloud right then, but it had scared him. The anger and need to hurt and kill had threatened to overwhelm him, and he would not let that happen. He would not lose himself.

He didn't look at Rache. Who knew what she thought of all this. She'd been less than friendly since the morning. She would leave soon anyway, heading back to the South. He didn't want her to go, but it would be better for her if she did.

Haltim led the way inside the boarding house. The inside matched the outside. Older, worn, but clean, and taken care of.

A thin wisp of a woman, her hair grey and red approached them. Not very tall, she dressed in clean and well-patched garments. "Well, Welcome to the Traveler's Fire. Three rooms will be 1 silver a week each. Two meals a day added will be an extra 2 bronze bits a day. Oh, and I need the first weeks payment up front."

Haltim smiled. "Well Bessim. It has been a long time if that's how you greet me."

"And who might you be? I know no Priests." The woman Haltim had named Bessim stopped and looked at him, and a smile broke out on her face. "Haltim? By the Forge, is that you?"

Haltim nodded. "Yes. I and my friends here, are in town, and will be for a while. And I hoped you'd still be here."

Bessim smacked Haltim on the arm. "Of course, I'm here. Where else would I be?"

Haltim shrugged. "Off married, doing whatever. I wasn't sure Ture was where you wanted to say."

Bessim sighed. "Haltim you always were a fool. Yes, I stayed in Ture." She glanced over and Duncan and Rache. "And who are your friends?"

Haltim pointed at Duncan. 'That is Duncan, and the girl is Rache. Duncan, I know from the Reach. He's the main reason I'm here. Rache, we helped on the road after bandits jumped her. She won't be staying more than a week; she is looking for a caravan or trader heading home."

"And where is home?" Bessim looked over at the girl.

"Renivit," Rache replied keeping her eyes on Duncan the whole time.

"Renivit? You are a long way. But I know of a few traders heading that way. We can talk about that later." Bessim smiled at the girl, looking from Rache to Duncan and giving a smile.

"Bessim. We need a place to stay. And not a lot of attention." Haltim spoke under his breath bringing her back to him.

"Haltim. What have you gotten yourself into?" Bessim studied Haltim, who to his credit met her gaze right back. "Ok, fine. I won't pry. I can give you all three rooms. And because it's you Haltim, I'll waive the first week payment."

Haltim chuckled. "Bessim. You never change. Thank you."

Bessim laughed back but walked out of the room. "Be right back with your keys."

"I trust Bessim. But let's keep a low profile. Duncan, you need to rest. Rache, I know you have questions, things made little sense today. Let's get in our rooms, let Duncan rest and then we will explain everything, at least as much as we can." Haltim stopped talking as they heard Bessim approach.

"Three keys. All the rooms are next to another." Bessim handed them a key each. Well-worn brass keys, smooth to the touch.

"Bessim thank you, I can't say how helpful this is." Haltim reached out and gave the woman a hug.

"Ok, go on. Rest. You can see you all need a bath and some rest. I serve food at seven. Better be here before then, food will be gone if you show up late." Bessim waved them upstairs. "Rache after eating we can discuss a few traders I know who are heading that way soon."

Haltim lead the two others up the stairs and each to their rooms. Bessim had given them three rooms off by themselves, off down a hallway. "Ok go rest, both of you. Come to my room at five bells."

***

Zalkiniv closed the door behind her and locked it before relaxing the iron mask she had forced herself into. She spat a curse at the door. The damned Amder loving fool Reis had taken drugs. And not any drug, something that had removed the Gods Blessing of Anger from him like water rising off mud.

That must have been why she couldn't control him last night. Why every speck of blood control had failed. She could feel the Gods blessing of Rage flowing through her, coiled with power. She drew her knife and disrobed. Taking the knife, she slashed a gash on each thigh, the blood flowing as she worked a quick binding into the room. She would be safe here from the old Amderite Priest, and using that anger, her other Rituals should have greater power, at least for the next fortnight.

Done with her binding, Zalkiniv started a bath. While she had no problem with dirt and blood, in this soft land it was expected. She did find herself curious though, what information would the Amderite share? *Fools, trusting fools*. This promised to be an interesting meeting.

Rache waited outside the Amderite Priests room, her skin clean but her senses telling her to leave. The Priest must have been doing something in his own room to protect himself. Her own bindings should keep her safe, she was Zalkiniv after all, and she had been working and using the blood for hundreds of years. This Amderite, from what she had gathered from bits of an overheard conversation between him and the Reis, was a minor Priest, assigned to the Reach. Yet, there was still an aura of power around him. Though part of his charge had been to watch over the Reis bloodline, which had to mean there was something special about him, didn't it?

Shaking her head, she calmed herself. These lands were strange. She had been this way once before the Godsfall. Before the war. And those memories were of no use to her. Too many things had changed, too much was different. But it didn't matter, once the Blood God returned, he would walk through these lands, spreading his gift.

The door finally opened, and it surprised Rache to see Duncan already in the room, looking ashamed and nervous.

"Ah Rache, good. Duncan got here a bit ago. He wants to explain things that happened today." Haltim waved her in.

Rache watched the Reis she had found. That drug, that Cloud he had taken had worn off. She could feel the blood now at least, the thread of her God moving through his veins. It pulled her, called to her. She felt an involuntary flush, but said nothing, sitting down in one of the two empty chairs.

Haltim closed the door and took the other chair, giving her a smile, she did not reciprocate. Her eyes were on her prize, the Reis. She wondered if she could save his blood if it came to killing him. There were workings that could keep the blood fresh, if it came to that.

"Rache, I need to explain things. Some of this won't make sense I'm sure. But you've traveled with us and while you're leaving here soon, I felt I owed you at least some background on what you've seen." Duncan sighed and lowered his eyes.

Rache knew that eye contact would be hard for him. The blood in his veins rang with passion when he looked at her, the blood called to her. Her workings just amplified that desire. He must be squirming inside, trying to hide from it.

"While you know a bit about my cousin, William. There're things you don't know. Some of it I will not get into. But some I will. It's about me, why I take Cloud." Duncan's voice was calm, but quiet.

"Before William left for the Guild, I helped him with his audition. The thing he made to prove he was good enough for the Guild. The place he had found was a ruin, old, old as the war itself." The Reis stopped and blew out a long breath. Zalkiniv could feel his blood, and this close, she could feel some of his emotions. He was nervous, scared. *I want a taste of that blood.* She banished the thought, not now.

"In the Reach, where William and I are from remember, I'm a scaver. I search old ruins and such for valuables to sell. It's frowned upon, but there's always a buyer. I never was one for forge work. But this ruin I'd never seen, the one William found. I searched it and found a few things. One, well, cursed me let's say." Duncan finally raised his head to look at her. His skin, pale, his eyes kept blinking, as if he wanted to close them and make all of this go away.

The nervous and scared feeling was gone, replaced with terror. That feeling would be nothing to what he would feel under the knife, his blood and his cousins blood shed to bring back the true God.

"The item that cursed me, is gone. Long gone. But because of the curse, if I lose control, if something makes me to frustrated, or angry, I fall into a rage. And in that rage, I hurt people, I get violent, I want to hurt and maim, tear and bite. I can't control it, it overwhelms me." Duncan shuddered his eyes closing.

"The Cloud. The stuff I took. It blocks all emotion. I can't feel anything. If I can't feel, I won't get angry, I won't hurt anyone, I won't kill anyone. That's what happened today. The Cloud kept me from hurting anyone."

He looked at her as if he was waiting for her to say something. She wanted to yell out that he was a fool. He should embrace the gift of the Blood God. Valnijz had chosen him to carry this gift! So that for now, until his death at her hands, he could give all these people a taste of the blessing to come. But she couldn't say that. Not yet. Not now.

"I understand." She said. There must be a way to overcome this Cloud he was taking. The will of Valnijz would not be stopped by a white liquid in a glass vial.

Duncan reached out and put his hand on hers. "I am sorry Rache. I should have said something before. But on the trip, I had dreams. Dark dreams. Blood filled dreams. I took Cloud at night to stop it from happening. It worried me that if I didn't, I'd wake up one day and find that you or Haltim, or even both of you were dead, because I'd fallen into that madness."

Rache felt another flush as he touched her. The pull of the blood was so strong. She'd done enough to make it stronger, and now she was paying the price. But she now knew why he'd taken it at night. The workings must have registered in some way in his sleeping mind. She might be able to overcome that. It gave her somewhere to start.

"I need to go. I need to think," she said, and stood. "Thank you for telling me." And she walked out the door.

***

Haltim watched Rache leave, a smile played across his face. The poor girl was smitten with Duncan that much was obvious. Even being near him she would get flushed. Looking at Duncan he saw how the young man was taken with her as well. The lad's eyes were still locked onto the door, about the same level as Rache's backside. Haltim swallowed a laugh, it would embarrass Duncan if he said something.

The day could have gone worse, all things considered. While they had missed getting to William in time, they had a place to stay, thanks to the marvelous luck of Bessim still being here. It had been a bare chance in his mind, but he was thankful the idea had come to him. Glancing down at his wrist and the hidden bracer, he said a small prayer of thanks. Whether it had been his idea or Amder's guidance, either way they were safe for now.

Bessim wouldn't turn him over to the Priesthood and forget the Tempered. He still had some connections in town, he'd get a message to William. How long it might take was a question, but they would do whatever they needed to do. His eyes rested on Duncan, at least the lad was calmer, Rache had that effect on him. Rache.

The idea was sudden, but it felt right. "Duncan, Rache should stay, at least for a while. Being near her, around her, it makes you happier, right?" Haltim sat down next to Duncan. "It's obvious how you feel about her. And a strong feeling like that, well that could help counteract the Blood Curse, or at least make it harder to come forth."

Duncan backed away shaking his head. "Haltim I couldn't ask her to stay. She wants to get home. She needs to tell her family about what happened to her father, and it's a long journey as it is."

Haltim held up a hand. "Duncan. If you want her to stay, I'll ask her. And here I thought all those stories about you back in the Reach were true, all those merchant daughters who got locked up at night to keep you away from them. Nervous as a boy." He gave a small laugh this time but saw Duncan's face darken.

"Oh, don't fret. I'm having a bit of fun. It's obvious you care for her Duncan, right?" he paused waiting for an answer.

"I can't explain it Haltim. Rache is different, something in me, the rush when she's nearby. I've felt nothing like it." Duncan paused. "Maybe this is..." He trailed off then, looking at Haltim.

"Say no more." Haltim stood placing a hand on Duncan's shoulder. "I'll go have a talk with Rache. I don't think it will be hard to convince her to stay here, at least for a while."

***

Rache closed the door behind her, letting out emotions she had held in. The blood blessed Reis was a fool. Though she had to admit that the use of that drug he had taken, Cloud, was an ingenious way to stop her blood bindings from taking effect. It made sense now, some part of him, some part of his sleeping mind had remembered the feelings and the rituals. It had shocked the poor little Amderite so much, he'd resorted to drugging himself to not have to face the power of the Blood God.

Now, what was she, Zalkiniv, the Immortal High Priest of the God of Blood and Rage going to do about it? She paced her room, pondering her options. She needed more power. But how? She had to find a way to stay here. Valnijz had been clear in her vision. He wanted both of the Reis bloodline. There was no other way. But that Haltim, the Priest of Amder, expected her gone soon. Her story had not centered around staying long term.

She drew her knife. She'd have to do a blood draw, a trance that would help her find a way. Because even if she stayed, how could she get the extra power to get past the drug he was taking? Rache scowled, her frustration growing to anger. Anger she could use.

She raised the knife, preparing to gash her forearm when a knock on the door interrupted her. Anger flowed from her. These blood blind fools! No one would ever interrupt her back on the other side of the barrier! Doing so would only mean a slow death, their blood not worthy of being given to Valnijz. The knock came again.

Setting her mouth to a thin line, she jabbed the knife back into its sheath. She buried her anger, holding on to it. Get rid of whoever this weak blood was and then use her anger to try to come up with some answers. She threw the door open to find the Amderite Priest of all people.

Haltim stood there, hand poised to knock again.

"Ah sorry Rache lass. I need to talk to you; I have a rather large favor to ask." Haltim pushed past her into her room.

"Your room..." the old Priest looked around. "You must have a draft or something, it feels cold in here, much colder than my room. I can say something to Bessim if you'd like."

"My room is fine," Rache answered. The sooner she got this fool out of her room the better. She looked forward to the day she could end his life, this wasn't the time or place.

"Odd. I'd think from being so far south." Haltim shrugged. "But that wasn't what I came here for. Now, what Duncan spoke to you about? I'm sure you may be a little uneasy, or even frightened of him. There's no need to be, at least for now. While I loathe the use of Cloud, the truth is I have no other way I can think of to control the anger in him, at least right now."

"So, right to it. Rache, I want you to stay. Duncan won't say it but being around you it affects the lad. And I've seen the way you react when he's near. You know what I mean, I need not come out and say it do I?" Haltim's gaze looked at her face.

Oh, Great Blood God! Was this old fool asking her to stay? Because he thought she was in love with the sacrifice? She suppressed the relief that filled her. She did let the smile out. Something she was sure he would misinterpret.

"But what about getting home?" Rache asked lowering her voice. She would stay, but the part she had created needed to be played out.

"Well, you weren't expected home for a while yet, your father was a trader. The added time wouldn't be a major concern. And we could send a message with a trader heading that way to whomever you needed to tell." Haltim stood and placed a hand on her shoulder. "Duncan needs you."

Rache felt sick to her stomach at his touch. Nausea first, then a hot burning feeling, as if her skin was being stacked with hot coals, centered on her shoulder. She moved, breaking the contact, turning away from his eyes as the pain faded.

"I guess I could stay. For a while. For Duncan," she whispered. Of all the solutions she could have come up with, having the Amderite Priest asking her to stay was not one she could have even dreamed of.

"Excellent!" Haltim exclaimed.

Turning back to the Priest she saw he was rubbing the hand that hand touched her. That wasn't a good sign.

"Well I'll tell Duncan. I'm sure this will lift his spirits!" Haltim said as he made his way to her door. "Yes, this is perfect. You'll help a great deal. I'm sure."

Rache watched the old Priest leave her room, the knowledge of how much the Blood God could touch the world, even here, brought a smile to her face that wouldn't leave. Not only did she have a way to stay now, the foolish priest wanted her to stay in close contact to the Reis she already had! Things could not have been more perfect if she tried.

***

Myriam watched as the last of the Potentials struck the anvil, one more was rejected, a dagger made no sound as it struck the anvil, but the rest passed with various levels of tone. It had been somewhat funny to watch the first Potential hit the anvil after the Masters finally got the room in order, the man had flinched visibly, as had some others.

Master Fargin stood, and with a meaty hand slapped the anvil the smack echoed in the room. "You have passed. You are now full Apprentices to the Guild. Tonight, is First Night, and the changing of the cloaks. For now, you are dismissed. Outside these doors Second year Apprentices and First year Journeyman await to show you to your respective dormitories."

Another Master so hooded in their blue cloak that she couldn't tell who it was stood and leaned in to whisper to Master Fargin, who shook his head. Apparently the other Master was insistent, and finally Master Fargin shrugged and turned again to the assembled Apprentices. "Class ranks will be announced tonight as well at First Night."

The murmur ran through the Apprentices at that news, but the real question was the one that Myriam needed to know. Where was Markin? What had happened to him? But no other announcements came as the Masters filed out first. As the last Master left the room, the Apprentices burst into talk.

"Where do you think that hammer maker is?" Gerad appeared next to Myriam. "You traveled with him, right? What's the story?"

"I don't know." Myriam knew Gerad was fishing for information, but she didn't have any to share.

"So, what about the hammer? My Master never said anything about light from that ceremony." Gerad pointed at the anvil. "So, what did it mean?"

Myriam shrugged, pushed past Gerad, and headed out into the hallway. The sooner she could get away from the questions the better. Gerad hadn't been the only one wanting to ask her about Markin, she was sure.

Entering the Hall her eyes fell on the one person who might be able to give her something. Master Jaste Noam. He was standing against the wall and watching the door. As soon as she had seen him, he had seen her, and with a finger, brought her to his side.

"Myriam. Good. Let's walk and talk. I'll show to you your dorm." Master Jaste's presence was enough to stop several others both Journeymen and Apprentices who at the sight of Myriam had started her way.

"Master Jaste, what about Markin? Is he being kicked out? Where is he?" the words spilled out in a rush, Myriam's nerves rose as Master Jaste held a single finger up to his mouth and led her out of the main passages.

Finally stopping after a few minutes of walking, he led her through a door into a small garden, one that was ablaze with red and orange flowers. "Here." Master Jaste sat down on a bench that was almost hidden against one wall.

"Markin?" Myriam sat down next to Jaste.

"He's fine. In fact, better than fine. He will be at First Night." Jaste picked a bloom before answering more. "Has Markin said anything to you about his hammer?"

"Only what he said in front of you. We never really discussed it much after he showed it to me. I knew he would get in, but…" Myriam shrugged. "How do you explain what happened Master Jaste?"

"I can't. And in fact, I've nearly a dozen Masters corner me so far and question me about Markin. I can't escape the feeling, though, that Markin knew something was different about the hammer. I expected nerves, but the lad was near terrified. Are you sure he never said anything?" Jaste pulled a few petals off the bloom he held in idle thought.

"Nothing. Do you really think Markin expected that? He looked surprised to me, or at least what I could see before that light drowned things out." Myriam could picture Markin's face that open-mouthed stunned look.

"I don't think he expected that no, but there was something different." Jaste stood, brushing the remnants of the bloom off his Masters cloak. "Myriam, I know you and Markin are, well, getting closer. And I'm not asking you to spy, but if you find something out, something that you feel you can share, let me know."

Myriam simply nodded. Balancing between the request of a Master and her feelings for Markin, whatever those were, wasn't going to be easy.

"Come on, I'll show you to your dorm, and, congratulations, you made an exceptional piece Myriam." Master Jaste led her back inside, and toward more questions than answers.

35

Duncan stood; his heart heavy. He hoped Haltim had some luck with Rache. He didn't want her to leave. He felt more connected to her than any other woman he'd ever even spoken to. He wasn't sure what it was, but even with the wearing off fog of the Cloud dose he'd taken, he'd been drawn to her.

Duncan took careful steps around the room, trying to keep calm. Taking Cloud wasn't a long-term solution, he knew that. There had to be another way, a better way to keep his anger in check. The sound of the door opening broke his concentration on his steps.

Haltim stood there smiling. "She will stay."

Bursting through the lingering fog, Duncan felt a leap of his heart. "Good... Good." He could feel his skin getting heated as he said the words. "So, what now? We failed at intercepting William. We don't have the money to stay here forever and taking advantage of the woman who owns the place, your friend, Bessim, isn't right." Duncan leaned against the wall. He both wanted to change the subject, and to get back to the task at hand. *Things with Rache gave him a jumble of feelings anyway.* No one would harm William if he could do anything about it.

"Well, there's a few things. As I said before, I still have some connections I can trust inside the Priesthood. I can see if I can use those connections to send a message to Will. As for money, you need to get a job." Haltim paused. "Before you ask ... I'm too old and risk being discovered. Rache might be able to get a job working an Inn where traders come in and out. Bessim might have something for her here."

"And me?" Duncan knew where this was going.

"Well you're the most useful, at least in terms of a job." Haltim kept going waving his hands up. "Hold on. You're young, strong, and can work. We need to find the right fit."

"Am I a man or a pack mule?" Duncan snorted. The Priest was right, but he didn't like it. Regular work wasn't any fun, if he'd wanted that life, he'd have never gotten into scaving. He didn't enjoy taking orders much and preferred working alone.

"Haltim I'm a scaver. I don't do other work. Not if I can help it." Duncan pointed out.

"There's not a lot of ruins here to scave there Duncan. Sure, there's run down parts of town, this is Ture, but even those places are clean. Nothing valuable there." Haltim sat on the edge of the bed, folding his hands in his lap.

Haltims face changed in an instant from thought to surprise. "Mucker!"

"Muck what?" The word confused Duncan. "Never heard of Muck whatever. And it doesn't sound like anything I want to do."

"Mucker, or Mucky. It's smelly, but it's like scaving. Sort of." The old priests face was lit up now. "Back in the Reach, you scaved, searched for treasures in ruins. Being a Mucker, is well, you clean the sewers."

Duncan felt the laugh coming and let it out. *It feels good to laugh.* "You are crazy! You think I will clean sewers?"

"Listen it's not about cleaning what flows through them. It's about cleaning out other things that end up IN the sewers. City this size, things get dropped in, or even thrown in. Yeah, it's junk, but I've heard of Muckers making a fair amount of money off jewelry, coins and other things." The old Priest rose. "I know it's not ideal, and I can't imagine it would smell good, but you can use the scaving skills you have to help us here, and now. We need to stay in town, try to get a message to Will. Money will help us do that."

Duncan felt his stomach churn at the thought of the smell down below in the dark. Now that the initial shock of what Haltim had proposed had worn off, the soundness of the idea stuck. But even so, sewers? He wasn't a small man, stooping in the dark, searching for treasure in that kind of filth?

"I don't know, aren't I too tall for something like that?" Duncan stood all the way upright. "Not made for crawling around in tunnels. And what else lives down there? I'm not a fighter, barring my current affliction."

"True, you're tall. But most tunnels are large enough for you to stand upright. And I know there're rats, and spiders, but what's that compared to the risk of the Valni back on your old scaving trips?" Haltim looked Duncan in the eyes. "I know it's not ideal lad, but it fits your skills. Unless you want to try to get work at a forge somewhere? But with the Guild in town, getting a job will not be easy."

Duncan sat down now. Work in a forge, something he could do, but didn't like. Or get work as a Mucker, crawling through the sewers looking for treasure.

"Wait, how do you know how big the sewers are, Haltim?" Duncan asked. "How would any Priest of Amder know?"

Haltim moved toward the one small window in the room, looking over a side street. He said nothing, watching the people below go about their business. Finally, his voice low, he spoke.

"Back when I was one of the Tempered, I and another member had to chase down a heretic. Well, someone labeled a heretic. They fled into the sewers. I imagine they thought that would keep them safe from me, and the rest of the Tempered. They were wrong." Haltim took a long breath and exhaled his breath disturbing the touch of dust on the glass.

"We chased him down there for most of a day. I terrified him, *we* terrified him. We cornered him in a section of the sewers that was more ruin that functional. The sewers here are old, some first work laid down when Ture was founded by Amder himself. But the oldest parts have fallen into disrepair."

"He was young, younger than you and William even. I had never asked what he had done to be labeled a heretic. This was my first runner like this. My partner had been a member of the Tempered order for several years. He was nice enough, normal even. But when we cornered the heretic, he changed. He drew his confession rod, a rod that if you spoke a word, an end would glow red hot."

"He demanded that the heretic repent, to give up. I thought it was for show, something to scare the unworthy." Haltim was slouching now, bent forward, his head almost touching the glass of the small window.

"But he wasn't. It was as if someone had poured another soul into the man. A man I had broken bread with, drank with, joked with. He took pleasure in it. He used the confession rod on the man." Haltim stopped talking for a moment, reaching up to wipe his forehead, now damp with sweat. "He burned out the man's eyes. He was a kid, only old enough to spend the day working, barely. He was screaming trying to take back whatever it was he had said to bring this upon him. And they... no... *we* burned out his eyes."

Duncan inhaled, loud enough for Haltim to turn towards him. "You did this?"

Head shaking Haltim looked down at his feet. "Not with my own hands. But I was there. I was a member of the Tempered, my order did that. Remember that Duncan, if you stand by while evil is done, you are as guilty as the person doing the evil."

"Afterward, we dragged the lad above ground and left him in an alley. I didn't know what to do. I hoped, somehow, that I'd find out what the young man had done would be worth this punishment. That he'd committed some horrible crime, so bad, so beyond forgiveness I could be at peace with what had happened." The old Priest turned back to the window, the sun in his face now.

"Instead, I found out that his heresy, what he had done, was say that he didn't think the Priesthood leadership, the Conclave and the High Priest himself, were trying hard to bring back Amder. That was all he had said. Words, overheard on a street corner. For that he was chased, hounded, blinded, and left for dead." Haltim tapped the glass with a finger, the soft click the only sound. Duncan was sure the old man was trying to gather his thoughts. None of this sounded like Haltim.

"I went looking for him the next day, but he was gone. When I got back to the Main church building, I renounced my membership in the Tempered, and was reassigned to the Reach. They wanted me gone. Out of their way." Hatim turned to Duncan. "And that's the story. Of why I'm not in the Tempered anymore, why I'm an outcast in the Priesthood, and why of course I know what the sewers of Ture are like."

Duncan stood looking at Haltim. He realized how much he looked like an old man, tired, worn. But there was a core of goodness, decency. He liked Haltim, which surprised him. He'd spent so much time disliking religion, all religion. But all this mess he'd found himself in, the Blood Curse, finding Amder's Hammer, chasing after William, all, Haltim had been right there to help him.

"Ok, I'll see about this mucking thing." Duncan replied. He wanted to say more. To tell Haltim he'd done the right thing, that he should have done more, that he should have left the Priesthood altogether. But none of those were right for him to say. Could he have done anything different if he had been in Haltim's place?

Duncan watched as Haltim left his room, quiet now. That had been a confession that he'd never expected. He still couldn't place this old man he knew, and liked, to a member of a secret order that involved torture and who knew what else. Haltim had left the group, but it was so out of place, so out of character.

I need to walk. Ambling, he passed Haltim's room, and Rache's. He considered knocking on her door for a moment but passed by. That was an issue for another day. He was tired. The effects of the run to get to the Guildhall in time, the depression of not getting to Will, the lingering aftereffects of taking Cloud, the whirlwind of the day. He was sure he had spotted a place to sit, a balcony on the side of the building when they had come in.

Sure enough, Duncan soon found a small door with four chairs out on a balcony. It didn't look like many people used it. The door was stuck, and three of the chairs had more bird droppings than he wanted to deal with. But one was clean enough for him, and he sat. Tired, stressed, and worried. He knew Haltim had said he might be able to get a message to Will, but that was a might, nothing concrete, nothing solid. *Hold on William, we will find a way to you.*

The rooftops spread out around him. Some taller, some shorter. He'd never seen so many buildings in one place. And somewhere, William Reis, was in danger.

***

Will couldn't help smiling. It was First Night He had made it into the Guild, though in a far more dramatic fashion than he'd ever wanted. His cover, Markin Darto, had held so far. Things were in truth far better than his fears had been this morning.

He entered the dining hall to find all the others already here. More than one turned toward him as he entered the room. Not that he blamed them, who wouldn't? But there was only one face he was happy to see, Myriam VolFar. Seated at a table with several other Apprentices, she apparently had saved him a seat, as she waved him over.

"Markin!" Myriam's voice rose as she grabbed his arm and hugged it. The scent of rosewater and spice clung to her.

"Myriam, thanks for saving me a seat." Will couldn't help but smile as she released his arm and introduced some of the others around them.

A few gave him a polite smile, or a greeting, but most acted like the others in the room, more than a few side glances and whispered murmurs with them. He shouldn't be surprised, he knew. He knew they all wanted to know what had happened, even Myriam he was sure wanted to ask. But no one would. He couldn't say anything even if they did ask.

As it was, they all sat, waiting, a small sea of Orange cloaks. A door on the other side of the room opened silently and in filed a far larger group of people, each wearing a grey cloak. Will felt a sense of foolishness, realizing that the hall was large for a reason, he and the others wearing Orange weren't the only ones at this feast.

Unsure of where to go or what to do, he and the other Orange cloaked newcomers sat there. The grey cloaked Apprentices ignored them and grabbed seats at the round tables throughout the hall but didn't talk. After all the grey cloaked students had sat, a new group entered. Four figures clad in Red cloaks, with hoods on entered first, Journeymen. They filed to a table, long and set against the wall. Following those comes three Blue cloaked Masters. Hoods on as well.

After they had arranged themselves at the table one Blue cloaked Master waved for the other Masters and Journeymen to sit. But that Master remained standing. The figure pulled the hood back to reveal the face of Master Reinhill.

"Apprentices new and old. Welcome. For those who have been here for a while, welcome to another First Night. For those wearing the Orange, congratulations! We have accepted you into the Smithing Guild. The oldest such Guild in Palnor and in fact all Alos. Founded by Amder himself, to explore, extend, and use the mastery of the forge to all who need it or can use it." Master Reinhill raised her hands for clear dramatic effect.

"This is First Night! Where the cloaks of Orange are exchanged for ones of Grey. A night of food, drink, and some revelry. Tomorrow will be one of the hardest days of your lives, I will warn you now." Master Reinhill paused as a ripple of slight humor moved through the Grey cloaked figures. "So, be careful of how little rest you get this evening."

"But now, feast." Reaching under the cloak, she produced a small baton which she used to smack, hard, the table she was standing at.

The peal that gave forth was like a crash, and several of the newer Apprentices flinched, Will among them. The doors on either side of the room opened, and in came food. Breads, cheeses, meats. Butter and mustard, pickled vegetables in small jars, each carried by silent and unsmiling figures.

The smell of the food arose a rumble deep within Will's stomach. Food was deposited on every table in equal portions. Even the head table with the Journeymen and Masters got the same food. After losing his breakfast before he entered the Guildhall, and not wanting to eat before the Anvil test, he hadn't eaten anything all day. He found that his hunger had returned in force.

"Everyone gets the same," the orange cloaked Potential on the other side of him said. "Hi, I'm Janko."

Will turned with some surprise to the man next to him. He looked like the prototypical smith. In fact, he was as normal looking a person as Will had seen in quite some time. "Markin, Markin Darto." Will replied. He took the offered hand with a firm shake. He could feel the callouses, the man knew the forge well then at least.

"I know. That hammer of yours, gave us all quite a fright." Janko gave a small laugh. "And here I thought I would be the best Apprentice this year. Instead I find myself a distant sixth."

"Huh? What's that? There's ranks?" Will hadn't thought about this.

"Informally. But each class sort of knows at the start, based on the anvil test. Some years there's a lot of controversy. Not this year!" Janko pounded Will on the back with a slap. "You blew the rest of us away. And you're from where? Dernstown? Right?"

"Um yes. You?" Will felt that ball in his stomach clench again.

"Here in Ture actually. My Grandfather was a Guild smith, and when he retired, he showed me some skills. Enough for me to get into the Guild at least." Janko smiled and grabbed a plate and helped himself to the food that had stopped coming out the doors.

Will did the same, grabbing everything he could find that looked at least familiar. "So... What's with these people serving the food?"

Janko paused for a moment. "Forgekeepers. All I know is they work for the Guild and the Priesthood. Have for generations. They live in the Guild here, somewhere. I'm sure you noticed, we all do, the Guild is far larger than it looks from the outside. The Forgekeepers don't talk to Apprentices, and barely speak to Journeymen. I'm not even sure if they talk to the Masters much. But didn't your Master, the one who brought you here tell you?"

Will felt that knot return with speed. "No, it must have slipped his mind."

Janko attempted a few times to talk but Will nodded and kept his mouth full of food so he couldn't say something stupid. This wasn't all that difficult, he still was hungry, though stress was making him less hungry each minute.

Myriam on the other hand was carrying on five different conversations. He wondered at her ability to do it. Of course, she wasn't here based on a lie, not like him. Though he was comforted by the fact that she wanted to include him in everything, though he didn't have much to say. Most of the conversations were about where they were from, and the journey here to Ture. He threw out a few facts about Dernstown from his lessons with Master Jaste but didn't go much farther than that. *Safer to be the quiet one.*

After what was to Will far too long, Master Reinhill stood again, and the room quieted down. "Now we have feasted." Reinhill reached under her cloak to take out a hammer. An old design by Will's estimation, wooden handled, flat headed on one end, and rounded on the other. She raised it once and brought it down, hard on the table.

A peal of sound came forth. Deeper than Will expected, he wondered what they made the hammer of.

"First Night! We now accept these applicants into the ranks of Apprenticeship. Each of you has proven your skill, and your basic knowledge of the craft. We carry a solemn charge from the fallen God Amder, to create and make, to use what we make for the good of all." Reinhill paused and smacked the table again, bringing forth another deep peal of sound.

"The Forgemasters of the Ancient World were members and set forth our rules and structure. We follow in their footsteps, and work to further their work." Reinhill once more hit the table, bringing forth the same peal of sound.

"Now, remove the orange cloak of the Potential, and take the grey of the Apprentice!" Reinhill raised the hammer again but did not strike this time. The red cloaked Journeymen who had been still and silent sprang into action, and from under the table brought forth several large packages.

"Markin Darto of Dernstown." Reinhill called out.

"Go!" Myriam whispered to him.

Will felt his legs lock up, why was he being called first?

"Markin Darto of Dernstown!" Master Reinhill called again, louder this time.

"GO." Myriam pushed his back and Will moved. That ball of nausea returned, and he hoped he wouldn't get sick and all the food he'd eaten come out into the world again. He stumbled twice and caught himself both times though an unnamed grinning grey cloaked Apprentice helped the second time.

He stood in front of Master Reinhill and the other assembled Masters and Journeymen. He cast his eyes down and the table, looking for the spot where the hammer had struck. Something, anything to not think about what was about to happen.

"Markin Darto, remove the orange of the Potential. Take up the first cloak of Apprentice for this forge group." Master Reinhill held up a grey cloak that on the outside looked like all the others. Yet the inside of this cloak wasn't plain, someone had lined it with red silk.

"Apprentice Darto!" Master Reinhill announced his name. Markin looked at her. A small smile flashed across her face. "Take the cloak lad, there are a lot of other names to call, and I don't want to be here all night," she whispered to him with a wink.

Will felt himself blush. He took off the orange cloak he had worn today, dropping it to the floor, unsure of what to do with it. Taking the grey one he put it over his shoulders and gave the Masters and Journeymen a small bow and walked back to his table.

"Good Job! Though I knew you'd be first. They had to make you first after the anvil test," Myriam whispered as Markin sat back down.

"I don't feel so good." Will mumbled and put his head in his hands. He wanted to yell, scream, what he had done, how he had cheated, how he'd broken the laws and rules of Amder to get here. But he kept his mouth shut. Coward indeed by using the blood of Amder to make the hammer to get into the guild, and coward in words by not admitting it.

"Bah, you're nervous. Besides being first doesn't mean anything, other than a larger target on your back!" Janko whispered with a swift clap on the back. Will heard other names called but tuned them out.

"Myriam VolFar!" Master Reinhill's voice came out.

"Oh hey, I'm fifth!" Myriam gave a huge grin and stood and went off to get her cloak. They called one by one, Janko and Gerad among them. Will payed no attention to the rankings, he didn't understand why others cared. He wanted to be the best smith he could. He wished Master Jaste hadn't told him about the Reis bloodline, or the Forgemasters, or any of it.

The last name was called, and a rather embarrassed looking boy stood up and grabbed his cloak without talking to any of the masters. Will felt sorry for him. The rankings were stupid he felt and placing someone dead last only made them insecure.

Master Reinhill made a motion with her hand and the other Masters still blue cloaked and silent stood. So did the red cloaked Journeymen. "This ends the ceremony. Eat, drink, and break nothing THIS time... And then report to the dormitories. On your beds you will find your schedule, first class is tomorrow morning, seven bells sharp!"

A small groan rippled through the grey cloaks at that news, but Reinhill ignored it as she and the others who had stood filed out. The Apprentices, all grey cloaked now, finished eating and in small groups or one at a time left the room. At last Will was alone with Myriam, sitting and thinking.

"Congratulations Markin. The red lining looks good on you." Myriam reached out and flipped one side of the cloak back, showing off the red silk.

"Thanks, I guess." Will wanted to tell her to truth. All of it. But what good would it do? Master Jaste had told him, he'd probably be Markin Darto for the rest of his life. He wished he'd thought about that before he'd left the Reach. Before he'd met Myriam.

"Walk me to my dormitory?" Myriam reached down and took Markin's hand.

Will wanted to, he wanted to walk with her, kiss her goodnight, and enjoy every second together. But he couldn't, not right now.

"Ah, I need to talk to a Master, about the Anvil test, after this, they asked me to. Sorry." Will hated lying to her, but he needed to be alone.

"Oh." Myriam let go of his hand, and then suddenly stood. She gave him a long look and quickly bent down giving his cheek a kiss. "Find me tomorrow then Markin Darto. Class First."

Will watched her leave, his thoughts as confused as usual. The smell of her clung to him, and he found himself rubbing the spot her lips had touched him. He liked her a lot, and she obviously felt the same, but again, it was a lie.

What was he going to do? Lies about his name and who he was weren't even the worst part. The truth would destroy anything with Myriam, he was sure of it. Standing he pulled the grey cloak back down, no longer showing the red lining and placed his hood up. He needed whatever semblance of privacy he could have.

36

Will was happy that the hallway outside was dim, and only the occasional voice could be heard. Time was getting late, most new members were in their dorms now, going over schedules and classes. But there weren't rules about wandering around at night in the Apprentices areas. You couldn't leave the Guild, and doors that were for other ranks just simply didn't open for an Apprentice. He needed clarity, but where was he going to be able to go? He wished Haltim was here, or Duncan even. Someone he could trust, someone who he could share the truth with.

His steps echoed down the hall; he did not know where he was even going. This place was a maze, but maybe that was a good thing, make him harder to find. The last thing he wanted was to answer questions about him, his hammer, or that test.

His walk brought him to a set of doors he remembered. The Anvil room, the test room. The place where in truth, he should have failed and been sent home. Looking back and forth in the hallway and seeing no one, Will pushed on the doors. Empty, the room felt smaller to him, the chairs still arranged as they had been this morning. And there in the middle, a silent judge to his lies, was the Anvil. It brought was a sour taste to his mouth. It should have caught his lie.

Will imagined this morning, if the anvil had shown the actual truth, striking the thing with his hammer, and instead of a sound, dead silence. No bright light, no sound, pointing to his failure. That's what should have happened. He had cheated to get in this place. Cheated with the blood, cheated by using another name. The sour taste in his mouth grew.

He could feel it under this cloak. The hammer. A symbol of his failure. He'd not believed in his own skill, his own abilities. So, he'd cheated. Lifting the hammer, he weighed it in his palm. It till shimmered and shone where the torchlight struck it. That was the effects of the Blood, not him, not his skill. His breath caught, and he choked down his sadness. He had betrayed the memory of every Reis who had tried and not get into the Guild by making this thing. He should have done it with his skill alone, his talent alone. He'd so wanted to be the one who made it he'd taken it too far, he'd cheated.

I'm sorry Da. I wanted this so much, so flaming much. I did this, and now I know, it was a mistake. I failed you. He would leave. Quit. He'd walk out the other door, the smaller one, the one reserved for the failures and rejects. They had to let him out if he wanted to quit, didn't they?

Will took the hammer and traced the carving he'd done of Amder on the side of the hammerhead. Without a word he placed the hammer on the anvil and turned to leave.

"William Reis, you are being a fool." A voice, one that he didn't recognize.

Will stopped dead. Did he want to look to see where that voice had come from? His palms felt sweaty. *His name, his real name, who said that?* He forced himself to look behind, to look back at the Anvil and the hammer he had placed there moments before.

There, standing next to the Anvil, stood a man in armor, the man from his vision back in the Reach. Haltim had told them back in the Reach, but Will couldn't remember. The last Forgemaster?

"William this isn't what Amder wants." The Forgemaster looked at Will before looking around the room an expression Will couldn't make out flitting across his face. "Still the Guild, though it feels different from in my day," the Forgemaster remarked. "We were more about the craft then."

Will turned toward the figure. "You're the Forgemaster, from my vision when I held the blood shard."

"Vision? I know nothing about a vision. Well other than this one." The Forgemaster gave Will a long look. "So, you're one of the last two. He last two of my line. Interesting. It's nice to meet you, as much as I am. My name is Simon, Simon Reis. Forgemaster to Amder, God of Creation and the Forge."

The Forgemaster picked up the hammer Will had placed on the Anvil "Very nice work. I'm impressed. I'd call you Grandson or something like that, but all the Greats would take a while, and I'm not sure how long I have here."

"Why are you here?" Will asked. This was all too strange for him. Yet, he wasn't scared. *I should be running away screaming, I'm taking to a man who's been dead for centuries.*

"Ah, direct. Good." The Forgemaster placed the hammer back where it had been. "Amder sent me. To talk some sense into that thick Reis skull of yours."

"Amder's dead," Will answered back unthinking.

Laughter boomed out of the Forgemaster for a second, shaking his head. "Well yes. You are a Reis, aren't you? Yes, Amder is dead, at least as much as a God can be dead, which isn't anything like how we die. But that's not why I'm here." The Forgemaster pointed at Will, almost poking at him to emphasize his words. "You are being a fool."

"What?" Will stated to say something else but he didn't know what to say. *Was this even real? Had the stress made him stumble, and he'd hit his head, and all this was a fever dream?*

"Do you think Amder would let anyone use his blood to make something if he didn't want them to? Amder may be dead as how mortals think of it, but that doesn't mean he's gone. And no God would let something as powerful as his blood be used to do anything without permission." The Forgemaster pointed to his hammer. "That results from your skill. Amder's blood was a blessing, not a stolen thing to hide."

Will paused. *Was this figure, ghost, whatever he or it was, saying that the use of the blood could have been stopped by Amder?*

"Yes. That's what I'm saying," Forgemaster Reis answered back. He tapped the side of his head and smiled. "Amder is letting me hear your thoughts, to help prove this all to you. You did nothing wrong."

Will felt more conflicted than ever at this piece of information. Amder wanted him to use the blood? It was all too much. He wanted to save Duncan and be a Guild Smith. That was it. "I'm not special. I'm not some chosen one. I'm me, William Reis. Sure, I'd be happy if Amder came back. Why wouldn't I? But, I'm not special."

The Forgemaster said nothing for a long moment, standing by the Anvil. "William, you aren't a chosen one. You have the skill; you have the knowledge. It's part of you. In truth, if there was to be a chosen one, it would be Duncan. He did open the tomb that held both the Hammer and the Blade. But, do you think Duncan would be here? Do you think he would listen to a God?"

"Are you saying the only reason I'm here and you want me to do this is because Duncan won't?" William could feel the heat rising on his face. "I'm a second-place pawn in the game?"

"No. Sparks. I wasn't good at this when I was alive either. Duncan couldn't do this. He wouldn't. He might do it to save you, but if it was to save Amder? He'd pass. You on the other hand are a believer. That makes all the difference in the world."

William's blood cooled. "Ok, I guess. This is giving me a headache. All this is ... I wanted simple and easy. And nothing has been since the day I took Duncan to that tower."

Forgemaster Simon Reis smiled at him and for a second Will was a kid again. "You look like my Uncle. Wish Duncan was here to see this."

The Forgemaster laughed at that, a big booming laugh. "Well, he was a descendant. Not surprised. And Duncan wouldn't be willing to see me. You are."

Will shook his head to clear it, rubbing his hand through his hair. "I wanted to be a Guild smith, to fulfill my father's dream. That was all. That was enough. Now, Duncan is cursed, and I'm hiding under a fake name and I don't even know why. Amder is dead. Why would the Priesthood be afraid of me?"

"Will, I know it's not the path you chose. But there's a reason for this. As for Duncan, he must walk his own path. I don't know what that path is, but he's got to go his own way. And from what little I know about Duncan that suits him fine. But you Will have a purpose."

Will stopped looking at the floor and faced the Forgemaster. "What purpose?"

The Forgemaster sighed and faced the Anvil standing in the room. "Will, did you know I didn't want to die for Amder? I wanted none of it. I wanted to go home after the battle, see my children, see my wife, travel, and do works in Amder's name. Fight the corruption that even then was spreading through the Priesthood. I wasn't prepared to die; I didn't *WANT* to die."

Forgemaster Reis placed his hand on the anvil. "I never dreamed that day would happen. That the Blood God would enter this world in the Flesh, and my God would call me to be the vessel for him to do the same. By my blood Amder died. If I had refused, or been a better fighter, maybe things would have ended differently."

The Forgemaster sighed and was quiet for a moment. "Will, I was the one who, though a sacrifice, gave my life, my blood for Amder to take a physical form. And only my blood can bring Amder back to life."

"I don't understand. You're dead, how can your blood bring a dead God back?" Will asked.

"Don't be silly, that's the other dead god. Not my blood as in my personal blood. But my blood, my bloodline. Will, you, your destiny, your purpose, your focus, is one reason, to bring Amder back." The long dead Forgemaster stood quiet, waiting for Will to react.

Will stood unsure what to say. Bring a God back to life? What? "Uh, What? How? Why?" Will shook his head and closed his eyes, trying to get clarity. "This isn't real. This can't be real."

"It's real. And stop acting like a child, Will. You're a full Guild Apprentice now. Act like it. You have the skill, you have the blood, but you don't have the confidence. Nor a few other things." The Forgemasters voice was as clear as it had been before Will had closed his eyes. *So that didn't make this dream go away.* Will opened them to see the Forgemaster there, as clear as before.

"What other things?" he found himself asking. "Not that I care because this whole thing is insane, but what other things?'

Forgemaster Reis gave Will a long look, face unreadable by Will. "Fine. I get it. You don't believe this. I can see why. I can. Amder being dead has been a fact for centuries. The Priesthood is powerful, and corrupt, and the Guild isn't what it once was. The other Gods were scared by the death of Amder and the Blood God and pulled far back from the world of mortals. But things are changing. They must change. And you, for all your self-doubt, are the best hope for that change."

Will shrugged. "Ok, fine let's say you are right. Why? Why me? Why does Amder need to come back? I'd love it if he did, but the world for all its imperfections for all the problems in the Priesthood and the Guild, even with all that, the world works, it's moving forward. Why me? Why now? And what 'other things?'— you didn't answer."

Forgemaster Reis vanished, only to reappear next to Will. He flinched at this reminder that this figure, this man, was long dead, and for lack of a better term, was a ghost. Forgemaster Reis waved his hand around the room. "William look around. This room, this place, even this room is wrong. This Anvil test? This was never part of the Guild. The Guild was supposed to take anyone who wanted to learn, to spread the joy of making, of creation, not choose only the best and train them to be better, but then use that skill to make money and gain power!"

Will nodded. He got that, but he felt his impatience rise. "You're not answering the questions."

The Forgemaster nodded. "Ok. Amder needs to come back. Because the Blood God, the one who cursed *OUR* bloodline, is coming back. Or at least is closer to it than he's ever been."

Will opened his mouth to speak but was cut off by The Forgemaster. "William, there is a good chance that your cousins' blood will be used to bring the Blood God back."

The Forgemaster continued. "As for the other question, the other things... that I can't tell you. Not yet, not now. I want to, William. You have one already, The Hammer of Amder, back at the Reach. But there's more. But I'm not the one who is to tell you, things must happen. I wasn't even supposed to come to you here. But, Amder didn't foresee your fear."

Will felt that knot of panic reform. They could kill Duncan. To bring back the Blood God. What? He'd stay of course if it meant saving Duncan, but this whole thing was still crazy. The Forgemaster smiled at him, and as William watched, vanished from the room before he could ask more questions.

He stood quiet in the room, looking at the hammer he'd made, the Anvil it sat on. Duncan was in danger of dying, the dead god Amder needed him to bring him back to life. To do so might save Duncan's life. Will took the hammer back hefting it. Duncan had helped him make this hammer, he'd not wanted Will to go or even try for the guild. And the truth was, if Will had never tried, the Blood God wouldn't be close to returning, nor would his only family be in this danger.

There was no more time for doubt. Will had a reason now for staying, outside of his own pride. Myriam would still be a problem, at least in terms of not wanting to lie to her. But staying could save Duncan, so he would stay. He stalked out of the room, back towards the dormitory, and the path laid out for him, leaving the Anvil in the dark, and the slightest hint of a hammer strike echoing in the emptiness.

37.

Duncan kept his head down as he made his way back to the boarding house. He wasn't from here and was out alone, and his thrice-hated Blood Curse made the possibility of violence a dangerous question.

He'd gone to meet with the Muckers and had been accepted to a preliminary job. He wasn't looking forward to it. *Just meeting them, the smell ...* He had a good sense for finding treasure when he was out scaving, but that was in the mountain ruins. Not moving hunched over through a stinking sewer, cleaning the gods knows what through passages and hoping to find something valuable. If he didn't need to job so they could stay here and figure out how to contact Will he'd have gone nowhere near the Muckers.

As he entered the Traveler's Fire, he spied Haltim sitting with the owner, that Bessim woman. He could swear, without hearing them that Haltim was flirting with the woman. Haltim, flirting? Too strange, even for his life these days.

"Ah Duncan. How did it go?" Haltim must have looked up and seen him. Duncan wasn't sure if that was a good thing or not.

"Well. I start tomorrow at least on a trial basis." He paused for a second. "Though I'm not sure about this. I'm tall for the job, and why do they go through people so fast? I guess it's the smell, but people never come back some days."

"It's only until we get done what we have to do." Haltim waved him toward an empty seat. "Join us? Talking about how much Ture has changed since I was here last."

Duncan shook his head. Listening to oldsters talk about the good old days didn't excite him. To be sure at times, he could get useful information, but that was back at the Reach. He'd found a few ruins that way, listening to the old coal merchants talk about former customers. *I just want to talk to Rache.* Even thinking her name made a smile start on his face.

"Oh no thanks, I'm sure the two of you have a lot of catching up to do," Duncan said, blurting it out and then taking to the stairs.

***

Haltim snorted and smiled. The lad was running right to see Rache, he was sure. "Young love."

"Forgetting when we were that age, old man?" Bessim asked arching an eyebrow at him. "I remember you rushing over here a time or two as soon as my parents were busy and not keeping a close watch."

"That was different." Haltim sat back in his chair.

"How so?" Bessim crossed her arms. Haltim knew that look, he'd been the recipient of Bessim's pointed retorts more than once.

"You're better looking!" Haltim gave her a grin.

"Still, glad to hear the lad found a job, even if it is being a Mucker. You better make sure he gets some work clothes and gets set up at a laundry... I'm not washing that stuff out." Bessim pointed to Haltim. "The whole place will stink worse than a stockyard at high noon otherwise."

Haltim held up his hands in surrender. "I'll talk to him about it, once he comes back down that is. I will not go up interrupt their ... conversations."

"I've got food to make, dinner in a few hours." Bessim excused herself, making her way to the kitchen in the back of the boarding house.

Haltim watched her go, remembering those days when they were both much younger, sneaking away when her mother was heading off to cook. He should have stayed back then. He should have left the Priesthood and stayed here with her.

A brief flash of heat on his arm shook that thought out. He knew what that meant. If he'd stayed, he'd have not been able to help Will or warn Duncan, and the chances were, they would both be dead now, and the Hammer of Amder if it had been found at all would be in the hands of the High Priest. Who knows what that man could do with the Hammer and the Heart?

The fact was they still needed to get word to William. *Somehow.* There were a few people he still knew, but could they get word inside the guild? Would they even be willing to help? By this point he was sure his name was known as an apostate, labeled a heretic or worse. The current set of Tempered looking for him, and he had no desire to be found by his old order.

He had to stay low, and hope that somehow, somewhere, a chance would present itself to get a message into the guild. And if nothing else, pray to Amder that Will could survive his first year in the guild.

38.

Duncan stretched, feeling the knots in his upper back scream with release. It was three months now that he'd been a Mucker. Three months of cleaning up the worse foulness and disgusting mess that people threw down the sewers. He'd found a few things of interest, a necklace gilded with Silverlace and set with fire eye gems, and a ring, solid and old, that he'd found behind some crumbling bricks in an old section of the sewers. It was made of pure lacnum, very rare here, only found in the far north. He only knew what it was from his old days scaving when he'd found a small broach made of the stuff. Both items he'd sold and payed for a full years' worth of lodging and board at the Travelers Rest for all.

He could have quit at that point but, in truth, while he hated the mucking part, it was the closest to scaving he would get here, outside of outright theft. And of course, there was Rache. They had grown close, but there was a limit with her. He wanted to be closer, but she always kept him a hands width away. There were odd things yet that nagged at him. She never left the Traveler's Rest, for one. Never. She came upstairs and downstairs, but he'd never seen her leave the building. Even on a day off.

It's as if she was waiting for something, but what he couldn't tell. And she would never say. He knew the main reason he kept coming back to the sewers though, it kept him away from other people. *And being away from other people meant he didn't get angry.* No anger, no Blood Curse. Except for the dreams.

Some nights, without warning, his dreams would come and be full of fire, blood and death. He would feel the ripping of flesh in his teeth, the screams and wails for pity and mercy. In these dreams he loved it, he craved the screams, the blood, and the rage. It consumed him, and he'd awake drenched in sweat, teeth gritted tight, sometimes having bitten his lip or tongue and his mouth full of his own blood.

Those nights he'd grab a vial of Cloud and drink half. The rage would go, the anger would fade, and peace would settle. He never knew when the dreams would come. He wished he had enough Cloud to take it every night, but he had to ration it. He hated those nights. What shook him more was one fact; the Cloud wasn't working as well anymore. He was sure of it. At first the effect would come in moments, seconds even. And he'd only have to take a sip, not a full half of a vial. But now? A few minutes would tick by before he could feel the rage leave him. A few minutes he'd find himself gripping the sheets, fighting to stay in his bed. Fighting to stay away from other people.

He had said nothing to Haltim about it. How could he? The old Priest sat in the common room and talked to that Bessim woman and ate food all day. He'd stopped wearing his Priest robes, and dressed just as a simple common laborer, and had even let his hair grow out some, but he did nothing. Whenever Duncan brought up getting a message to Will, Haltim would give him the same lecture about biding time and finding out the best way to contact his cousin.

Haltim assured him that Will safe, but he wouldn't answer how he knew that. He'd tap his heart, like that meant anything. Duncan had found himself more often annoyed with the old man. *He was the one working, he was the one bringing in money, he was the one whose only family in the world was in danger, and yet no one else was doing anything!*

Stretching again, Duncan took stock of the bare room he lived in. He hadn't even unpacked. He kept one pack with traveling clothes, a small store of money hoarded away, and of course the Cloud, hidden near the bottom.

Ture, being the capital would have places he could get Cloud. That wasn't the question. What was the problem, was where? Ture was huge, and Cloud wasn't something he just 'ask around' on. Maybe Haltim would know and be worth something.

Duncan snorted, Haltim would be much more likely to lecture him than help.

The only other thing was a delivered package of clean Mucking gear. Bessim had refused to wash any of his work gear after he had got the job. He wasn't blaming her for that, it was awful stuff. The smell the first few days of the job made him sick more than a few times. He had stuck with it for Will's sake and had gotten able to control his response to it. He didn't like it, but some other Muckers had given him tricks like taking a cloth and dripping mint oil on it and wrapping that around his mouth and nose while he worked.

Throwing on his gear, Duncan exited out of the room. He paused for a moment outside Rache's door, wondering if he should knock. No, better to talk to her tonight. Rache always looked tired if he saw her before noon.

He had asked once why, and she'd claimed the cold northern nights made her unable to sleep well, though he didn't see how that could be. Ture was far warmer that the Reach was! At least to his Reach born senses. The only good thing about Mucking, was he was out of the hot Ture sun. The sewers were dark, and cooler. Still smelled horrible, though.

No one spoke to him as he walked. His gear marked him, and who wanted to spend time with someone who cleaned sewers? No one reputable at least. Even the two pieces of jewelry he'd found he'd had to go through a person recommended by the other Muckers. A strange fellow, Duncan had never even gotten a good look at him, he'd been wrapped in clothes and hidden by a wall and counter. But he'd paid a fair price for the finds. He'd dealt with fences before back in the Reach. Merchants who did a little business on the side. Nothing harmful, but not wanting to ask questions nor be asked any in return.

The other Muckers were a mixed lot. Duncan had expected them to work like a crew, but he realized they had no interest in socializing. They got their assignments from a board, and the arrangement was after you did your route, you could explore the older sections of the sewers that weren't in use as you felt fit. That was that. You marked when you got in, and when you left. Simple.

The only other Mucker Duncan had spoken over three words do was the bossman, Talmon. A stooped middle-aged figure, Talmon claimed to have been a Mucker for twenty years. He knew all the routes and made the schedule. He was fair about it, and didn't play favorites, so no one complained. And even Talmon wasn't exactly a talker.

As Duncan entered the Muckers headquarters, he cursed. The glows were out. Two baskets with the silvery hand sized globes. Stuff rots in sewers. And the gas rotting things can give off, burns. There were times however, when something blocked a sewer vent, there would be a gas buildup. That meant no open flames. It meant the glows. And it meant worse than usual stench.

"Glows," Duncan cursed, not wanting an answer. At least a torch killed the smell a bit. And when your skin was cold even through your gloves, a torch could warm you. Not the glows. The glows only gave light, and not a particularly warm light.

"Yes, Duncan the Tall. Glows. The Southern Fork is more clogged up than I am after a feast day!" Talmons voice called out from the back end of the room.

"Really ... a bathroom joke? In the sewers?" Duncan answered back. Talmon didn't say much, but he loved his bad humor.

A chair scraped across the stone floor and Talmon came out of the back office. Talmon shrugged. "Get your glow and hit your assignment. You are eastern bound, harbor line." And then the bent man walked back toward the small room he used as an office. Duncan liked the man; he didn't try to be anything other than what he was.

Even better. The harbor line was part of the old system, and parts were closed, and had been for years. While most of it still stood fine, they had covered the vents and pipes and closed off with years of growth and change. The plus side was that because of all that change, the parts he had to check weren't a huge number and he'd get time to do some serious scaving. The downside was animals and rumors of other things came in from time to time from the connections to the water in the harbor.

One of the other Muckers had told him a story his second day working, about a worker, gone to check the harbor line and never come back. They had searched for him for a night as was customary. The only thing they ever found was the skin off his hand. It was like it had been cut off, flayed. They all claimed some sea creature had done it. *Walked like a man, covered in scales.* They claimed they had seen it vanish into the water when they found what was left of the hand.

Duncan didn't believe a word. People disappeared in the sewers sometimes, but they usually drowned, or got lost and died of thirst. Or they succumbed to their thirst and drank the sewer water. *What was worse, dying from lack of water, or dying from whatever was in the water.* He wouldn't even be surprised if a murder happened down here, at least off the main lines. But he'd worked the harbor line before, and nothing had ever come of it, so he wasn't worried now.

39

Duncan grabbed a glow, giving it a firm shake, and was rewarded with a blue silver glow. Each glow had a small hook with a small strap of leather tied to it. Duncan tied his to the end of his pole and started off, the glow swinging with his steps. It was dark, smelly, and wet. *Typical sewer workday.*

He'd completed one pass of the main line when his pole hist something different. He'd already found and pulled up several bunches of blackweed, that seaweed that didn't mind the lack of light. But this felt metallic. Hard.

Duncan smiled despite himself, something worth scaving! He reached into the foul water, thankful for the long waterproof gloves and grabbed a roundish pendent out of the water, holding it up to the glow, he gave a slow soft whistle.

Black it was, or at least parts. Decorated it with rubies, dark red ones, unusual for most valuable work. But these were clear of obvious flaws. The pendant while small was down in the shape of a red drop of blood, black stone and red gems. As he looked at the pendant, a shudder stole up his spine. *The rubies were as dark as blood. Could he squeeze blood out of Talmon? How much could he get out of the man? No one would hear him scream down here.*

He slammed the door on those thoughts; that was the last thing he wanted to think about. In fact, while the whole thing was more valuable, it gave him feelings he wasn't ready for. *It was the dark and the smell, that's the reason he was feeling this way. No reason to panic.* Studying it for a moment more, Duncan glanced around and took out a small knife. He pried out the gems, and with a toss, threw the rest of the pendant back into the water. He always kept a few small bags and pouches with him, and placed the gems in a small pouch, hanging it around his neck, and under his shirt.

The rest of the shift was uneventful, more blackweed, a large dead longfish, its toothy smile and rotting body having gotten caught on a grate and unable to free itself. A few well-placed pushes with the pole and its body slipped back out into the harbor, to be made a feast of by the innumerable scavenger birds that lived in the harbor.

With his main shift over, he had more time to explore and search the older areas, but with the gems he already had, Duncan was content. And if he admitted it to himself, the pendant had unnerved him anyway, not quite sure he wanted to stick around here.

He spent a second wondering where the thing had come from. It obviously was valuable, but it was a waste of time to spend much thought on it. The water down here, when it flowed, carried things from all over the city, and a lot of them ended up in the harbor line.

The way back to the Muckers headquarters was the same as when he left this morning. Though about halfway back marks on the wall forced him to detour. Muckers left those marks for each other, there was a scheduled increase in water flow, and no one wanted to get caught in a torrent of whatever filth needed the extra power to get moving.

Back at the Muckers base, Duncan made his report, to Talmon and said his farewells. He felt increasing itchy down here today, oppressive almost. He felt a sense of relief breaking back out into the sunlit world. He took a few back-alley ways to the one merchant who bought their stuff.

He could have made it faster taking the more direct routes on the main roads, but the looks he got from people, and the way they avoided him after a shift in the sewers made it very clear he wasn't welcome. *He could break their bones every time they smirked at him, gouge eyes, and leave a trail of blood and death from here to city walls! How their screams would echo, a chorus to light the land on fire.*

Duncan gasped and collapsed against a wall, grabbing his head. He hadn't had thoughts like that in weeks, months even. Now twice in one day? Dreams were one thing, but active waking thoughts? His stomach churned. Why now? He had no answers, but sat for a while, his breath labored.

***

The Underpriest gripped the black iron dagger, the sharp grooves in the handle making small cuts in his hand. Blood dripped from the cuts, only to be sucked up by the dagger. The High Priest, may his name be struck from the rolls finally, had been gone for months. Fear had kept the others in line, but he, one of the twenty, was done waiting. He had sacrificed five slaves to the Blood God under a black moon, and Valnijz had spoken to him. The god was tired of waiting and angry.

The High Priest had been in power too long, had forgotten his place. Valnijz whispered a plan into his soul. If the High Priest returned with only one of the sacrifices, this dagger, an item of power on its own right, would give Zalkiniv to the Blood God.

He, Girin, would be raised up, as the new High Priest. He would return the Destroyer to life. He would be above all! And the world would weep in ruin as they died, for the glory of Valnijz. The others of the twenty would fall in line, or they too would be first given to the Blood God upon his return.

40

Duncan stood, his hands helping push himself up against the cold stone wall. The chill his hands had felt good, it helped push away this most recent attack. He wished he had Cloud with him. He'd have to bring some once more. When he'd started work as a Mucker, he had brought a small vial with him, every day. But as the days had passed, he's stopped bringing it. There had been little point, except for his dreams at night he hadn't needed it.

Why today? Sweat dripped down, leaving a trail down his face and onto his shirt. For the moment his thoughts were clear, and the most recent event faded away some. He needed normal. Get rid of these gems, go take this outfit to the cleaner, grab a shower there and change into the clothes he kept there. And then, head back to the boarding house. Order. Normality. Routine.

Near the city wall, in the shadows of several old buildings, he spied it. One look could tell you it wasn't built with care in mind, which meant it was far newer than most of the buildings here. Why the City Guard and the Inspectors ignored it he wasn't sure. It could be a payoff, or some other reason, but he'd heard they would walk by the place, ignoring it.

Duncan had only been here twice. Dirty wooden door, stained brown with who knew what, a strange smell, not quite musty, but different. A very large and high counter. Plain and wooden, and for a place that claimed to buy and sell things, completely empty of any merchandise.

He walked in and as all the Muckers did, rapped his fist on the wooden counter five times. From a door in the back, came the sound of cloth moving, and then, the buyer walked into the room. As before the figure was swaddled in cloth head to foot. Only the eyes were uncovered, and even those were impossible to make out in the dim candlelight, for the place was only lit with one candle.

"Yes?" the buyer asked. The buyer's voice was stranger still, raspy, and cold. He wondered where the person was from, the accent was as strange as the sound, with odd emphasis on letters.

"I have a find I want to sell," Duncan replied. It was all a careful back and forth, line by line, repeated the same way every time. Talmon had told him before the first time he'd come here what to say. The buyer wouldn't even respond if you said anything different. If you kept going off from what was expected, the buyer would leave, and he'd never come back for you, ever.

"Show me what you have found." the buyer said, keeping to the ritual.

Duncan reached in, under his shirt and pulled out the pouch with the rubies. He poured them out onto the counter, next to the candle.

"This is what I have found." Duncan found the whole thing stilted and silly, but, well, who was Duncan to judge? He'd done a few things back in the Reach that might be frowned upon. At least with this method there wasn't any exchange of more personal information. Nothing to lead the curious to him.

The buyer paused, and looked down at the dark red gems, a few of the faucets catching in the light of the single flame. He picked them up, one by one, holding them before the candle, peering at them. There were six, and one by one he repeated this, not saying a word.

When there was one left, the buyer stopped and looked at the gem. Nothing marked it as differing from the others, at least not in Duncan's eyes. Finally, the figure looked at Duncan. From under his various cloth coverings he pulled out a pouch of coin and pushed it, along with the last gem, to Duncan.

It confused Duncan. The buyer always bought everything. No one had ever said anything different to him. Why hadn't he taken the last stone?

"I brought six, not five," Duncan said, trying to figure this out.

The buyer stood still, not saying anything.

Duncan shifted his weight, from side to side. If he kept talking, there was a chance he'd say too much and no longer be able to use the services of the buyer. But this made little sense. He could use a different merchant, but this was the only one who never got caught, turned no one in, and never got asked questions, at least, that was what everyone said.

With a nod, Duncan grabbed the coins and the final gem and left, hearing the buyer return to wherever he had been before.

What was he going to do with the last gem? Duncan wondered what by the forges of Amder all that had been about? He didn't need a ruby. Money was always useful to have. Once they got Will and got out of this place, money would be very helpful. If they got that far.

Rache! He'd give the gem to Rache! The gem would help him get past whatever barrier was there, and she wouldn't keep him at an arm's length anymore. *Yes, that was a good plan.* Give the girl the gem. He felt better, like something made sense. Off to the showers, a change of clothes, and then to present Rache with a gift. Rache would love it.

***

Zalkiniv yawned and stretched. Twelve bells sounded in the city outside. The time was later than normal, but she had spent half the night on a working. Every night that she had the strength to do it, she'd work the blood to lessen the impact of that foul drug the blood blessed was taking.

Standing she examined this form in the mirror. This body had proved useful. Duncan was enamored of Rache, the persona she'd made up. Which made it all the easier to get the hooks into the Reis. He was a foolish young man, chasing money and distraction. Hopefully the other one, the Smithing one was as easy to manipulate.

Duncan would have been killed long ago if it wasn't for the Blood he carried, and her need for the other Reis. The Scaled One had made that quite clear and there was to be no change in the plan unless the God demanded it. And so, she waited. Worked the blood and thought about how to get access to this William Reis, and how to get both of them, Duncan and William out of Ture, back past the barrier by the Reach, and back to where she belonged.

Zalkiniv wasn't sure yet how she could do this. With enough blood it might be possible to control Duncan Reis, but that left the other threat, the main threat, this William. The one in training to be a Forgemaster. *Dangerous.* If this other Reis completed his training, Amder could return. All the work of years would be gone, destroyed in the hammer blows of a dirty stinking blacksmith.

Zalkiniv paused, a familiar set of footsteps was coming up the stairs. Duncan was back, early this day. Zalkiniv checked the body in the mirror again, ruffled the hair. Perfect.

The knock came, hesitantly.

"Come in." Zalkiniv answered. Duncan. The call of the blood he carried could be felt from here, but there was something strange today. *Something had changed, something new.* A greater hunger hovered over her prize. Something old, something dark, something powerful.

"Hi Rache. How are you today?" Duncan sat down for a second then stood again, wiping his hands on his shirt. Was that a slight quiver? Zalkiniv watched her prize carefully.

"I'm fine Duncan. You're back early today." She smiled, letting him know she noticed. "Are you ok? Somethings different about you."

"Me? Yes, I'm fine. Great. Well, see I found something, a gift for you, while I was Mucking." Duncan reached into a pocket.

"I'm not sure I want something you found in the sewers Duncan." Rache gave a small laugh, feeling his blood move in response. She wanted to laugh. The responses were so easy to read and typical, it was like reading a book. But even so, that odd feeling remained.

"No! Nothing like that, well, yes like that, but..." Duncan stopped talking for a moment. Rache watched him, he was more than nervous. *Excited? Scared?* This went beyond what she had been doing to him. Her blood workings had magnified his feelings, but nothing on this scale. What was going on? There wasn't another power at play per se, but that odd feeling, old, strong, but dim.

"Here., I found this and though you might like it." Duncan handed her a cloth, folded up, but clean. She could feel something hard inside, oval.

Rache cocked her head. That odd feeling, was coming from whatever this was. What had the boy found? Flipping the cloth back, Zalkiniv was unable to breathe. *A Claret stone?*

Claret stones were old magic from even before Zalkiniv was born to some slave mother. Ancient even then. They were blood worked and reworked into looking like a gem, and power, the power they could hold. How had a Claret stone made it here? Here into the heart of Ture, in the seat of the hammering fool Amder? *Where had this child found this?*

"Do you like it? I found it today. Well that and more, sold the rest, but kept one, for you. As a gift." Duncan stammered out. He looked away once she looked in his eyes, trying not to explode.

He'd sold the others? How? To whom? She wanted to work the blood now, rip the truth from him. She bit down inside her mouth, tearing a small but ragged cut on her tongue, feeling the blood spurt, and feeling the claret stone echo with each pulse. She would pay for using her own blood, but this was to important.

She waved her fingers in a small pattern and whispered with blood flecked lips a minor working. Enough to question this fool and have him forget it.

"Where did you find this?" Zalkiniv asked, letting her rage and anger flow with her words, giving them extra power.

"In the sewers. I was near the harbor line; I found a pendant. Black stone, these rubies set in it. Made me feel strange. Pried the rubies out, threw the black stone part back into the water. Took the rubies to the fence we use, he bought all but one. He doesn't talk, did not say why." Duncan answered, his eyes, turning red from the rush of blood through his body.

While she did not know of this pendant, items like that were very rare and valuable. One set with that many claret stones had to be from someone very skilled and blessed of Valnijz, how had it come here? Why had he not bought all? There was no reason for a criminal to not buy all the stones.

"Who is this fence? What is his name?" Zalkiniv watched Duncan's face. She would have to get information fast; the working would run out soon, already the blood in her mouth was fading.

"We don't know. We put items we find on a counter in a wooden shack. He comes out, wrapped in cloth, we can't see his face. He takes the items, gives the coin in a bag, then leaves." Duncan shuddered, his face turning even redder.

Zalkiniv spat a curse, then ended the working, but first sending Duncan to his room. She'd have to work again tonight, but this time to pair the claret stone with her own blood. The stone would make her own workings far more powerful, and she should be able to use it to set a permanent shield against the old Amderite. And giving her more power to work over this Reis fool.

Then, she'd turn her attention to finding this fence, and get the rest of those stones back! Zalkiniv held the stone tight in her fist. After months of waiting and trying to find a way, the Blood God had given her a path forward.

41.

With a shudder that forced him to grab a bedpost, Duncan became aware. He sat down, gasping for breath and feeling his blood thrum, as if he had been straining hard and hadn't been breathing. His head snapped around why was he in his room? He had been in Rache's room and had given her the ruby he'd found and then things got fuzzy. She'd liked the gift, but after that things sort of slipped away from him.

He collapsed back onto his bed, rubbing his temples. The cool sheets felt good under him, and his pressure in his skull faded. He also noticed that itch he had been feeling, that odd presence was gone. He was less on edge at least. By the sparks, he hated this Blood Curse.

Laying there Duncan closed his eyes, trying to finish his calming down. He wiped the small beads of sweat that had formed off his face. He missed his old life. Scaving, hanging out with Will, not feeling lost and confused. Even girls back home he'd had no small string of dalliances with. Here? Here he was always finding himself lost and confused by Rache.

Standing, Duncan stood still for a moment gathering himself. He needed to see her. He left his room and knocked on Rache's door.

"Come in." Rache's voice came from behind the door.

He pushed open the door to find Rache behind a changing partition.

"Rache, did I look ok when I left here? I don't remember going back to my room." He watched the shadow of her changing playing on the wall, wishing he could see more.

She stopped moving for a second, then continued. "Um, yes. I thanked you for the gift of the ruby, and then you left."

"Ah ok, odd. It's been an unsettling day anyway." Duncan sighed. "Coming to eat?"

"In a while, I've got an errand to run." Rache shot back, coming around from behind the partition. Clad in her old traveling clothes, she gave the picture of someone used to the road. *Where was she going, she never left this place.*

"Want company? Might not be a good idea to walk around like that, in some parts of town." He didn't want her to go alone anywhere. "Let me go with you."

Rache laughed. "I'll be fine Duncan. Besides, I can't have you come with me, it's a surprise."

"What?" Duncan scratched his head. Why was it every time he talked to her, he got fuzzy?

"You gave me a gift, now I need to return the favor." Rache sighed and rolled her eyes.

"Oh! I wasn't expecting anything in return! Really." He moved himself to stand in the doorway. "Going alone, as the night falls…"

Her eyes flashed for a moment, and his blood gave him a chill. "I will be fine Duncan Reis. Now move."

He tried to come up with an argument, but instead moved out of the way, and watched Rache walk past him and down the stairs.

He stood there, unable to move. *I must go after her.* If he couldn't go with her, he'd at least follow at a safe and discreet distance. He came down as quiet as he could, but no Rache in sight. Cursing his luck, Duncan flew out the front door, but Rache was nowhere. He'd lost her.

"Everything ok my boy?" Haltim said and came outside after him.

"Yeah, Rache went out and with night falling, I wanted to go with her to make sure nothing bad happened to her, but she refused. I would follow, but she's gone." Duncan paced the porch.

"Well I'm sure she will be fine. Why did she go out?" Haltim sat down in a nearby chair. Duncan could feel the old priest observing him.

"Well I found something, a gem. I gave it to her as a present. She said after I gave it to her, she had to go out, and when I asked why, she said it was a surprise." Duncan sat down next to Haltim. "I guess she's returning the favor."

"A gem? A very nice present." Haltim sat back in his chair considering something. "A word of advice, if a woman tells you no, listen the first time. A fool's errand and dangerous to try and force your choice on her."

"Duncan, how have you been? I know you don't like to talk about it, but, now that we have a moment here, how are you. I mean regarding your condition." The old priest looked down at his feet for a moment and rubbed his right wrist. *He rubs that wrist often. Maybe it hurts.*

"Ok. Not great. I have dreams sometimes. Today was different, I was walking after work, and I wanted to hurt everyone I saw, it was almost overwhelming. And I wasn't mad Haltim, I was annoyed." Duncan started out into the gathering night. The shadows of the buildings merging together, deepening the darkness. "I hate this. Can't we find a way to warn Will? Are they still even after him? It's been months. We are here, waiting, and nothing. No word, no way to contact, no nothing."

"I know Duncan. All I can say is this, that for now, Will is fine. Don't ask how I know; you won't like the answer. But he's safe, for now. But that could change at a moment's notice. The people involved are dangerous and powerful. And rich." Haltim sighed. "There are things I am working on. I hope that soon we can get word to your cousin. By Amder's forge I pray we can."

Duncan turned towards Haltim and snorted. "You've said that exact thing before, or very similar. I'm not sure you mean it anymore. All you do is sit around, talking to Bessim and eating. That's it. All on the money that I have brought in. Me. Not you. Me." Standing, Duncan walked back inside but paused at the doorway. "Next time, try to think of something to say that at least justifies your being here."

He could hear Haltim about to speak, but he stalked away. He could feel his annoyance turning to anger, he had to get away, calm down. He went back to his room, and without a thought opened his sack and took out a small vial of Cloud. *Cloud could fix it.* He'd take a half dose, a small half dose, and then he'd be fine. All those visions of death and blood, gone. Anger and frustration, gone. A small vial.

It still made him grimace as he swallowed the thick sticky white liquid. He gave a half second thought to who made this stuff this cloyingly sweet, and then, he didn't care. He didn't care about anything.

***

Haltim watched the man go. Man. Duncan wasn't a boy anymore, neither was Will. He knew that the words directed at him were out of frustration. Back in the Reach Duncan had been confident, in control. He'd been taken from that; from the life and world he knew. The Blood Curse had seen to that. With these stresses of missing William, the trials of the heart with the young Rache, he was sure Duncan often felt his life was barely staying together.

"I wish I knew how to fix this. If we could get a message to Will, somehow. That would help." Haltim whispered to himself as he rubbed the bracer on his arm. It never came off, and Haltim wasn't even sure if it could. It didn't hurt, except for when Amder was trying to tell him something, and even then, it got hot, but not burning.

Haltim always wore something long sleeved, so no one could see the thing. They would ask too many questions about it. Often at night, alone in his room he'd look at it though. The metals shimmering in perfect balance, made from that cloth that had protected Amders Hammer. Blessed by a God. The Anvil and Hammer etched into the metal.

His thoughts drifted. This gem that Duncan had given Rache. It was reasonable for a man to give a woman a gift, even more so one that he was pursuing. As if in response, the bracer on his arm grew warm for a second, then faded, as if wanted to get hot, but couldn't. Haltim shook his head and snorted. Nothing could stop that from warning him, he was being paranoid.

Heading inside, Haltim stopped to grab some paper. He would send yet another message to an old friend still in the Priesthood, one of the few who might be willing to help. The smell of fresh bread wafted through the common room making Haltim's stomach grumble. Well, after dinner he would.

***

Zalkiniv cursed her luck as she gave her left palm a slice. She needed more blood for this to work, and she hadn't attuned the claret stone yet. She would have done that first; its power would be useful. Binding the stone would take more power than she had free right now. With the Blood blessing, yes, but draining that much would be foolish. But if she waited till after then she might never get her hands on the other stones, and she wanted them all. Night had fallen, and these back streets had little enough foot traffic. There were other dangers, but to the High Priest of the Blood God, those dangers were nothing.

She reached out, drawing on the half-a-day old traces of Duncan's passing, and the claret stones' movement. There, the place he showered earlier. The trail left the building heading deeper into the city, and stronger now. The water must have been dampening the working. Water always was a problem. This part of the city was quieter than even before. It was old even if it had some upkeep on it. Old and empty. The sounds of two people yelling at each other echoed through the air, faint. Sounds of some animal fighting, the tang of blood touching her senses.

The trail led to a small shack, leaned up against another building. Ramshackle. This was the place? Zalkiniv snorted, this would be easy. Ending the working, she rubbed her hand, all that remained was a faint pink line, and even that would fade.

The door wasn't even locked! She couldn't believe her luck, who would leave this place unguarded, unwatched? Pushing in she saw a small room a counter too high for the space, and s single candle, still lit, but near the end of its time. The shadows thrown by the single flame danced in the corners, but she wasn't concerned. It would take a lot more than shadows to disturb her. Otherwise the room was plain and barren. Empty except for the partition in the back, behind the counter.

Vaulting over the counter a smell wafted around the room, one that tickled a memory, like the description of the clothed figure that the Reis had mentioned under her working. If she'd been back where she belonged, she'd access the blood memories again, but there was no way to do that here. Looking around the corner, instead of another room, it ended at a small round sewer entrance! Someone had removed the cover, and a ladder led down underground. Curious. There was no smell of sewage, or other foul things.

It was dark down the passage, and she had no light. She could take the candle, but it wasn't going last long anyway. Another working then. She took her knife and cut a shallow gash on each cheek and smeared blood across her eyelids, working the blood into sight. Everything took on a reddish tinge, but she could see through the darkness now, and in daylight.

The ladder was not old. The ropes used were too clean, and not damp. It was also spaced oddly the rungs a bit too far apart, which tickled her memories yet again. The rungs were too far apart, as if whoever used it had legs that were far too long. Dropping down into a dry tunnel, she stopped to take stock of the situation. The tunnel she was in ran in two directions and was empty in both. In fact, she couldn't even sense any water in either direction, but on the very edge of her senses, a faint telltale tang of blood came from the right.

Human blood. A smile broke out on her face. Interesting. But she needed to be careful. While she had power, she only had her own blood to work with, and if she were attacked by too many at once, she wasn't sure she could hold a large group of attackers off with only her blood for power. The claret stone would have erased her fears, but it wasn't ready yet.

Her footsteps soft and silent, Rache leaning on her centuries of knowledge. Knowing how to creep along was useful when she was moving up the hierarchy of Valnijz. She had dispatched more than one rival and used their blood, to power her own schemes. Subterfuge had its place, as much as she loved to dance in the blood and rage, uncaring and unthinking.

The floor showed signs of foot traffic, the dry dirt and dust showing the passage of boots and shoes. The smell of blood was stronger now, the smell made her mouth water. It was tinged with a bitter hint, terror. She savored it for a moment. She'd been working her own blood and the Blood Blessing for a while now, and neither was full of this level of pain and terror, she had missed it. The tunnel ended at a door, but what was on that door made her stop in surprise.

There, laid into the door, was a symbol, and one she would have never expected. A fang and scale, over a single red drop of blood, the symbol of her master, the Blood God, the Scaled One, the God of Rage and Death, The Destroyer, Valnijz.

Zalkiniv started at it for a long moment. This was much unexpected, but useful. Then, with the rush of an old thought, it came to her: cultists. When she had been first inducted into the Higher Priest castes, before the war, before the fall and the creation of the valley, she had heard of a plot to found a group of Blood God followers here, in Ture, and other capitols. She hadn't been involved, some other Priest had, one she had killed in fact a few years later. But against all odds, a cult had survived these long years? How?

If they were cultists, she needed them. In fact, she could use this to expand her power and abilities far greater still, greater than even with the claret stone. If the other claret stones were here, her power would dwarf what it was back on the other side of the barrier. Well what her power was without the shaft, or the spearhead.

Holding the claret stone close, she pushed through the door. A large stone room, lit by a few lamps lay before her. The floor in the room's middle, stained black and brown with the old blood of thousands of sacrifices, overlaid with the new blood of the man who was strung up from the ceiling. He had been at least half flayed, and his blood collected into a ritual vessel with four ports on it for the blood to flow into a pattern.

She knew this ritual, though it was ancient. The room appeared empty except for the corpse, but something else half-remembered came to her. The swaddled figure, the lack of talking, an Axessed! As if on cue a soft breath came from a back shadowed corner. A figure appeared, hunched over, but walking into the light. It was gray to white, scaled from head to toe. Its hands and feet clawed, but the claws were yellow with age. An ancient Axessed then.

42

Axessed were a creation of the old times. Ritual blood workings had created these man reptile creatures as special agents of the Scaled One. Believed to be creations made in the true image of Valnijz, only a very few had ever been born. They had abandoned the ritual after the war and the creation of the Valley. With the Valni now in existence, and far easier to be born and more of them, the need for the Axessed had dwindled and vanished. But, here stood one, and this thing had led the cult over the centuries, keep a small base of power for the Blood God alive.

"You are not one of mine." The Axessed whispered. Its voice was dry, old. "I will give your blood to my master."

"I think not Axessed." Zalkiniv grabbed her knife and slashed her forearm. The pain giving her working a clarity she had been missing. A cut this deep would need other blood to fix, but she doubted that she'd need to work for that after taking this cult over.

The Axessed paused, and she could imagine the thoughts, confused, unsure of how this young woman knew of him, and what she was doing.

"I am Zalkiniv, High Priest of our God. I am here on the behest of our master. A mission. And you will bow." Taking the blood, she ended her other workings, and with a burst of power, gave the working enough power to reach the Blood God. She wanted no doubts in the Axessed mind that she was who she said she was.

A mist formed around her, one of her blood, it shone wet and red in the flickering torchlight. A voice came from it, one she knew well. The familiar groans and screams of rage and pain echoed in its tones. "She speaks for me, do as she says. Her mission is most important. But know this, you have done well Axessed. Your reward will be great once I return."

The red mist fell, only a bit of it left wafting as the working had drained it of all life, all power.

The Axessed looked at her for a long moment, finally kneeling. "Forgive me. I had not known."

"You do well to beg forgiveness." Zalkiniv knew the only way to make this work was to make sure the creature knew she was in control. "But I will not harm you, not yet at least. We must talk of other things, and how you can help me."

The Axessed stood, his form silent. "How did you find us, why are you here in this place?"

"This is why." Zalkiniv held out her hand, the claret stone shone dark red in the middle. "You gave a man this stone and bought more like it. Where are they, and why did you not take them all back?"

The Axessed walked forward towards her, towering over her. She had forgotten how tall these things were.

"Where did you get that High Priest? I gave it to a man yesterday. His blood, it called to me, I did not understand it. I gave the stone as a test, to see what he would do." The Axessed started at the stone, unblinking.

"That was foolish. But lucky." Zalkiniv answered. It made sense of course. The blood gift that Duncan Reis carried had called out to this creature. But it did not understand what had happened or what had caused it.

"High Priest, how did you get the stone?" The creature would not take its eyes off the Claret.

"The boy, the human. He is part of my mission. His blood has been blessed by our master; the blade of the spear kissed him." She closed her hand around the stone, making the creature look away. "I have some control over the boy, he gave me the stone as a gift. I knew what it was, and I tracked its passage back to the shop above, and then, to here."

"The blade? Someone has found it?" The Axessed stood upright at this news, brushing its head on the ceiling.

"Yes. But our Master has not returned yet. I need one more human. The one you met and one other, also part of his bloodline, are descendants of the Forgemasters, of the Forgemaster, the one at the battle. Our lord has ordered me use both to return him to this world." Zalkiniv locked eyes with the creature. "You and your cult will help me."

The Axessed resumed its hunched position and kept its eyes on her. She knew it was deciding what to do. While the Axessed had been creations of the Priesthood, they had always had an independent streak. They loved the blood but didn't always fall into line. Unlike the Valni, which could be controlled with the right equipment and knowledge.

"Yes. We will help. The return of the Master comes before all." The Axessed reached under the altar and from some unseen cubby pulled out a small bag which he upended into its hands.

Zalkiniv let out a hiss at the sight of all the claret stones. That much power would make her impossible to stop. But she'd need a mighty working to bind them all to her. A working she did not have the time for, nor the blood for, yet.

"No, keep them for now. Too many questions might get asked." Zalkiniv walked around the dead suspended man in thought. "I will keep the one I have and bind it. That should give me the strength I need. It might even give me the strength to get to the other one our master wants."

"Where is this other one? Why have you not taken it?" the Axessed walked as well, circling opposite her, always keeping her in its gaze.

"He is in the Guild. There is potential he may become a Forgemaster, a turn of events the Blood God will not accept. But being in the Guild has presented problems." Zalkiniv pointed at the creature. "Do you know of a way to get in? To access that place?"

"No." The Axessed let out a sound reticent of a groan.

"Pity. Then the way forward is the way I've been on. Waiting for the foolish priest to find a way. But at least you can help me now, with this." She opened her hand again the claret stone dark red, near black in the dim light.

"Summon your followers. Now. The ritual will go faster, and I have limited time tonight." Zalkiniv Sat down on the blood stained and sticky floor, closing her eyes. For a moment she could almost be back where she belonged, back in the temple, back in the sacrificial chamber.

The sounds of the Axessed shuffling off to do her bidding brought a smile to her face. The creature was for now obeying her orders. An eye would have to be kept on the thing, but with no Valni here, it was an asset. And it had dropped an entire cult of worshippers in her lap. She did not understand how the thing could summon the cultists, but she didn't care.

On the edges of her senses, the blood of others appeared. The cultists must be massing. She was unsure how long she had been building the power for. She could feel the nervous energy in their blood, the unsure nature of their hearts. What had the Axessed told them? No matter, they would learn their true place, and the true power of the Blood God, tonight.

They filed into the room, not a sound being made. Good, the creature knew enough to keep them from bothering her at work. They stood, some excited, some nervous, two afraid, and one, one in abject terror. Good.

Eyes opened Zalkiniv stood. Dirty robes, stained black with blood and whatever else clad each worshiper. Old forms, but that was to be expected.

"I am Zalkiniv, High Priest of Valnijz, the Blood God, the Rage Incarnate, and the Scaled God of Destruction. And you are mine to do with as I please." Zalkiniv raised her knife to eye level, blade horizontal. Making a quick slice down her arm, she let her own blood drip onto the floor.

"I will claim your blood tonight. Each will give some, and one will give all. You will witness the Glory that the Blood god will bring to all who oppose him, and further the steps to bring about our Gods return!" Zalkiniv motioned the closest figure forward.

She took the arm of the figure and slashed it. Deep enough to draw forth a rich red of fresh blood, but not enough to damage anything. She only needed blood tonight; they might need other parts another time.

Each figure came forward, and to each she cut. Their blood fell but flowed toward her, mixing with her own. Rivulets of red, moving in ways no liquid should. She smiled at the ecstasy. She had missed this so. Each she could feel was worried about what she had said, about one giving all. And as she had planned the one soaked with terror was the most worried. A beautiful bouquet to her senses.

She worked the blood she had now, using it to start the binding. The Claret stone writhed her grasp. Holding the blood of thousands of ancient victims, concentrated down, the stone was in this moment a living thing. It gave off a beat, a counterpoint to her own heartbeat, her own blood.

She knew to use the stone she would have to force it to be in unison with her own. There was only one way. The knife was in her hand again, its edge still wet with the blood of those around her. She worked, for this was the most critical point. The full sacrifice would only work one way, the one given to the Blood God must be killed not by a knife, but by rage.

A slash through her hand between bones, sent a surge of pain through her, giving her working the edge she needed. "There!" she whispered, pointing with the skewered hand toward to one figure reeking of fear. Releasing her working the blood flowed, faster than a blink into each of the others assembled, even the Axessed.

The effect was immediate, and wonderful. Each of them erupted into wordless howls, anger, rage, as bloodlust took each one, and it directed all at the scared one. The figure stood, trying to make a break for the door, but that was a foolish gesture. The Axessed moved faster, and it blocked the door before two steps could be taken. The mob descended on the cloaked figure who gave forth a single scream, ending in a gurgle as one of the others ripped out the throat.

The Axessed joined in, reaching forth and ripping something out of the now dead figure. Bloodlust filled the room and a rising chorus of screams and rage joined in. At the moment of its height, when the room was about to descend into pure chaos, Zalkiniv spoke a word. And all froze.

She made her way around the now destroyed figure. Blood filled that part of the floor, blood and other parts. Taking the knife from her hand she plunged her damaged hand into what they left. Gripping the claret stone in the other she placed it on her own breast.

She threw open the working, taking in the last ebbing flows of blood of this death, given to the God of Blood and Rage. Everything slowed, and a tightness filled her chest before air flowed in. Beat, beat, beat... the Claret stone in rhythm with her own. She had done it. It was bound.

The stones' power flowed into her. They had concentrated each drop of ancient blood in the Claret stone. The memories, the potential of their lives, and what they had done before it had been cut short, all of it there for the taking. Each drop held the final scream of each victim. Exquisite.

She held the stone and worked through it to close her wounds. She was hungry, thirsty, but sitting with more power than she could have believed. Holding the knife once more, she released the word that held the others. The rage was spent now, and each stood unsure of what had happened. She could feel their confusion but said nothing.

The Axessed knew though, and she locked its gaze. Unblinking it stared back at her. Its feelings were mixed. Anger? Disappointment? Envy? Its blood was hard to read. But it knew what she wanted, and it gave a whisper of some word, and the cult members left, leaving trails of blood behind them.

The Axessed itself bowed low and started to leave.

"I did not give you leave yet. I have one final question. How did the stones get to where the human I am with found them? They are valuable artifacts." Zalkiniv pointed the knife at the creature. "How did they get there?"

The Axessed stood straight, towering over her. She felt no fear of this creature, and it knew it. "I placed it there High Priest. His blood, it called to me, and sang to me, as the stones do. I needed to know why, and what was different about that piece of flesh." The Axessed crouched down, kneeling.

Zalkiniv gave a tight-lipped smile. "That is a poor choice. These stones are more powerful than you can imagine. If they had been lost due to your failure…" Zalkiniv smiled for a moment and pulled her knife free once more. Through the claret stone she worked, and the blade glowed red to white hot. The Axessed, to its credit, didn't move though a spike of worry clear enough to be read shone through its blood.

She pressed the knife against its left eye, the scaled being giving a scream, hissing with the sound of blood streaming from what she left of its eye. "Never place the sacred items of our Master in danger, do you understand me?" Zalkiniv removed the knife from the eye. The blade was cool now, and the creature's blood was bound in the blade.

The Axessed nodded, its head down. She could feel its hate and anger now, they must be strong. It feared her more than it hated her, *at least for now*. Perfect. If it stayed in line, it was useful.

Without a word, she left the room, walking back toward the ladder and the shack. She had bound the claret stone, she had a group of cultists to use, and an Axessed to use. Tonight, could not have gone better if she tried.

43

Will was bored. After his encounter with his ancestor, the last Forgemaster, he'd been full of fire and ready to go. But as the days stretched on, the luster had faded. He was learning things, but not quite in the way he had expected.

Smithing classes didn't challenge him. He'd picked up a few new techniques, refined his hammer technique, and at least in that aspect of things he was still the top of the current class. In truth, about every Master Smith he'd worked with praised his work and his work ethic. That was not the problem.

The problem was the other classes. The political classes, the etiquette classes, the "how to deal with rich nobles who want to hire you" classes. He hated those. But here he was being lectured about how to get the best payment out of a noble for what should have been a simple smithing job that wouldn't take more than a week to make. Demanding payment upfront, asking for what to Will was an exorbitant sum.

He hated it. What made it worse, the former Journeyman, now Master Regin, taught one. Regin wasn't fond of Will and liked to put him on the spot every time he could. If a question came up, he'd always have Will try to answer it first, and then, if Will got it wrong, he'd point out how bad his answer was.

Regin took great delight in this. *He's a petty man.* Will would tell himself, but that didn't make the class easier. Other students wanted to know why young Master Regin had it in for Will. Rumors swirled about it. Regin and Markin had gotten into a fist fight on the road. No, they had grown up together and Regin was the better of the two and Markin resented it. No, they had both been after a girl, and she'd gone with Regin, no Markin. Myriam also tried to quell the rumors, but that just started more rumors over her.

Will had considered getting the real story out there more than once. *He simply doesn't like me because I'm better than he expected.* That was the truth, but it was such a dull answer, the rumor mill would never believe it. The rumors made for drama, and for a place like the Smithing Guild, drama of any kind made for good gossip. So, the stories and rumors continued and swirled.

He wanted more forge time, he wanted to create, to help others, and not sit and listen to a lecture on metal fatigue, when he could tell more about the stresses metal go through than almost any Master in the building.

He'd perked up in a Smithing class with Master Greenmar one day when the subject of the Reach came up. Greenmar had been accurate in his descriptions of the Reach, and what it provided to the Guild. And he'd cut down an Apprentice who had made a rather disparaging remark about miners. But other than that, it was dull. *After all that trial, all that trouble, I'm here, and I'm bored.*

Will found himself, alone again, in the Anvil room. He liked it here. It was almost always empty, and it helped him refocus. He'd study the Anvil itself, how it was made, what it was made of, even the minute etchings he'd missed and not seen the first time he'd been here. He'd rest his hand on the thing and swear he could hear hammer blows, and the sounds of the bellows working in the distance.

"Markin Darto. There you are." A feminine voice broke his recollection. Myriam walked in with a smile on her face, looking happy. *Hopefully the smile was for him.* He was happy to see her as well. More than once over the three months she had expressed some annoyance with his slow-paced romance. Nothing aloud of course, at least not to him. But the occasional tighter lipped smile as he begged off spending time together, or the eye roll as he always insisted in studying in the packed areas, and never alone with her in a small study room.

Will liked her, a lot. At least he thought he did, he found her, confusing. He kept expecting her to decide to stop expressing her interest, but she never did. This both made him rather happy and confused him.

"Myriam. Good to see you! Are you looking for me? Why?" Will stood from the chair he'd been resting in and turned toward her. *Calm down.* Her smile still made his face break into one in response.

"I was looking for you, Markin, because I have a problem. And you kind sir, may be able to help me." Myriam tossed her hair, exaggerating her motions, and gave him a fake pouty look.

"What can I do for you, fair maiden blacksmith?" Will had to smile at her antics.

"You good sir, must help me with Master Frondigs class. I can't keep the different folding patterns straight in my head. You do it without effort while I on the other hand get double up v patterns mixed up with a crossbar." Getting down on one knee Myriam held up her hands in supplication. "Teach me oh wise one the ways to metal fold!"

Will's laugh escaped him. "Ah Myriam, you make things fun. Sure, I can help." He'd been doing folding patterns since he was old enough to hold a hammer.

"And I'm hungry, so teach me as we go to the kitchens and get something to eat at the same time." Myriam jumped up and helped Will out of his seat.

"Yes, food sounds good." Will opened the door to the main hall with a bow. "After you my good lady."

As they walked down the hall Will explained his method of remembering the patterns. There were only so many patterns people wanted. There were a few off the wall ones, the circles were cracked-iron hard to do, but no one liked them much. By the time they got to the kitchen Myriam had at least made a way to remember them by.

"Now we feast!" she announced as they entered the kitchens.

One thing Will liked about the Guild, even during off dining hours, there was a kitchen/pantry for each guild group. Masters had their own, Journeymen as well, and of course, Apprentices. Rumors were that the Masters food was expensive and rich stuff, roasts from the grasslands, rare wines from the south, and spices from all over the world.

The new students were not so lucky. Will found the food of good quality, and good quantity. Better heeled Apprentices complained, but they always did. To him it was good.

"So Markin, let's eat! How about I make a specialty of my home, and you from yours? I've had nothing from Dernstown before. On the road you always just went along with whatever I made." Myriam searched through cabinets for ingredients.

A surge of panic flew up his spine. Sparks aflame, what had Master Jaste told him about food in Dernstown? No one had asked him about it before.

"Um yes, sure." Will searched through food stuffs, including the cold box, trying to remember lessons from months ago on a rickety cart. Garlic, ah, he could make Klah, if that hadn't been from the Reach!

"I'm making a chicken dish, my Da made it all the time." Myriam was busy mixing spices into something. "You know, cooking isn't that different from Smithing. Add the right ingredients, the correct amount of heat, use the right tools, and there you go!"

Will nodded. The only thing he could think to make was Klah. That was it. His mind had gone blank, and that was the only thing he could think of. Could he make it and play it off as a Dernstown thing? And who knows if they ate Klah in Dernstown? Not that far from the Reach on the other side of the mountains, so who knew, could be they ate a ton of Klah there.

Will didn't feel the confidence he was trying to give himself. But he had to do something, right? He could make nothing, and make Myriam wonder why, or make Klah and try to play it off. Klah it was.

"Oh Yeah I see your point." Will answered back, aware of the long silence while he tried to figure out what to do.

"What are you making?" Myriam had returned to her work, and the smell of chicken fat filled the air.

"It's a side dish, eaten a lot with other dishes, I figured it might go well with your dish. It's called..." Will gulped. "Klah"

"Klah? Sounds strange. But make away!" her voice didn't give sign to any knowledge of the stuff at least.

Will grabbed the garlic and a few other things he would need, and a large loaf of bread, square. Garlic, oil, seasoning, a few other ingredients went into a nearby mortar and pestle and were ground up into a thick paste. Will cut four large thick slices of bread and put it all down on the table in the corner. "There, done."

Myriam laughed. "Don't go through any effort for me." She was still cooking though she appeared near the end.

She placed her dish on the table and took a long sniff of the Klah. "Gah strong stuff you Dernstowners eat. Good thing I'm not being courted, I'd drive off any suitors with my breath after this."

Will flushed, he knew where that comment came from. But he had a mission, something far more important than a date. *When everything was over, and if he was still alive, I might just have to come and find her.*

Still alive. He'd never considered the thought he might not make it out of all this alive. If the High Priest of Amder found him, he was most likely dead. If Valnijz returned, there was no way any of them would survive.

"Hey Markin? You ok? Looking a little pale there." Myriam waved her hand in from of his face.

"Yes sorry, remembering something." Will tried to calm himself. He had no appetite now, but he forced himself to sit. "Looks good."

"Thanks!" Myriam cheerful nature didn't lighten his feelings.

"So, try this! Chicken with a mustard pepper sauce. It's a little spicy, but not bad." Myriam trailed off as Will took a bite. Almost at once his throat tried to force itself closed to save it from the heat his mouth was feeling. A bit spicy?

Will stood, looking for something to drink, anything. Swallowing he blew out a long breath and sucked in cool air. Cool, anything cool.

"Did you like it?" Myriam was busy munching on her chicken, not even appearing to notice the heat.

Will found a clean looking, though at this moment he didn't care much, mug and filled it with water from a nearby large cask, drinking it down. Followed by another. Sparks above, it was like someone had thrust a red-hot piece of forge clinker down his throat. He liked strong flavor, but Reachers liked Garlic and Onions, not whatever flame inducing peppers Myriam had used. "Yes, it's nice." He managed to say before his mouth filled with spit, trying to quench the flames.

"Good! I'm glad. Here, let me try this Klah? You called it?" Myriam smeared a large amount on a hunk of bread and took a large bite. "Wow, this is pretty good." She took another bite and threw Will a thumbs up.

"Glad you liked it" Will managed to say, still blinking tears and sweat away. He smeared some Klah on bread as well and took a bite. If he closed his eyes, he could imagine he was eating lunch by a forge somewhere in the Reach, helping a neighbor, or doing a short-term job. That was if the lingering burning in his mouth didn't tell him otherwise.

They ate the rest of the meal in silence though Will tried more than once to talk. The sauce she had made things too hot for him to think.

A series of short chimes sounded, marking off the time, reverberating through pipes placed throughout the Guild.

"Oops, that's my sign, have to go, meeting some others to study the lineage of Western Bantin. Want to come?" Myriam asked, then took once last large bite of Klah laced bread, this time swiped through that fire-starting sauce she had made!

"No thanks. I'll pass tonight." Lineage of nobles, not a fun way to spend time.

"Ok. I'll look for you later." Myriam gave a nod and left, leaving Will to his thoughts. He cleaned up, putting the leftovers in the cold box for anyone else who might want them. Let someone else enjoy the heat of that dish of Myriam's!

44

Will awoke with pain, which based on what he had eaten last night, wasn't a huge surprise. Still, a quick wash of his face and he started to feel better until that he remembered what day it was. He had a class with Master Regin today. *Jumped up, self-important, Master Regin.*

Master Regin's class, "Noble Houses and Pricing Structures" was the first thing for the day. Will got there early, so he could grab the seat farthest from the former Journeyman. Regin was always late, and there was one seat that couldn't be seen from where he entered.

Having claimed his chair, Will put his head down in his arms, still not feeling totally better. Over time the rest of the class filed in, in ones or twos. Will didn't know most, first names on those, but nothing else. A few had tried friendly overtures at first, but he'd turned them all down. It just safer that way. For them and himself.

"Class." Master Regin's voice interrupted Will's rest, and he raised his head, trying to hide his reactions to his man.

"Good Morning Master Regin." Everyone answered in unison. It was a stupid thing, and no other Master required or even asked for. But Regin had demanded it the first day. *He just likes hearing his name with the word Master.* Will's thoughts were sour.

"So, pricing structures of the Eastern Dukedoms. For a minor lord, landed, can someone give me the breakdown on say, a dozen ornamented parade spears?" Regin launched into his normal question-and-answer style, asking Apprentices questions and tearing apart even the slightest flaw in their answer.

Will was glad for his seat; he'd have to get here early more often. By now Regin would stand next to his chair and poking holes in anything he said. Back here, Regin pretty much ignored him so far.

"Markin?" Regin's voice asked from beside his chair.

Sparks alight. Will felt annoyance rise with himself, he'd not been paying attention, and once again, Regin was here to bother him.

"Yes, Master Regin?" Will answered but kept his head down at first but raised his head to make eye contact. Regin would dock his answer if he didn't.

Master Regin looked at him with an odd expression for a moment as if he was trying to figure something out.

"Apprentice Darto, please compare the goods of the Eastern Dukedoms and the Merchants Alliance of Ture and give me a fair trade for each for say, 50 daggers. Each made of Steel with Goldlace etching." Master Regin took a large breath and held it, staring at Will.

Will rattled off a good guess which he was sure Master Regin would tear apart. But still the look on Regin's face didn't change. Was the man trying to stare a hole through Will's skull?

Odder still after Will finished his answer Master Regin looked at him again and sniffed! No traditional pointing out how wrong he was on everything. Strange.

The class ended and Will along with everyone else got up to leave, but Master Regin got up and left quicker than they did. One last look at Will and was out the door. His dark blue Masters Cape flowing behind him.

Will was glad to be out of the class, but why had Regin acted that way? It was odd, and odd could be dangerous. Before he could think on it more, he spotted Myriam looking for him.

"Markin!" Myriam ran up to him. "Thanks again so much for your help with the folding patterns. Aced three questions today in class and made a fairly decent double x pattern. Master Trikin was actually complimentary."

"Good! I'm glad I helped, but I'm sure you would've gotten it without me." Will bowed, continuing the game from yesterday.

"Never good sir. As a reward, you must accompany me in a walk through the main courtyard garden!" Myriam grabbed his arm and hand, leading him onward.

For a moment Will wanted to pull his hand away, and find an excuse to go elsewhere, alone. But for once he let her lead the way, the proper choice to make her happy it appeared as she looked back with such a grin that he laughed out loud.

The courtyard garden was a maze, large plantings and hedges, the exact sort of place young Apprentices go when they didn't want to be seen, or disturbed. Will knew why she had led him here, and finally for once, he didn't fight it. *This is just going to cause more pain, when she learns the truth.* Will silenced the voice and as they walked, unseen by all through an archway of blue flowers, he pulled Myriam to the side, and kissed her.

***

Haltim read the note in his hand again, not believing what he was reading. An old contact would get a note into the guild! This would put Duncan at ease. He had been fighting some doubt himself, and only the presence of the bracer on his wrist had kept the worst of those feelings at bay.

Rache had come in late last night, from wherever she had gone after her and Duncan had talked. Haltim still hadn't seen this gem Duncan had given her. Duncan should be up by now, even with those dreams. The stairs made their normal noise as he climbed them. He'd mentioned it to Bessim once, but she pointed out that it was near impossible for anyone to sneak into the place and rob anyone upstairs with the noise.

Duncan's room was dark, but he could hear a stirring inside as he listened at the door.

Haltim gave a single knock before opening the door, pushing it open. Duncan was in bed still, and one look made Haltim rush towards the lad. Sweat was all over his face, as the skin of his face was red, and cast into a grimace as he writhed in bed. Another one of those nightmares?

"Duncan!" Haltim reached for the young man, not thinking about the Blood Curse, but helping his young friend. Duncan's eyes opened, and a grin came across his face. A grin not of joy, but of insanity. His hands grabbed Haltims shirt and face, squeezing his head tight. Pain bloomed, and Haltim let out a gasp.

"Duncan, stop!" Haltim managed to say as he felt something in his jaw go POP! With another flash of pain.

But Duncan's face didn't change, anger and rage writ large. Flailing now Haltim tried to grab something, anything that he could use to hit Duncan to shock him from his dream locked anger. With a burst of heat on his arm, he knew what he should do.

He took the bracer covered arm, and as hard as he could hit his sleeping attacker, right between the eyes.

The effect was sudden. The sound of hot metal hitting flesh, that tiny sizzle and the hands released, grasping at the air. Haltim forced himself back, moving his jaw in pain but otherwise undamaged. Duncan thrashed around on the bed, in an agony of some nature, as his back arched, and hands grabbed the sheets.

Then like quenching a red-hot metal bar, he relaxed, and the rage leaked out of him. The normal color of his face returned, his mouth relaxed, and like that, he was sleeping.

"Duncan?" Haltim whispered again, the pain in his jaw still there, but he was at least able to speak.

The lad's eyes opened, and he half sat up, wiping the sweat off his face. He saw Haltim and knew immediately what had happened.

"By the sparks Haltim, what did I do? Did I hurt you?" The young man sat all the way up, wiping his face again, this time with the sheet he was wrapped in.

"It's fine lad. Are you ok?" Haltim didn't want to bother him. His hands still trembled, as he choked back the nausea that nearly made him sick. He had been sure he was going to die for a moment, until Amder had reminded him of the gift he carried on his arm. The lad didn't need to know that though.

"The dreams Haltim. They were worse than ever. And the Cloud I took last night, did nothing. I had taken a half dose." Duncan shuddered. "I was ripping the skin off people's faces in the dream, I was doing horrible things, blood everywhere, body parts ... And I loved it, I wanted even more."

Haltim watched as Duncan began to cry. He wished he could remove the curse, remove the Rage Gods taint from this young man. But the only one who could would be Amder himself, and nothing would ever happen in that direction if William died. Haltim also knew that if Duncan died with this Curse still laid upon him, what would happen to his soul was an open question.

"Hush Lad, and I'd advise not to take more Cloud. You remember what happened to your Uncle ... he took so much he was lost to the sky. I'll see if I can come up with a better plan." Haltim knew there wasn't one, but he could at least try to help the lad feel better. Hope was a powerful force.

"You think I want to take it? I hate it Haltim. I *HATE* it. It took my Uncle, and then, because he had to go look for him, my own father. I hate every drop, every vial I see. But I can't handle the dreams without it. It's getting worse every day. Every day I wake up wondering if this is the day, I lose control, and kill someone, or more than one." Duncan shuddered as memories overwhelmed him. His breath caught for a hitch as he wiped off his tears. "Yesterday I saw a fist fight, two idiots, and taking swings out on the street. And you know what? The moment one started to bleed? I got aroused Haltim. *AROUSED*." Duncan slipped off then, skin flushed, but silent.

"I can't imagine that Duncan. I can't. But look here, I came to give you good news." Haltim held out the note that had been delivered this morning.

Duncan looked at it. "Who is Garon?"

Haltim laughed for a second. "That's my late brother's name. I've been using it as I try to find people to help us. I can't very well use Haltim." By the sparks his jaw hurt.

"So, what's it say?" Duncan didn't take the note. Haltim hoped the message would cheer him up some.

"It's from an old contact, who has agreed to slip a note to William! We can get him a message!" the words rushed out of Haltim's mouth.

A spark of excitement touched Duncan. "Finally!!" And he smiled.

"Yes, come downstairs after you've cleaned up, and we will figure out what we need to say. It will have to be short, something that can be hid. The Guild is rather stringent on their rules." Haltim made to leave the room but Duncan stopped him.

"Haltim, what do you mean late brother? Brother as in fellow Priest, or, like a real brother?"

"Real brother," Haltim said, his voice lower. *I never told them about Garon.*

"What happened? You never mentioned him before." Duncan's voice came from behind him.

"I know. Garon was, well, Garon. He was younger than I by a few years. Three to be exact. He vanished one day in Ture. We grew up about eleven or twelve blocks from here. Not rich, above being poor. Garon was always looking for ways to make money. Reminds me of you in some ways, with your scaving back in the Reach." Haltim could feel the throb in his jaw still, but ignored it, thinking back to those horrible dark days.

"One morning he swore he had found something valuable. He wouldn't show it to me, or our parents. He would sell it, find a merchant who wouldn't ask questions, and sell it. We'd have money for days. He wouldn't even tell me what it was, said he'd found it in a house. Garon was part of one of those city of Ture groups that keep houses from falling apart. Unlike Mucking, finding stuff in the houses is rare, very rare. At least anything valuable."

"He left and was never seen again. We searched for him for days. Our parents spent all the money they had trying to find him, and we ended up living in a house like Garon had been fixing. I actually joined the Priesthood because of it."

"So, trust me, while Will is your cousin and not a brother, he's like one to you I know. I know what it's like to lose family." Haltim turned back to Duncan, who was watching him with no expression. "I won't have you go through that."

Duncan said nothing, just nodded in return.

"Ok, enough of that. Get dressed and come down. I'll be waiting." Haltim exited and all Duncan could hear was his footfalls.

45

Zalkiniv's head hurt. Everything had been going as planned. With the power of the Claret stone now bound to her, she had taken control of the Blood in Duncan's body and tore through whatever barrier that thrice-cursed drug was doing. This time with the additional power she'd been able to watch his dreams and had reveled in the sheer brutality.

They would need his blood to bring her Lord back and watching him suffer was fun. But watching him tear apart her foes outside a dream would be intoxicating. She could always make a new blood blessed toy, after her Master was reborn.

She'd even watched as that old Priest had entered the room, and her plaything had attacked him. It was perfect! Duncan would rid her of the old Priest right now! She'd find a different way to get into the guild, using the cult and the other stones. The pleasure of the coming kill had made her moan. Until the Amderite had entered done something.

A flash of heat, so hot that she could feel it herself had struck Duncan, breaking the link between her and the Blood. She wasn't sure what it was, but it had come from something on the Priest's wrist. He always wore long-sleeved shirts, or robes, was that why? He wanted no one to see what was there?

The break had been sudden, then the pain had come. Pain didn't bother her; she's experienced enough of it to be able to ignore it. But the control snapping like that made her thoughts muddled, and the storm in her own blood, arousal, pain, confusion, made it hard to plan what to do.

Why Haltim had been in the room to wake Duncan was unknown but it must have been something important. She needed to find out what exactly had broken her control of his Blood. She doubted it was permanent, more like shears cutting though cloth, one and done. If he did it once, he could do it again.

Her stomach lurched again for a moment, but Zalkiniv's iron will kept everything in check. Enough! She was the High Priest of the Blood God, and whatever body she wore would listen to her. Standing, she splashed some water in her face and checked the mirrored metal sheet in the room. There! On her forehead, the slightest hint of a mark.

What had the Amderite done! She had put the fool down as a weak idiot, like all followers of the Forge. Weak and slow. But... she needed to reevaluate. If he could break the link between her and the Blood that was a serious threat. Another splash of water cleared the mark.

Someone drew her attention to the stairs outside, Duncan. She could hear and feel him going down the stairs, in a hurry by the sound. His blood was still flowing with the remnants of her workings, drawing her back in.

"Not now. Soon." Zalkiniv whispered to the empty room. Time to be Rache and find out what the Priest needed.

***

Duncan could still feel the echoes of both the dream and whatever had ended it. The faint hints of anger tinged the fading images of death and blood, and somehow the echoes of a forge beat in counterpoint. It made it head hurt. He had tried to kill Haltim! He hadn't been himself, but still, there had been a moment... No, he was better than that, it was the blood curse. The Taint was getting stronger, somehow. But Haltim, killing him? Had he already sunk that far? Was he doomed to this forever? Living on the edge of killing or hurting those he cared about?

If Haltim had a way to contact Will, to get a message to his cousin, then maybe he could get out of Ture, get free, and go somewhere alone, where he couldn't hurt anyone. Live like a hermit in the mountains and go back to scaving, only go back to the Reach to sell and get supplies. Stay away from everyone.

It wasn't a great plan, but it was the only idea he had. There was no cure, and the Cloud wasn't doing it anymore. Haltim was right though, taking more Cloud was as big a risk. He could still remember the look on his Uncles face, Will's father. He'd taken two or three full doses of Cloud, at least that's how many empty vials had been left on the ground near the chair he'd gotten up from. When he had gotten up and walked away, into the Skyreach, and never seen again.

They'd been empty eyes. Dead eyes. No feeling, no memories, no caring, no sorrow, no love. Empty. He'd 'gone to the sky' as Cloud addicts say. Taken so much and all feeling was gone, all emotion, all thought. And he'd wandered off to die, free of his pain, free of anything.

Duncan had no intention of dying. So, more and more Cloud wasn't the answer. But nor could he live his life with others. He'd hurt them in the end. Even William. But for now, he had to do whatever it took to get a message to Will. That had been the whole point of coming to this place, and by the sparks he was going to get something good out of this.

Haltim was sitting at a small side desk, ink and writing needle on the table.

"Haltim" Duncan called out to break the Priest's concentration. Haltim had been sitting there staring at the paper, sighing.

"Ah Duncan. Glad you came down." Haltim waved him to a nearby seat. Duncan could still see a red mark down the side of the face from before and felt a flash of guilt. He knew that there was nothing he could have done, but still, Haltim didn't deserve that.

"Ok, why? Who's this person who has agreed to help us? You said an old contact? Friend, I assume?" Duncan pulled up his chair to the same table. "You trust this person?"

"Trust? Yes. Her name is Faranir. She's one of the Forgekeepers." Haltim waved off into the air "But she's not important. What is important is getting a short message to Will that says exactly what we need it to say, that fits on this small piece of paper!" Haltims voice rose as he spoke.

"Why only on this paper?" Duncan didn't get it. "And what's a Forgekeeper?"

Haltim shook his head and sighed. "I forget you and your cousin don't know this sort of thing. Forgekeepers are servants who work in the Guildhall and the Temple. Cooks, servers, cleaners, that thing. Faranir is one. I know her from my days here, there's a lot of overlap with the Priesthood and the Guild for those jobs. As for why this paper, because whatever she brings in must be small. If she gets caught, it's the end of her work, and depending on who finds her, more."

Duncan nodded. It sounded unreal him, but everything about Ture was crazy to him. If one thing this time in the Capital had shown him, he didn't like people that much. Give him the

Reach any day of the week against this mess of backstabbing, secrets, heat and sweat. But he was here, and their goal was in sight.

"Ok, so warn him about the High Priest. Tell him his life is in danger that the High Priest is looking for him." Duncan shrugged. "Doesn't look that difficult."

Haltim shook his head. "If it was that simple, I wouldn't have asked for your help." Haltim looked around the boarding house for a moment. "I'm just worried that if anything arouses suspicion, the message could get tracked back to us, and then we'd be in real trouble."

Duncan snorted. "I don't know, we've done a decent job so far."

Haltim picked up the writing needle. Long metal and sharpened at one end to a slanting point, it shone in the sunlight. "See this? It's a simple writing needle. Dip the sharp end in the ink, then write away. Simple, easy, no fuss. This same writing needle, in the hands of a trained member of the Tempered? Pain, agony, and you'd give anything to make it stop. Trust me, the High Priest would send every tool he had to find us." He threw the needle on the table.

Duncan picked up the needle off the table and looked at it. What could they say to Will that would make sense? His cousin wasn't stupid, but William had always been weak with subterfuge. "I know what to say!" Duncan blurted out.

Haltim grinned "I knew you'd figure it out lad!" He took the needle again, dipped it in the ink and was ready... Poised.

Duncan thought for a moment. "Markin, bandits on the trials again. Grandfather is staying with me, moved to Ture, we needed to get off the road, Travelers rest."

Haltim wrote each word. "I don't get it."

"It was there right back there, where those bandits attacked us, the ones that I... Defeated. You're Grandfather. He'll get it. I'm stretching with the Travelers rest, but I'm hoping Will can understand that part." Duncan shrugged.

"Don't you want to add anything?" Haltim looked at the words on the page. "Have room."

"No. Will would worry more. He can barely keep from worrying most days." Duncan eyed the paper. "I hope that works."

Haltim nodded. "I as well. I need to get this to Faranir. Now. The sooner I get it to her, the sooner it can get to Will."

Duncan watched as Haltim cleaned up the writing supplies and made to leave. "Wait... Haltim. What you said about the needle. You were a member of the Tempered, did you do anything like that? Do you know how to do things like that?"

Haltim said nothing, a ghost of a sad smile crossed his face and he left, carrying the note, and the answer to their long wait.

46

Regin wrapped his cloak around himself, the dark blue of the Masters cloak made the few people out and about in this section of Ture move out of his way without a word. He needed the speed of travel which the cloak gave him. He walked through checkpoints and guard stations as he got closer to the Holy Forge, the Seat of the Church of Amder. No city guard would dare stop him.

He had the bastards now. Jaste and that Markin Darto. Maybe even that Myriam girl, though maybe not. Jaste and Markin had been so damn superior on the trip, and Markin had been less than deferential to him, a senior Journeyman. Regin was a Master now, and he was sure of his suspicions.

There was no way some stonemason from Dernstown knew that much about smithing. Jaste had sent him on ahead so Regin couldn't investigate more, and he had even sent him away when they were on the road. He'd been suspicious even then, Master Jaste sending him away on purpose? Jaste had broken one of the cardinal rules. Whoever Markin Darto was, he wasn't from Dernstown. He was a Reacher.

A Reacher. Jaste had always been less than strict on the rules. A known quantity, his lack of subservience to the Church had raised concern before. But this, this was large enough to have him decloaked and turned over to the Tempered. And Markin, if that was even his name, they would hand over to the Tempered as well.

He'd had no proof though. Only suspicions, until class. Regin smelled it on Markin as soon as he got close by. *He'd known that smell.* He'd searched through the Apprentice kitchen right after, finding the small jar of the stuff, even labeled! Regin had brought a sample of Markin's handwriting. They matched. *Klah.* The smell was undeniable.

Approaching the final set of gates, Regin bowed low before them, and the four guards dressed in Silverlace chased red steel armor. Beautiful and crafted with the full might of the Guild. Better still it had been blessed by the Priests. No one was sure what blessings the Priesthood had given upon it, but it was sure to be many, and powerful.

"Guildmaster, what is your business?" One armored figure spoke, his face unseen and unknown.

"Audience with the High Priest, I have news." Regin kept his head down.

"Enter. The High Priest is waiting for you." The figure stepped to one side to let him through.

Regin had met the High Priest more than once, and as the newest Guildmaster, had only just seen him at his own cloaking. Regin liked the man. He knew that some older GuildMasters and even Priests didn't. They didn't see that the Priesthood needed a strong hand, and the Guild was one finger of that hand. Ready to do whatever was needed to promote and glorify the church of Amder, and the Guild along with it. *And get rich doing it.*

The doors swung open to the main hall of the Church. Embossed and decorated, the glints of metalwork and red gems shone from the ceiling. The Pews were empty as always, but clean. No one came here to worship, why worship a dead God? But they kept up appearances, it was good for the common folk's morale.

Regin made his way to a side door where another two guards stood. They also stepped aside as he approached, the High Priest must have sent word. The faint pink red light flickered down the hallway as he entered. *What was that?*

And there, in a round chamber, it was. Floating a few feet off the ground, looking like nothing more than a huge chunk of pink and red tinged crystal at first glance, and the pattern of its shape and lines of goldlace gave it the form of a heart.

"Master Regin Hamsand, why do you come here now, and demanding to see me?" High Priest Bracin Monsteen walked into the room, his bulky frame made all the larger by the robes he wore.

Regin went down to one knee and bowed his head. "Forgive my High Priest, but I have something of import. But High Priest, what is that?" Regin turned to the floating rock. "I feel as if I should know what it is, and the feelings it gives…"

"Ah. Guildmaster Regin that is the Heart. The Heart of Amder to be precise. The source of all our power, all our wealth." Bracin's face was lit by the glow, looking more rapacious than usual to Regin. "Consider it an honor for you to even see the Heart, very few Guild members ever do."

Regin didn't know what to say. *The Heart of Amder? This was how the Priesthood did what they did?* While Regin liked to think he was a practical man, this seemed, wrong. And why show this to him? A brand-new Master? He lowered his eyes; something was wrong here.

"A newly minted Master of the Guild has information for me? Doubtful." Bracin stopped, and Regin looked up. The man was standing in front of the heart, a calculating look upon his face as the Heart shone brighter and the pulsed faster the closer the High Priest got to it. "Well Master Regin? I have much to do, and far more important people than you to meet with."

Regin stood. "High Priest, it's about a new Apprentice in the guild. I have reason and evidence he's not who he says he is, nor where he's from."

Regin watched as the High Priest's eyebrow arched, and the skin on his forehead folded up. "This is why you asked to see me? This minor matter? I had pegged you at one point as a Master of the Guild with some promise, but this? You've wasted my time Regin, and that's a bad thing for anyone, even a master of the guild."

Regin heard a soft rustle and saw two cloaked figures in the shadows he hadn't seen before. The robes, black with orange and red threads, the robes of the Tempered. Regin felt the blood drain from his face.

"No, High Priest, you're not understanding." Regin blurted out before shutting his mouth.

"I'm not understanding?" High Priest Bracin pointed a chubby finger at Regin. "You waste my time, and now you insult me?"

Master Regin threw himself down and bowed his head. "I meant I didn't explain it well, the Apprentice, he's a Reacher! A Reacher in the Guild! I don't know his real name yet, but he IS a Reacher. I know the ban on Reachers in the guild is absolute, and I know the Priesthood set the ban, so I came here."

Regin heard the footsteps of Bracin and saw the boots in front of him, but he dared not raise his head. Clean boots, made from rare black leather from the north. Some kind of barking fish or some nonsense. Regin knew how much things like that cost.

"Master Regin, stand." Bracins voice, moments before full of anger, was calm now.

Regin stood and watched as the High Priest examined him. "Master Regin, let me be clear. You say that a Reacher, has somehow made it into the Guild? How could that be possible? You will tell me everything, and you will tell me now."

Regin swallowed. His eyes flicked to the two Tempered cloaked figures, the light of the Heart only barely illuminating their robes. "Yes, High Priest."

Regin launched into his idea, how Markin Darto knew too much, how his entrance had been handled. How Master Jaste had kept him away from the Potential when they were traveling, and how he'd smelled Klah on the student. The High Priest said nothing, only giving the slightest of nods.

"So, you're claiming a Markin Darto, who claims to be from Dernstown, is in fact from the Reach. And that you're former Master, Jaste Noam, conspired to get a Reacher into the guild by creating a fake identity, and keeping you away so you wouldn't get suspicious. Adding in the knowledge of this student, and the finding of Klah?" Bracin crossed his arms waiting for Regin to respond.

Regin knew his idea was only that, but he felt it had to be true, there wasn't anything else that it could be. "Yes, High Priest." Regin kept a straight face and tried not to look at the Tempered.

Bracin stood still for a while, then turned to the Heart. "Do you see this Heart Regin? This heart, a Heart of an actual God, is the keystone to all the power we have. All the power of the Priesthood, and the Guild. Without it, we wouldn't even exist. The Guild might, but you'd be no better than Potters or Carpenters. You'd not have the power, or the money, or even the influence you have."

"I will tell you something Master Regin. I will tell you because from this moment on one of two things will happen to you. Either your information is correct, and you will be elevated, and you will have a debt of gratitude from me, or you will be turned over to my associates, and no one will ever see you again." Bracin reached out and his fingers touched the Heart.

Regin watched in amazement as the heart turned dark where Bracins fingers touched it as if the essence in the Heart ran away from the man. From the High Priest?

"You see Regin, there're things here that you aren't aware of. Do you know WHY we say no Reachers in the Guild? I doubt it, few know the truth." Bracin smirked at the dark area, then removed his hand watching the light return to that section.

"No High Priest." Regin didn't know. And, who cared? *Reachers were dirty rock grubbers. Who cared about a bunch of backward Miners?*

"Have you ever heard of the Forgemasters? That order created by Amder to help the less fortunate?" Bracin stuck his finger out and touched the heart again, removing it after the light faded away from his finger, as if he were playing a game.

"Yes, but they all died long ago." Regin had heard of them but discounted the stories. There had never been many of them, and it had been centuries since any were around.

"The Lead Forgemaster was, at the time of the Fall, a man named Reis. This man was the one who Amder bonded with, or in some ancient accounts welded himself into to take physical form the day he and the Rage God fought. He was a Reacher." Bracin turned away from his game with the Heart.

"His bloodline, his descendants exist to this day. And none of them can ever be trained in the Guild. None. Ever. If they did, there is a chance, a small one, but still a chance they could become a Forgemaster. And if so, could in fact end the power that the Priesthood has, and of course, the Guild." Bracin reached out and placed his hand, soft and heavy on Regin's shoulder.

"You Master Regin wouldn't want that would you?" the High Priest asked his eyes locked into Regin's own.

"I'm not sure I understand. How could that happen?" The story confused Regin but wanted to know more.

"Because Regin, a Forgemaster, could, if given access to the right tools, and to the right materials..." Bracins hand rose from his shoulder and with a speed that the man's bulk denied, slapped Regin hard. Blackness quivered on the edge of Regin's vision, pain made him gasp as he went down. A Guild Master Smith he was a strong man, he had to be. But this blow was far stronger than he expected.

"A Forgemaster *COULD BRING AMDER BACK TO LIFE!*" Bracin roared at Regin. "*DO YOU GET IT NOW YOU THICK BRAINED CRETIN?* We would lose *EVERYTHING.*" The High Priest flicked his hand and the two Tempered rushed forward each grabbing one arm, hauling Regin to his feet.

Regin felt a weakness gather in his gut. What was going on? Bring Amder back to life?

"As it so happens, I ordered the ending of the Reis line. There were two left. But someone betrayed me, by one of our own, a thorn in my side, a Priest named Haltim. He and the last two Reis descendants fled. I sent some hired help after them, but they vanished as well. So Regin, here is where things stand." Bracin poked Regin in the chest.

"If you're right, and this Apprentice is one of the missing Reis boys, I may let you live. If you're right, and he's not a Reis, I may let you live, but not without a penalty. But, if you're wrong, well you will never work a Forge again, and I will fill your life with pain, for as long as it lasts." Bracin waved his wrist again, and the Tempered dragged Regin away, towards a dark door on the far side of the room.

"But I helped you!" Regin yelled as he tried to set his feet against the Tempered, to stop them from taking him who knows where. "Bracin! I gave you information!"

"Yes, I know. Thank you. But if you thought you were ever going to walk out of here, well, you were sadly mistaken." Bracins voice was distant, and the last sight Regin saw of him, was the High Priest standing in from of the heart, with a large smile on his face.

47

Will could not stop yawning. He'd spent the last few days in a happy daze since that walk with Myriam in the garden. Since then they'd been near inseparable. That small voice in his head kept telling him this was a mistake had finally gone quiet. Myriam made him happy. Happy to wake up, happy to be here, in a way he'd never expected. Master Jaste had said that he'd pretty much always have to be Markin Darto, so the lie was one he'd always have to tell, right? Will pushed the thought aside again and stretched.

He'd been studying in one of the smaller side rooms of the Apprentice wing for the entire afternoon, since Master Regin's class had strangely been canceled. Rumors were flying that Regin was in fact missing, a fact that if true Will found himself not feeling overly upset about.

After five bells though, the place was getting to him. It was quiet, still, and he needed food, as the rumble of his stomach reminded him. Klah! Maybe there was some left in the kitchen from when he'd made it the other day.

Gathering his study materials, Will headed out into the side hallway this room was down, seeing no one. *Not a surprise, this place was full of odd little study rooms.* You had to cut down four side passages and a room in the middle of that to get here.

As he walked back to more trafficked areas, the size of the Guild got to him again. It made his head hurt, thinking about how large this place was inside, versus how normal it looked from the outside. He knew Amder himself had helped create the place, but still, it stretched his mind.

Will joined into the flow, keeping his head down and made his way first to his dormitory. He didn't feel like carrying the Rules of Mid Rank Nobilities in Trade negotiations any more than he had too. His room was sparse, and the same as when he moved into it. Other students had brought things to make their rooms more individual, wall hangings, mementos from home, the like. Will's only addition was a small smooth metal ball he had made in a class on advanced smelting techniques. Will only liked it because it had layers of copper and blued steel, and the pattern was pleasing.

Will had only placed his books on the small study table when Master Jaste burst into his room.

"Markin! There you are. Put your hood back up and follow. Quick and don't ask questions." Master Jaste's skin was pale, and he was out of breath.

"What?" Will wasn't sure what to say.

"Do it now." Jaste looked behind him. "Don't ask questions yet. Follow!" Jaste looked around and made a beeline for the dorm exit.

Will swallowed his confusion but did as Master Jaste instructed. His hood back up he followed Jaste as the Master led him through a maze of hallways and passages. Cutting through rooms to end up in a small room, not much bigger than a closet. It was empty, and the air was stale.

"There. That should at least give us some time." Jaste leaned against the wall, lowered his head and took deep breaths.

"Master Jaste? I'm confused. What's going on? What happened?" Will felt the growing knot in his stomach. *Someone had figured it out, someone knew the truth.*

If it was about his family Master Jaste wouldn't have led him on this chase, he would have pulled him aside and let him know. The truth had come out, Markin Darto didn't exist, he wasn't from Dernstown, and knew Jaste had helped him.

"Someone found out, didn't they?" Will asked. He knew that this day would come. Lies always do get found out. Myriam... oh Amder, why now after he finally got over his fears with her finding out, only to have this break now? *She will hate me forever.*

"What happened was Regin. Thrice cursed Regin!" Jaste slapped his leg, the thwack loud enough to make Will flinch. "The damned fool found out somehow, and instead of cornering us, he went straight to the Priesthood. And to the High Priest himself."

Will slid down the wall to the floor. It was over. All. The ruse was over, and he'd be kicked out of the guild.

"I hate him. Regin." Will spat. "Well, back to the Reach for me then."

Master Jaste looked up. "Will, you do not understand. It's not back to the Reach. It's being turned over to the High Priest's private little army and whatever life you have left being in extreme pain. It's them extracting every piece of information from you, and killing you, me, that Priest from the Reach, your cousin, everyone connected with you."

Will's stomach knot twisted. "But why?"

"You know why. You're a Reis. He may not know yet, but he will. His men, the Tempered they call themselves; they will extract everything. Everything. The High Priest will never allow a Reis to study here. The odds of a new Forgemaster are too high." Jaste stood up all the way, looking as if he was about to pass out.

"How? How did you find out?" Will couldn't process this; it was too much.

"My friendship with the gate guards. One of them passed me a note, asking me to come see him. I did so and he let me know. Then I came running for you. The fact is they are likely already here, looking for both of us." Jaste looked around the bare room. "I used the fact that the Guild has some secrets of its own to get time."

Will didn't care about secrets, he cared about survival. "So, what now?"

"We run. We run and head for the Reach. Full tilt. Get you back home, then you, your cousin, and anyone else you have with you, goes into hiding. The Skyreach Mountains cover a large area, and enough canyons and valleys to hide for a good long time." Jaste stepped out the door looking both ways. "Come on, it's time to go."

Will stood. "But what about clothes, and the like? And my hammer! And Myriam, if they know about me, they must know about her. We can't leave her here."

"William... I have money. We can lose ourselves in Ture long enough to buy supplies and get the scaled one out of here! And, look the hammer needs to stay. If anything, it would single you out, there's not many Wight Iron hammers out there in the world." Jaste sighed. "We both knew this was a risk. A large risk. But we did it. And it worked. And would have kept working if that damn fool Regin hadn't stepped into it." Jaste sighed again. "Myriam will be fine, I think. Her reaction to finding out the truth will be an honest one, I take it?"

Will knew what he was asking. "Yes. She doesn't know who I am. Not really."

"That's something at least, that should protect her, though they will ask questions. But I'm confident the Guild will protect her, at least enough that she will be safe." Master Jaste looked Will in the eyes.

"I know you hate Regin. And right now, I'm not happy with him. But no one deserves what's happening to him now. Regin didn't return to the Guild. There is only one reason, High Priest Bracin turned him over to the Tempered. His life, or whatever is left, is over." Jaste ducked his head out. "Now we leave."

Jaste took off down the hall, Will following as fast as he could. Jaste may be older than Will by a good bit, but he was also leaner, and faster. Will still wasn't built for running, and his heavy footfalls echoed down the hallway.

Cutting left several times, Jaste stopped and held up a hand to halt Will. "Quiet." Jaste looked around, and his head pulled back, even paler. His eyes locked onto Will. "When I say now, run down this hall and take your first three rights, and then two lefts. You'll be in front of a small nondescript door. Go out that door and you'll be out of the Guild. Take this!" Jaste pulled out a leather wallet, one that could be easy to hide under the clothes. The weight of coins was heavy, but there didn't feel like many, gold then.

"Master Jaste..." Will stopped talking, as voices yelling in anger and the scream of someone in pain came to him from around the corner that Jaste had looked around.

"No time Will. I got you into this ruse, and I'll get you out." Jaste swallowed and looked up for a moment. "Amder bless this." Jaste shot Will a small smile "You should ask, not me."

Will knew Jaste was planning to give himself up for him to escape if it came to that. "We should do this together."

Jaste shook his head. "You won't escape if I don't distract them. You're more important than me."

Will grabbed Jaste by the shoulder. "You're an Anointed Guildmaster of the Smithing Guild! I'm a three-month-old Apprentice. By the sparks, I'm nobody! I don't care about my name, my blood, any of it!" Will kept his voice to a whisper.

Jaste sighed. "You will be a problem about this won't you? Fine, we don't have time to argue. Lead the way, and I'll follow."

Will froze. Going first raised warning bells. But Jaste was right, they didn't have time to argue. Taking a deep breath, Will launched himself down the hallway. He didn't care much about the footfalls now. It was a race. Get out, get lost in Ture, or die in pain locked in some torture chamber.

Yells and curses came down behind them as he and Jaste made their break for it. He could hear Jaste running behind him but staying behind. Will knew he was covering his back. No time to argue it though. Pain climbed up his shins as he ran.

Left, another left. The yells behind them got louder, and Will pushed himself to run faster. He risked a glance backwards. Jaste was there still, but Will could see three robed figures now. Black with orange and red, each holding a rod, its end glowing white hot.

The sight made Will run faster, surprising himself. As he ran though, he could feel it, each step he was leaning more forward, he was close to losing his balance. And then, as if the Scaled One himself was cursing him he heard and felt a small pop in his right knee, and he tripped.

With a curse he went flying forward, falling and hitting the hallway floor hard. Pain bloomed in his shoulder as it hit first, then his head, smacking against the flagstone floor. Amder curse it! Will raised his head, looking at his approaching death. So close!

He saw Jaste's face. For a second their eyes met, and Jaste set his mouth in a straight line, and with a small nod turned and launched himself at their pursuers.

Jaste threw out his arms and tangled up all three priests. Will saw Jaste pull something out from under his cloak, but didn't have time to look further, he had to get up, and he had to run. He hated it, but he'd mourn Jaste later. There wasn't time to waste.

Will took off, his knee hurt, his shoulder hurt, his head hurt, but he wasn't caught yet. Right turn, right turn, then the door. A scream echoed in the distance, a scream of pain. Will prayed to Amder that was a pursuer, one of those Tempered Jaste had called them, and not Master Jaste.

The door, small, weather beaten, and innocuous. And freedom. Will burst through the door, entering a small courtyard, full of wagons and crates. Foodstuffs. This must be the place where food enters the Guild for everyone. Will threw off his cloak, and without stopping ran out into the alley, cutting through alleys, ending up in the road where he could lose himself. Safe for now. Alone, in pain, but safe.

***

Jaste hoped Will had gotten away. For a moment he had thought they had made it. Then Will took a tumble, and Jaste knew there was only one way for this to work, only one way for William Reis to escape. *I wish I could tell the lad more; there's so much he doesn't know.* About a lot of things. No time now. Jaste grabbed a robe of a Tempered, pulling him down. Jaste was a Smith, and you don't get to be a Master Smith by being weak. The figure stumbled down with an oath and jammed a glowing rod at Jaste.

Jaste knew what those were. The ends of those things never cool, a weapon of torture, of pain. Jaste rolled back and swung the small hammer he had brought. He felt it contact a Tempered and felt the bone give way. The figure yelled in pain and went down hard.

Jaste rolled away again, and for a second wondered if he'd manage to do this, to get away. Then, pain. White hot metal pushed against the middle of his back. The scream echoed down the hallway as the pain made him drop his hammer, falling to the flagstones with a clang. Another bloom of pain as another rod hit his shoulder.

"Traitor!" One of the Tempered yelled as he pushed down on the rod. Jaste screamed again, and felt the blackness approaching. Pain, all he could feel was pain. Jaste Noam was gone.

***

Myriam stood in Master Reinhill's study angrier than anything else. She had been pulled out of class, to a world that didn't make sense.

Markin Darto wasn't Markin Darto. He was, at least according to the Tempered who had just questioned her for the last two bells, named William Reis, and wasn't from Dernstown, but the Reach.

She had nearly laughed when she had been told that, Markin wouldn't have lied to her, there's no way that man could be lying about everything and everyone he'd told her about. She'd told them as much, even asking them to go get Master Jaste, he'd fix this mess.

"Jaste Noam is dead." The Tempered had said clearly, raising his confession rod and making the end glow. "Helping the imposter escape. He maimed two other Tempered in the escape."

Master Reinhill's breath caught at that news. "Master Jaste would never do such a thing, he's an anointed Master of the Guild and I will speak to the High Priest about this…"

"*JASTE NOAM IS DEAD*. He's the Master of nothing. His name is to be stricken from all rolls, and his works destroyed. His name is nothing, and he leaves nothing behind." The Tempered slammed the glowing end of the rod into his chair behind him, and it burst into flame where it struck.

Myriam didn't know what to say. Master Jaste dead? Markin … not Markin, *Will* … gone? Shock filled her. She had chased after this lie for months, and finally, when he had given up the chase, she finds this out?

"I don't know where he is, I didn't know." Myriam blinked back a few tears, real ones. But her sorrow was quickly turning to anger. How could he?!? How?

You knew he was hiding something. He ran from you; he was always evasive. You knew something was off.

The Tempered snarled at her. "Apprentice Myriam VolFar, you will be questioned again I am certain." He jabbed the rod at Master Reinhill. "And you will be as well. The Guild needs to learn it's place." With a long look he left, holding the still glowing confession rod as if he would force an answer out of everyone he met.

Master Reinhill sprung up, and thanks to the fact that the Guild required buckets of sand all over the place, put out the chair before turning to Myriam.

"How are you?" Master Reinhill leaned against her desk.

"How am I? The Master who brought me here is apparently dead, and the man I care about, isn't the man I care about. He's a stranger." Myriam could feel her sadness and anger return. *I don't know if I want to cry or find this William and beat him to near death with a piece of forging steel.* "I don't know what to think!"

"Myriam, I don't know what to say to you. Jaste Noam, if this is all true, knowingly brought in an Apprentice from the Reach. That's forbidden. I can guess why he did it, but it was a dangerous gambit. It might have worked, if not for Regin." Master Reinhill shook her head. "Sparks alive. What a mess."

"A mess? A *MESS*? Master Jaste is dead!" Myriam couldn't believe what she was hearing. If anything, Master Reinhill was just sad, not angry.

"Apprentice VolFar. You don't understand. The Priesthood has spoken. Jaste Noam is no longer a Master. He is dead, and my first act once I leave this room is to destroy everything he's done, made, or written down. You may stay, of course, you were an innocent in this. But now I am down two Masters." Master Reinhill gave a sigh and kicked the burnt chair over. "And I must replace a chair. I liked that chair."

Myriam couldn't follow this. "Don't you care?" *She's already given in.*

"I care, but I can't do anything about it." Master Reinhill sat, finally, in her own seat. "The Priesthood has spoken."

Myriam didn't like that answer, and the more she thought about it, the angrier she became. "You said you knew why Master Jaste had done this? And what was that about Master Regin?"

"Jaste Noam did this because of the name. Reis. He loved the idea of the Forgemasters. The last Forgemaster was a Reis. I'm sure the man thought that maybe, if a Reis became a Guild Master, maybe the Forgemasters could come again. A silly idea, Amder being dead and all that." Reinhill paused. "As for Master Regin, the High Priest has him. He won't leave that Temple alive."

Myriam didn't understand this. Forgemasters? An ancient order of Amder's? And why was Master Reinhill so… submissive to the Priesthood? This was the Smithing Guild!

"Don't worry about it child. Forget everything I told you. Leave this room, go back to your studies and try to move past this. It's safer, far safer for you, and the Guild." Master Reinhill waved toward to the door. "Leave."

48

High Priest Bracin hit the wall, his meaty hand turning red and stinging at the blow. *That idiot Regin had been right, and not only had he been right, the imposter had been one of the missing Reis men!* Someone had tipped the Master who had brought the Reacher in, and he'd warned the boy, and they had fled. The Tempered had almost got them both, but the Guildmaster, this Jaste Noam, had sacrificed himself to save the imposter who had fled into the city.

His men were right now bringing in all the items in the room. While the man had gone by 'Markin Darto', his real name was William Reis. The descriptions they had gotten from confused guild students lined up with the notes he had about the last two of the Forgemasters line.

Now William Reis was somewhere in Ture. The other Reis and Haltim's location he was unsure of. But if one Reis was here, there was a chance the other was to. Haltim was with him, the former priest was from Ture. While it had been years, Bracin was sure the fool still had contacts in the City.

The knock on the door distracted Bracin from his frustration as a Tempered came in bowing low. "Forgive the intrusion High Priest, but everything we could find in the dorm of the imposter is here in this sack." The Tempered raised a sack. It was only half full that Bracin could see. *So, not a man of means this William.*

"Master Reinhill wasn't happy with the way things went," the Tempered added, keeping his back to the Heart.

"I do not care how any Master of the Guild feels right now. They harbored an imposter and a traitor." Bracin stared at the Tempered for a moment. "Bring me a table, I want to pour this out and look over it." Bracin waved the Tempered away.

"Master, in here? The Heart is right there..." The Tempered looked up, confused. High Priest Bracin turned toward the bowing figure. "I am the High Priest of Amder, and you will bring a table here. Now!"

"Yes Master." The Tempered stayed bowing low and left the room.

Bracin sighed. Some Tempered held more reverence for the Heart than was necessary. The Heart was a tool. He was sure that there was a connection to whatever was left of Amder in the thing, but who cared? *Amder was dead. Amder would stay dead if he had anything to do with it.*

"And you'll have to deal with it." Bracin said to the Heart, watching the thing flash in response. He liked to think it hated him. He found it amusing to have power over it. Watching the light in it run away from his touch, seeing it flash in anger, it made him laugh. He, a mortal man, had the power of a God to mold and use.

They brought the table and with no ceremony, Bracin upended the sack. A few changes of clothes, a metal sphere, a silvery hammer, a few books and scrolls, a folded piece of paper all spilled out. This was all? Pathetic.

The sphere was a hunk of metal, nicely made, but junk. The clothes were only useful to get a better picture of what William looked like. The books and scrolls were the normal Apprentice studies. He'd have someone look through them, in case this Markin wrote some notes or anything in them that was pertinent. That left the hammer and the folded paper.

Bracin picked up the hammer and was surprised by both its weight, and its craftsmanship. Bracin may not be the most pious man, but he knew good craft, and this hammer was an excellent example of metalwork. He flicked it with his finger, and the telltale moaning echo confirmed his suspicions. Wight Iron. Very nice indeed then. Worth a fair amount of money. If William Reis had made this, it impressed him. And that wasn't good. He needed no Forgemaster to come into being.

He held up the hammer examining it closer. Decoration of some kind, but it was hard to see in the dim light. Bracin carried it closer to the heart holding it close to see the abstract figure of Amder.

Heat. It immediately glowed, and a white silver glow enveloped the tool that pulsed in time with the heart. Bracin yelled and dropped the hammer which clattered to the floor with another low moaning sound. But the glow continued and grew. A hazy light came *OUT* of the thing, reaching toward the Heart. And a matching hazy light grew from the Heart itself, toward the tool. Pinkish in hue, it reached for the white-silver glowing mist coming from the hammer!

Bracin looked around for something to push the hammer away from the heart but, seeing nothing, took a deep breath and reached out to push it away himself. His fingers brushed the hammer and a force stronger than he pushed him away, sending him flying against the wall. Bracin was a large man, and yet the blow knocked the wind out of him.

He watched in horror as the white and pink mists met, and as they joined Bracin could hear it, the hammer blows of a god. He knew what it was, horror and doubt gripping him. *Amder was here and judged him.* Bracin swallowed but resolve grew after the initial shock.

"By the Blood Gods dead soul, you will not stop me!" Bracin pushed himself to his feet, and with a huge heave launched himself at the hammer. This time there was no push, and he could push the hammer away and break the connection. The anger of a god washed over him for a moment, coming close to overwhelming him.

A quick look yet told him that whatever that connection had been, both the heart and the hammer were different. The hammer's decoration, the etched figure of Amder was different, the lines glowed now, red and yellow. The heart, its glow had grown stronger, mightier. Bracin spat on the hammer. Therefore the Reis line should have been ended years ago! He had never understood why his predecessors had allowed the line to continue. He would have ended it himself if that traitor, Haltim, hadn't interfered.

Bracin carefully picked up the hammer, throwing it onto the table. His eyes fell on the table, and the note. Probably useless, but worth a look. He unfolded the note reading the short thing with disinterest. Eyes widened as he read again, this was it! It wasn't too late; he could end this threat now.

Bracin bellowed for a Tempered, he had to move. But if he did everything right, today would see the end of the chance for Amder's return. And the Priesthood of Amder would go on, stronger, more powerful, and richer than anyone could ever dream of. Already the King and Nobles bowed before them, but only here. What heights could they go when they had an army of Heart blessed weapons, and armor? All Alos would fall before them!

***

Will sat against a wall in the unknown street he was on. His stomach felt horrible, he had a headache, and on top of it all, he did not know where he was. He'd spent a single night and part of two days in Ture before the Guild trials. He was lost.

Master Jaste was dead, he was lost, and powerful and dangerous people were after him. And who knows what had happened to Myriam. He hoped, he prayed to every God that she was safe. "Pull yourself together William." He whispered under his breath. He had money, and he'd escaped his pursuers, at least for now. One small bonus to all this, he'd no longer have to go by that silly name, Markin Darto. He was once more, William Reis, from the Reach.

Dragging a sleeve across his forehead, Will inspected his surroundings. He was in a side street, decent foot traffic, so didn't look to unsafe. He should put more space between him and the Guild, which had its own dangers.

All he needed was supplies, and to get out of Ture. That was all. Get out, get back to home, and forget all this. *Forgemaster? Ha. Savior of Amder? Ha.* Go home. But he couldn't go home, at least not for long. He had to find Duncan. Haltim could help, he knew people, right?

The Priesthood was still after him, they would never stop hunting him. His existence was a threat to their power and wealth. He was fine with their power and wealth. If it meant he got to live his life in peace? Sure, who cared?

They wouldn't see it that way. He needed someone he could trust. Will needed Duncan, Haltim. He needed time to figure this out. Time to get free. Time to plan. But not here. He'd wasted enough of what little time he had.

Will made his way through the crowd. He didn't have his grey cloak to hide his face, but he didn't need it. And the dark grey cloak would have attracted far more attention as they weren't supposed to be out of the Guild.

Will followed the flow of traffic through the city. Not paying attention to where he was going, if it was away from the Guild it was good enough for him. He found himself in a section that was frequented by travelers. More varied costume, more variations on skin tone, and even accents. A good place to get supplies, and a good place to get rest before bolting out of town. He thought about getting supplies and going, but night was falling fast, and he was exhausted. Dealing with the gates would be nerve wracking enough, who wanted to deal with that when he was so tired he couldn't think?

Will moved down the street, taking in the names of shops and various business, trying to make a note of where he'd need to stop in the morning. Cobbler, leatherworker, Grocer, and even a small shop selling metalwork. He passed more than a few inns and boarding houses, most looked either too busy, or loud, or deserted, which meant traders knew enough to stay away from them.

As the sun fell, Will spotted an Inn that had traffic, but wasn't overflowing. The sign above read "The Broken Wheel." Even had a trader's wagon wheel nailed above it. Will knew traders from the Reach, and once glance at the horses and carts outside the place made him feel at home. Places like this were for normal working traders who had a set route. Clean, safe, and had decent but not opulent accommodations. Exactly what he needed.

Will made his way inside to a long narrow main room. Half the tables were taken up, as it was dinner time for most, though food would be served until late into the night. Clean floor, swept often, serviceable tables and chairs. And no Guards, no Priests, and no one who looked like a threat.

"How can I help you lad?" a woman from behind the bar asked. "Need a meal?"

Will nodded. He'd been going to get food when he'd had to flee the Guild. He'd forgotten about it in the panic and danger, but his hunger had returned with a vengeance now that the immediate danger had passed.

"And a Room please. One night." Will spied a small table with two chairs on the back side of the main room. Hidden in the shadows, but fine with him. It felt good to sit, his legs and knees hurt from the mad sprint earlier.

The woman approached his table. "Food will be 1 silver bit. The room will be three. Half now, half in the morning."

Will reached for the purse Jaste forced upon him during the escape. Opening it all he saw was gold coins, no silver. "Um... all I have is gold." Will kept his voice low. He didn't think there was a large theft risk in this place, but why be careless?

"I can change ya. What kind of Inn do you think this is?" The woman took a coin and held it up to the light. A grunt of acknowledgement later she headed back into the kitchen. She reappeared carrying a tray laden with food.

"Change." She held out 6 silver bits, each uniform and square. "You don't look like the drinking type, so some weak ale with the meal. Want something stronger, come find me." With that a flagon of watery beer was placed on the table, followed by a plate of food. Roast, flatbreads, and some roasted vegetables he couldn't quite identify, and merciful above even a small tart for dessert.

Will ate his fill and devoured it. Keeping one eye on the door on the far side of the room, in case. But nothing more than the usual trader came in or out. A few locals too by the look, who stood at the bar and had a few drinks talking to the innkeeper the whole time. Will ate his last bite and leaned back, full. *Master Jaste would enjoy the meal, he liked good food.* He pushed away thoughts of Master Jaste. That loss was fresh, too hard to deal with. Get out of the city and then deal with the guilt.

The innkeeper was a good one and noticed when he was done with his meal. Cleaning the table, she took a small key out of her pocket. "Room four. Up the stairs, last door on the right." Will smiled for a second, all business, but it made him feel relaxed.

Will found the room and locked the door behind him. Myriam. Sparks, he hoped she was ok. It would be his fault, and only his if something happened to her. He should have kept her even farther away, not even been friendly. *I wanted to pretend that I wasn't dangerous to know.* And what had he done? He'd followed his heart and not his head, and now... now he didn't know. Those Priests, would they hurt her? Will sat on the edge of the bed, head in his hands trying to figure this out.

Will knew there was nothing he could do for her. He couldn't even get her a message an apology. Master Jaste had said he didn't think the Priesthood would do anything to her, but those same people had killed him for running. He laid down on the bed, and sleep was a long time coming.

49

Haltim sat back in his chair, relaxing after one more amazing meal that Bessim had worked up. The boarding house was full as more of the traders were in this evening. Duncan had gone to bed after another day of mucking, and he hadn't seen Rache all day, unless she and Duncan had gone out for a walk earlier. Yesterday had been the last time. She'd come down wearing that ruby stone the lad had given her on a simple woolen necklace.

Haltim liked the girl, but every time he saw her now, something in his mind itched. He couldn't quiet his thoughts, somehow, somewhere, something about the girl bothered him. That was a minor concern in the whirlwind of things going on however. Duncan's mental health and getting news that Will had gotten their message were far more important right now.

The door flew open, as a series of armed guards stormed in, followed by three men in robes. Robes that made Haltim stand, but then collapse into his chair. Robes of black, with red and orange. The Tempered. They had been discovered.

"Haltim Goin. You are your companions are needed for *conversations* with High Priest Bracin. Immediately." The Tempered who spoke spat out Haltim's name. He reached under his robes, pulling out the once familiar metal rod.

Thinking, Haltim stood, making a show of age. "I'm sorry my lad, but I'm here alone. I'm frail you know but..." he could not finish as the Tempered uttered a word and drove the rod into his gut. Haltim howled in pain as the now glowing end tore through his clothes and into his skin.

"Someone silence this traitor. The High Priest wants to have a long talk with him." The Tempered turned towards the guards. "Search the building, find the companion. Young man, lanky. Goes by the name Duncan."

The Guard bowed and motioning his men went upstairs, weapons drawn. Haltim was in pain but felt a slight swell of pity for the men. If they awoke Duncan in his current state, there was a good possibility that would be the last thing they ever did.

Not a minute later a scream of rage and anger came from upstairs, loud enough to make even the Tempered turn pale. "What was that?" one of the other Tempered said before it became clear as to what had happened.

Duncan came down the stairs, but on all fours, like an animal. His face contorted and twisted in rage and anger, twisted up in hate. Blood flowed from two slicing wounds on his back, but much of the blood on him was on his hands and face. His hands were red with it. Haltim knew what had happened. Even though they were arresting him he said a quick silent prayer for their souls.

Duncan launched himself at the nearest person, lost in the Blood Curse. This person wasn't a Tempered, but an innocent merchant who had flattened himself against the wall. Duncan's arm flew out and ripped the man's throat out without hesitation, blood fountained from the corpse as a look of near ecstasy flashed across the features of the killer.

"Duncan!" Haltim tried to get the lad's attention. He didn't want the deaths, no deaths. Not even the Tempered. Each death would weigh on the man when he came out of his rage. But his voice didn't make it through. Duncan charged at the next figure, one of the Tempered.

The robe ripped away as Duncan tore at it, revealing a middle-aged woman whose face was terrified of the man beast that Duncan had become. Her face changed to a scream as that same man beast broke her elbow as he bit down hard, drawing a new fresh fountain of blood.

Haltim stood, his stomach burned still form the injury the Tempered rod had inflicted, but he had to do something. He only knew one way, the bracer. Haltim ran at Duncan, and for once the man, caught in the throes of his curse did not notice. With a wild swing, Haltim's bracer, the bracer Amder had forged, touched Duncan.

A noise like the touch of hot metal to meat filled the room as Duncan went flying from the hit, and Haltim collapsed. He raised his head to see Duncan lying on the floor, with a groan escaping his blood-covered face. The two standing Tempered stood still, unable to move for a moment, before raising their rods and with no more hesitation sending waves of burning pain into the prone form of Duncan Reis.

Haltim closed his eyes as the screams of pain tore through the air. He had stopped Duncan from killing anymore, but the bracer couldn't stop this. Maybe he should have let Duncan go, but innocents were in his path. The Curse made him incapable of picking and choosing his victims.

Duncan's screams ended, as Haltim opened his eyes again. The lad breathed, but the pain must have been too much for him, and he had blacked out. The two remaining tempered were still thrusting the glowing hot rod ends into his body, but no response. One of the Tempered stopped and spat at the body lying there.

'Go get the other guardsmen, the High Priest will want to know what has happened." This Tempered held the red-hot glowing rod in front of Haltims face. "And you, the betrayer of the order, betrayer of your vows, do not think we will go any easier on you than your insane friend."

Guardsmen filed into the room, hauling Duncan's body up. "Chain him, tightly." The second tempered ordered. "He's crazed."

Two guardsmen pulled Haltim up and placed daggers at his back. "That one, make sure he stays up. I'd be fine with a knife slip, but the High Priest wants to talk to him. So, let's get him there alive."

The last sight Haltim saw as they dragged him and Duncan out the door was the sight of a weeping Bessim, blood spattered and terrified.

***

Zalkiniv could smell the blood long before she got near to the boarding house. Something had happened. She had been tightening her grip on the cult. They had caught a guard who had been sniffing around, and they had tortured him for several hours before his heart gave out. The blood had been powerful, pain and fear had made it almost intoxicating.

The group that the Axessed had made served her now, though she could tell that most served her out of pure terror. No matter, their feelings made their blood more powerful for her uses. She hadn't drained a full member since that first night, but that would soon change. She needed to bind the rest of the stones to herself, and that meant blood. Fear laced blood was even better.

The Axessed would be an issue. The creature was attached to its little group. It hated her, as much as its primitive brain could. While she could kill the beast, she wanted to come up with a good way to use it first. Use the Claret stones to drive it to a frenzy and release it onto the streets of Ture? The crazed scaled monster tearing through the teaming throngs of this city made for a good fantasy.

The blood smell changed all thoughts. Blood, and fresh. If something had happened to her sacrifice, to the Reis lad she had, her God would not be kind. The Rage God was not known for forgiveness. He might even turn her over to the Axessed, which would not be something to be enjoyed. Having her thousand years of life ended by that thing was not in her plans.

Stepping around the corner she took one glance at the boarding house and cursed, ducking behind a trader's cart. A small contingent of armed guards bearing the livery of both the city of Ture, and the Priesthood of Amder were there! What had happened? Where was Duncan Reis?

She cared not about the Amderite, being free of him would be useful. But her prize?

"Rache, girl, hide in here!" A whisper came from an open door.

Zalkiniv glanced that way, to see a pale Bessim motioning her. So, the owner of the place had survived, she could tell her what had happened here.

Zalkiniv crept to the door and slipped in, Bessim closing it behind them.

"What happened?" Zalkiniv asked, her impatience making her be more forceful than she thought.

Bessim wrung her hands looking down at the ground. "It was... horrible. Someone or somehow the Tempered discovered that Haltim and Duncan were there. I don't know how. They came in by force. Three of those Tempered Priests and three or four guards. Before I knew what had happened, they had hit Haltim with one of those rods they carry and arrested him. But when they went upstairs..." Bessim swallowed and paused, getting even paler before Zalkiniv's gaze.

"Go on. Something happened with Duncan?" Zalkiniv could guess what had happened, but she needed to know if her prize survived!

Bessim nodded, leaning against a wall. "There was a scream, and then... He came down the stairs like a wild animal!

Blood covered him! He ripped the throat out of an innocent man and then he screamed and was attacking one of the Tempered when Haltim did something. I don't know what. But Duncan fell and stopped attacking. The Tempered hit him again and again with those rods, and he screamed over and over in pain until he blacked out. The Tempered got more guards and took them both away, towards the temple I expect. They left those guards here for you!"

Zalkiniv said nothing and turned away from Bessim. Anger suffused her. Her prize, taken! She couldn't care less about the pain, but how had the old Priest stopped him? That was twice now the Amderite had turned off the Blood Curse, something that should have been far beyond his power. *Yet, he had done it.*

Bessim thought the Tempered had taken them to the Temple, but thought wasn't good enough. Zalkiniv needed to know and know for sure. There were other ways, but one way always worked well, and it got rid of a loose end. Zalkiniv turned back to Bessim, lowering her eyes, and putting a slight quiver to her cheeks. "What will we do?"

Bessim laid a hand on her shoulder. "I don't know, but once those guards leave, I'll sneak your belongings out and some money. They will look for you. They don't think I know anything, so there's a good chance they will let me go."

Zalkiniv nodded and without a word unsheathed her knife, plunging it point first into the underside of Bessims jaw. Blood fountained and the in dying light of Bessims eyes she could see the question of why.

"It doesn't matter why woman. Your blood will serve a higher purpose now." She watched as consciousness fled from the woman's body. She must work fast, while the woman lived yet, and her blood was warm.

Zalkiniv took her Claret stone and with Bessims blood began a working. The old woman's feelings for the Amderite would allow her to ride the blood to the old man. The odds of them keeping Haltim and Duncan apart were low. They'd want them both secure, and hidden.

The Claret stone pulsed in time with her heart, following the blood, flying through the streets in her mind. There! The Amderite temple, but that was no surprise. *But where in the Temple?* Like her own, the place was huge, and ancient. Added onto over the years, it was a maze of passages and rooms. The blood must find a way!

There! Down, down, tunnels and hallways, till, there. A room, one floor up from the bottom. Both men, chained and unconscious. She dared not look closer. The Temple was warded elsewhere. They had let the wards slip in the lowest levels, probably never thinking that someone would dare attack from below. The time for hiding was over. She was Zalkiniv, the High Priest of the Blood God, and she would have her prize again.

50

Will awoke with a headache, pain in his shoulder, and knees that reminded him of his hate of running. At least it wasn't the same shoulder he hurt getting to Ture. He was on the run now from the two most powerful organizations in Palnor, if not all Alos. The Guild and the Priesthood. No one in the Guild was going to do anything to help him, outside Myriam. *Maybe not even her.*

She'd be furious with him and hurt. She had every right to be angry with him, he just hoped she didn't get sucked into this more. *I really do hate running.* Will winced with every step he took down the stairs, this better not slow him down. He grabbed a roll and a weak beer, nodding to the innkeeper. The streets were busy with their normal trader traffic though there was a tension in the air.

Will hit up the shops he'd made a mental note about the night before. In short order he had everything he thought he had to have, and had money left over. He gazed over a horse seller's stall, a horse would make the trip faster, and save him from dealing with some of his aches. *No, no horse.* He wasn't sure how much money he would need for his trip home, a horse was a high cost, and ... he didn't ride. As he made his way toward the gate, he kept his head down and his new light brown cloak.

The Gate he had chosen to exit Ture came into view. There was a line this morning to exit, which made Will's stomach flip. He knew trying to leave this way was probably stupid, but the only other gate he'd gone through was the Guild gate, and he couldn't go that way. This was the closest exit, he'd asked around, though he'd had a few strange looks while asking.

"What's with the line today?" Will asked the woman in front of him.

The woman turned towards him, showing the face of a farmer, her clothes worn but serviceable.

"Are you a fool? It's because of the murders last night! A boarding house ... some criminals were there, and the guards went to arrest them. They killed a guard, some merchant, and even the innkeeper. I heard that one was more animal than man and even ate one of the dead." The woman shuddered.

Will paused. Murders? "I hadn't heard. Did they catch them?"

"Do you think they'd have a checkpoint if they had caught them? I heard they caught two, but there was a third. A young woman. She vanished, so they are doing these checkpoints. Don't worry, you're not a young woman." The woman gave a laugh. "I want to get back to the farm. Got fields that need tending to."

Will shuffled forward in the line, ignoring the woman's rambling comments about her farm. Murders. Could they be related to his escape? He doubted it, but it could be a trick to put checkpoints up. A story.

The farmer in front of him trailed off, she must have realized that Will wasn't listening. He focused on being calm. He was sure that whatever this checkpoint was, if he looked and acted like something scared him, that would arouse more suspicion. Will was close now; the gate was four people in front of him. He was glad he was traveling alone. The line for groups or traders with carts was twice as long as the solo traveler's one. He could hear the traders complaining about how much time this was taking.

Then he saw it. A poster, hung up, with three faces. One was Haltim's, one was Duncan's, and one, was his! Will almost lost his breakfast. What were Haltim and Duncan doing on the poster? By Amder's forge light, was that woman's story true? But it was Duncan and Haltim who had been arrested? What was the girl they were after? *The crazy man ... could that have been Duncan!*

The Blood Curse ... Oh Amder above! Will drew his hood tight and tried to step out of line. He had taken two steps when he felt it. The hand on his shoulder and the dagger pressing into his side.

"Don't run boy. I'm sure the High Priest wants you alive. We've been watching you since you got in line. The reward for your capture will be very nice, very nice." The breath with the voice smelled of old beer and a foul sourness.

"I don't know." Will tried to say, but the dagger dug in, silencing him.

"Shut up. I don't know why, but I know you're a wanted man. That's all I need." The figure pushed him towards the guard post door. He was captured. They had captured Duncan and

Haltim. It was over. His line was done, Amder would never return, it was over.

The guard post was a simple door in one of the side towers of the gate. They pushed in Will, the figure behind him digging the dagger point into his side just below his ribs, hard.

"Evening Captain. I have your prize." The figure pushed him towards a man who looked annoyed. The Captain covered his mouth and nose as he spoke to the man who had captured him.

"Go away and return to your sewers Spider. Your finds are never worth the effort. You reek of the underbelly of Ture." The Captain of the Guard went back to carving a pair of dice.

"Captain... it's the one from the posters. The one you're looking for," Spider whispered. Will wanted to turn and look at the man but was still hoping that he could somehow escape this. He had to keep his face hidden.

"You? You've captured the one man that the entire Priesthood is outraged about? The Apprentice who killed a Master in the Guild? I doubt it." The Captain sighed and threw the dice on the table, giving a grunt of annoyance when they didn't show the numbers he wanted.

"I swear it." Spider moved back behind Will and dug the dagger into his back again. "Look!" Spider ripped the hood off Will's head.

Silence filled the room for a second. Will closed his eyes.

"GUARDS!" The Captain yelled, leaping to his feet.

Four men came running out of another door, weapons at the ready. "Take him to the Priesthood! Now!" The Captain pointed at Will.

"See? I told you. Pay up." Spider's whine came and Will now caught, looked at the man. Dirty, and unshaven, the man was a mess. Patch worked and damp clothes covered him, but the dagger in his hand was shiny and well cared for.

The Captain drew his sword. "Go back to your sewer Spider. I might share the reward later with you. But I'm the one taking him to the Priesthood, not you."

Spider spat on the floor. "Damned Guard. He's MINE! I CAUGHT HIM!"

"Don't raise your voice to me pest. I'll cut you here and now and let whatever animals you live with underneath this place eat what's left." The Captain's sword was drawn now, and one of the Guards had moved to block the exit.

Spider looked around and with a muffled oath, turned toward the exit. The Guard there glanced at the Captain who gave him a nod and moved away. Spider slipped out, still mumbling into the crowd.

"Now Prize. Let's be off." The Captain motioned and two of the Guards grabbed Will's arms and the other kept the point of his sword at the base of Will's neck.

"Struggle and I'll push it through." The Guard with the sword whispered to Will. "Might be worth it, I know what the Tempered do to people. A quick death here and now?"

"Stop that." The Captain yelled as he led them forward. "He's the High Priest's now."

Will felt a blow to the back of his head, a sharp pain, and then nothing.

***

Zalkiniv paced around the room, gripping the Claret stone tight in her hand. The blood-stained altar to the Rage God stood empty. She had choices to make and make now. Her prize was in the hands of the High Priest of Amder. And while he didn't have the backing of his god, he had access to men, and resources.

Her blood workings might work on him, but they might not. While Amder himself was not in tune with his Priests, they still had power from him. They had access to the Heart of Amder, the living heart of a dead god. That gave them power. Power that her blood workings couldn't stand against.

The Scaled one brooked no argument. She needed her sacrifice. Either she sacrificed this little band of Blood God worshipers tonight, and the Axessed as well, to allow her to bind all the stones. Or she could use the cult and the Axessed to raid the Temple of Amder, and steal her prize back.

The Claret stones would increase her power to heights not seen since Valnijz himself walked the land. But would that be enough? The raid was riskier, it could wipe the cult out in moments, and while she believed the Axessed would fare better, would that be enough?

The hissing breath of the Axessed came down the hall, and Zalkiniv waited for him. The raid would be easier one way, the Axessed wouldn't argue. All these centuries here, alone in Ture had given the creature an unhealthy sense of power. Sacrifice of what it had built would make it angry, even for the betterment of the true God. Killing Amderites would make it happy. *It would make me happy as well.*

It was decided, a raid. And a raid tonight. The Axessed had said there were ways into the Temple, those ways were not guarded well, or even that often. People, arrogant people always tend to forget what's under their feet.

The Axessed lumbered into the room, the nearly transparent scales reflecting the torchlight. Its breath was steady, but always carrying that alien note of something not human. "High Priest, I have news."

Zalkiniv wondered what information this thing could give her. She already knew her prize was in the Temple, and this creature had no way to get information from beyond the barrier.

"What could you know that would interest me?" Zalkiniv asked grasping the Claret stone that was bound to her tightly.

The Axessed locked eyes with her for a long moment before bowing. "I have caught a man, a man who knows things."

"You interrupt my thoughts to tell me about a man?" the more time she spent with this creature, the more she knew, it should not live after she was done in this place. *The Blood God offered to reward it, but Valnijz would not stop her.*

The Axessed left the room and pulled back in a dirt covered man who stank of sourness and the sewer. He sobbed as he was pulled in. "I don't know anything, I don't know. Let me go, don't hurt me."

"What could this person know that would interest the Blood God?" Zalkiniv mouth soured. It wasn't the stink that bothered her, his blood, it was polluted. Drink, and other things flowed through him. *Disgusting.*

"The Guards, they put up signs, this sign. This man knows about the other human." The Axessed help up a poster. Three men. One, the Amderite Haltim, one her prize, and one...

Oh, Great One, give your blessing on tonight. Zalkiniv turned to the sobbing wretch. "Speak." She reached through the

Claret stone and set the man's blood. The figure splayed out, unable to move except for breathing and talking. 'Tell me about this man on the poster."

"I found him, I did. I brought him to the Guards, they didn't pay me. It was my find, and they didn't pay me." The man spoke. His words spilling out now. "Spider brought them their prisoner, and they offered to hurt Spider."

"Where is he now?" Zalkiniv pulled on the blood harder, the man's bones stretched, and joints cracked in response.

"They took him to the High Priest of Amder." The man, this Spider managed to say, before a loud crack and his body collapsed.

Broken neck. Zalkiniv waved the Axessed over to take the body. *That one's blood wouldn't be worthy of feeding even the Valni.*

She didn't know how, but the other prize, the one in the Guild was now out, and in the grasp of the Amder temple. Both of the bloodline were within her grasp. The choice was obvious now.

"Gather the cult. Now. The Church of Amder has captured our master's prizes. We must take them." Zalkiniv pointed at the creature. "We will all go. If we fail, you know what fate befalls us both."

The Axessed said nothing but kept its black eyes on her as it bowed low and left the room. She watched it leave, wondering if tonight was a good time to end the creature. It was far too independent. Zalkiniv turned toward the altar, removing the rest of the claret stones from their resting place.

"I'll need you, even if you're not bound. I'll not let the beast keep you." She smiled at the dark red stones, the crystalized blood of ages past.

She cut herself, the stones covered in her blood. This wasn't a real binding, but at least she'd be able to draw a little power out. The rush that this provided made Zalkiniv almost moan in pleasure. No time for that now, there was work to do.

Settling down, she closed her eyes and began the first of several workings. She would survive tonight and have her prizes.

***

Myriam paced in the small study she had used with Markin, *William*, and fought with her feelings. She still couldn't believe the Guild wasn't going to do anything. Two Masters dead, or at least one dead and one missing, and nothing.

This morning had been horrible. Rumors flew that Markin had killed Master Jaste and fled in a fight over *her* of all people. Regin had gone after him. Or she had helped Markin escape and she had killed Master Regin. She'd tried to follow Master Reinhill's advice and ignore it, but after several hours had come back to this small room to hide.

Myriam kept finding herself coming back to something, something that only a few days before would have been unthinkable. If the Priesthood caught William, he'd die. She was sure of it. He was a no name Apprentice, regardless of what his last name was. That whole Forgemaster nonsense was, well, silly. But the thought of Markin, William, whatever his name was, being killed was one she didn't want. She was still furious about his betrayal, both mad at him and at herself for not seeing it. But death? No.

But if she did what her heart said, her life as a Guild smith would be over. She could do it, they did allow for it, but she'd never be let back in. Ever. The rules were absolute. Once she quit, she was outcast, and gone. The Guild or William? *A Guild that was impotent, worked with murderers, and didn't do anything to defend itself from a corrupt and evil organization.*

Her Grandfather would never talk to her again, she was sure. But if she left, if she went after him, where would she go?

There was only one place she knew of, the Reach. If she could find his family there, she could figure out where to go. The Guild or...William. A faint smile crossed her face, she liked the name William at least, she had always sort of thought Markin Darto was a rather silly name.

Two hours later Myriam found herself outside Master Reinhill's office again, knocking on the door.

"Come" Master Reinhills voice came, tired.

Myriam walked in to see a very tired looking Master. Papers and messages covered what had been a clean desk yesterday. "Master Reinhill, I formally give notice of my desire to leave the Smithing Guild."

Reinhill sighed and sat back in her chair. "Myriam. I haven't slept since the night before last. I've spent the better part of a day trying to find a way to fix all this. And now you want to leave?"

Myriam nodded. "I have to."

"Your leaving to go after him aren't you." Master Reinhill closed her eyes and slipped into silence. Myriam wondered if she had fallen asleep. "Have you thought about this? He may not want you to help him. What if whatever you had together was all part of the act?"

"That wouldn't... he...I don't think he did that. It wouldn't make sense." Myriam had thought about that, but it wouldn't make sense. Even if it was true, which it wasn't, did she want to stay here? Knowing that if the Priesthood came for her, the Guild would let them take her away? No, better to leave and be done with it.

"Maybe." Reinhill was silent again for a long pause. "I can't stop you, so go. Might be safer for you in the long run. We will miss you Myriam. You are a great Apprentice, and the Guild will be all the lesser for it."

Myriam turned to leave the room, unsure if she knew what she was doing. Throwing away her dream, for what? But she wasn't safe here. Not with the Tempered around. She had to leave.

"Myriam." Reinhill said. "I have something for you."

Myriam turned back, to see Master Reinhill holding a small package. "What?"

"Your leaving alone, going places that I don't want you to tell me about. But you're traveling alone. I want you to have this, on the promise that once you're safe, you will get it to a trader or merchant who can bring it back to me. If anyone finds you with this, I will deny giving it to you." Master Reinhill held the package towards her. "Take it."

What was she talking about? Myriam took the package, not sure what Reinhill was getting at. It was cloth of some kind under the wrapping that was obvious as she took it. She opened the wrapping to see, red.

A Journeyman's cloak. Myriam understood as soon as she saw it. Only the most foolhardy and desperate bandit or robber would try and attack her if she was wearing this. It was, as much as Master Reinhill could make it, safety for her.

"I can't do anything about the death of Jaste or Regin. I can't do anything about the disappearance of this William Reis, but I can at least try to keep you safe." Master Reinhill's voice was barely able to be heard. "Go, before those warped Tempered show up again, and set fire to the whole Guild."

51

Duncan struggled to open his eyes, without success. *Pain. Everything hurt.* He remembered being in bed when someone had burst in, and that was it. Everything after that descended into a red haze of anger. His lips were dry but covered with something sticky, metallic...blood, it was blood. He hoped it was his blood, but in his heart, he was afraid of the truth, the Blood Curse had overcome him, and whoever had burst in, was dead now.

Awareness returned. Someone had chained him to a stone wall, he could feel the lumps on his back, his arms shackled near his head. Two lines of pain cut down his body, and his shirt was stuck to his skin. His legs were affixed to the floor, and the shackles hurt, a dim pain, but noticeable. The air smelled of... smoke, a distant forge like smell, but the stone under his feet was damp and slippery. His bare feet were cold on the stone.

"Duncan? Are you awake lad?" A whisper came to him. Haltim? Oh, Amder above, let it be Haltim.

"Haltim? Is that you?" Duncan struggled to open his eyes and turn his face toward the sound.

"Yes. So, you're awake, that's good at least." Haltim's voice was soft, calming. But Duncan could hear the quaver in it. Haltim was afraid.

"Where are we Haltim? What happened? I was asleep, and someone burst in. And that's all I remember. Why can't I open my eyes? Why do I hurt so much?" Duncan took a deep breath and gasped at the shock of fire a simple breath gave him.

"They discovered us. I don't know how. Three Tempered and some guards came to arrest us. A guard burst in to arrest you. Haltim's voice left no doubt. The Curse. That wasn't Duncan's blood on his face. It was guards. Oh, Amder above, what had he done?

"Tell me everything Haltim." Duncan let the chains hold him up. The shackles cut into his skin, but he ignored it. Everything hurt anyway, what was more pain?

"You killed him. Savagely. Bound down the stairs and killed a merchant. Ripped the arm off one of the Tempered before the other two drew the Rods of Confession and used them on you. I've seen no one take as much pain as you did. They must have broken ribs in their fury. They dragged you here, and me. The High Priest of Amder has us now. May our souls be safe," Haltim whispered.

"What are we going to do Haltim?" Duncan was at a loss. Everything was gone. If the Priesthood had discovered them, there was a chance Will had been discovered. All that time, all that hope. Wasted. Duncan's thoughts drifted back to the day he had met Rache. Even with the blood taint, he'd been happy. He'd never see her again. And Will, he hoped a fool's dream that Will might come out of this and be safe.

Silence was the initial answer as the situation sunk in. Duncan waited, he needed to know there was a way out of this, that this wasn't the end.

"I don't know Duncan. I don't know. Rache made it out. I don't know where she was, but they didn't arrest her with us. So that's good, right?" Haltim's voice rose, seeking assurance that not everything was bad.

"Rache alive? Ok. I hope she finds her way home." Duncan sighed and tried to feel his face with his fingertips. It was puffy, swollen in places from the beating he had taken. Dried crusty blood was sealing his eyes shut.

He pried his right eye open with his fingertips, taking a moment to get used to seeing things, anything, again. The stone cell was round, and right next to him was Haltim. The old Priest had red and puffy injuries; they had beaten him too. Chained on a round wall next to each other, but not close enough to touch. What was with these shackles? The ache they gave him.

The only other thing in the room was a small table with a few items on it he couldn't make out. Torture? All that would do would make him drop control, and then the Curse would take over. He wasn't sure what would happen then, but nothing good for him. *Nothing good at all.*

"Haltim I'm sorry. I should have told Will back when we made that hammer of his about that tomb, I knew he wouldn't approve, so I didn't tell him. But things would have been different." Duncan lowered his head. Everything was wrong. They would die, die screaming most likely.

"Nonsense. Look lad, if you had told Will, he would have helped you open the thing. I know it. And he could have gotten the

Blood Curse. William is a great many things, but he's not as strong as you are, at least in the mind. Will would have lost it." Haltim shook his chains the sound hard and cold in the stone room. "These chains are like regret. Regret will keep you a prisoner. Don't let it."

"They hurt Haltim, these chains." Duncan tried to push it away. "I hurt everywhere, but these shackles, I ache from them."

"Preaching like always?" A voice came from the darkened doorway. Duncan couldn't see the face, but the figure was large, a bulky frame. The voice had a fleshy quality as if spoken by someone who lived on the finest foods and wine.

"High Priest Bracin! I'm sorry High Priest, but I am unable to bow. If you'd release me, I'd be happy to follow proper form." Haltim's tone was formal, but the quaver was still there.

"I'm not a fool Haltim. You should have been replaced years ago in the Reach. To close to the bloodline. Even my predecessor before his ... accident saw that. But I never thought you'd go against the Priesthood like this. Helping them escape? Foolish." The figure moved into the room, and Duncan could see him clearer now. The man was large and thick. There was strength in him, one he was born to. His features were round and heavy. In the dim light and with only one eye Duncan couldn't see much else of the man.

"High Priest? Of Amder? Could you explain exactly what we are doing here?" Duncan felt his anger rise a tick. "I mean I was asleep in my bed, and next thing I know I'm here and hurt like a blacksmith chased me down after spending time with his daughter!"

"Duncan Reis. One of the two last living descendants of the Reis line. Last of the Forgemaster's blood." Bracin studied Duncan for a moment. Eyes darted over the chained figure, dissecting him. "You know why you are here. Be glad you are, the guard was ready to skewer you and leave your body in a charnel pit after what happened at the boarding house. And those chains? Those are Heart blessed chains. Interesting that those would give you pain. Very interesting."

"What happened?" Duncan licked his lips, cringing inside at the taste of dried blood. "I told you I don't remember." Heart blessed chains. What was the man talking about?

"You became a wild beast according to my reports. You killed two men, ripped the arm off a third, a woman that time. One of the Tempered. My Tempered." Bracin regarded them both for a moment, a frown stuck on his face.

"You will happy to know you will soon be reunited with your friend." Bracin turned to the table and picked something up. Duncan couldn't see it, but Haltim could because the old man gave an audible gasp.

"Where did you get that?" Haltim asked his words rushed.

"Friend? Rache?" Duncan blurted out.

"Rache? The girl? She's vanished. But everything I have says she's a nobody. No... Not her." Bracin gave a wide smile, the torchlight reflected his perfect white teeth. "Haltim here understands."

"How did you get that??" Haltim asked again, panic in his voice.

"Oh this?" Bracin held up what was in his hand. Duncan could see it now, and the last vestige of hope fled. A hammer. A hammer that Duncan knew well, Williams hammer! The Wight iron shone in the light, a dull white glow.

Duncan tried a lunge at the man, but the chains held him fast. "Where is my cousin??" Red clouded his vision, if this man had done something to Will ... the dull ache from the shackles expanded into a burning, the pain cutting into the anger.

"He's on his way. We picked him up not long ago, trying to leave the city. Had to get rough with him I'm afraid." Bracin swung the hammer a few times in the air. "He does do good work. But that's expected, considering the situation."

Duncan felt his anger growing and could hear his blood roaring in his ears. "What did you do?" he growled out. All he could feel now was anger and rage. He wanted to rip this vile bloated man's throat out with his teeth, feel his blood spurting, destroy, kill... The pain from the shackles burst over him, and a gasp escaped his lips. It was enough to force the anger away, at least for now.

"*DUNCAN!*" Haltim's voice snapped him back to awareness, but only barely enough. He was still poised on the edge of falling into the full effects of the blood taint. He could feel it, growing in his mind.

"Oh, made the other one mad, have I? I know what happened in the boarding house, boy. You won't be getting that close. Amusing in a way, chains made with the power of Amder's heart, holding the last two of the Forgemaster's line. You won't be breaking those." High Priest Bracin tossed the hammer again. "I like this thing. I'll use it to break your ankles and your cousin's ankles. In case something odd happens and you get out of those shackles, you won't be going anywhere."

A rattle down the hall distracted Duncan for a moment. He was fighting the curse, trying to keep control. He needed Cloud and needed it soon. This High Priest turned at the sound. "Looks like we are about to have a nice reunion. I thought about keeping you all in separate cells, but I like this room. And after all the headache you all have caused me, watching each other die is justified."

The wooden door, as thick as a sapling swung open without a sound, there, suspended between two black robed Tempered was Will, head down, out cold, but Will. It was good to see him again, even like this.

"*WILL!*" Duncan yelled, then the happiness at seeing him vanishing as he realized Will was hurt. Anger fed into the curse, and again he forced himself to try to stay calm.

As they shackled him to his place on the wall, the High Priest examined his newest prize. "You three have been a headache of hammer blows for months now. I'll be glad to have this business behind me. I will wait until that Forgemaster attempter wakes up. So, for now, hang there, and know you will never see the outside of this room again."

"Bracin, you don't understand, the Blood God, he's trying to return." Haltim spoke the words quickly. "I don't know what you believe in anymore but listen to me."

"You're that desperate? Haltim, you are a fool." The High Priest snorted and shook his head, leaving them alone.

Duncan watched the man leave the room, trailed by his Tempered. His rage was still there, he wanted to hurt that fool of a man. But that same anger fought with his thoughts about Will. *Sparks Will, wake up.* Duncan could see his cousin's chest still rise and fall, but nothing else showed him even alive.

"I'm sorry Duncan. I did not know Bracin was this bad. If I had known the Priesthood had become this corrupt…" Haltim trailed off, he didn't know what else to say.

"Done what?" Duncan spat at the ground his mouth dry but the taste of blood still lingering, driving him crazy. "This is what I always thought of the Church, of the Gods. A death is too good for all of them." Duncan pulled on the chains as hard as he could, feeling his muscles strain, and with it, the pain the shackles gave him grew. Muscles tensed, as he could barely concentrate on anything other than the hurt. Fire, his world of fire, it broke over him again, drowning his anger. With a tremor that ended in sob, he gave up, and the pain stopped. The ache remained, a reminder that these chains, Amder forged according to that man, had punished him.

He forced his head up and looked at Will, who still unconscious, hanging there. "I'm sorry Will. We tried." He hung his own head and waited for the long night to end.

***

Myriam walked away from the Guild as fast as she could go without getting winded. Ture was busy, but she knew generally where she needed to be. She still had a store of coins that she'd brought with her, which thanks to Master Jaste she had not needed to use after joining his party. She wasn't wearing the Cloak yet, she had debated that point with herself, but with the city still in a bit of a buzz about murders and something happening in the Guild, she didn't want any attention.

Her traveling pack had all her clothes and supplies, she just needed to get out of the city, and head toward the Reach. From there, she could figure things out.

In line, she waited to leave half listening to the trader and his partner in front of them in their cart.

"Did ya hear about those killers caught yesterday? One even tried to leave here, through this very gate." The older man said. "Killers. They found another body last night, old Bessim over at Travelers Rest. May the Gods bless her."

"Bessim? That's a right shame. Staying at her place a few months back. Clean, and a good price. Hope whoever takes it over keeps it that way." The younger man spat over the edge, landing on Myriam's boot.

"Oh pardon." The younger man bowed his head. "Didn't see you there."

"It's fine." Myriam side stepped away from the man's line of sight. "Don't need to worry."

"Where are you going?" The older man asked her. "The Guards are all worked up after catching someone yesterday. Solo travelers may get a lot of questions."

"Oh, I was heading to... the Reach." Myriam wondered if she should even say that, but she already had. "Moving there, have family there."

"The Reach? Long way." The older man gave her a long look. "Look here, if you want, I can tell the guards you're my Granddaughter. You come with us to the cart, we can pass through the gate. Can take you as far as Kilvar. An apology for my partner's wayward aim here."

Myriam wasn't sure. They appeared decent men, but all the way to Kilvar would be a decent length of travel. A week at least.

"My name is Ottor Kalin. My partner here is my nephew, Wert Kalin." The older man nodded to the Gate. "Going to need an answer soon."

Myriam nodded slowly. "Before we get closer, come here." Ottor shrugged. "Ok, why?"

"This." Myriam opened her pack just enough so that the older man could see the red cloak, the Journeyman's cloak. "I'm taking care of something for the Guild. Quietly."

Myriam watched with some amusement as this Ottor's face cycled through a series of emotions. Shock, then a careful appraising look at her, and finally a smile.

"Well far be it from the Kalin family traders to stand in the way of Guild business. You are more than welcome to travel with us, no questions." Ottor returned to the man who he has said was his nephew and whispered something in his ear.

Myriam didn't know what he had said, but the younger man's face turned a bit pale, he turned to her with a wide-eyed glance before nodding.

Good. They may have only been traders, but now they won't attempt anything underhanded, or even be tempted to. Thank you Master Reinhill.

In short order Myriam found herself sitting on the back of a wagon, heading toward Kilvar, and from there, the Reach. She was still angry with William, hurt and angry, but right now, she had nowhere else to go.

52.

Zalkiniv stood before the assembled cult. The displays of power had bolstered the group, and in ways the Axessed couldn't match, bonded them to her. They were now more an extension of her will, and through her the Blood God. Tonight, they would die, but useful deaths. Each death would bring blood, both theirs and the defenders. Blood born in anger and rage; blood full of power she could use.

"Tonight, we move against the followers of the soot god. They took a prize the Scaled one seeks. Your life, your death, your blood, belongs to our Lord. Kill every guard, bleed out every Priest, and slaughter every servant! On this evening, we claim revenge for the Gods Fall!" raising her knife she beckoned the Axessed to stand next to her. Her knife flashed down, cutting the creature on the arm.

The Blood dripped down but rose again as a mist in response to her working, flowing around the thirty odd cultists. It touched each of them on the forehead, leaving a mark. "This mark will grant you a tiny part of our Lord's power. Kill and maim! Rip and tear! Leave no one alive but prisoners. None of them are to be touched until we find the prize!" As the last mark was left on a forehead, she pointed towards the door, and the Axessed who watched her with unblinking eyes. "Go, and the Axessed will lead the way!"

The left in a rush, no words spoken but a guttural growl and the occasional sound of teeth snapping shut. The working she had made would increase their blind anger and hate to be true, but its primary effect would be, at the moment of their deaths, to transfer the power of that blood to her.

As the last of the cult left, she followed. She must have the prizes back; they would not disappoint her God tonight. The tunnels flew by as they walked, turns upon turns. She trusted the Axessed in this regard, the creature would not lead them astray. Regardless of its feelings towards her, the chance to feed, the chance to kill in the name of their Lord would not be something it would back away from.

After a long amount of time, they stopped at a ladder leading up, metal and much finer workmanship than any of the others they had passed, it stood alone. The tunnel was dry, dry and old.

Zalkiniv gritted her teeth. The closer they had gotten to the place, the more on edge she had gotten. Being this close to the seat of the soot stained fools' power was not one she enjoyed. While he was dead, there was power here. She felt it like a low rhythmic hammer blow, out of reach. It was irritating.

It did not matter however, tonight if all went well, she would have her prize, and the Priesthood of Amder would have a blow struck against it larger than any since the Godsfall. All because of the Deathless High Priest, Zalkiniv.

"Go." Speaking a single word, she motioned to the Axessed who stood still, its scaled skin reflecting the torchlight. Without a word the creature climbed up the ladder, making short work of the rungs, skipping them two or three at a time.

The blood rage induced cultists followed, her working still driving them to the edge of rage and madness. Only when they had all gone up and the first scream echoed in her ears, did she ascend. Power was hers.

***

Will winced and let forth a groan. By the sparks he had hit that bar hard. His head hurt, his arms hurt too, why did they hurt? He discovered why as he tried to rub his head. They had chained him up, the shackles limiting his movement.

"Will!" a voice broke in, it sounded like... Duncan?

"Duncan?" Will opened his eyes to see two people he missed most. People he trusted, people he loved. People who had both seen much better days. Duncan covered with what looked like dried blood, and red welts on his face, and Haltim with no blood on him but as many red welts on his face.

"Duncan! Haltim! What happened to you? You both look horrible!" Will was worried, but happy. The people he cared most about were here, and alive.

"Well sorry Will, being captured by the evil Priesthood of a God that shouldn't be evil, and then being beat to near death while that happened, makes you look rough." Duncan gave Will a half smile, which in truth made Will almost laugh. Duncan was still Duncan.

"We need to get out of here. Any ideas?" Will asked as he looked around the room. "Not much to go on. Oh, I see they raided my room in the Guildhall." Will could see his hammer, the one he and Duncan had made sitting on the small table, along with a few small items. "Myriam, Amder protect you."

Will stopped his searching and turned back to Duncan and Haltim. "What are you all *doing* here? When I left the Reach, you all were there and fine. I know the blood curse was weighing on you, but I thought if you didn't get angry, things were under control."

"But I get discovered, you all turn up here, in Ture, captured by the Tempered, and I end up the same way!" Will didn't get it, none of it made sense.

Duncan and Haltim gave him a quick explanation of what they'd been doing since they'd seen each other last, and what had happened along the way. Haltim noticed that Duncan didn't mention Cloud at all.

"What about Master Jaste, can he help us?" Haltim asked. "He's a Guildmaster, and he's one of the few who might be willing to help get us out of this. Or at least try. It's a tiny chance, but it can't hurt."

Will closed his eyes and swallowed. He'd been trying to not think about what had happened to Jaste, he wanted to put it out of his mind until he was somewhere safe. "Jaste is dead. He found out that the Priesthood was coming after me, and once again, got me out in time. But only by sacrificing himself. I'm sure he's dead. Killed by the Tempered."

Silence held for a moment as Duncan and Haltim absorbed this information. "I'm sorry lad, I know you don't like the idea of someone giving up their life for you. Anyone. And to have someone like Jaste do it..." Haltim trailed off.

Will nodded and was about to respond when the first scream tore through the air outside the door, and the sounds of battle came.

"What by the sparks was that??" Duncan asked as the noise got louder. Will nodded, whatever was going on, it didn't give him a good feeling.

They could hear the pounding of steps outside the door, if muffled. More yells and the sounds of screams came to them. "Someone or, something is attacking the Temple!" Haltim yelled.

"Yeah, but who? Why?" Will didn't get it. "Isn't the Priesthood powerful? How could this happen?" All three men looked at each other. The real question was if the people doing this were friendly or not.

"Well, if they get us out of here, I don't care who they are." Duncan spat on the floor. "Being alive fixes a lot of bad feelings."

Haltim shook his head. "Lad, while I'm no friend of Bracin, and what he's created, there's a lot of good people in the Church of Amder. Having them killed isn't an act of someone good."

"I don't care. I told you before Haltim. I'm sick of Gods, Priests, and powerful people. I want to be left alone, not kill anyone and be alive. No one pulling any strings, no one making choices for me." Duncan locked his gaze with Will. "You know what I mean Will, don't you?"

This Forgemaster stuff, Gods, it was unwanted. He knew one thing though, that if he didn't make it, if he didn't find a way, regardless of how hard it was, everything he held important, everything that meant anything to him, would be gone. Wiped out in a wave of destruction by the rebirth of the Blood God.

"I know Duncan. But there comes a time to fight, and a time to rise to the occasion. We can't run away from our blood. We can't run away from the path and expect everything to work out. I know what will happen if we don't. And I'm not willing to let what I *want* determine the fate of everyone else. I made that mistake already, I won't again." Will kept his eyes on Duncan, trying to read his cousins expressions.

"You've changed." Duncan said the words but nothing else. There wasn't a noise for a moment, then footsteps, rushed, came down the hall.

"Quick, pretend to be unconscious. Quietly." Haltim whispered and fell back into his chains. Will and Duncan glanced at the door and followed suite. The door opened, they could hear the latch, though the hinges made not a sound. And then a voice, not known by William, laughed.

"*RACHE?*" Duncan's voice made Will jerk up, and Haltim's too. Standing in front of them stood a young woman, pretty, dressed in a simple brown traveling garb. The only thing that stood out was the blood on both hands, and the glittering dark red stone that adorned her neck, tied on a simple woolen string.

Standing next to the woman was a huge figure, bulky and muscular, it stayed in the shadows, but they could hear its breathing, labored, almost sibilant.

"My prizes. Already for me." The woman drew her knife, and to their surprise, made a shallow cut on her cheek, followed by another of the other side. Muttering she did... something. Will felt cold, wrong, and then pain exploded in his body. He screamed a long scream before the pain stopped as fast as it began.

"Rache? I don't understand," Duncan said, his voice questioning. Will could barely see through the sweat and tears that the pain had brought.

"By Amder's forge. She's a Blood God follower," Haltim whispered.

"Finally, you understand old man. Do you know how long I waited for this? It was hard to keep things from you. But I needed my prizes. And I'm not just a follower. You know my name even if you don't think you do." The woman who Duncan knew as Rache walked towards Haltim. As she approached the old Priest, she took her knife and sliced a small nick, right between his eyes. As the blood dripped down, she took her own thumb, blood covered and smashed it into the cut.

Will watched in terror as the Priest convulsed. He wanted to scream, to stop her, but no sound would come from him. A sound not human, one of horror and pain tore from Haltim's throat. "Who am I?" the woman asked. "Say my name."

"You can't be…" Haltim whispered and then convulsed again. "Can't be…"

"Say it." The woman commanded again.

"Zalll… Zalkiniv." Haltim hung his head and wept.

"Superb. They still teach you things." Zalkiniv sauntered towards Will, who got a good full look at her. Long dark hair, wide eyes, attractive. Those eyes though, hard, cruel. An oppressive feeling of malice, hate, violence clung to her. The closer she got; the more nausea rose in him. "So this is the subject of so much angst and trouble. William Reis."

"Who are you? Why did Duncan call you Rache and who is Zalkiniv?" Will didn't understand any of this. Duncan and Haltim knew this woman?

"Many questions. But none are important. Your blood, your cousin's blood, will pave the way for the return of my Lord." The woman smiled and whispering something Will couldn't hear, placed her hand on his chest.

53

Pain. Agony. A scream tore through his throat. Visions of the future swam in front of him, a future bathed in the red of blood. The ground soaked in it as they drained bodies. All races, all ages, all sexes, it didn't matter. All taken by the Blood God or became his servants. The Reach, with blood flowing down its valleys and canyons like water after a storm. And above all, the scaled form of Valnijz, the Blood God.

"You see? My future, our future, is coming. Your God will lose, I have you both. The last two of the bloodline. You're mine." The woman removed her hand and Will gasped in relief though red spots swam in front of his eyes.

"How..."

"She's the High Priest of the Scaled One. She's, well her spirit, is immortal." Haltim whispered as he kept his head down. "All this time, and I even invited you to stay! How could I not see it?!"

Zalkiniv approached Haltim again but keeping her hands off this time. "It wasn't easy. I used a lot of blood to hide myself from you. A lot of my own blood, at first. Then, once I had power over him, the Blood blessed here." She waved towards Duncan who had been silent this entire time. Will could see a look on Duncan's face that made his breath catch. One of rage.

"I must admit, I was surprised by how much effort I put into having to hide. I wouldn't have expected a simple Priest to have that much power. How *DID* you end my control on Duncan those times he attacked you? Something about you? Some item?" Zalkiniv turned towards the bulky figure who had come in with her. Will had almost forgotten it was there, it was so still, unnaturally so. "Remove his sleeves, I want to see what's on his arms."

The figure stepped more into the light as Will gasped. It was, a man, or moved like one, well-muscled, but hairless, small scales covered its body, shining in the light. Blood covered its mouth and jaw, and it's scaled and clawed fingers. He didn't know what it was and didn't want to know. The same wrongness, the same feeling came off this creature.

The figure walked towards Haltim and without a word ripped the clothing off his arms. The fabric gave way with a loud tear. One arm was bare, but the other, a large metal bracer, multicolored shone in the light. At the sight of it the large scaled thing flinched and backed away.

"What is that on your arm? Some gift, some power from the sooty one?" Zalkiniv drew a knife. "Answer old priest. Or lose the arm, and I'll examine it my way."

Haltim said nothing, but Will saw him glance at Duncan. Haltim was pale and sweat beaded on his skin. Haltim was terrified, Will could tell that easy. He shared the emotion.

"Fine, I will figure it out later." The woman turned toward Duncan. "You've been quiet my prize. Bit hurt, are we? The girl you fell for was an act. A lie? Your blood is all I want." Duncan spat at her face but did nothing else. "Good, stay angry, that will help."

A long scream echoed down the hall drawing Zalkiniv's attention. "That was one of mine, so it looks like more help is here. Time to get moving." She motioned to the creature. "Take that one." She pointed at Will. "Remove his chains, hold him. Do not let him go. He will want to, soon." She flashed a smile at Will that made his skin crawl.

Turning back to his cousin, Duncan, she held forth something in her hand, Will couldn't see it in the dim light, but it glittered in her palm. "Do you recognize this? There's more you know. They called to you. To your blood. Do you remember the day you brought it to me? How you felt the rage and anger well up? And you wanted to hurt, to kill? Because they called to your blessing."

"It's not a blessing it's a CURSE!" Duncan yelled the last word. Will could see it in his face, Duncan was on edge, and about to boil over. "It's a blessing." The woman continued. "You will see."

She raised her hand and with her other hand she slashed with her knife, slicing a long shallow cut down the center of Duncan's face. Blood welled up instantly, dark red. A howl tore through Duncan's throat. A cry of pain, anger, rage.

The woman, Zalkiniv pressed the thing in her hand into the cut and muttered something he couldn't hear, but Haltim understood it, or knew what it was, because the old priests face went paler still. "Fight it Duncan! Fight her! You are *NOT* the animal."

Duncan went silent, and before Will could open his mouth, he looked up. His face transformed. The stress and fear which had been writ clear, were gone. All that was left was anger, rage and the desire to hurt, to feast. Zalkiniv muttered something else, and the shackles flashed. Duncan strained against them as his bonds began to glow, orange, then red, then white. A sound, one that should never come from a human throat tore through his cousin as he ripped one arm free, then another. He removed his leg shackles, not bothered by the sound and sharp smell of burning flesh. Duncan was free.

"Now, as a test, kill that one." Zalkiniv turned and pointed at Haltim.

"NO!" Will yelled as Duncan walked toward Haltim. Will couldn't see his face, but he could see Haltim's. Haltim. A friend, mentor, almost a surrogate father, was crying.

"Duncan! Don't do this!" Will yelled struggling in his shackles. The large man thing hadn't freed him yet, but stood there, unmoving, watching the scene unfolding.

Will could see Duncan's hands reach out and take Haltim's head in between them. Will closed his eyes and lowered his head. He couldn't watch, he wouldn't watch. A scream of pain, one that made Will want to cry with him erupted from his old mentor.

"Wait. Let him live for now. This could be fun." Zalkiniv's voice came to Will through hearing his out blood in his ears. "Let him live, for now."

Will opened his eyes. Haltim was breathing, but unconscious. His face already had swollen red blotches on it from Duncan's hands. "Duncan!" Will whispered. He knew Duncan couldn't control himself, he knew whenever this wore off, the pain he'd feel, and the guilt, would drive him mad.

The creature she controlled turned toward Will and without a word grabbed a shackle and jerked back with a hiss. Will could feel a surge of heat, as where the thing had grabbed the shackle had glowed, the red glow of heated metal, for a tiny moment of time.

"Well? We need to get moving." Zalkiniv pointed at Will with her knife. "Take him."

"High Priestess, the metal is painful." The creature spoke, its voice low, deep, but with that slightly sibilant hiss that betrayed snake like characteristics to go along with its scaled form.

"Axessed, pain is just pain. Take him." Zalkiniv stroked the arm of Duncan giving him what Will could only call a *hungry* look. "Our lord wants them both."

The Axessed said nothing at first but looked back at Haltim who was still unconscious. "Should I free him?"

Zalkiniv nodded, her eyes still locked on Duncan. Will couldn't see Duncan's face, but he could hear his cousins breathing. Hard breathing, as if he had worked a forge for hours, his shoulders were hunched as if he were on the edge of exploding.

"What did you do to him?" Will yelled at the woman.

"He's mine now. He's mine body and soul. The Blood God's blessing flows through him, and is in control, and I am in control of it. From now, until his death, Duncan Reis is no more. He is my tool to use, and I plan on using him, often. Take them. We must go," she said to the Axessed, who ripped the shackles off Haltim. Will noticed that those didn't glow in response. Haltim's form fell to the ground with a thud, his breathing labored, but breathing still. "Damn it Haltim, wake up!" Will yelled at the Priest but got no response.

The creature then turned towards Will and ripped his shackles free. This time though the same glow and heat came, it ignored the effect, though Will could see its eyes half close in response to the obvious pain. Will tensed for a moment, he could escape if he timed this right. He hesitated though, that would mean leaving both Duncan and Haltim to this thing, and this woman.

The foot shackles came off and Will fell to the ground as well though not for long as the creature grabbed him by the shoulder and without effort lifted him off the ground. Will was strong, and this thing lifted him like he was a feather pillow! The creature had a long sniff and Will imagined it was tasting his thoughts.

"Grab the Priest, it's time to go." Zalkiniv turned towards the door, but they had taken too long. Three armed guards came in the room, followed by the one-man Will was not happy to see, High Priest Bracin of Amder. "Who are you? What are you doing with these people? I am the High Priest, and you will answer me!"

Bracin yelled before he got a good look at the thing holding Will and Haltim. Will found a small measure of satisfaction at seeing the man turn a noticeable shade paler at the sight of the Axessed.

Zalkiniv laughed. "So, this is the High Priest of Amder? I'm not even impressed. Duncan? Axessed? Kill them." It threw Will to the far side of the room, along with Haltim, slamming his shoulder hard against the stone wall and feeling something crack in response. Pain came, but Will tried to put it out of his mind. He reached down to Haltim with his uninjured arm and tried to help the man sit up.

"William." Haltim's voice came, weak, whispering, but there. His eyes opened a tiny bit and Will's fears were realized, Haltims eyes were full of blood! "I'm dying William. But I must tell you something, Amder made it very clear."

"Say nothing Haltim, save your strength." Will glanced up to see the Axessed who had been fighting with a guard take a large cut to the arm not even flinch and grab the man by the throat. Will looked away wincing, not wanting to look. He kept his eyes on Haltim instead, though he knew what that creature and worse, Duncan, were doing.

"Haltim, you will not die." Will tried very hard not to look at the struggle before him but glanced around. He scrambled towards the table where he had seen something before, his hammer! He had been right. The Tempered must have taken his stuff out of the Guild! Grabbing it Will felt, more complete, less stressed. He made his way back to the wall where Haltim was, hiding the hammer with his body in case Zalkiniv was watching. But she watched the carnage with a rapturous expression.

"Will, I can't see." Haltim moved weakly, taking his hand and putting it on the bracer on his wrist. "Will listen. Amder made this, it's made from the cloth that covered the hammer you found. It's blessed, I used it, I used it to." Haltim's voice trailed off his breathing hard.

"Used it to what? Free Duncan? She said you did something right?" Will blinked back tears, Haltim should not die like this, here, with these people.

Haltim nodded, his head moving slowly with great effort. "My head hurts. Can't think straight. Bracer broke her control, don't know if it will now, it's stronger than it was. Take it, it will help."

Will hesitated. He glanced back and saw that only one guard and the High Priest was still standing. Bracin turned pale at the sight of his guards dying and with a shove pushed the last guard towards the Axessed and Duncan, running out the door.

"No time. Take it. It doesn't like to come off, but now...." Haltim tugged off the bracer and held it out for Will. Will hesitated and reached out, his fingers brushed against it and hammers filled the air.

54

Will jerked back, but he was no longer in the cell, but back in the Anvil room, in the Guildhall. Or at least it looked like the Anvil room. The sound of the forge and hammers filled the air, but in the distance, as if coming from a forge far away.

"William Reis," A voice came, strong, but one he had heard before.

Will turned and there by the anvil stood the last Forgemaster. He stood, holding a hammer by the Anvil. Will felt his knees give way with the shock. *What was going on? A vision, now?*

"Oh, get up. You don't have time for that. No one ever had time for that. I hated it when I was alive, being dead doesn't make it better." Forgemaster Reis scoffed and flipped his hammer in the air. "It's good to see you again, William. I was happy you managed to escape from the Guild. I am sorry lad, about Master Jaste."

"Forgemaster, I don't understand, where's the cell? The others, Haltim, Duncan?" Will looked around again. "Am I dreaming? Unconscious?"

"Not dreaming, and not unconscious, well not dreaming literally. You're still in that cell Will, and all the same people are still there, though Bracin isn't." Forgemaster Reis's face turned dark at Bracin's name Will noted. "You are here for a quick talk."

"I don't..." Will said, but the Forgemaster held up a hand to silence him.

"You don't understand." Amder sighed for a moment. "I didn't want to have to go about things this way, but the Blood Gods followers have forced my hand. Haltim was supposed to tell you what to do, but he can't."

Forgemaster Reis pulled forth a bar of metal from somewhere and placed it on the anvil, with a snap it glowed, and he hammered it, a rhythmic hammering that began to intertwine with his words. "William, the time for the remaking is here. We can't wait any longer. Valnijz is planning on using your blood and Duncan's blood to be reborn to spite Amder. We won't, no, we can't let that happen."

"You must take Amder's heart out of the Temple. For too long the Priesthood has used his heart for its own ends. This must stop!" The Forgemasters voice rose, and he slammed his hammer down on the anvil, hard, drawing a series of reddish silver sparks from its surface. "You will need the Heart to recreate Amder, to make him live again."

"But I don't..." Will asked again. But the room shimmered, faded.

"No time to answer. I've done all I can. But I can tell you this, she's safe." The Forgemasters voice came again but faded out. And Will was back in the cell. One arm useable, Haltim wheezing on the floor near death, and fighting still going on at the one door in and out of the room.

And on his wrist, was now the bracer. An almost pleasant warmth came from it. And with that warmth some pain and exhaustion faded. His shoulder still throbbed, but he didn't feel like he was about to fall over. A choked scream came from behind him, probably the last guard. The Forgemasters last words came back to him. She was safe. Myriam, it had to be.

Relief spilled through him, like a cold waterfall, washing away that fear. She hadn't paid for his foolish mistake. That was something at least. The cost of knowing him hadn't been her life.

"Bracer might stop Duncan, might not. Her hold is strong." Haltim whispered. "Don't know about..." the old Priest stopped talking at that point and slumped down even more. Panic rose in Will and he hoped Haltim hadn't died there. *No, his chest still rose and fell, though slower than it should.*

"Get them up Duncan. Axessed? Chase down that fat fool of a High Priest." Zalkiniv ordered her minions around. "Hurry, I want to get out of here!" Will turned to face this woman, he wasn't scared, or even worried. Her face was one of joy, even excitement. *She loved this, the violence.* A wave of disgust rolled over him. Will knew what he had to do.

The creature, the Axessed, didn't even acknowledge her order, but ran out the door after High Priest Bracin. Will couldn't help feeling sorry for the man when that thing caught him. Bracin was an evil man and corrupt didn't begin to describe him, but still being torn apart by that thing, wouldn't be a fate he'd wish for anyone.

Duncan approached Will and Haltim. Blood spattered him from head to hands, arms and shirt. His face, that face was one of hate. *Duncan, I'm sorry.* Hate and anger, one that lived to exert pain. A rictus grin, and as he watched in horror, Duncan bit the air, tasting it, the same way as the Valni had, so long ago.

"Duncan don't do this, it's me, William! It's Haltim! You know us! This isn't you, she's done something, and she's using the Blood, the thing you hate!" Will pleaded with Duncan. He knew that Rache or whatever her name was had said it was useless, but he had to try. "Remember the tower? Back in the Reach? When those Bandits attacked us? You killed them, but you fought it off, the taint. Do it now! Reject her!"

Duncan said nothing and had no reaction. He reached forward and grabbed Haltim's robe, and dragging the dying man upright, and then, with his other arm tried to grab Will. "By the sparks Duncan, fight!" Will yelled as he tried to move out of the way, but with whatever control she had had over his cousin, he moved fast, faster than Will expected.

"Now, you come with me, or Duncan will be entertaining me on our trip. I have a very sharp knife, and I know more ways to use it that any person you have met. I can make him scream for days. I need both of you, but I don't need you whole, just alive." Zalkiniv smiled, a smile of joy. "Before long you will know nothing William Reis, you will live in the pain and rage like Duncan."

Will could feel the hammer under his jacket, its weight comforting him. She hadn't noticed it yet but would soon. He had to act now before that thing came back. Will reversed his body weight pushing it toward his cousin instead of away. For a moment Duncan stumbled and Will took advantage, throwing his arm with the bracer forward catching Duncan right across the cheek.

The effect was instant. Duncan gave out a howl of pain, great pain, his face stuck in a rictus as he fell backward, releasing both Haltim and Will. Zalkiniv grabbed her head and fell to her knees as whatever connection she had was struck by this Amder blessed bracer.

Will grabbed Haltim as he fell, screaming himself as the old man's weight hit his injured shoulder, jerking it downward. But he had to move, he couldn't stop! He turned away from the pair that were down for the moment and he made for the door, making it through before either of them recovered. The bracer hadn't broken the control she had over Duncan, but it had slowed him down. Through the door, Will decided to bar the place shut. It wouldn't stop them, but it would slow them down. He could hear the woman, moaning but it sounded like she was recovering, and Will wanted no part of that.

Will let Haltim slump to the stone floor, wincing as the man hit the hard floor, but no time for gentle. He grabbed the bar and with his foot slammed the door shut, sliding the bar into place. He tried to ignore the sharp spike of pain in his shoulder again, Amder above if he made it through this day alive, he would sit down and cry!

Haltim was breathing still, but the slow breaths were uneven now, an even worse sign. The red blotches on his face were already turning dark, a sure sign of pooling blood. "By the sparks Duncan!" Will whispered as he hoisted the old man back up, forcing the pain out of his mind. He took the hammer out from its hiding place with his other hand, and the feeling of the metal in his hand was one of relief, something at least felt good, right.

Will did not understand where to go, or even what direction. But standing in the hall wasn't going to get them anywhere, so half dragging Haltim with him, Will set off down the hallway, trying to find the Heart, and a way out.

***

Bracin panted as he slammed yet another door behind himself. He'd done that now five times, running or at least fast walking through a series of rooms and hallways. Everything he'd planned, everything he'd built, was in danger of destruction. Blood God followers! Here in the heart of Ture! Bracin couldn't understand it. All his life he'd heard of the horrors of the Scaled One and his faith, how they use people, bleed them, made them monsters, and he'd not believed them. Oh, the Valni were real, but that was from the actual blood of a God. And they were far away, beyond the barrier.

But a religion being able to do that? Ridiculous. But here they were, and the power they held was true. He'd been having fun with a young pretty acolyte, when the first scream had broken the mood. At first, he'd thought one of the many prisoners had escaped, but injured, and he'd ignored it. But then the sound came again, and with it the distinct sound of fighting. Fighting! He'd summoned guards, and a few Tempered and headed off, not sure what was going on, but sure that whatever it was, they could handle it. He'd stayed in back of course, with a Tempered and a guard behind him, in case. But then this roving mad army of people in dirty blood-stained robes had appeared and had torn through what he had assembled. They fought like wild animals, and wounds that would stop a man cold only made them fight harder, angrier.

Right then he'd grabbed the three nearest guards and ran for his prizes. The two men of the Reis bloodline were too valuable to escape. He didn't care if the attackers killed them, but he hadn't been sure then what they wanted, until he'd arrived at the cell and learned the truth. Blood cultists, a young girl wielding power beyond anything he'd expected, and a monstrosity that gave it away. Because Bracin knew what the thing was.

He'd been a studious acolyte, though not pious. But learning the history of the Church of Amder had been useful in his rise to power. And a large part of that history dealt with the fight against the God of Rage and Blood, the Scaled One, Valnijz. He'd never expected to see one, but the moment his eyes fell on it, he knew, an Axessed.

He'd run once he'd realized that there was no way his guards would win, even armed with Heart forged blades. These attackers didn't break, they didn't flee. They were in some kind of blood frenzy. But he should be safe here, in a nameless room with nothing in it. He wasn't even sure how he got here or where he was. The Temple of Amder was old like the Guildhall, and as a result had lots of empty space. But there was no way those people, or that Axessed thing would follow him all this way. Stay low, stay safe and wait. He'd make a more dignified return to the more used parts of the Temple later. A slow smile spread across his face as the thought occurred to him. If he was lucky, he could find a body of one of these Blood God followers, a little blood use of his own, a minor cut, and he'd be a proud defender of the Temple. Maybe quiet the more traditional members of the clergy.

The door flew in, erasing his smile, and the sinking feeling of dread replaced it. There in the doorway stood the Axessed, sniffing the air and moving into the room with a smooth gait.

"Prey." The Axessed whispered, as its gaze fell upon Bracin. Sweat and tears began as panic filled him.

"I can pay you, I can... whatever you want, leave me alone. Take others, take as many as you want!" Bracin tried to force himself into the corner farthest away from the creature.

"Meat is all I want. You are meat." The Axessed moved closer, sniffing the air again. "I can smell your fear. Good, it will make you taste better."

Bracin felt panic overwhelm him and closed his eyes. In quiet desperation he prayed to Amder for help, for deliverance, for safety. He was the High Priest! He deserved an answer! But silence and the feeling of a cold stone wall was all he got.

Pain, as one large scaled hand grabbed him by the arm, and with a crack, broke it. Bracin screamed then, a scream of terror, but no one was near to hear it. The scream cut off as the Axessed fed.

55.

Will paused, catching his breath. Haltim may be an old man but dragging him around with one good arm was tiring. *Where was everyone?* He'd heard over one set of running footsteps, but he didn't know where they had come from, things echoed down these hallways. Unsure if they were friendly or not, or who would even be considered friendly in this place, he'd hidden in alcoves, and even played dead a few times, when he'd been sure they were heading his way. Haltim's breathing was barely noticeable now, and Will knew time was short for the old priest. But he didn't want to leave him here, in this place of corruption and betrayal.

Steps came again, and Will began the same lurching walk he'd been doing. His shoulder burned now, and Will wondered if he'd done more damage to it with this dragging of Haltim. The steps came closer and seemed to head his way. There were several doors in this hallway, all barred, meaning, more cells. How many cells did a Temple of Amder have and why?

A voice called out from a nearby cell, one he didn't want to hear. *I know that voice.* It couldn't be. It can't be him. Will wanted to take Haltim and run, but he had to be sure, Master Jaste would have wanted him to. He turned toward the door that the voice he recognized had come from, throwing the bar open.

He took up his hammer again and dragged Haltim into the dark room, closing the door behind him. "Who is that?" A voice came from the far side of the room. A voice Will knew, a voice weak, but recognizable. A voice that Will didn't like and would have been happy to never hear again. Regin. Jaste had said Regin was the one who had turned him in. Master Jaste was dead because of this man, all of this was because of the man chained up against the wall.

"Who is that? I have nothing else to tell you just let me be please." Regin's voice broke a few times, and Will felt himself wince in sympathy. He should just take Haltim and go. Leave and never look back.

He should. But he wasn't going to. Will paused listening for a moment then, he as silently as he could, place Haltim down on the floor. His eyes took a moment to adjust to the gloom as the only light was coming through the small opening in the door the guards used to look in and check.

It was Regin! Will felt pity for the man as he looked him over. They had beaten Regin, hard, and recently. Bruises and raised swollen areas covered what Will could see, and worse. Burn marks, some quite long covered his arms in places. Will didn't like the man, but did he deserve this?

Will knew in his heart that while he didn't like him, Regin had been doing what he thought was right. Will had been breaking the rules. Master Jaste had been breaking the rules. Unjust rules, wrong rules, but rules. "Amder help me." Will approached the chained man.

"What was that? Who?" Regin asked again. His eyes peered toward Will, and slowly, widened as he could see who was talking. "Markin? Markin Darto?? What? How? I don't understand!" Will shook his head, unsure of how to answer that. What did he tell the man?

He knew the whole Markin Darto name was a lie, and one now dead. Did this man deserve the truth? Could William be true to himself if he kept up the lies? The faint sound of hammers filled the air for a second, and Will with a deep breath knew what to say.

"No. My name was never Markin Darto. My name is William Reis. I am from the Reach. This you know, at least some of it. I will be honest with you Master Regin. I don't like you. I find you arrogant, annoying, and quite possibly one of the most irritating people I've ever met. Amder above, I'd like to leave you here, and have you see what fate brings you." Will paused, listening for footsteps, but silence filled the air except for Haltim's barely audible wheeze.

"I am a descendant of the last Forgemaster. I have been tasked by Amder himself to bring him back into this world. The Blood God is also trying to return, and wants to use my blood, and the blood of my last living relative, a cousin, to return to life. That is who I am that is why I was in the Guild." Will kept his face on Regin's face, which had gone from surprise, to outright shock.

"I... what? Forgemaster? Amder?" was all Regin croaked out.

"For now, I will free you. Come with us or stay here. You should know the Temple is under attack however, by Valnijz cultists. They came for me and Duncan, my cousin. I escaped, he could not." William took his hammer and with a final check for footsteps, hammered the shackles that bound Regin to the wall.

Regin fell to the ground with a groan, unable to say much else. Will listened for footsteps, because either way, they wouldn't be friendly. If it was the cultists, they would be dead. If it was that woman, that Priestess, and Duncan, and that thing, the Axessed, they would be dead. And if by some chance it was the Tempered and the Guards for the Temple, the odds were they would be put back in chains and killed or beaten for as long as they still lived, which wouldn't be long. Will could wait no longer, they had to get moving.

"Well? Are you coming or staying?" he did not want Master Regin to go with them but leaving him here to this charnel house didn't sit well with him.

"I'll come," was all Regin said and slowly came to his feet. Will was surprised that Regin said nothing else, some biting comment about how Will was a fool, or delusional, of a fraud. *He just must be saving it up for later.*

"Help me pick Haltim up." Will asked as he heard a faint yell in the distance. "We must get moving." Regin again didn't complain and helped Will get Haltim to his feet.

"He's nearly dead. Just leave him here," Regin said as he got a look at Haltim's face. "He's barely breathing."

Will felt a fury in his gut start to build. "I will never leave this man here in this damned cell. Never. I know he's dying, but I will get this man out of here. You can help or stay." Will felt his shoulder scream again with the weight and locked his jaw as they moved.

"Fine," Regin followed helping hold up Haltim's limp form as they made their way out of the cell and down the hallway. "Where are we going, anyway? How do we get out?" he asked.

"I have no idea. They brought here me in a wagon, unconscious," Will said, "We have one more thing to do before we leave this place. Something we must do. I have to get the Heart."

Regin nearly dropped the part of Haltim he was holding up. "Are you crazy? They aren't going to just let you walk out with the Heart of Amder! It's big, magical, and the source of power for the Guild and the Priesthood."

"I know. But it's needed, I can't bring Amder back without it." Will pressed on, looking for stairs as they passed hallways and doors

"And how do you plan on getting the Heart out of here?" Regin said, staring at Will. "We are carrying this... person."

"Haltim."

"What?" Regin said and might have said more but at the moment the sound of a large bell rung through the air.

"His name is Haltim. And what was that?" Will stopped mid stride at the sound of the bell.

"Nothing good." Regin answered, as they moved again, as fast as they could carry the body of the old Priest.
"Haltim is a mentor, friend. He's a Priest of Amder, and a not corrupt one, there's enough of them." Will pushed a door open on the right side of the hallway to be greeted with stairs. "Here, up!"

Regin didn't answer but followed Will's direction. As they made it through the door, Will closed it behind them, wishing he had something, anything to wedge it closed, but he knew it was a fruitless endeavor. He barely had the clothes on his body right now. No money, just his hammer and this bracer.

At that moment, the faint sound of hammers came again, which Will associated with Amder trying to communicate. Could he do something to make this work? Will took a deep breath and took a heavy swing at the doors latch and handle. As the hammer struck, a sound echoed down the hallway, the moan of Wight Iron, overlaid with a pure note that rose out of hearing. And with a single stroke, the doors latch, and handle were hammered flat, and broken.

"How?" Regin looked at Will with a look of disbelief obvious in his face, and while Will waited for the snide follow up, none came.

"I told you why. Do not doubt me." Will shut his mouth. That was out of character for him, but Regin wasn't anyone he needed to explain himself to. They ascended the stairs, and found they were out of the dungeons and crypts, and into a more ornate section of the Temple.

"Regin. Master Regin." Will spoke quietly. "Do you know where the Heart is? I've never been in this place."

Regin had been silent since the door closing, and while it was hard to make out with the bruises and welts, he looked at Will with wide eyes and an opened mouth. "I don't know, maybe." His voice was low, a whisper.

"Lead on then." Will motioned him forward with the hammer. His shoulder sent a spike of pain as he did so. Will tried to block it out by examining Haltim. The old Priest was still breathing, sort of. Will just didn't want him to die here.

Regin lead them down a series of hallways, pausing occasionally and muttering. Will couldn't make it out but didn't think about it too much. His thoughts were on what he would do if they ran into Guards, or those attackers. *Or worse, Duncan.* He knew there had been nothing he could have done to save him, but leaving him in the grips of that woman, that High Priest, left an empty hollow in his chest. He hoped Duncan would forgive him if he ever came back to himself. He had to come back. There had to be a way to make him come back.

"Here." Regin stopped at a large door, unmarked but impressive.

"Are you sure?" Will was surprised, he had expected a monstrosity of gilded metal. Not this large but simple wooden door.

"As much as I can be, yes." And with that Regin pushed the door open before Will could stop him.

And there, hovering in the air, was the Heart. It was large, as Regin had said, the size of three or four anvils. Crystalline, pink and white. It tuned in the air, casting its glowing radiance around the room. Will gasped at the sight, and the sound. For it thrummed. A beat more felt than heard, it pulsed with the rhythmic power of a hammer blow. Deep and wide, it shook Will to his core. The heart of a God, the heart of his God.

He turned to Regin who, to his surprise, was staring at him, and not the heart. No, he wasn't staring at Will, but at his hammer! It was glowing! Brighter than the day they had forged it, the hammer in his hand glowed with a silver-white light, and the light pulsed in tune with the Heart. Will knew why, though he hadn't expected it, maybe he should have. It was the blood. The blood used in the forging. The blood that had started all of this. "Blood calls to blood," Will whispered.

"What did you say?" Regin asked jerking his eyes away from the hammer.

"Nothing, just a thought." Will looked behind them. While he thought he heard a few yells in the distance, he was still rather surprised at the lack of activity. Where was everyone? An attack of the Temple like this should have meant that the place would be swarming with Guards, Priests, who knew what else. Maybe Amder was helping, but in that case, they needed to not waste whatever time they had.

They moved into the room, and Will motioned Regin to place Haltim down against the wall. Haltim collapsed down, limp. His face was black with blood now, rather than the pink of healthy flesh. "Regin, close the door, I need to figure out how or what I'm supposed to do with that." Will pointed at the Heart.

56

Regin stood, turning back to Will. "You didn't call me Master Regin. I am a Guildmaster, and you will treat me as such."

Will resisted the urge to hit Regin with his hammer. "When you act like one, you'll be one." He turned away and toward the Heart, tamping down the fury that had appeared in his gut. He knew Regin would say something to that effect at some point, the man was too self-righteous not to.

He heard the door close, but Regin said nothing. Will felt a struggle, he didn't like ordering the man around, but he, with everything else wasn't about to let this man, Guildmaster or not, walk all over him again. Too much pain had come out of that choice.

The Heart stood before him, the light from it making him squint in the dim room. The thrum in tune with the hammer in his hand was even more noticeable this close. What's more the light off the thing made his skin feel tight, as if the heat from a forge fire. There was no heat coming off this to make it feel that way. If anything, the room was cool, comfortable almost.

Amder, Haltim, Forgemaster Reis, how by the sparks do I take this out of here? Will wondered. The thing was far too big to move alone. Will reached out a hand to touch the heart, and the sound of hammers, strong sprung to his ears.

Will was alone. Alone in a Smith shop, by the look. A clean and well stocked Blacksmiths shop. Every tool he'd ever even heard about was laid out against the wall, and the forge itself was a work of art. Even the Anvil gave a shine to the room.

"Ah there you are." The voice came from the other side of the room, and there, a large figure, indistinct was quenching something. The telltale hiss of metal in liquid filled the smithy for a moment. He could hear the figure, but its outline and details shook and faded in the forge light.

"Amder?" Will said stunned and fell to his knees.

"Oh, get up." Amder snorted and pulled out a billet of metal out of the quench, holding it up and clicking his teeth in annoyance.

"I hate being dead. Things don't work right." Amder threw the metal into a pile of same shaped lumps and placed his tongs on the bench.

"William Reis. We meet at last." Amder came nearer to Will, and Will could tell his first impression had been right. If this was Amder, he was just a ghost of an outline now.

"I know, I don't look like anything, I'm dead." Amder leaned against the Anvil. "I hope, soon, I won't be."

Will nodded. "But Amder my lord, don't get all this. Why me? I know what the Forgemaster said, but I still..."

Amder held up a hand. "I know. You have the skill, the knowledge and the blessing needed. Your whole family has had my blessing since the day of the Godsfall. It was the one gift I could give in a short time on that day. You and your cousin, Duncan, both have it."

Will felt a sting of sadness well up at the mention of Duncan's name, but tamped it down, not yet, not now he told himself.

"I'm sorry William. I am. Duncan has been captured by my brother. I wish it wasn't so, but he has been taken as a thief takes an unwatched coin purse." Amder sighed. "I should have seen the possibility, but I didn't. I was always blind to what depths of madness Valnijz has sunk to."

"Brother? You and the Blood God are brothers?" Will didn't know that information, he wasn't sure even Haltim had known.

"Well, yes. More so than the other Gods. Valnijz wasn't always this way, full of Rage and Anger, blood and hate. Back when we entered the world, we, he and I, were the Gods of Men. The others watched the natural world, and they had their people. But he and I were the Gods of Men. I was to be the God of Creation, of making things, craft. He was to be the God of inner life, Emotion and Thought. But something twisted him."

"What could twist a God?" Will blurted out. "I'm sorry Amder my Lord, I know I shouldn't question." *It didn't make sense, they were Gods, right?*

"I don't know and please call me Amder. I'm not a formal God. We got into a fight, an argument, over something minor, and he left. He disappeared for years, and when he returned, he was as he is now. The only thing he wanted was blood. Rage and pain. He changed his appearance, taking on the name of the Scaled One." Amder's figure shook its head. "I lost him. As Duncan is now lost to you."

"We can save Duncan!" Will yelled feeling the anger rise. "He's the only family I have, I'll not let them have him!"

Amder said nothing for a long time, finally walking over to the forge, and started poking at the coals there. "I hope you can. I had plans for him as well you know."

"Amder, why didn't you stop my Father from using Cloud?" Will blurted out, the thought had occurred to him with all this talk about Duncan. "He gave up, and left, went to the Sky. Why didn't you stop him?"

"I couldn't. I can't make you do anything. I can guide, I can help, and I can plan, but I can't make you do anything." Amder reached out and grabbed a red glowing coal. Will flinched a tiny bit, but the figure of his God didn't notice. "You have your own minds. I don't pull strings like a puppeteer. Not my area anyway. That was supposed to be the sphere of my brother, before..." Amder paused, and though he had no features, Will would have sworn the God was scowling at the coal in his hand.

"I need to return William. Things are spiraling out of control. My Priesthood, corrupted, the Guild, corrupted." Amder tossed the coal back and forth for a moment. "Take this!" and threw the coal to William. Reflexes took over and Will grabbed the coal, only to expect burning heat, but the coal for all its glow, was cold.

"It's not hot?" Will asked, unsure what to do with it.

"No. It's not, because the faith is dying out. There would have been a time that even being in this room would have been too much for a mortal to bear. But now, it's fine. That coal should be hot enough to melt any metal, and now it's as cold as coal dug up from the ground." Amder plucked the coal from Will's fingers and threw it back into the forge. "You William Reis, are my hope."

Will knew Amder was right at least about the corruption, and the fact that the faith of Amder was dying out. Outside the Reach the true faith was small, why worship a God everyone knew was dead? Even in Ture, where the Temple of Amder stood, it wasn't about worship of a God, it was about making money, and making power.

"So, are you dead? Really?" Will asked. "I'm talking to you, right? If you could do this why couldn't you have kept the faith alive?"

The figure of Amder, or shadow, Will wasn't sure which term fit, stood up straight in front of him for a long minute and then much to the relief of Will, laughed. "Ah, you Reises... know how to be blunt. It's one reason I always like your family. I can talk to you now, at this, the limit of what I can do now, is only because, and you're touching the Heart. My heart. That's it. If you weren't, I could send a messenger, like I did before, but I couldn't talk to you like this."

"Ah." Will didn't know what to say. "Should I be... back in the Temple? I've been here for several minutes, and we aren't safe. Haltim is about to die. The followers of the High Priest, all those cultists, that Zalkiniv person, that creature thing, and my cousin are out there."

Amder nodded. "All true. But time doesn't pass the same here, I may be dead, but I am a God."

"How do I take the heart then? What do I do? Everyone keeps telling me to remake you, reforge you, but no one wants to tell me how to do it." Will crossed his arms in thought as he planned out what to do in his head. "I know we needed the Heart, we have the Hammer, but what else? Anything?"

Amder gave a nod, the edges growing a tiny bit blurrier as the head moved. "Heart, Hammer, Forge. That will start the process and, it must be the Forge in the Reach. Under the Church of the Eight, there's a Forge. A special forge. It can start the process."

"Start?" Will could tell that God or not, Amder was holding something back.

"We will explain later, we don't have a lot of time right now." Amder waved his hand dismissive, "Now get out of here. Take the Heart and go."

"How? The thing is huge! How do I get it out?"

"You already have." Amder said, and the forge faded to white and then, vanished. Will stood, back in the Temple. The

Heart in front of him was gone! Will was surprised, because in his hand a small pinkish white heart shaped crystal sat.

"Neat trick," Will muttered.

"What is?" Regin asked as Will whirled around. Regin was sitting next to the still and quiet form of Haltim, his back to Will, had the old man died? He ran over to Haltim was too late? Tears came to his eyes. He had been almost a father to Will over the years, he didn't deserve this. His death was on William. *And Duncan...*

"Is he dead?" Will stood there, looking at the body of Haltim. *Mourn later.*

"No, he's still breathing," Regin's voice broke through the inner struggle. Haltim wasn't gone yet!

"Markin!" Regin jumped to his feet "The Heart! It's gone!"

"William, not Markin. And I have it, here." Will made his way to Haltim's form, waving the crystal in his hand at the now stunned Regin, who was standing there with his mouth open, trying to process.

"How..." Regin said before snapping his mouth shut and shaking his head in disbelief.

"You wouldn't believe me if I told you," Will replied and knelt by Haltim's body. His face was black now, too much pooled blood, but he was breathing. Will held the heart up to Haltim. "I have it Haltim, I have the Heart. I can return Amder to life, assuming I can get to the Church of the Eight, get to the Hammer, get the Forge working, and deal with whatever Amder isn't telling me, that is." Will felt a small smile cross his face for a moment.

The Heart, which hadn't glowed since it had shrunk, burst into light, its pinkish radiance illuminating the crags and lines of the old man's face. Will had never really paid attention to how old Haltim was.

"Don't mourn me." Haltim's eyes fluttered open for a second. Blood red and broken, but they still were able to focus on Will's face.

"Haltim! You're awake! Oh, by the sparks, it's a miracle! Come, we need to move and get you and us out of there, somehow." Will felt that smile, which had burst forth into a full grin. *Finally, something good.*

"No Will. I'm dying. The Heart gave me enough, Amder gave me enough for a short talk." Haltim's eyes closed again, but his voice remained, though weak. "It has been my honor, my privilege to see you grow up my lad. You're a true man of the Reach."

Will felt the joy fade. "Don't say that, we need to get you to a healer, something. Regin quick, grab his other arm and let's get him up."

Haltim loosely waved his arm in a dismissive wave. "Will, I know you don't want me to die, I don't want to die. But it's too late. I'm at peace. You're ready. Go. Bring Amder back into the World. End this madness." A ragged breath and Haltim's eyes opened but then closed again. "The Hammer, the one I hid, it's wrapped in leather, under a mound of old robes in a storeroom in the Church." Haltim's voice got weaker as he spoke. "Go. Leave. I'm at peace."

Will felt the tears on his cheeks, he hadn't even known he was crying. "Haltim, Haltim!" Will shook the old man, but he was gone, for good this time. Will bent his head into Haltim's robes for a moment, overcome by grief.

"William, we need to go. I'm sorry." Regin spoke from behind him. "I don't know what I believe about all this, but it's obvious that old man cared about you, and you him. Don't die here."

Will lifted his face, looking at the face of his dead friend, mentor, even surrogate father. He wouldn't let them win. Zalkiniv, Valnijz, corrupted and wrong Priesthoods and Guilds. None of it. Amder would return.

He spied his hammer against the wall and grabbed it with his good hand after shoving the Heart into an interior pocket of his tunic. It was time to move.

57.

Zalkiniv found herself unable to speak or even think, the sound of hammers overwhelmed all thought. Blinking as it faded, she took stock of her situation. *Her prizes!* Duncan was unconscious still, though her link to him was returning, and he was still nominally under her control. The other one, and the Amderite, were gone. The Scaled One would not be understanding if they managed to escape.

Trying to clear her head, she worked to remember what had happened. One look at Duncan's face made it clear. The same mark as that time in the Boarding House. The bracer. She had seen the two men talking, but watching her new pet kill the Guardsmen here had been such a joy, she hadn't given it much attention. *Foolish, she should have separated them.*

The door was closed, so they had fled. She checked the door, but as she had expected, it was barred. This couldn't stand. She had to recover what the Blood God demanded, there was no alternative path. Cursing the luck, she drew her knife and walked over to Duncan. The link was growing stronger yet, soon he would be awake, and she would send him on the hunt. That bracer, whatever it was, had limits then. Before it had broken the link totally. The Claret stone had made the difference this time. *Even here, the Blood God wins.* She reached down and drew blood from Duncan's scalp. Easy to get blood, and she needed it fast.

She had to get the door open and open now; she worked the blood taint and the lingering rage still present to break the door open. It was a working avoided. It was messy, loud, and workings on objects weren't easy.

She could feel the pressure building as she worked the blood, a resistance to her power. Both ears popped as it grew, and beads of sweat appeared on her face as she pushed with the blood. No door, not even one here in the Temple of the Soot God would stop her!

With a huge boom, the door flew outwards; the pressure ending immediately. The echoes of the boom spread down the halls and rooms, sure to draw attention. She could feel some of her cultists still around, her link to them from the working earlier still there, but far less than when they started. Three or four left now, down from the twenty she had started with.

She needed her Hunter. The Axessed was gone, having chased after that fool of a High Priest of the Dirty One. She knew it was feasting even now as the man it had chased had no real power. No, she needed Duncan up. She could work his blood to follow the other Reis, blood calls to blood.

She was about to make him hunt down the last of his family, and blood ties like that can be hard to overcome. Some deep lingering bonds can wreak havoc with control. Her uninjured hand took some of the mixed blood and smeared a symbol on Duncan's body. "Awaken," she ordered as his eyes flickered open. For a split second she could see the man inside, terrified, angry, sad, but then it disappeared, swallowed by the working. Rage and hunger filled him again as she sighed with the feeling of hate.

"Go, find and hunt, find the other of the blood." Duncan froze for a second, and then without a word took off. Zalkiniv followed him, keeping within sight of the man as he moved through the halls. He moved like a Valni, the almost loping gait, the grunts and growls he made.

The first stop came in a room where someone had been held but was now freed. Duncan froze for a long minute in the room as Zalkiniv took in the feelings that lingered here. She wondered why the prey had stayed here so long, and why had he freed whoever had been held here. They had passed other cells with prisoners, some alive, some dead, and this William had passed them by. But this one, he hadn't.

Duncan's sudden movement interrupted her musing, as he ran up to a door. Another barred door. Zalkiniv spat. Their prey had made it out of the cells and was now roaming the halls of the upper temple! Duncan flung himself at the door, trying to batter it down. "Stop," she ordered. Where was that creation of old, the Axessed? He could have broken these doors without her having to resort to more blood workings. But the thing hadn't shown back up since chasing the High Priest.

Working again, she felt the same pressure as before, though the resistance was even stronger this time. So, there was still real power left in this place, old power, but real.

Hundreds of years of neglect took its toll, even on faith inspired power. And with another huge boom, amplified even more because the space was narrower, the door gave way again. Without her Claret stone, there was no way she would have been able to break through, and that bothered her. She had stretched her powers thin, with the bindings on the cultists, and Duncan.

She needed to recuperate, but there was no time, the Scaled one would not forgive her losing the prize now! Duncan moved through the door and she followed, the halls were dressed here, well-made carpets, hangings, ornate decorations. All displaying the wealth and so-called power of the Priesthood. Zalkiniv ignored it all. Duncan was moving faster now; he must be getting closer.

He threw open a door to a large open room. And for the first time in a long time, Zalkiniv felt the loss of control. The air in the room set her teeth on edge, and her skin itched. Something important had been here and been here recently. Against the wall, was the body of Haltim, the old Amderite Priest. Her quarry had been here but had left Haltim's body behind. She was surprised he had carried the old man this far.

Her target had left but Duncan hadn't moved. He stood, stock still, almost rigid. She tested the bonds and with an oath sliced her arm, deeper than she meant to. He was trying to break her control! She could feel the inner struggle, whatever was left of who he had been was fighting hard. She didn't know if it was the room, or the sight of the old man's corpse. But either way, he was fighting. She took the Claret stones out of the pouch she had them in and worked to bind him closer to her. Force this resistance away.

It wasn't working! She had taxed her powers, and this place had weakened her. Zalkiniv screamed in frustration and anger. He was breaking free! *She couldn't lose this one too!* Changing her working, she did the only thing she could think of, she made him collapse, knocked out. Duncan fell, collapsing onto the floor with a thud.

She still had Duncan but her other needed sacrifice, the one her Lord had ordered her to go get was gone. Frustration welled up as she kicked the cooling corpse of the old Priest, feeling a level of satisfaction in hearing a crunch as a bone broke. Duncan could awaken at any time. She wasn't even sure if moving him was an option as that might bring him round. But she couldn't leave him here either.

Finally, at that moment, she could sense it. The Axessed! The large form appeared outside the door to the room, its bulk blocking most of the light from the hallway. Blood and viscera covered its form, it must have feasted well.

Her thoughts clicked into place and a plan came to mind. "Come, I need your help, grab this prize, and let's move. I'm not sure how far ahead the task the Scaled One set us on is now, but we need to follow." She pointed at Duncan's prone form, but the Axessed did not move.

"No. I will not go into that place." The Axessed voice came low, a whisper. "Feeling is wrong."

"Do you think our Lord will care how you *FEEL*? Come, take the prize!" Zalkiniv raised her voice, she only had one chance at this.

The Axessed took a faltering half step into the room and stopped. She could hear it breathing ragged, then it stepped farther in, its scaled skin blood stained and all glittering in the light from the hallway. "Smells... wrong." The Axessed whispered but continued to move, faster this time.

Zalkiniv moved to the side, allowing the Axessed to pick up Duncan. One chance, one try. She would have to move fast and work fast. Her Lord would not care if he got what he wanted. She watched as the Axessed paused and then bent over, grabbing Duncan to lift him up.

Zalkiniv struck, the knife she had gripped in her hand slashing down, point first to the base of the back of the neck. There was a slight resistance as it broke through the scaled skin, and then deep, plunging into the gap between the vertebrae severing the spinal cord. The Axessed gave forth a rush of air, trying to make a sound but failing. But with its spinal cord cut, the best it could do was twitch as it collapsed. Duncan's body still out rolled away, as Zalkiniv worked. She took her knife and ripped it sideways, shearing through muscle, and several major arteries. Blood fountained as the creature gave a shudder. Fresh blood, laced with ancient centuries of power, and today, only a short time ago, feasted upon the terror of the former High Priest of this place.

All she needed to regain total control of the prize. She worked the blood, seeing in her minds eyes as the tendrils of power and control overlaid the unconscious form of her prize. *Tighter control, he would only be an extension of her will.* Power flowed into her, and she laughed with the joy. She hated the creature anyway. At last its life faded, and the blood oozed. But the power was hers and more important, Duncan was hers again.

58

Will heard the booming sound behind them and almost fell over Regin as they ran. "What was that?" Regin yelled as he caught himself on the wall. "No idea. But it can't be good." Will paused for a second catching his breath. "Defenders or attackers, either one we don't want to find us."

Regin nodded in response and took off again, down the hall, and toward escape. Will followed, hating every running step. Running still hurt, but the physical pain was minor. The real hate was the fact that he was running away from Duncan. Could the Heart free him? Maybe the Heart and the bracer? But finding out would mean getting close. Which meant both could fall into the hands of that person. That Zalkiniv person. Or that creature of hers.

Will hated it. Maybe he could save Duncan, maybe not. But if he tried, the odds were they would lose the only chance to bring Amder back into the world, and the Blood God would be guaranteed to return. He wanted to scream in frustration. He wasn't even sure where Regin was leading him. Or why he was following a person who he didn't trust.

But none of that mattered now. Only escape mattered. Getting out of danger mattered. *Forgive me Duncan.* Will ran after Regin. Regin skidded to a stop and turned into a small room and gave a yell. Will drew his hammer up as he ran and followed, expecting to fight. But instead, he found Regin smiling and holding up a cloak of Red and a cloak of Dark blue. Guild cloaks!

"Here! Put this on!" Regin threw the red cloak to Will as he put the Blue one around his own shoulders.

"How did you know this would be here?" Will asked as he slid the hammer back into his belt and fastened the cloak around his shoulders. His one shoulder still screamed at him, his legs hurt, but they had a chance now. The Cloaks held centuries of respect, centuries of power. The obedience to what the Cloaks represented could with luck, get them out of Ture and on the road to the Reach.

"I've been here before; I remembered this room. If Guild members come and didn't have their formal cloaks with them for whatever reason, they keep a few here. Master Jaste showed them to me." Regin's face turned thoughtful for a moment. "We should find him, Jaste I mean. I need to apologize, and he could help.

He'd leap at the chance to. He always did kind of like thumbing his nose at the Priesthood."

Will blinked back sudden tears. Regin didn't know. In all the chaos, he didn't know. "Master Jaste is dead, Regin. He helped me escape the Tempered. In the Guild. They killed him." Will looked down at the floor, remembering the sound of Jaste yelling at him to run.

"By the sparks... What have I done?" Regin sat on a nearby bench, needing its support as he took in the news. "I'm sorry William. So sorry. If I hadn't been so damn blind, so wrapped up in power, I should have seen the truth. His death, it's my fault."

Will looked at the man. Regin was truly sorry. He still found it hard to trust him, or even like him. But he was different now. Whatever the Tempered and the High Priest had done, it had stripped Regin of his pride and arrogance. "Yes. It was. But you helped me escape. You helped me carry Haltim to a place where he could find peace. You helped me recover the Heart. And you will help me escape and get to the Reach."

Regin looked up at Will. His face, pale. The bruises and welts from his torture were still there. But there was something different in his eyes now, something Will hadn't had a good look at before now. Strength. He still didn't like him, but he knew, Regin wouldn't betray him again.

"Yes. I will. I'll do whatever I can to help. What about that girl? Myriam? She traveled with us, the Tempered would know that." Regin asked his face drawn, red and dirty.

"She's safe. I have it on good authority." Will didn't want to get into how he knew, at least not now.

Regin blinked and wiped his eyes, standing. "Let's get out of this blood-soaked horror. We will need money, and I know how we can get that. Follow my lead in the city, and with the gate guards. If all goes well, we will be on the road to the Reach soon. I hope."

Will nodded. "Will we have time to get to a setter? My shoulder, I hit it earlier, before we found you. I can barely use the arm." Regin nodded and lead them down a hallway, and a series of turns before there, in front of them was an Ornate door, but guarded by a dozen men.

Regin pulled Will to the side, pulling him around a corner and out of the line of sight of the guards. "Remember, follow my lead." Regin took a breath and stood straighter, Will nodded again. What was the man up to?

Regin walked around the corner and straight towards the guards. Will took a deep breath and followed, hoping the man knew what he was doing. He never thought his life would be in the hands of Regin of all people.

"Halt!" one Guard, only differentiated by the two gold bars on his chest plate, yelled as he drew his weapon. Will could feel the heart in his pocket thrum as soon as the man did so. God Forged weapons. No normal guards then.

"Master Regin of the Guild. And this is my Journeyman, William. We were in the temple when it was attacked. I was beaten as you can see, and my Journeyman's arm was injured badly, he can barely use it. We need to get him to a setter. A Smith with only one good arm ... Difficult." Regin gave the man a smirk that made Will wonder if he was right to forgive the man anything.

The guard who had spoken eyed them both, taking in the cloaks and the hammer he could see on Will's belt. He opened his mouth and shut it again. Regin just stood there, saying nothing else and still giving that man a haughty look that screamed two things, contempt and superiority. Will was worried. *This was taking too long, it wouldn't work. They wouldn't get out.*

Finally, the Guard who had spoken nodded to them and waved to the others to let them pass. Will followed Regin out the door, and into the bright sun, blinking and unable to see for a minute. Regin walked still stalking down the road, a steady pace, as if he had not a care in the world. Will followed, as they walked through crowds that had gathered outside the temple. That same crowd parted however for the two Smiths, some even bowing as they passed!

Regin turned off the main road once they had gone two of three blocks, enough so no guard could tell where they had gone. He walked a short distance, making a series of turns down a few side roads before glancing back at Will and pointing at a decrepit house and going in. Will followed, looking behind them, but no one was following.

He walked in to find Regin sitting on the floor, breathing hard. "By the sparks, I am glad to be out of that place." Regin said as he leaned back and closed his eyes. "Just give me a moment."

Will looked around. The Building was empty, abandoned. "I thought for sure they had caught us," Will said as he drew his hammer and flipped it in his hand, the metal calming him.

"I did too, for a moment. That Guard captain, he was the captain for the whole temple. I prayed and hoped that the cloaks would command enough respect to get us through. He almost didn't let us go. I was sure he wanted to throw us into a cell to question."

"Why didn't he?" Will asked. "I know the cloaks mean something, but still…"

"The cloaks mean a great more than something, at least here in Ture. The Guild and the Church rule this place Will. He may not have totally believed us, but to throw a Guilder into a cell, even on a day like this, could be suicide. He wouldn't be killed, but he'd lose everything he had, everything he worked for. The risk outweighed the reward."

"That look you gave him…" Will turned to Regin to find him, eyes open observing him. "I thought for a second you would turn me in."

"I knew I had to project power along with the cloak. People expect Guild masters to be arrogant assholes. Jaste was a rarity. So are some Guild masters who teach. Most of the masters who are out in the world really are arrogant pricks, Will. He expected it. If I hadn't, he might not have let us through, regardless of the consequences." Regin stood back up, wincing as he did so.

"So, to get out of Ture we need money. Money for someone to fix this shoulder, to look at your other injuries, supplies for the road, all of that. I had money, before they captured me, but it's gone now.

You said you had a plan?" Will asked as he kept an eye on the outside, but no pursuit came.

"I'm still a Guild master. I can command certain resources," Regin remarked as he took a deep breath. "Just follow my lead again. Until we get out of town, it might be better if you refer to me as Master Regin.

Will knew he was right. He still found himself not wanting to listen to the man, but he had gotten them out of the Temple. And if he could get them out of this place, and on the way to the Reach. It might be worth it. "Agreed. Why did you introduce me as William to the guard though? Why not use Markin Darto?" Will asked, curious.

"I wasn't sure if he knew that name or not. If the High Priest had been looking for a Markin Darto, he might know that. He'd never let us go then. So, I went with your real name." Regin threw up his hood, covering his face. "Let's go Journeyman William."

Will felt stupid. Regin was right of course. He should have seen that possibility. "Yes... Master Regin." Will threw his own cloak over his head and followed Regin out the door, and into the metropolis of Ture.

59

Zalkiniv led her pet Duncan back down the stairs, moving toward the entrance to the sewers and unground passages they had come up from. The power of the Axessed flowed through her, that power and a quick working of some of its residual blood would lead her straight back to the lair.

She called out to the blood of the few remaining attackers, as a little insurance in case anyone surprised her. While Duncan would be more than enough for most encounters, he wasn't immortal, and she would rather throw these blood crazed fools at guards than her prize. Three finally appeared, all covered in blood, some of their own, but most of it belonging to others.

She was a little surprised at how well they had done. She could feel these three were still under the sway of the blood craze she had worked on them. And more, they had all not fought it. They, in fact, had reveled in it. True believers then. Useful.

The blood sense led them down and farther down until finally, the access cover to the sewers they had come up from. They still had seen no guards or Priests, no alive ones anyway. Bodies they had seen, guards, Priests, and dead cultists.

As they made their way down the ladder and back into the sewer tunnels, her thoughts turned to how to reclaim the other Reis. The Blood God wanted both and losing one wasn't in her plan. Her advantage was singular: Duncan was the only family he had, and he cared for the man. That she could exploit. That she could use. But she needed to find out where that William Reis had gone. And who was he traveling with now? With the Amderite dead, she wasn't sure whom else they were looking for.

Her thoughts were still moving when they finally arrived back in the chamber of sacrifice. Of twenty cultists, the Axessed and she who had left, three cultists, her and Duncan had survived. But power flowed through her, and her control of the blood-blessed Reis was absolute.

She didn't like using her prize as a hunter, but she saw no other way. *Blood calls to Blood.* Duncan could find and lead her and the others to William Reis, and whoever else he was with. She could use the cultists, but the other Reis would run from them. Capture William, and take them both beyond the barrier, sacrifice them to the Scaled one, and bring forth the return of the God of Rage and Blood.

In the torchlight she took a long look at Duncan, strong and lean, his face locked into a grimace of controlled rage, he was hers to command. But, if he came out of the sewers looking like that, he'd draw too much attention. Far too much. For one, he was covered with blood, his clothes sticky with it, and little of his skin wasn't splashed with now dried blood and gore. All of them were the same, her included.

"Water. Clean. We must remove the outer blessing. For now." She ordered the cultists, not caring what they thought. When the world fell to her Lord, blood would be the sign of his favor, until then, subterfuge was the way.

They returned soon carrying between them a very large tub of clean water. Where it had come from in a sewer wasn't clear, but she couldn't detect any trace of foulness in it. She disrobed, and got into the water, the blood on her skin melting away. Zalkiniv felt even more naked without it, as if some part of her was melting away. She turned to one cultist, a woman "Clothes. Find me some." The woman said nothing, but left, and arrived back soon, carrying serviceable travel clothes. They must have a storeroom or something down here. She had never asked.

Climbing from the tub, she turned toward her prize. "Disrobe, and wash." He did so, and her gaze lingered over his form. A worthy sacrifice. She could see some of his veins through his skin and feel the blood coursing through them. Strong blood, surging blood. He lived in a world of rage now. Anger and hate. She could amplify that even further before she sent him out to hunt. And she knew how to do it.

Duncan took longer to wash as he had more blood on his body. But he stood from the tub, his skin pink and clean in the flickering light. He looked better the other way. After the sacrifice her God might let her have the body. She doubted her Lord needed all his blood. It would be amusing to wear the form of one of the last of the Forgemasters line.

"Clothes," she said, ordering the same woman again, who returned with clothes for Duncan, which fit, though were a little small. It would work, it was all for show, just enough not to cause panic. *Not yet at least.* A tall young man in ill-fitting clothes wouldn't draw attention, he looked like a simple day laborer.

She took her knife once more, and though its blade was black with blood, used it to nick Duncan's ear, drawing forth a small well of blood. She dipped her finger in the blood and touched each Claret stone, each one drawing forth a font of power.

The hardest part, she released her control, and let part of him out.

"Oh gods! What have I done?" Duncan's voice came back, a dry whisper of sound. "Haltim. I killed Haltim!" She could hear the sorrow etched into his soul. Not the emotion she needed, but it could be twisted, turned, used.

"Duncan. It's me, Rache," she whispered in his ear from behind him. He couldn't move, she wouldn't let him. But twisting his emotions needed a temporary break in her domination.

"Rache? I had such bad dreams, I killed Haltim. You were there, but it wasn't you. Where am I? I saw William, my cousin, but he's not here, I know it. Where did he go?" Duncan asked, his voice falling lower with each word.

"He abandoned you. Us. He left us to die Duncan. He got his hammer, and left us," Zalkiniv whispered, running her fingertips through his hair. "Left us to die while he ran. He blamed you for this."

"He left me to die. No, Will wouldn't do that," he responded, but the twinge of doubt was there. Good.

"He blamed you. He said if you hadn't come to Ture, this wouldn't have happened." Zalkiniv could feel Duncan's emotions. Sadness, confusion, worry. *Easy to change for her.* Through the blood she pushed his feelings, changing them. Anger, rage, frustration. His face transformed as his emotions changed. From a slight frown to gritted teeth and a clenched jaw. His skin changed with it, flushing with the red blood that Zalkiniv craved so much.

"My fault? This is all *HIS* fault. If he hadn't wanted to join the Guild, never would have left the Reach. None of this would have happened... It's *HIS* fault." His voice grew harsh. "He left us to die. After all, I've ever done for him. I protected him. I kept him safe when we were kids, and this is how he repays me?"

"He laughed as he left. Left us to die." Rache felt his blood rush, the hate spilling out, he was hers.

"Left me? Left you? You're innocent. How could he! Always so better than me, always so honorable. I kept food on the table for us, I dealt with the whispers and looks of not being an 'honorable' Reis, and he leaves me to die!" His voice rose to a shout, anger blossomed through his blood, anger and more.

"Where did he go?" Duncan screamed, the anger escalating with the help of Zalkiniv and the stones.

Perfect. "Find him. I don't know where he went. I can help you though, find him, and bring him here... bring him to me." Zalkiniv reached through the blood one last time, pushing Duncan to compliance. "Bring him to me."

"Bring him to you? Here?" his voice turned to a growl. "I'll make him come here. He must pay for leaving me... Leaving you." Duncan's body trembled, and the rage and anger churned through his blood.

Zalkiniv laughed. So easy to manipulate. It was intoxicating. But she needed her prize, and this was the only way. She'd follow, at a safe distance. The risk of losing both needed bloods was too great.

"Go, find him." She whispered one more time, as the trembles stopped, and muscle tightened. Duncan left the room, heading straight toward the main ladder up and out, and into the city of Ture. She followed at a safe distance. Blood workings like this could be tricky things, if the subject got pushed too far, or asked to do something he could rebel at, that could make things fall apart. Which was why she had only asked Duncan to find his cousin and bring him to her. If she had asked him to kill him, that wouldn't work. Even with the Blood, there were some lines that were too far.

As Duncan exited the sewers and through the light from above, she watched him pause and head out, walking out of view. Ascending herself, she glimpsed him walking towards the center of Ture, ignoring those around him. *Blood calls to blood.*

60

Duncan's height made him easy to spot, she watched him push though the traffic, his face set in an angry grimace. More than a few people took one look at him and avoided him entirely. *Good, all that much faster.* She heard snippets of conversation as she walked. Someone had attacked the guild, no the Temple, no Amder had returned and struck down the High priest. One man was yelling to a small crowd that there had been a coup and the King was dead. Farther along another man screamed that they must purge anyone not of Ture for the Glory of Amder.

Still Duncan walked, and she followed. Main streets, then side streets, then back to a main street.

"I tell you; the king is dead!" A voice cut into her thoughts, turning to the voice, it was the same man as before, and the same crowd, and this was the same street! They had gone in a circle! Zalkiniv felt her ire leap forward. Something was wrong! Duncan should have made a beeline for his cousin. Straight towards him. But they were going in circles. In fact, she could see him now, taking the same turn as earlier.

Fighting the urge to take her knife and silence the yelling fool nearby, she instead slapped her hand in frustration against the wall. Somehow, that other Reis had hidden himself. The question was that protection accidental or purposeful? Did he know she was hunting him? Too many questions.

A tiny blossom of fear formed in her stomach. They left her with no other recourse. She had to commune with the Blood God. Valnijz could answer if he wanted to. Her failure at losing the other Reis gave her pause in contacting him. He was not a forgiving god, dead or not. She had been a servant of her master for many years, if approached correctly, just maybe he could be convinced to help.

The trip back to the cult was easy, with the chaos of the city, no one payed attention to her. A simple working through the Claret stone she wore around her neck, the same one that Duncan had given her, was enough to bring him back to the safe darkness of the cult.

She sat him in the corner and ordered him to do nothing. Compliant, she nicked his other ear, as she needed a touch of his blood, and a lot of other blood. She eyed the remaining cultists, feeling the remnants of the rage and hate in the workings she had done to them. She could feel them, the last of the anger and rage, warring with the falling excitement of the killing of the Amderites. They would work for her needs.

Disrobing, Zalkiniv took the spot of blood from Duncan and spread it on the edge of her knife. She could have used her own, but she wanted to save this new strength, with all the obstacles they had already faced, power could be useful.

"Come, kneel." She ordered the three robed cultists. All three complied, though she could feel a hint of confusion and in one man, a touch of fear. Good. Closing her eyes, she began her working, reaching inside herself, and through the blood on the knife, reaching into the Blood that Duncan carried. The howling dark, the screams of pain and anger came, distant now, but growing closer. The dark grew to a dim red, then the hint of the brilliant crimson of fresh blood. Screams of pain echoed in her head, but the voice of Valnijz was not among them.

No word escaped her as with one motion, her knife sliced through the throats of the three kneeling in front of her, their blood drenched her form, and with the end of their lives she pushed harder, begging for her Lord to speak with her.

A moan came now, a moan that grew to a scream to a roar. "*FAILURE!*" the word came, as she fell to her knees. "*FAILURE AND WASTE*"

"My Lord, I ask forgiveness, I had him, but..." Zalkiniv was cut off by the Scaled Ones roar. "*I DO NOT ALLOW FAILURE! I KNOW WHAT HAPPENED. I KNOW WHY YOU FAILED.*" The Blood God was not happy.

"He is still here, in Ture! But my workings can't find him! Even blood calling to blood doesn't work! Please, help me find him so I may take him and then bring you back to this world to wreck your vengeance!" Zalkiniv knelt then, cutting her thighs in contrition, the blood flowing sacrificing power to appease Valnijz.

"*HE HAS THE HEART! EVEN I CAN NOT FIND HIM.*" The Blood God's voice was louder than ever, and she dropped her knife in shock. The Heart? The Heart of the Soot god?

"*I CAN NOT FIND HIM. BUT I KNOW WHERE HE IS GOING, AND I KNOW WHAT MY BROTHER MUST DO TO RETURN.*" Valnijz voice made her scream, so loud, her ears rang.

"*HE RETURNS TO MY BROTHER'S TEMPLE, IN THE CITY OF THE REACH. HE WILL WORK TO RETURN MY BROTHER TO LIFE. BUT THE BARRIER MUST COME DOWN FOR THIS TO HAPPEN. YOU HAVE ONE CHANCE. GO, RETURN HOME. MASS MY CHILDREN AT THE BARRIER, WHEN IT FALLS, THEY MUST TAKE THE TEMPLE AND KILL ALL WITHIN. EVEN THE OTHER CHILD OF THE FORGEMASTER. DO THIS, AND I WILL ALLOW YOU TO LIVE. FAIL ME, AND YOUR BLOOD WILL BE BANISHED TO THE DARK, NEVER TO FLOW AGAIN.*" The screams and moans that had formed the voice of the Rage God broke apart then, separating into uncountable screams and moans. Her audience was at an end.

A shuddering breath came as she stood, unsteady on her feet. So, the other Reis had the Heart. The only good news was that the barrier, the one thing that had kept the Valni from overrunning all the west and the Skyreach Mountains, would fall. If she hurried, she could cross back over, take the parts of the Spear, and call an army of Valni to cross and slaughter everyone in the Reach. But they had to hurry.

If the Heart wasn't in his possession, she'd intercept him on the road, but with it, she would be unable to track him, and she didn't know this side of the barrier well. It was a race, her to base of power, and this William Reis to the Reach.

Duncan stood still, his mind lost in the Rage induced dreams she had fed him to keep him docile, and the cultists were dead. A quick search of the rest of the safe house yielded food, water, in fact a running pipe of clean fresh water, clothing and some money. All they needed to get started.

After a new bath, hopefully the last one in a long time, she used a working to close any wounds on herself and on Duncan. When she was back across the barrier, she could go back to wearing the ritual scars. She summoned Duncan to her side, he was a simple tool now, but useful.

"Stay quiet. Let me do the talking," she whispered to her prize. No flicker of acknowledgement crossed his face, but she would have been surprised if there had been. She could feel his emotions and knew he was experiencing bloodlust and hate on a scale that many would go insane at. She could smell it on him.

Climbing back out to the surface, she had to orient herself. The sun had set, but it wasn't dark yet, and they still should be able to make it out of the city. But which gate? The closest gate was crowded, and well-guarded even in good times. With the news of today spreading everywhere, she was sure a small army would be there now.

So, a smaller gate then, and one not too far, before they closed the gates for the night. Drawing her knife, she nicked her thumb, a tiny cut that drew forth a bead of blood. She needed a drop for this working. She reached out with its power, and there, a smaller gate, the Water gate. Used by poor fishermen, ones who couldn't afford a boat.

She brought Duncan to her side, and flashed a smile on her face, all the world looking like a young woman and her beau, out for an evening's walk, except for the pack on Duncan's back. But that could be explained away, an overnight camp? Away from the prying eyes and ears of protective relatives? Easy enough to say, depending on the guards.

They arrived at the gate, to find four guards, which was far more than the normal one. But a quick look and sensing made Zalkiniv smile even more. All were elderly, and two were asleep. Easy, if she played it right.

"Halt!" One guard, hunched with age stood in front of them "What business do you have leaving Ture?"

"Oh, well my... Fiancée here, we wanted to get out of town, for the night. With all the noise and everything, people aren't leaving us alone." Zalkiniv threw the old guard a pout.

"Oh... I see! Well... We are under orders to not let anyone out at night, with all the business today." the old guards voice trailed off.

"Please? We wanted to get out earlier today, but it was so crowded." She hugged closer to Duncan, drawing up a small working to use in case this didn't work. There were only four guards, and Duncan would have no problem ripping them apart, if need be. Doing so would mean a search through this gate when it was discovered, so that was a last resort.

"Let them through." A different guard said, not even bothering to stand. "They aren't the killers were looking for, anyway."

"Killers? You mean there's a description?" Zalkiniv was curious, maybe this could hold up the other Reis. This was a race now.

"Only one, strong young guy, the story is he was in the Guild, and went crazy, broke into the Temple and killed a bunch of Priests and guards and vanished. That's what I heard at least." The Guard waved them through. "Go on."

"Have fun! Take care of her, she looks like a nice girl!' the first guard clapped Duncan on the arm as they walked by.

Duncan froze, and Zalkiniv held her breath. She could feel the rage blossom, and felt him tense, ready to tear this man limb from limb. *No, not yet.* She quietly stopped him, using her new power over him to force him to just walk away.

The gate fell behind them as they walked, the sound of its closing brought a new smile to her face. They were out of Ture, and on their way to power.

61

Will followed Regin through the streets of Ture, a different Ture than a day ago. The city was buzzing with rumors and stories as Will could hear as they walked. What was interesting was the reaction of people to their cloaks as they moved. Many gave way, growing silent as they passed, but more than a few chased after them. Regin was impassive to the noise and questions, he walked through it all.

A few more turns and Regin stopped and entered a small house, unremarkable but for a sign, a sign of a silver sun. Will did not recognize it, but he had agreed to follow Regin till they got out of Ture, and so far, he hadn't been led astray.

As he followed Regin inside, he blinked at the light change. It was dim inside, very dim. There were a few well-dressed merchant looking men inside, and sitting at a huge desk, sat a strange woman. Will had seen nothing like her. For one, her skin was green! Not dark green of a forest, but a sea green, and her hair was white, or at least a light blond.

"Ah, a Guildmaster and Journeyman. What brings you here today? The city is full of rumors and half-truths, could it be you have valuable information to trade?" the woman sat back, her eyes unblinking and dark. Dark enough that Will wondered if they had any color at all.

"Mistress Shal'ton. I am Guild Master Regin, and this is my Journeyman William. We find ourselves in need of coin, we have urgent business outside of Ture, and because of some unforeseen issues, no funds." Regin answered her, and to Will's surprise, lowered his hood, showing his welts and bruises.

"Well, you have a story to tell Master Regin. I wonder how those marks got upon you." Shal'ton settled back in her chair and with a single long finger waved one man over. "Chairs for our guests, and refreshments? I gained some delightful Korba fruits yesterday."

Regin sat and waved for Will to do the same. "Yes, some refreshment would be good. It has been a long day."

"Food as well then and bring them some drinks. Water though, this should prove to be an interesting tale." Shal'ton looked at Will with a small smile. "Your Journeyman here doesn't speak much. And still wearing his hood, how rude."

Head bowed Regin turned toward Will and nodded. "Take off the hood William, don't be rude." Will didn't understand what was going on but did so. The woman, this Shal'ton made a small noise in the back of her throat at the sight of Wills face and grinned.

"Well now, a nice handsome young Journeyman that shouldn't exist." Shal'ton turned back toward Regin. "So, information you have. Be truthful, and money you will have."

Will felt panic grip him again for a second, what did she mean? His hands reached under the cloak and gripped the Heart. The whole walk its weight had given him strength, and now, he might need that strength.

"First the price Mistress. Thirty Gold bits each, and no rumors afterwards." Regin leaned forward, his face inches from the strange woman's.

"Thirty? That's a high price for information. There're already dozens of rumors flying, I could promote one of those as the truth. And I doubt the Priesthood or Guild would argue, they won't even comment on the current rumors." Mistress Shal'ton said as she made a small face and sat back. "Please Master Regin, your breath leaves something to be desired."

Regin smiled. "And why would a Guildmaster of the Smithing guild, come to you, looking like this, and with bad breath, uncleaned teeth, and needing Gold?"

Shal'ton said nothing but sat back, thinking. The refreshments appeared, and Will looked at them, a rumble in his stomach reminding him how long it had been since he'd eaten or even drank anything. With the blur of everything from trying to flee, capture and escaping the Temple, he hadn't even thought about it. Now the food, as simple as it was, made him hungry.

He poured himself a glass of cold water, and with a smith's eye took notice of the craftsmanship and materials of the cups and pitcher. Silver and some red material he wasn't sure of, it looked organic to him. But well crafted, and everything had an ocean-based motif, seashells and waves. The water was refreshing, and as cold as water from home, which was a pleasant surprise.

The fruits, Korba fruits he thought she had called them, were oblong things, purple fading to green. He wasn't much a fruit eater, but anything would be good now. He didn't know how to eat these things. Pick it up and take a bite? Peel it? His answer came when Regin, who watched this Shal'ton woman with care, took a fruit and bit into it.

Will followed suit and was happy to find the fruit as cold and fresh as he could ask for. The taste was unlike anything he'd ever had, sweet, but not sticky, with lots of juice and a decided crunch. He liked them, and before long he'd polished off three in short order.

"Your Journeyman is hungry I see." Shal'ton smirked at Will. "Thirty gold bits?"

"Yes Mistress. And no rumors." Regin sat back, arms crossed.

"Fine," Mistress Shal'ton said and waved to another of the men, who took a writing rod, ink and some paper out of a drawer. The man set up nearby, pen waiting to write down whatever Regin said.

"Please, tell me what happened today." Mistress Shal'ton

Regin turned to Will and shrugged. What did he want Will to say? "I guess. Tell her what she wants to know." Will said taking a long drink of water.

Regin nodded and began to tell this woman everything. The bare truth. His capture, the assault on the Temple by followers of the Blood god, the death of Haltim, the disappearance of Will's cousin. The Heart, Will's ancestry, and why they had to get to the Reach again Regin left out.

Throughout the story, this woman said nothing. Will noted that she didn't even raise an eyebrow, if she had those, it was hard to tell. As Regin ended his tale, she tapped her finger on the desk a few times and nodded to another of her workers, who vanished through a small door.

"Interesting tale. Some I had heard, some I hadn't. It doesn't paint High Priest Bracin in the best light, and he's a... dangerous man." Shal'ton then turned to Will. "Your turn Reacher."

Will felt a surge of panic. "My turn? And how did you know I was a Reacher?"

Mistress Shal'ton took a long sip of water, eye locked on Will, but said nothing at first. "I'm not paying you each thirty bits of gold from information without information from both of you." Shal'ton shrugged, "You don't have to say anything, but then only Master Regin here gets paid."

Regin nodded at Will. Smug idiot Will thought to himself. Why had he trusted his man? He hated to lie, he hated keeping things from people. And here he was having to give half-truths and partial information, all the things that made him feel sick inside. He swore he would not do this kind of thing anymore!

Then don't. Tell the bare truth. The thought came to him. Don't hide, be forthright. Will took another long sip of water. Could he do that? Stop the lie and be honest?

"I'm waiting Journeyman. Mistress Shal'ton said, facing him and ignoring everyone else.

"Fine," Will said and under his robes grabbed the heart with his free hand.

Will spoke, telling things from his side. About Master Jaste, about running from the Guild only to discover Duncan and Haltim were here in the city, looking for him. His capture, the showdown with that Zalkiniv person, the creature, an Axessed, the High Priest, and he came to the final piece, the Heart. Shal'ton had not said a word, though the man taking notes, copious notes, had looked up in surprise more than once. Will didn't get into talking about Myriam however; that wasn't needed here.

Will reached under his robes and removed the Heart. Shal'ton reacted then, gasping. "I have been tasked, tasked to return Amder to the world. I have already found the Hammer, I know where the Anvil is, and I have this now. With this I can return the God of Craft and Creation to Palnor, to all Alos. The Blood God is moving, and unless we are fast, my cousin will die, and the Scaled One will return to this world first. And not just Ture, not only this land, but the world itself will drown in the blood of millions of victims."

Mistress Shal'ton stood, saying nothing. Master Regin was white and staring at Will with equal parts of awe and questioning. The two other men in the room one taking notes and one waiting both had stood along with Shal'ton, but unlike their boss, looked scared.

The third man returned and stopped at the tension in the room. Will put the heart back under his shirt, its heaviness reassuring him again. The third man, who was carrying two smallish leather bags placed them on the desk. "Mistress?" he asked carefully.

Shal'ton looked at Will for a long time. Dead quiet fell over the room and the tension grew. Was she going to turn them in? Have her men attack? All three, while well-dressed looked like people who knew how to fight. Will might be stronger than them, but he was a Smith, not a warrior!

"Forgive my questioning. This falls to the Law of Waves." Mistress Shal'ton turned to the man with the notes. "Burn those. Now." The man hesitated but brought the papers to the nearby fireplace and set them ablaze.

"Law of Waves?" Will asked. "I'm sorry I don't know what that means." He turned to ask Master Regin, but he looked as confused as Will.

"When Amder fell, defeating the Blood God, my people, the people of the sea, swore an oath, to do whatever we could to help the true servants of Amder. Amder sacrificed his life to save all ours. We are a people with few numbers and would have been easy for the Blood God to end. When the Scaled one fell, they made the Law of Waves." Mistress Shal'ton bowed to Will. "You are the agent of Amder's return. I will help."

Will sat there, unsure of what to say. He hadn't expected this. Leaning to Regin he whispered, "Have you ever heard of this?"

Regin shook his head. "No, I knew of her, and we know her people never cheat or lie. So, I went here. This ... I had no idea. But she's, because of her people, the most trusted information broker in Ture."

Will nodded, that would be true, but still, this was crazy. And more than a little convenient. He wondered if Amder was stretching whatever powers he could to help them because this was too easy.

"Gold. Thirty each, as agreed. And, we will get you out of the city. The cloaks are helpful, but many questions about the Guild are circulating right now. And of course, horses." Mistress Shal'ton took the writing rod and began notes.

"Um, I can't ride a horse," Will admitted. "No need in the Reach."

"Ah true. And learning now would be painful." Shal'ton gave him a long look. *Sizing me up like a prize catch.* "A cart then? Still faster than on foot."

"I came here on a cart, that would be fine," Will agreed.

"Good." Mistress Shal'ton paused for a moment and then looked at Will. "Be careful. Amder's return will change many things in this city, in the kingdom, and as you say, in the world. Not only agents of the Blood God might not want that to happen. I wouldn't go showing what's in your pocket to any more people unless you had to."

Within an hour, Will found himself defrocked of the Guild Cloak, sitting on a cart, a bag of gold on his hip. They'd even found a setter who had pushed his shoulder back into its socket, whatever that meant. All he knew was that it felt better, much better. A cart laden with travel supplies, and with whatever Mistress Shal'ton had done, they had ridden out a gate without the guards saying a word. They hadn't even inspected the cart, just waived him and Regin through.

He was free of Ture. Next stop, the Reach.

62

Will's eyes dropped, nearly closing for the fifth time. Regin wasn't much for talking, and every attempt at conversation was met with shrugs or single word answers. Not that Will minded a great deal, considering it was Regin. Regin. *If anyone had told me I'd be escaping Ture with Regin by my side, I would have thought they were insane.* Still, without Regin he'd be inside the Temple right now or dead. He'd not have the Heart; he wouldn't be on the way to the Reach.

The rocking of the cart as it rolled north, and toward the Skyreach mountains, which were appearing in the distance lulled him. Will tried to not think about people who weren't here, Master Jaste, Haltim, Myriam, or what had happened to Duncan. Even the thought of his name made him feel guilty. Guilty and wrong. There had been no options other than fleeing, but still, it was hard.

He knew the only chance Dunc had was to return Amder to the world before Valnijz could return. Only then would there be a chance. If Valnijz returned first, or even at the same time, Duncan would be gone. A glance back at the fading sight of Ture made him sad. So much had happened, so much changed.

They continued, Regin taking smaller roads. When asked he had replied that he wouldn't feel safe until they made it to the edge of the mountains, then he'd hit the main roads. It made sense of course. While they had escaped, who knew what their actions would bring about? The High Priest most likely dead, scores of Priests and Guards dead, and the Heart missing. With the chaos, and deaths, he wasn't sure anyone left in the Priesthood even knew about him and Regin. *That's not a risk I'm willing to take.*

Sun setting, Regin pulled the cart into one of the many side clearings these merchant routes had for carts and wagons. "Let's camp here, up in the morning early, and get back on the road."

Will nodded. He needed to be away from anyone, even Regin. As they had traveled the heat of the lowlands had slipped away, and he'd felt more like himself than he had in months. It also reminded him more and more of what coming south had cost him.

Camp was simple, bedrolls in the cart so not to have to deal with wet ground from the dew, campfire, simple food and drink.

Will made the dinner, a simple affair of toasted bread and cheese, and a piece of that Korba fruit each. Mistress Shal'ton had put an entire sack of the things in the cart, and since neither knew how long they would last, better to eat them now.

After dinner, Regin fell into a sort of melancholy reflection of his own, staring into the fire and poking it, and Will found himself wanting to be alone. "Going to walk into the tree's over there for a few minutes, got to take care of, something," Will told Regin, but got no response.

Will made his way into the woods nearby. Near enough he could still see the firelight at least. The woods were still strange to him, these trees dwarfed anything in the Reach. Will leaned back and sat at the base of one tree, some huge looming thing.

Haltim. Master Jaste. Duncan. The names came to him, and tears fell down his cheeks, wet and cold in the crisp air. He didn't hold it back. Haltim had tried to save him and died. Master Jaste had tried to save him and died. Duncan… Duncan had tried to save him and now faced a fate worse than the other two. Turned into some monster, a killing machine in the service of the Scaled One. Lucky, carefree Duncan. His life had been shattered by that sparks be burned blood taint.

Will wept. Wept for his friends, wept for his family. Wept for the never would be with Myriam. The blame for this fell on the one person who had made it through this, himself. If he hadn't tried so hard to be in the Guild, none of this would have happened. Valnijz wouldn't be close to returning. Haltim would be alive, and Master Jaste, too. Duncan would still be scaving and living the life he wanted. This was HIS fault.

But was it? None of them had to do this. Duncan had opened the tomb that held the hammer and blade, all on his own. He hadn't told Will about it, he'd done it. Master Jaste had taken the risk to get him into the Guild, knowing the move was risky. Even more risky, had dropped everything to get him out. Haltim, he'd wanted to help. He knew there was danger but accepted it.

Wiping his now cold tears from his face, Will felt better. He'd held that in for a while. There hadn't been time to grieve, to feel sadness, to move forward. Now that there was, it was better. He was still sad, but it was a dull sadness now, not a sharp one.

And that would heal in time. A hard lesson to learn, but a necessary one.

The Heart lay heavy in his pocket. He kept it on his own person. Was it because he didn't trust Regin? The idea made him uncomfortable. *The man helped me, and yet I still can't bring myself to fully trust him.* There was no safe way for two people to transport the Heart of a Dead God. He considered trying to reach Amder, to ask why all this pain had to happen, to ask if Haltim and Jaste were at peace, if there was another way to rescue Duncan. In his heart he wasn't sure he wanted those answers. They well could be exactly what he wanted to hear, but they might not be. He wasn't ready for that, not yet.

He'd have to sooner or later. There were some glaring holes in Amder's plan. From the last talk they had, there had been things Amder had been keeping from him, and that couldn't be good. But, just for now, he'd trust. He'd try.

Cheeks now dry, he stood, brushing a few leaves and grass from his back. Taking a long breath, the cool air felt good, clean. He walked back toward the fire, and his improbable travel partner, Master Regin.

Back at the fire, Regin was still staring into it, but Will could see his mood had changed. Before he'd been pensive before, worried almost. Now, that was gone. Regin looked up when he returned but said nothing. Will for his part got ready to sleep, he wasn't even sure how long it had been since he'd woken up in Ture, expecting to leave the city, only to get captured.

"William. Will. I am sorry," Regin said. "When I met you, back on the road to Ture, with Master Jaste, it bothered me. I was jealous. You knew things I didn't even know. It all came so easy to you. By the sparks, it was annoying. And when Master Jaste sent me away early, I knew something was wrong. I knew he was protecting you. I didn't know why. But I didn't care. I only wanted to take you down a notch."

"Well, I didn't like you much either. I'm still not sure if I do." Will sat by the fire. "You turned me in to the Priesthood."

"I know. I've been sitting here, running that over and over in my mind. Why did I do that? Why turn you and Master Jaste in? Did I want power? Did I want revenge? And I must admit, I did it because I wanted to be better than you." Regin poked the fire, watching the line of sparks waft into the air. "I wanted to have you gone. I was jealous. Simple, silly, sad jealous."

"Ok." Will didn't know what else to say. *Where was Regin going with this?*

"But when the High Priest, that Bracin man threw me in a cell to be beaten, tortured... all because he could. I saw it. This was me. This was what I was heading towards. The pain made me see it. All my choices, all the choices I had made, were leading me down this path. I'm a good Smith William. A very good Smith. I wouldn't be a Guild Master if that were not true. You could be great. One in a Million. And now? Knowing you're to be a Forgemaster? The first Forgemaster in hundreds of years? It was silly, my jealousy." Regin threw his stick into the fire and stood.

"I am yours to command. You are to be the Forgemaster of Amder. I will follow you from now until the end of my days." Regin bowed to Will as he said these words.

"Uh... I don't know what to say," Will croaked out, unprepared for this.

"Don't think about it, the end of my days might be blood-soaked soon, if recent events are to be believed," Regin answered back with a small smile. Will felt, surprisingly a small laugh come forth at that. Things had been rough and downright wrong, but they were still here. And the laugh, as small as it was, felt good. A small part of his soul felt better for doing it, and that was enough for tonight.

63

Zalkiniv and Duncan walked for a good two miles before they spotted anyone else. A merchant it appeared, one leaving Ture. He had stopped off to the side, and setup a small camp. He wasn't alone, there was a long-armed guard with him. But two men, only one armed would be easy prey for Duncan.

It didn't appear that the merchant and guard had spotted them yet, which made it all the easier. She led Duncan off the road, near a small cove of small trees and some bushes. "Duncan my pet, it is time. We need horses, and supplies. You will get them." Zalkiniv looked at Duncan, feeling the blood in him. Still locked him into the blood rage she had induced in him. Outwardly calm, inside he was killing, raging. She reached through the Claret stone at her throat, preparing to release her weapon on the merchant and guard, but paused for a moment.

Something else besides anger and rage, faint, so faint, but it was there. Sadness. Somewhere, deep inside, some tiny part of the man Duncan Reis was before still existed. And it was in pain, sadness, hopelessness, horror. She smiled, all the better. She wanted to soak it in, revel in the pain. "Go. Kill them." She pushed Duncan toward the merchant's camp. And watched the carnage.

Duncan transformed as he moved, going from a walk, to a run, to a half-crouched leap. He was almost upon his targets when he gave forth a huge scream, full of hate and anger. She saw the guard bolt upright and try to draw his weapon, a spiked club that hung at his side, but it was too late. Duncan moved faster.

One arm grabbed the guard by the throat, and without hesitation, crushed down on the man's throat, fingers breaking through the skin. Even from where she stood, Zalkiniv could see the red fountain of the man's blood spring forth. Duncan pulled his hand back, ripping whatever was left of the Guards throat out with it. The merchant had stood opened mouthed for a second in shock, turned to run.

Duncan grabbed the now dead Guards club, and without a pause, leaped after the man, taking a few steps, and caught the merchant. Duncan was under the sway of the Blood rage now, and showed it as he raised the spiked club, and smashed it down on the merchant as he cowered and then fell.

Duncan rained blows down on the merchant's prone form, blow after blow. Zalkiniv walked down to join him she could hear his grunts of effort as he continued to beat the dead form of the Merchant, who now no longer resembled anything like a person from the waist up.

"Good. Thank you, Duncan." She laid an arm on Duncan's back, and once more, through the Claret stone, pushed the Rage and Anger inside. Duncan straightened up, and as the club, slick with blood slipped through his fingers to fall on the soaked ground, snapped his teeth, hard, as if trying to bite the air.

"Don't worry my prize. You will get to kill again, before your time comes at my hand." She savored the scent of carnage that filled the camp. They did need to take the horses which were spooked and grab all the food and water they could. She thought about hiding the bodies, then thought better of it. The fear they would bring, the rumors, would prime the area for her Lord.

In a short time, they were both mounted, though she'd had to perform a small working on both horses to calm them. Horses were harder to work on than that predator had been. That had at least been a creature that interacted with blood, instead of plants, but she would work horses, if she had to. Duncan sat rock still as she worked harder to calm his horse. Animals were good at picking up human emotions, and putting a raging person, not to mention one half covered in blood was not something the horse wanted.

She'd leave the blood she decided. If any bandits or thieves on the way investigated, the sight of a man covered in dried blood might give them pause. If time wasn't of importance, they could have carved a swath of death through this land. Soft and weak people, ripe for the culling. But time was important.

Spurring her horse forward, she could hear Duncan following. They headed north, towards the mountains, toward the barrier, toward the Mistlands, and toward the return of the Scaled One. The time was soon, and the land, the world, would learn the true Rage of a God.

***

Will awoke with a start, a dream, one of screaming pain and anger faded from his mind. He suspected it had something to do with Duncan, but what? Thinking about it made him depressed.

He was doing the only thing he knew he could to help, but still, Dreams like that... Will shuddered at some images that still clung to him.

Daylight streamed from above, more than Will wanted it to. They had overslept! Understandable with the chaos they had been through, but time was important. "Regin! Wake up! We slept more than we should have. Let's get moving!" Will shook Regin, giving a wince as he used the arm that the setter had fixed. Better, but still sore.

Regin for his part groaned and mumbled something before sitting up. He blinked for a few moments in the morning sun before awareness returned. "By the sparks I hurt. But you're right, we need to get moving." Will could see his welts had faded some, from red to a yellowish red. The man was going to more bruise than anything else soon.

Breaking camp, they got back on the road, eating as they rode. Korba fruit again, and Will added a chunk of some super salty sausage he found in the provision bag. "So, Regin, who was that woman, that Mistress Shal'ton?" Will asked. "I have never seen anyone like that."

"I didn't know her. But she is a knowledge broker. True knowledge, not a rumor monger. And she has a reputation, because of her background, of being fair." Regin worked the horse to move a bit faster. "She's a Saltmistress."

Will had never heard the term. But given the Ocean was not something Reachers thought about much, he wasn't surprised. "Some connection to the Ocean Goddess?"

Regin nodded. "Saltmisstresses are always women. No one has ever seen a male, or even heard of one. There aren't many of them, but they all are honest to a fault. Mistress Shal'ton is more of an oddity than most. Every other Saltmistress lives near the ocean, or on it. But Shal'ton appeared in the river harbor five years ago, just walked out of the water and set up shop. Made quite a stir. The rumor was that even nobles showed up and spoke to her."

Will listed to Regin explain the history of the Saltmisstresses, or what he knew. But his mind kept going back to the comment about nobles. Nobles. Why in all the chaos, had no one going to the court? The King lived in Ture. "Regin, why didn't anyone go to the Court? Couldn't they have helped? Why didn't we?"

Regin laughed, a barking affair. He continued laughing for a moment until he realized Will wasn't laughing with him. "Oh, I thought you were making a joke. The reason no one goes to the Court, is that the court, and the King, has no real power. Ceremonial power, and useful as a figurehead. But all the power in this land, lives in two places, the Priesthood and the Guild. No noble with money, no King with his army, has more power than those two organizations."

"But, couldn't they have helped?" Will asked. It made little sense; they were talking about the King!

"Could? Maybe. Would they? No. One word of things involving the Temple of Amder, and the Court and the King would show you the way out, by force. I don't think you understand how powerful the Priesthood of Amder is, William. And why the source of that power is sitting in your pocket, is so insane. Without that, without the Heart, they have no power." Regin gave Will a look, questioning. "You really don't know how dangerous this is do you?"

Will listened but didn't respond. Regin knew more about this than he did, but still, that the King of Palnor was nothing more than a puppet sat wrong with him. His hand crept to the now familiar weight of the Heart of Amder, when this was over with, things would change. It needed to change.

Regin said nothing more, and they traveled, moving north, ever north, toward the snowcapped reaches of the Skyreach mountains, and home.

64

Days later, Will awoke to find a light dusting of snow on his bedroll. A sight that brought the first real joy he'd had in quite some time. They had passed several large towns and villages on their way north, taking a different route than they had taken when Jaste had taken him to Ture. At least they didn't go near Kilvar, if Will never had to smell that place again, he'd be happy. They had only stopped to get supplies and moved on.

But here they were, only a day or two out from the Reach, and home. Home made him think of Duncan once more, and the smile fade from his face. By the sparks, he'd give a lot to know what was going on with his cousin. Where he was, what was going on.

He knew he had to be alive, because if he was dead, the Blood God was back, and this whole trip was pointless. No, Duncan was alive, somewhere. Guilt still gnawed at him about leaving him behind. It didn't matter how much he knew there hadn't been any other choice, he still hated it. And even if everything worked out, Amder returned, Duncan saved, blood taint somehow removed, he'd still feel guilty.

"I hate snow." Regin awoke, wiping the snow from his face. "Too cold, too wet, and stays around for too long."

"Snow is great. It looks good, gives you access to water when melted, and at least in the Reach, is a sign that the Forges will not run too hot." Will stood as he spoke, stretching in the cold morning air. He was glad for the traveling furs, the snow had frozen some of it stiff, and it's crunching reminded him what the cold could do if you weren't careful.

"You can keep it. I hate snow." Regin stood, stamping his feet, cold in his boots. "Will, I do have a question though."

"About snow?" Will smiled but faced as Regin looked serious and shook his head.

"We are close to the Reach. What exactly are we going to do when we get there? How do we get inside this Church of the Eight? How are you going to reforge or rebuild a God? I don't understand." Regin stoked the fire back from the coals as he spoke. "I'm sure there is a plan, but... do you even know it?"

Will knew he was right. Amder hadn't been exactly forthcoming with details. Which meant Will would not like the answers. *Anytime anyone doesn't want to tell you everything, it means you won't like it. Gods included.* They could go straight to the Church, but that replacement Priest, the one Bracin had sent, was there, and anyone Bracin liked, Will did not.

Going home was a bad choice as well. He was sure it was being watched, again, by that Priest and whatever men he had. He doubted word had reached here yet about the events in Ture, but word would come soon enough.

Will didn't have answers. He needed them, and the only way to get them, was talk to a dead God. Or at least try to. He'd never tried to speak to Amder directly. The last time it had been when he'd touched the Heart with his bare hand. Would that do it now?

"Will?" Regin asked as he made breakfast. Regin made all the food after Will had burned three separate meals.

"I don't know. There's only one person, or way, to get that. I have to talk to Amder again." Will sat by the fire, the weight of the Heart pulling harder this morning. "Hopefully I get answers. Amder was less than forthcoming about details."

Regin nodded and then laughed. "Sorry Will, find it odd but yet amusing to be talking about a God, a dead God on a first name basis."

Will smiled, lessening his fear about talking to Amder, and the lingering guilt from earlier. Regin was right, who talked to a God like that? Will wasn't much for formality though, and the God has told him to just call him Amder.

"After we eat, I'll try to talk to him. I guess. I don't know how, but I'll see if I can figure it out." Will poked at the fire, its warmth lingering on his face. "I want to be home Regin. The Reach is where I fit. Ture, Ture was too big, too crowded, too everything."

"Well almost there right? I'm sure we will figure it out." Regin said the words, but Will wondered if he believed it. This trip had changed his opinion of the man. Which would have shocked the fire out of him a few weeks ago. Regin had changed that was clear. And he admitted to himself, maybe he had changed too.

Breakfast was a simple affair, Bread, cheese, and hot tea. They had run out of Korba fruit a few days back, and even those salty sausages. They ate in silence at first. Will looked at the bread and wished he was back in the Reach. "I want Klah."

Regin took a long sip of his tea. "Klah. How I found you out."

"What do you mean?" Will was confused. Then he remembered, he'd eaten Klah back in the Guild, right before Regin's class! "By the sparks! That's how?"

"Yes. You smelled of it. I know what Klah is, and what it smells like. Real Klah. Only Reachers eat the stuff. I knew at that moment you weren't who you said you were. I suspected, but that decided it." Regin sipped his tea again and looked sheepish. "Sorry."

"No, we've covered that. A lot of things changed in the cold dark corners of the Temple. We've moved on." Will wanted to smack himself. Klah, of all things. Klah had been the final clue he wasn't Markin Darto from Dernstown.

Breakfast finished, Will cleaned up, as Regin packed up the camp. He would try this, and if it worked, or if it didn't, they needed to get on the Road. This close to the Reach he was sure they'd pass Traders, and the chance that someone Will knew would see them was high. While his information was a little out of date now, he knew of at least five mines near here, all of which he had worked at or had deals with.

Camp cleaned, and the cart packed, Will put out the fire. They did everything quick, and it was time. Blowing out a long breath he reached under his coat and pulled out into the cold clear air, the Heart of Amder. Sunlight shone on the Heart, casting pink and white light rays on the snow. Regin let out a whistle but said nothing.

Will felt a lump in his throat, but with a deep breath, took off a glove and with a nod to Regin closed his eyes, and touched the Heart.

And nothing happened.

Will cracked his eyes to see, everything as was when he closed them. Closing them again, he let out a breath he hadn't realized he was holding in, and this time in his head, asked, Amder?

A roaring sound came to him, and warmth covered him, the warmth of the forge, the smell of burning coal and hot metal came to his nose. Comforting him, he knew this place, it was a part of him.

"*Oh, open your eyes,*" Amder's voice ordered, and Will complied. It was his forge! The one at home, his real home, in the Reach! He had missed the place. All three forges were lit, something he'd never seen in his life and there was Amder and... The Forgemaster!

"Good morning William." Forgemaster Reis smiled and clasped him on the arm. "I'm proud of you son. You've come far, and though things went sideways there, you are here, with the Heart and close, so close to fixing this."

"*Yes, good point. Great job William!*" Amder joined in the praise, his indistinct form stood facing the forge, poking the coals, bringing forth bursts of white light from them as he did so. "*Now for the hard part.*"

"Hard part?" Will blurted out. "Getting out of the Temple with the Heart, escaping that madman Bracin, and getting out of the Capitol wasn't the hard part?"

Forgemaster Reis lowered his arm, shaking his head. "Amder always had a way with words. No, those were hard, but this might be harder."

"What aren't you telling me? How do I get into a Temple that most likely has people in it who want to kill me? How do I use the Heart, the Hammer and the Forge to bring you back? I need to know, there's no more time to wait to find out."

Amder's form moved toward him but turned away. It was the Forgemaster again, who spoke. "William. You must figure the first part out yourself; we don't have an answer. I'm sure you will figure it out. Amder has stretched his powers to the limit already. But I'll be here, to help you. As much as I can."

Will couldn't believe this; this wasn't an answer. Figure it out for yourself was another way of saying "I don't know." It's what his father said when he young when Will asked questions his father either didn't like or didn't understand.

"Fine. How do I bring you back?" Will raised his voice. "Can you tell me that at least?"

Forgemaster Reis picked up a hammer and from somewhere produced a cherry red billet of metal, hammering it as he spoke. "That's easy, actually. Take the Heart to the Forge, put it in the fire. That bracer, the one you wear on your wrist. That will make the billet, the start for the rebirth. That's all!"

Amder's form shuddered. *"Tell him the rest."*

Forgemaster Reis didn't look up from his hammering, turning the metal as he struck. He said nothing for a long moment, then taking the red-hot billet he threw it into the forge, handle and all. "Didn't work." He mumbled something else then turned to Will.

"This is serious William. So, it will be hard." Forgemaster Reis reached into the Forge and pulled out a small glowing crystal, a shard of Amder's blood! Will knew what it was the moment he saw it. "You couldn't have used this, to make the hammer you wear, if you hadn't been one of my bloodline. Nothing would have happened. But you are, and as a result, you could make something that if all goes well, will continue down the Reis line, for generations to come."

"I don't get it, what are you telling me?" Will could see the Forgemaster was going somewhere with this, but where he wasn't sure.

"This is the blood of Amder. He will need it again. ALL of it." Forgemaster Reis pointed off to the east. "What you call the Mistlands, it's full of the blood of two Gods. One of which, you need." Forgemaster Reis tossed the Crystal into the air and caught it. "Every speck."

Will couldn't believe his ears. "How by the sparks do I bring crystals bigger than me all the way back to the Reach? There's quite a few, Gods have a lot of Blood! And it's covered with a mist that turns anyone it touches into a blood mad howling animal!!" Will was yelling, but he didn't care, this was insane.

"No, no. You don't have to go get them!" Forgemaster Reis laughed. Will noticed Amder was not laughing. "They will come, on their own. I imagine it will be a strange sight, though rather pretty in its own way, glowing crystals flying through the sky. All the doors, windows, everything in the Church will need to be open, there must be a clear path for them to get to the Forge." The

Forgemaster looked down and then back at Amder, whose form nodded to the Forgemaster.

"William, what keeps you, what keeps the whole land safe from the Valni? From the followers of the Blood God?" Forgemaster Reis laid a hand on Will's shoulder.

"The barrier." Will answered, a feeling of dread forming in his stomach.

"The Barrier. Right. The Barrier was made, back soon after the Godsfall. Before the Priesthood fell to corruption, it was the first thing made with the Heart. The Guild made each of the markers, Guildmasters worked those on the Anvil in the Guild, and the Priesthood used the Heart, the only time they ever took it out of the Temple, to make the barrier. It has stood for a long time. Working, keeping the Valni out. Working mostly, I should say." Forgemaster Reis closed his eyes. "The Barrier, it has to come down. For Amder to return, he needs that power for the rebirth. Without it, no Amder. One reason Amder has been so limited since the Godsfall, keeping the Barrier up takes his power."

Will said nothing, dumbstruck. This was what they meant by hard. The Barrier had to come down. Which meant Valni, and whatever else it kept out, could come through. The Reach would be defenseless. A horde of blood crazed almost humans could descend on the Reach, killing everyone and everything.

"What about the other things made with the Heart? What happens to them?" Will asked. "Or is it only the barrier?"

"Everything made with my Heart will lose its power. Until I return and choose to give it back. I will do so with the barrier, most of the rest, I will not." Amder shrugged. *"But this isn't what's important, is it?"*

"I have to sacrifice all the people of the Reach?" Will couldn't believe this. He felt sick, and tears came on their own. "I've lost Haltim, I've lost Master Jaste, I've lost *DUNCAN*, and now you say I have to give up the one place in the world I care for?"

"I don't know." Amder replied. *"I can't tell you what will happen when the barrier comes down. I don't know if those things my brother made will attack or not. All I can say is that it has to come down. Once I'm reborn, I can remake it. I can power it back*

up without effort. But while I'm being reborn, it has to come down."

Will blinked back his tears. Anger filled him. "You knew this would be the choice. Give up the Reach, to bring you back."

"I didn't want to say anything last time. You had lost Duncan, and Haltim. It worried me what you might do." Amder sighed. *"Easy choices these are not."*

"Easy choices?? The only easy choice I've had since I started down this road was if I wanted weak beer or weak wine with dinner back in the Guild!" Wills teeth ground against each other. He was worn out, tired. All this work, to find out this at the end*? How much more will I have to sacrifice?*

"What do you want to do William?" Forgemaster Reis asked. "Because when it comes down to the core, you're the only one who can make this choice."

Will brushed the Forgemasters hand off his shoulder. He didn't need a ghost of the past to tell him what he knew, that regardless of how much he hated this choice, regardless of how sad and sick it made him, there was no other way. If he didn't, they would lose everything. Not only the Reach, but everything. He didn't have to pretend to be happy about it.

"What do I want to do? That doesn't matter. I'll do what I must. That's all I can do." Will looked around the forge. He knew it wasn't real, but it felt so much like home. Home. Will wondered if even if everything went perfect, would this ever be home again? He'd be a Forgemaster, *THE* Forgemaster. He'd be all over the place, doing who knows what. Would he ever be able to stay here, stay in a place he loved, with people he cared about?

"Fine. It will get done." Will turned to leave the Forge, the exit stood before him, dark and cold. "I won't ever see Duncan again, will I? He's gone. Like the others." Will walked through the exit, not looking back at the God he was to bring back to life, or the ghost of the last Forgemaster, but no answer came from either.

Will opened his eyes, gasping in the cold air. The Heart thrummed in his hand, pulsing with its light, a steady rhythm. Before that pulsing had brought him some level of hope, but now… Will pushed the thought aside, he had a job to do. He put the Heart back in his inner pocket and shook himself. How was he going to get this done?

Regin stood from where he'd been sitting. "That took longer than I thought it would. You've been standing there for at least half an hour. So, get the answers you needed?"

"Yes. I know why nothing was said earlier. The barrier." Will pointed in the general direction of the one thing that kept these lands free of the Valni. "It has to come down for this to work. It's powered by the Heart, always has been. But in the process, the reforging of Amder, it has to come down."

Regin's frown appeared as he considered the implications. "But doesn't that mean that those things can attack?"

Will held up his hammer flipping it in the air, catching it by the handle each time. "Yes. That while it's down, the Valni, and whatever else the Blood God has to throw at us, will be free to do so. Getting the existing Priest and whatever guards or men he has out of the Church, is up to us."

"That doesn't sound like something we can do alone." Regin paced around the remains of the fire kicking a mix of snow and dirt into the cooling coals. "Even if we get the Priest out, and his men, I guess we could sort of blockade the place, long enough for you to do whatever you need to do."

"Won't work. According to Amder, every window, door, inside and out has to be open." Will flipped his hammer again in thought. "I don't see how this works. The Reach has what, ten or fifteen Guardsmen in the whole place. And these aren't professional fighters, just miners and smiths too old to swing a hammer or pick well anymore, who work as watch men. The worst we have here is the rare animal attack. No one attacks the Reach. There's no one else up here to attack us."

Will flipped the hammer again. Sunlight filled the clear blue sky that reflected off the hammer, its silvery sheen nearly white as the snow right now. No one ever attacked the Reach. Why? Because the miners and smiths here were a tough bunch. An idea came, and Will stopped flipping the hammer.

He wasn't sure he could do it. But it was the only way. He may never get Duncan back. He may be the last Reis ever. But the Scaled One, and his brood would pay for what they have wrought. "We need to get to the Reach as soon as we can. I have a plan." Will climbed into the cart. "I'll tell you on the way, let's go."

Regin climbed in with him taking the reins as he started the cart forward. "Good. I had faith you would."

65

Zalkiniv watched as Duncan killed a farmer who was walking his fields. The kill was brutal as it should be. There wasn't any real need to kill the man, not in terms of survival, or travel. He'd seen them, and she didn't need stories of a young woman traveling with a "thing" covering the countryside. Duncan was a thing now, dirty, dried blood spattered, and worse. The longer she kept him under the control of the Blood, the more animalistic and savage he became.

Duncan returned to her side, fresh red covering patches of old dried blood. He smelled, but that didn't make any difference. She reached out through the Claret stone at her throat and smiled. There it was. The other reason she had him killing often. Hate. Whatever was left of Duncan Reis, hated her. Each kill she had him make, each brutal attack, made him hate her more. That hate couldn't do anything, but she enjoyed it all the same. Locked inside his own body, powerless to stop himself from killing men, women, anyone who got in their way, or even saw them.

These lands were fat and rich, and the people would be great sacrifices once the Scaled One returned. The harvest she would make! They rode towards the mountains at a brisk pace, with her prodding of the horses to keep up the pace. They had run through two sets of the animals already, with her having pushed the things past their breaking point. But horses were easy to get still, traders and merchants, farmers and whoever else came across. While the route they had taken was not the busiest, there was enough traffic to provide for them.

"My pet, we will be in the Mountains soon enough. Do you remember the trip down? You, me, and that fool of a priest? Each night, me working your blood, twisting it, drawing forth more and more power from your blessing. And Haltim, your dear friend, a blind idiot to what was going on right in front of him." Zalkiniv could feel a tiny surge in hate, but it was buried again in the tide of rage and anger she had placed on the man.

Once they reached the mountains, she knew they would have to take a route that avoided the Reach, at least for now. They would make for the cave, and the one weak spot in the barrier. The bodyguards she had placed there would still be there. Even if the barrier stopped her from feeling them, years if not decades of obedience to her wouldn't break that easy.

The Valni wouldn't attack them either, they had been bound there. Still it had been far longer than she had thought to get this done. When she had crossed over the first time, she had expected to be gone for a day or a few weeks. But she'd been on this side of everything for months now. She was sure the Temple of the Blood God was running red often. Some fool may have even set themselves up as the new High Priest. Nothing she couldn't handle, and with the blade and shaft, none would stand against her for long.

The day ended as they crested a ridge to see the Skyreach Mountains. Soon she would be back across. The horses were breathing hard, and one was bleeding from a scored hoof, but for the final sprint, they would make it. She knew that whatever William Reis was up to, he hadn't brought Amder back. The Barrier was still up for one. The first thing she would do upon taking back possession of the Shaft of Valnijz would be to call the Valni in droves, pull them from all the ruins, caves, and buildings they hid in. Every single one.

And one very important Valni. She hadn't forgotten that one Valni, one special and lucky Valni, had tasted the blood of William Reis. That would lead her army, the moment the barrier fell, an arrow straight for the man has he tried to bring back his God. She would throw every Valni at that problem. If they killed the man, so be it. She could use his blood even if it was off a cold corpse if she also had Duncan's blood.

They rode through the night, pushing the horses close to exhaustion. Zalkiniv drew power off the Claret stone to keep herself and her pet fresh. Morning came and Zalkiniv smiled. Today was the day she would be back where she belonged. Where her word ruled. Her whims were the command that moved a people. No one would stand against her, nor could they.

"Come prize. Leave it all. We ride fast now." She pushed her horse, feeling its fight to flee and its exhaustion. Duncan's horse was even worse, as the blood on the man brought it to the edge of bolting. One last working then. Hide the exhaustion, block the pain, and give them false calm. They would run until death, and they would give their lives for the glory to come.

The working was quick and using the Claret stone, didn't even need blood to take effect. The horses took off, running like the wind that flew down the mountains. Duncan followed right behind her, his rage at the edge, balanced to be pushed into action. On they rode, the rocks passing by as they moved up this trail, the old trail they had used on the way down. She spied the building she had first approached them at, working to cloud their judgement of her. The smile on her face grew, so close to her goal now.

Her horse stumbled, and the spike of pain almost broke through her working. She looked down to see a rock, sharp lodged deep in a leg. No matter, they must keep moving! She pushed the animal to ignore it and they rode on, leaving a trail of blood behind them. At last she spied it, the afternoon sun lighting the small cave entrance that marked the way under the barrier. She could feel the thing, being this close to it. It made her sick to her stomach. Stopping her horse, and Duncan's, it was time to walk. Both horses were foaming at the mouth now, sides panting, and bleeding.

She released the workings on the beasts as they both gave forth a sound like a scream and collapsed, one twitching, but the other dead as soon as it hit the ground. "Come prize," Zalkiniv ordered Duncan, as they climbed up the scree and lose rocks to the cave. The way was steep, but it wasn't far. Not but a quarter of an hour later they stood in front of the cave. Time to cross back over, and ready the attack.

66

The domed homes and buildings of the old quarter of the Reach laid out in Will's eyes like a set of beehives. He was sure he could even point out which one was home, his home. As his eyes traveled the newer buildings, peaked roofs instead of domed roofs, and newer styles gave way to the Reach proper. A whiff of smell of the forges and smelters, still lingering after the winds blew through town brought a sense of peace for a second. Home. Just... home.

Will took a deep breath and let it out. At least he was doing this here. He hoped his love of this place, of its smells, and sights, and of its people would translate to the thing he would attempt. To convince the miners, smiths, merchants, smelters, took take up arms. To defend their home, to defend the Church of the Eight, to buy him time. He couldn't even be out there with them if this worked.

I'll be asking them to die for me. His smile faded.

"It will work William." Regin stood next to Will. "You're asking them to fight for their homes, their lives, even their God." Regin pointed in the general direction of the Mistlands "Against an enemy they know well, one they have known of for generations."

Will nodded. He knew all that. But asking them to take this risk without joining in the same risk, sat wrong with him. Even Regin couldn't join them. He needed Regin to help him, he wasn't sure if he would need another pair of hands in this process. That he, a not even trained Apprentice in the Guild, would use a full cloaked Master of the Guild as an assistant was something that amused him, if anything in this business was amusing. *I won't mention that to Regin though.*

"Let's go." Will and Regin climbed back into the cart and made their way to the Reach. Will sat straight up in the cart, no cloak, and no hood. If he would do this, he would do it his way. No subterfuge, no hiding who he was.

"Sparks. William Reis!" Barnibus Steenir the gate guard stood up straight at the sight of William. "We all thought you were dead! You and that cousin of yours vanished, along with old Haltim. We spent a month looking for you!" Barnibus stopped the cart and gave Will a long look. "Where have you been? Why no notice? What are you doing back?"

Will climbed out of the cart and clasped Barnibus's shoulder, looking him in the eye. "It's good to see you. And the Reach. I will answer the questions, but... I need you to do something. Send word. I need to speak to everyone. Every mining house, every smelter, every merchant. Every man, woman and child who can swing a hammer, all. Main Square, tonight."

Barnibus stepped back for a second, and Will could see him trying to make sense of what Will was asking. "I don't know. Why, William? You're a Reacher, but this sounds, crazy."

Will nodded. "I know. But I wouldn't ask if it wasn't important. Please. On my honor as a Reacher, and as a Reis, this is important."

Barnibus said nothing but ran his hand through what hair he had left shaking his head as he did so. "I don't know. You show up out of nowhere, with someone I don't recognize, and all you'll say is get everyone in the Reach together?"

"Yes. It's important." Will paused and sighed for a moment. "If you don't, it will be the end of the Reach. And a lot more. Again, if there is any goodwill left toward me, toward the name of Reis, here, please, do this."

Barnibus looked between Will and Regin for a time. "Ok. I'll do it. I may regret it, but I'll try."

Will smiled. "Thank you. And let's not invite the new Priest in the Church of the Eight, ok?"

"Bah, we don't like him anyway. Him or his men. Five armed men who wander the place. He came around a lot when you vanished at first. Made many people mad, asking questions, getting into people's business. Those guards of his made a mess of a few mines, looking for you and Duncan. And Haltim. Besides, he and his men haven't left the Church since a month after you vanished. Set up getting supplies delivered to them and that was it."

"I'm sorry. I am. I'll explain everything tonight." Will paused. "It is great to see you, I've missed home."

Will walked toward Regin brow furrowed. "Come, we need to go to each of the main entrances to the Reach. I will have to tell each guard the same thing. Barnibus is a good man, but I doubt he will reach enough people."

Regin nodded. "You are in charge; I swore my oath. Point the way."

The afternoon passed as Will and Regin spoke to each gate guard. At each gate more and more people met them, word had already spread through the Reach he was back. Will was rather surprised, they had sent out search parties for weeks after he, Duncan and Haltim had vanished. He hadn't realized how liked they all were, even Duncan.

At each gate he told them he'd explain everything tonight, and while there might have been grumbles, no one demanded an answer right away. Will was thankful for that, tonight would be hard enough. The lower the sun sank, the more his stomach sank with it. Regin wasn't much help, he didn't get nervous doing this, the man was born with a silver tongue and no nerves.

Will could feel the pit inside growing by the minute. His heart beating fast and sweat, actual sweat, here in the cold air of the Reach clinging to his hands.

"Almost time William. Are you ready?" Regin climbed into the cart, ready to drive it into the center of the Reach, to the main square. Will had no idea how many would show up, but whoever didn't would hear about it by morning. As the miner shifts changed out, the story would spread.

He reached under his shirt, and took out the Heart, it pulsed, pink and white, its light even visible in the reds and yellows of the sunset. "Yes. I guess I am." Will didn't feel ready, but he didn't have a choice. He climbed into the cart and let out a deep breath, placing the heart back under his shirt.

Regin said nothing, which Will was thankful for. How much more would Amder ask of him? He had dreamed of being a Guild smith and making tools for the common man. And yet here he was, about to try to rouse the Reach, and bring a God back to life. The cart started forward, its metal shod wheels clattering on the stone street, heading toward the square.

Will could hear the crowd before he could see it. A murmur, a buzz, the sound of muted voices, but growing each turn of the wheels. "Sounds like a crowd," Regin remarked, a trace of a smile crossing his face.

"Your enjoying this aren't you?" Will's voice rose with an edge. "Why on earth would you enjoy this?"

"William, Look at this from my perspective. You're the chosen Forgemaster of Amder. You have been picked, selected, whatever you want to call it to bring a *GOD* back to life. And yet, speaking to his crowd has you terrified. These are your people. They respect you, sparks aflame, they like if not love you. You're one of them. I doubt that there is anyone else, not even your cousin you talk about all the time, who could draw a crowd like the one we can hear. They are here for you. I find it amusing that you don't get that." Regin drove the cart deeper into the Reach as the noise grew.

Will face locked into a scowl for a second, but it passed as the first signs of the crowd came into view. Half the Reach must have crammed into the square. People everywhere. Men, women, children. Every inch of standing room taken, and even more, younger men, teenagers, hanging from roofs, and even standing on piles of ore and rock. At the sight of the cart the sound of the crowd changed, as if a wind swept over them, the sound vanished, as eyes and faces watched them.

Someone had cleared a place on the steps leading into the Golden Chisel, put an ore crate there for him to stand on. Will let his eyes cover the crowd, stop here and there as faces of those he had known well, miners and smiths, merchants and townsfolk looked back. Most wore smiles, happy to see him again. Others wore worried expressions, and yet even a few wore not-quite scowls.

Will nodded to Regin who stopped the cart. Will climbed down, and with a few nods made his way to the steps and stepped up onto the crate. The nerves he had battled all the way here, faded. Maybe it was because he had no other choice. Regin was right, these were his people. If that was the case, what he said here tonight might strain that relationship to the breaking point. *No point in worrying about it now.*

"Reachers!" He raised his hammer high, its slivery sheen almost glowing in the torchlight. It had its intended effect, as the few remaining murmurs and whispers left the crowd, and all attention was on Will. "I have come here, because I both owe you an explanation, and something to ask of you. Something hard. Something I would never ask if I had any other choice."

Faces expectant, Will saw more than a few of the throng cross their arms to listen, heads cocked, pondering his words. Good. They would listen at least.

"I must apologize to you all. I left without warning. Duncan and Haltim too. We did not mean to cause worry, or concern. I left, to join the Smithing Guild, in Ture." Will said those words as a few faces broke into surprise and a few whispers started. "I know how that sounds hard. You know as well as I that Reachers never get into the guild. I know why now, which is why I joined the guild under a false name. And it worked. I was in the Guild for several months. Until they discovered my ruse, and I had to flee Ture."

"The reason no Reacher gets in is, the Priesthood of Amder, has fallen to corruption and greed. They allow no Reacher for one reason. Because of my name. Because I am a Reis. The Priesthood fears the return of a Forgemaster!" Will could tell, they were listening now, and a few older men in the corner were whispering and nodding. *So far so good.*

"When I left, Duncan and Haltim discovered that the Priesthood was after me, that there was a death sentence, given down by the High Priest of Amder himself, to kill me. And Duncan, and anyone helping me, meaning Haltim. They defrocked Haltim for standing against this man, this High Priest. And they fled into the night, trying to find me, to warn me. That's where I have been." Will could feel it now, his voice was calm. He was being honest, and the crowded responded. The anger written on many faces wasn't directed at him, but at the Priesthood, and more than a few glances toward the Church of the Eight.

"I must tell you this. Haltim is dead. Duncan... Is lost." A voice yelled out in the crowd, and a surge of anger that Will could feel, spread. "He isn't dead but captured. But not by the Priesthood of Amder, but by the followers of the Blood God! There is one way to save him, and only one." Will reached under his shirt, taking the Heart into his hand. *This was it. The moment.*

He held up the heart, and to the credit of the spirit of a dead God, the Heart shone bright, brighter than a full moon, illuminating the throng in silver and pink, it shone on faces now full of wonder and awe.

"This is the Heart of Amder! With this, and the Forge and Hammer, which lie in the Church of the Eight, I can restore Amder to life! I can bring back the God of the Forge and Creation. I can bring back the one who gave his life to save us all from the Scaled One, the Blood God, the One who lives in Anger and Rage, Valnijz!" Will's hammer shone along with the Heart, shining with a light that pulsed once more in time with the Heart, lighting up the night sky even more.

"But I can only do this with your help. Because there is a danger. Valnijz is close to returning as well. Duncan's life is to be sacrificed to the Blood God! The only chance of stopping is to bring Amder back first."

A man yelled from the back of the crowd. Will couldn't hear him, but the people did and yelled in clear assent. "I must get into the Church! But that is not all I will need help with... The danger is worse than you know." Will put the heart back in his inner pocket while the crowd stood silent, listening. He had them, but to ask this, was asking a lot.

"We have all lost friends, family, and ancestors, to the Valni! Those cursed by the blood mist. The barrier, the only thing that stops them stands, strong, to protect us. To bring Amder back, the barrier must come down, if only for a short time. I ask, I beg you, stand. Gather every weapon, every hammer, every sickle and club. Every dagger and shield. Every scrap of armor and stand with me! Stand with the Reach. Stand with Amder! Amder will restore the barrier when he returns." Shock went through the crowd, some turning pale, some yelled, others shook their heads in disbelief.

"I know. I am asking you to risk much, to lay down your life to give me time to bring a God back to life. You know me. I am one of you! So, I ask of you this, to stand strong, to give me the time to bring Amder, the God of the Reach, the God of all Palnor, back to the world! Are you with me?" Will held up his hammer, and asked Amder to help, give them a sign, and to his credit Amder answered. *This better work.*

Will's hammer shone brighter than it ever had, and the silver glow turned gold and red, and the faint sound of a ringing anvil filled the ears of every assembled person in the crowd. The sound of a God. The sound of *their* God. A yell, with the raising of fists, hammers, and tongs, whatever was nearby filled the crowd. "AMDER, AMDER, AMDER." the sound of the name of a God echoed off the walls of the square, spreading through the streets, and lifting Will's spirit. He had done it; he had bought time.

***

What Myriam had just seen was incredible, and somewhat shocking. She'd been in the Reach for a little over a week already, and she had almost given up hope of William ever getting here.

When she had arrived, she'd asked about William Reis. Everyone she asked had been somewhat guarded but spoke glowingly of the man. How trustworthy, how dependable, and how he was gone, and no one had seen him, or a person named Duncan Reis. It had only been two days ago she learned that they had no other family. Some old Priest of the Eight was missing as well.

She liked the Reach though, and the longer she spent here, the more she could see how William was from here. Just about everyone she talked to had the same general attitude. Hard workers, friendly, but distant. They didn't trust those from elsewhere. She had kept her red cloak hidden away since the day she saw the Reach in front of her, the less attention she drew the better. She had simply described William as a friend from Ture.

That had raised a few eyebrows, no one had known that was where he was going. The only place she didn't look was the Church of the Eight, and the Priest there. Though thankfully she was told the new Priest didn't like it here and avoided coming into the town proper.

She'd been staying at the main inn, a place called the Golden Chisel, when word had come that William Reis and another man were here and wanted everyone to be in the main square tonight. Said it was important, and he'd asked this on the name of Reis. To her surprise carried a lot of weight, because the square quickly became a mob.

When William pulled in with Master Regin, of all people, she'd nearly screamed. Regin was supposed to be dead! But there he was sitting there, smiling and nodding. And he and William were getting along? Regin had been an insufferable ass before, what had changed?

William was different, though he looked the same. It hadn't been till halfway through the speech she realized what it was. The fear was gone. What was left had been tested, and strengthened. Just like a forged hammer, the weakness had been removed.

67

Zalkiniv stumbled several times as they made their way down, into the depths of the earth. The barrier made her feel unbalanced, and the total darkness didn't help. There was only one way to do this. The cave had been made many years ago for this purpose. Duncan followed, she could hear his breath and feel his blood behind her. A dim light came into view and as they descended a small drop, the reason became clear. One of her guards was there!

The man stood, facing the barrier, holding a torch. Waiting. They were loyal, the blood workings that kept them alive made sure of it. The room the barrier passed through wasn't very large, but big enough for both her and Duncan to stand in front of the barrier. She could feel the weak point. Put there for a traitor by the Amderites. She would use now it to deliver half of her Lord's prize.

"Wait here." She ordered Duncan. She needed to go through first, she needed to know how the barrier and the Claret stones would interact. Duncan was also a question. He wasn't a Valni, but he wasn't human either. Being prepared on the other side, the side he was crossing to, would make it so she could take control, if something happened.

With a breath, she stepped forward. And screamed. The Claret stone at her throat burned. Burned like a drop of molten steel, and pain, overwhelming pain, filled her. Zalkiniv was used to pain, pain was an old friend. This pain was more than even the High Priest of Valnijz could take. But her forward momentum made her fall forward, and as quick as the pain had come, it faded. Still she stayed down, her mind unable to concentrate.

What had that been? She hadn't expected the Claret stone she wore to react that way. She was thankful the other stones were still in the bag. If she'd been wearing them... The thought made her shudder. Standing, she brushed loose dirt and rock from her legs and took a deep breath. She was home. The air showed her the way. The faint smell of blood and smoke filled her nose, a heady smell. And the air felt like home, it was warmer, drier.

Turning to Duncan on the other side of the barrier, she could feel the sense of worry return. The Claret stone reaction hadn't been expected. How would this man, touched by the blade of Valnijz, and for the last few weeks been kept in a total state of rage of hate, react to passing through the barrier? There was no time to waste on idle thought. Things must be started.

"Come Duncan. Come." Zalkiniv beckoned the man and watched as he stepped forward and screamed.

Time slowed as she saw smoke and small flames erupt from his body. All the dried blood, left there on her whim, burned off, filling the space with a foul smoke. What worried her more, was the change in the eyes of the man. Deep inside her prize there had always been a small part of the person he had been before. A small tiny speck of the real Duncan Reis that resisted her still.

As he burned the rage and hate, the induced rage and hate, fell away like the dried blood off his skin. And the real Duncan Reis was in control. Eyes filling with tears, his face changed. While the pain was still there, her bond shattered. And she knew, he was free.

When his eyes fell upon her, hate and anger returned. Not a hate and anger of the Blood God, one of blind rage and torment. No, a hate born of betrayal, and an anger sprung from being used to be a killer, a murderer of innocents.

"RACHE!" Duncan screamed the name he had known her by. Duncan lurched forward, crossing the barrier to her, determined to stop her, punish her, something. *An error, such a shame, for him.* As he moved forward, to her side of the barrier, she reacted. Her knife drawn, she plunged it into the guard who had been waiting for her. True to their oaths he fell, as obedient as always, giving his life, his blood, to her.

She reached through the Claret stone, and with a working, froze Duncan in mid stride. "Ah Duncan. Such a foolish man." Zalkiniv reached out and brushed remnants of burned blood off his face, the flickering light of the torch in the still smoky cave giving the hard angles of his face a dark shadow.

"Such a fool. If you had stepped back, and run, I doubt I would have been able to stop you in time. You would have been free! As free as you could be with the Blood you carry. But free!" she laughed then, watching his eyes, knowing the anger and pain, sorrow and sadness that roiled beneath the frozen paralyzed exterior.

"But you didn't. And that should tell you why Valnijz, the God of Anger and Rage, is the true God of Man. You chose him as you stepped forward. You delivered yourself, once more, to me." She reached down and wetting three fingers in the still warm blood of the fallen guard and drew a symbol on Duncan's face. "And you will never be free again while I live." Her symbol drawn, she gathered her might and made her working. Binding the man in front of her back to her side.

His own anger and hate of her helped the working. The emotions needed to be tweaked, their target changed. Their target changed from her, to his very much alive cousin, William Reis. The cousin who had abandoned him, left him to die, to hurt. How dare William Reis leave him to die after everything Duncan had done for him! A simple as that, the spark of Duncan that had lived in his eyes, vanished, and the animal, rage and hate, returned.

"Good. Follow me." Zalkiniv released the paralysis and reached down to grab the torch. She ascended, Duncan following, once again under her control. She could feel that tiny spark still there, howling in sadness. It brought a smile to her face, all the better for the upcoming sacrifice.

***

Will sat down in the Golden Chisel, his nerves getting the better of him. The crowd had responded, and much to his surprise a group of miners and a few smiths headed off toward the Church of the Eight. Bent on kicking out the Priest and armed guards that were, in one miner's loud exclamation, "squatters in the Church of Amder." For the moment he happy to be here. The place hadn't changed at all in the time away though that wasn't surprising. It had only been a few months, yet, so long ago.

Regin sat down at the table and sat back with a sigh. "That William, was one of the best speeches I'd ever heard. You had them in the palm of your hand! You're a natural!" Will didn't feel like a natural. He'd been terrified inside and wasn't sure how he'd kept the doubt of his own words out of his voice.

"Don't feel like one. But doesn't matter. It worked." Will closed his eyes but opened them at the sound of something heavy being put on the table, and the smell of glorious food. The innkeeper stood there, having put two large flagons of weak beer and a massive trencher of meat, bread, vegetables, and a rather large crock of Klah on the table! "By the sparks, thank you!" Will exclaimed. The smell of the food banished any remnants of fear, replacing them with hunger.

"How much?" Will took out his coin purse, while Regin, ever the opportunist, was already eating, munching away on a spiced sausage in one hand, and his flagon in the other.

"Nothing. You've been through a lot, and based on what you said, Reachers got to stick together. And if you will really be a Forgemaster, well..." the innkeeper left off and gave a shrug.

"Please, let me pay you." Will shook his head. "I don't want to be any different from any other Reacher walking through your door."

The innkeeper gave a laugh. "True Reacher you are William Reis. Fine, two silver bits."

Will paid the man, and turned his attention to the food, tearing off a hunk of brown bread and smearing a thick layer of Klah on it. One bite and he sighed in contentment. "Regin, I'm home."

The meal continued, in silence. The Chisel was crowded, and much conversation about what Will had said, and the plans. But people left Will and Regin alone. There were a lot of nods toward Will which he returned, but it wasn't the Reachers way to bother a man who was eating. If they had questions, they'd wait to ask.

Will sat back at last, feeling full, and for the first time in a long while, content. For this moment, everything was good. Regin stood and moved his chair next to Will. Sitting down, Regin leaned in close, "Are you ready for this?" he said, voice low.

Will's first reaction was to ask for what, but he knew where the question was coming from. Everything was moving, and fast. This meal was likely the last one he'd have before the rebirth. If he even survived this. How little that bothered him. This time tomorrow he could be dead, or captured by the Blood God, the Reach in ruins. Or, he could be successful, Amder reborn, the Scaled One not coming back, and Duncan rescued.

"Yes. I am." Will wasn't sure what he felt. For the first time, he realized he wasn't worried. He wasn't scared. It might all fall down around him, but he was here, at the end of it all. He had made it this far, beyond his expectations. And soon, it would be over.

Regin said nothing else and sat back, lost in his own thoughts. Will took a long drink of his weak beer, he was tired, but sleep was something he would not get much of tonight. If any.

As if to prove him right, the group of people who had gone to the Church of the Eight to evict the current Priest and Guards came in, and with them, the Priest! He was bound, and gagged, and clad only in a sleep shirt. They must have taken the Church by surprise.

"Here ya Priest." A miner pushed the Priest toward Will and Regin. "Those guards of his put up a fight, but not much. After we took two out, the rest surrendered and dropped weapons. We let em flee. Though not sure how far they will get, running out into the Skyreach in the dark."

"You took out two guards?" Will didn't want any of the guards hurt. He wasn't sure if they even knew what was going on.

"We didn't kill em. Just knocked out. They are outside, hands bound and disarmed." The miner shrugged. "Figured once they woke up, we'd let em leave. But we weren't sure what to do with this Priest, so we brought him to you."

Will nodded. *I should have expected this.* Still, they had taken the Church so fast was a good sign. "Thanks." Will shook hands with each Miner, drawing smiles from them each. As they group dissipated into the crowd, he turned his attention to the Priest. The Priest flushed with anger. He raised a finger to lecture Will, but it trembled to the point that he had to put it down.

Will pulled a chair out and crouched down next to the Priest. "I will untie you. But I'd recommend you take a seat here. We can talk. After we talk, you can leave town, or stay. But I'd save any thought of trying to turn the people of the Reach against me." Will drew a small knife, the Priest flinched in response. "I'm freeing you." Will shook his head and cut his bindings and gag.

Will returned to his seat, keeping his eyes on the Priest. He was young, far younger than Haltim had been. Will didn't trust the man, Haltim and Duncan had filled him in, in that dark dungeon cell, what had happened when they fled the Reach after him. No, not trust, but considering all the Death to come, leaving the man unhurt appealed to him.

The Priest stood and sat in the chair. "How dare you! The Church of Amder rules this country! When the High Priest hears of this attack, an army of Church Guards, even Tempered Priests will fall down upon this place!" The Priest sat up straight, crossing his arms.

"Doubtful." Will took a sip of beer. "The High Priest is dead, and someone attacked the Church... I doubt they are even giving two thoughts to this place right now. What's your name Priest?" Will took satisfaction seeing the look of shock on the man's face. Haughty people annoyed him, and this man had it in spades.

"Lockseed," The Priest mumbled. "Priest Lockseed." Will nodded and smiled when Regin shook his head at the man. Sweat was coming off him, soaking into his collar "Don't worry Priest Lockseed. I have no interest in harming you. Though by rights, I could. You tried to have my cousin killed, and the former occupant of your office. Who was a second father to me."

Will enjoyed the paleness the man could produce as the words Will spoke sunk in. "I knew the name was familiar! You're the one the High Priest wanted dead! You and your cousin... Duncan! That was it." Realizing what he had blurted out, the Priest snapped his mouth shut.

"Yes. Let me be plain. I'm about to bring Amder back to the world. During this, the Valni will attack. All of them. The Barrier will come down. You can either stay or help defend the Reach, help with the wounded, and earn your place here. Or... leave. Flee. Run back to Ture if you will make it that far." Will took out his hammer and placed it on the table, it still shone with a silvery light, feeding off the proximity to the heart in his inner pocket.

True to what he would expect, the Priest laughed. "Fool. Amder is dead. There's no way to bring him back! And besides, there's no way the Priesthood would let you." His voice cut short and Will reached into that inner pocket and drew out the Heart, its light pink and white flaring anew. Silencing the inn as the Reachers stopped talking and watched.

"How did you get that!" Lockseed stood, knocking his chair over. "That's not possible!"

"I took it. From the main Temple. Away from that Bracin. Or you could say Amder gave it to me, either way I have the Heart, I have the Anvil, and unknown to you, I have the Hammer of Amder, hidden in the very Church you've been living in all this time. I have what we need. Amder will return, tonight!" Will stood, taking up his hammer and pointing at the Priest with it.

"Your choice. Stay, redeem yourself, or flee, and know the old order, the corruption and greed that the Church of Amder has spread will end with the Gods return. There are no other choices." Will waited for the man to answer. He didn't much care which way the man went, though a Priest would be useful, if only for the required training in healing all their order had.

If he had thought the man pale before, it surprised him to see the man turn as white as the fine linen shirt the man wore. Will stood, the man was too scared to answer either way. Will waited for a moment, then shrugged. "Stay or go. But I will not wait for you to answer." Will put the heart back where it was safe and walked out of the Golden Chisel. One more task and it would be time to begin.

"Well Markin, or William, I guess. Quite the speech." The voice behind him was one he'd never expected to hear again.

He turned around and there, standing here, in the Golden Chisel, against all reason, was Myriam Volfar.

"Myriam!" Will jumped to hug her. He had missed her, she was here, and safe! His joy however was short lived as the slap she gave him brought spots in front of his eyes.

"You LIED to me. Everything was a lie. You and Master Jaste. I get why you did it now, maybe, but you still lied. Everything I thought, everything ..." Myriam's voice caught. "And you lied."

Will knew she had every right to be angry, he *had* lied. He'd hated it, he'd not wanted to do it, but he had. "I know. Sparks aflame Myriam. I kept you at an arms distance for months, trying to find a way to figure this out. I didn't want to lie to you."

"I know that. It makes so much sense now. Why you were so obviously interested but hiding it at the same time. All the little things, how you avoided talking about yourself, your past. It doesn't change the fact it hurt to learn the truth." Myriam grabbed a chair and sat at the table with them.

"And you, Master Regin. You were supposed to be dead. And why suddenly are you two being all friendly?" Myriam pointed a finger at the young Master Smith who sat there with a smile on his face. "You were quite the ass on the trip to the Guild, and yet here you are, all forgiven."

"Let's just say I've been shown the error of my ways." Regin shook his head. "Forgive me Myriam but why are you *here*?"

"I was going to ask the same thing." Will sat back down rubbing his jaw that still stung from her slap. "You are supposed to be safe in the Guild. I was told that."

"You were told she was safe, not in the Guild." Regin added.

"Can I say something here? Or are the two of you going to argue about my safety?" Myriam broke into their conversation. "I am safe. I came here because I wasn't sure where else to go. After the day you fled, and Master Jaste was killed, the Guild pretended like it was something to be forgotten. Rumors flew of course, but the Masters did nothing. I was questioned by one of the Tempered, and after realizing I was in danger there, I left."

Myriam shrugged. "I couldn't go home, and not knowing where else to go, I came here after I found out that your real name was William Reis and you were from the Reach, and not Markin Darto from Dernstown. I've been surprised though that no one has been looking here for you besides me or looking for me."

Will looked at Regin who slowly nodded, Will looked at Myriam, she needed to know the truth. He couldn't lie to her again, even if it was just a lie of omission. "Myriam, the reason no one is looking for us, is that the Priesthood is in tatters. The High Priest is dead, the Tempered mostly killed off. You could have stayed in the Guild and been safe there."

"What do you mean, dead?" Myriam's face fell. "What happened?"

Will explained his capture, being reunited with his cousin only to lose him again, the death of Haltim, the attack of the Blood God followers, finding Regin who had been beaten and tortured, and finally recovering the Heart of Amder. Myriam's face at the end reflected the strangeness of the truth.

"I'm sorry William. I'm so sorry." Myriam sat back in silence.

"Will. Call me Will." Will shook his head. "I have a task, but now, I have to figure out how to keep you safe as well."

"You don't have to keep me safe. I'm helping you, and I don't want to hear another word about keeping me safe. I might not be of the bloodline of the Forgemaster, I might not be chosen by a dead God, and I might only be a first year Apprentice, but I'm coming with you and I'm keeping YOU safe." Myriam looked him in the eyes, her pale blue ones locked onto him. "And when this is over, we are going to sit down and have a very long conversation."

Will nearly laughed, but not at her, but at himself. He'd not been listening to her again and trying to keep her at an arm's length. "I'd be honored to have you help."

Regin nodded. "You have skill, and who knows what we will have to do in the Temple."

"One last task, then we go. Stay here, both of you." William stood and walked outside.

68

Zalkiniv burst from the cave, smiling at the sight of the camp. Exactly where she left them. At her appearance the guards lined up, leaving the picket guards. "Mistress you return!" her personal bodyguard stepped forward and kneeled in front of her. "We have been waiting as you ordered."

"Any trouble?" Zalkiniv didn't think there would be, armed guards and a small mob of Valni bound to the place would not be a target most would attack. Though there was always the possibility of an Underpriest getting ideas of taking the shaft of Valnijz. "Speak!"

"No mistress. Some wild animal attacks, a starving Cattro, but nothing else." Her bodyguard stood, she could tell he was eyeing Duncan behind her, but made no move to question her.

"Good. Bring me the Shaft, and your fastest runner, now." There was little time to waste. She needed the shaft to summon the Valni, and the runner to bring the blade to her. The Blood God would be reborn here as the blood flowed. If the working was done in time, every death her Valni made would feed into the final ritual, the return.

A man appeared, another of the mute guards bearing a wrapped bundle. The shaft! She could feel its power from here, a hunger grew in her. Grabbing it and tearing the covering off brought forth a moan of excitement. With the Claret stones, and the Shaft, her abilities could summon an army of Valni greater than any other since the creation of the creatures. A growl broke her thoughts, a growl from her prize.

Duncan stood, hands clenched, knuckles white and eyes locked on the shaft. She could feel his hate from here. Interesting. She had given little thought to how he might react to the shaft; the Blood must be overwhelming. She was almost envious; his pain and anger were such pure emotions. All the better for the sacrifice. Duncan would provide the anger and hate and rage. And that William Reis would provide the sorrow and terror of the victims.

The runner also appeared, who she sent off to the Temple, with orders to bring the Blade and the twenty Underpriests to here. She marked the runner with her knife in her personal blood, by cutting her lip, so that all who he spoke to would know, this was her words and orders. They would come, they dared not refuse.

At the thought of William Reis, she walked to Duncan, and gave him a smile. "Let's get started my prize. Starting with how we will find that cousin of yours." She drew her knife and cut a thin slice on Duncan's arm, the blood dripping down. She gathered the blood in her hand and smeared it on the Shaft, the power blooming that brought a shuddering breath.

Reaching through the shaft, she began her working. *Blood calls to blood* as she summoned the Valni. Dozens, hundreds, thousands. She pulled the blood, tainted by the mist, pulled by a power far greater than anything they could resist. They came! From caves and ruins, packs of Valni new and old.

But there was one more, one special Valni. She brought the Claret stone into the working, searching, for one Valni. The stone was hot still, almost burning, but passing through the weak spot in the barrier hadn't done it much harm. Still, she didn't want to try taking it through anywhere else.

And there! Still alive, healthy, powerful. Good. She pulled him harder, bringing him to her. The Valni answered, and her guide would be here soon. She needed more blood for this next part, for the matter was that the Valni didn't normally capture. They killed. They destroyed. She would revel in this otherwise, but she needed William Reis alive, here, to give his blood to the return. The Blood God had given her permission to have him killed, but it would be sweeter yet to feel his sorrow and fear.

The working she had in mind would force the Valni to capture the man. No serious injuries, but brought here, alive. Hurting him was fine, the pain would add to the final working. But not dead, or unconscious. Blood was in short supply here. In the Temple she'd order the sacrifice of slaves until she had enough. She just had to wait for the barrier to fall.

There was one blood source here, her guards. They stood still, in a line. Unmoving, not speaking. Loyal. But what was loyalty compared to the return of a God? The Valni gathered, she could feel them, and already within sight several hundred of the beasts. The one she needed the most hadn't been too far, and in under an hour the Valni who would lead crouched before her. Hair half missing, several broken fingers, what clothing left was so covered with blood and dirt the colors couldn't be seen. Who knows who it had been before the God mist raised him up?

It was time. She drew her knife and without a warning sliced the neck of a guard, then another down the line, they fell, never saying a word, giving their blood to her. It would have been better if they had been full of fear, or at least she would have enjoyed it more. But blood was needed, regardless of emotion. Soon twenty men lay in the dirty sandy ground, now stained red and wet with their blood. Only her personal bodyguard remained. "Mistress." He spoke and still kneeling looked up, offering his neck to the blade.

She cut, watching the blood fountain for a second before closing her eyes. This working would be difficult. She would have to touch every Valni. Everyone that answered her call. She must work, they must not harm her sacrifice.

*****

Will entered a square looking different from the one he had left. Night had fallen, and yet the place was full of activity. Groups of men and women raced around, most carrying hammers, pickaxes, some axes. Most Reachers had no training with swords, but they could use the tools they used every day as weapons. But Will had a problem. He would be in the Church, working the Amder forge, he wouldn't be here helping. And he wouldn't know what to do either, he was a Smith. He needed someone, anyone, with background or training in warcraft. The town guard wasn't much more than a group of old miners, and the town council was the same.

As he looked over the square his eyes spied a group of wagons belonging to a small caravan, and from the look of the horses, it just had arrived a few minutes ago, they hadn't been here for the meeting. The animals were being tended to, but the action going on surprised one very confused looking trader. Trader. Caravan. The words hung in the air for a moment before the idea came to him.

Caravans had guards. Guards that knew what they were doing. Guards that... Often... had been part of the army, or at least some military training! There were the two guards from the Church still, and the Priest, but there were reservations in trusting those people. No, he wanted a good, experienced caravan guard captain. Someone who could organize a working defense.

There, in the last wagon he found what he was after. A large man, counting out coins. A line of five other guards stood before him. Payday then. Will didn't have an eye for soldiers. But he had an eye for their equipment. Two of the men didn't appear to take great care of their gear. Small rust spots dotted the chain mail, and the pommel of one sword was loose. So, not them. But the rest were in good care, and the one counting the money... his gear showed what kind of man he was.

Everything showed care. Nothing ornate, nothing decorated and useless. Everything well-worn and used. But of good quality. Will watched as he paid each man, though one man with less than well cared for gear complained about the amount, before grumbling and heading towards the Golden Chisel.

The large man, the captain looked at Will. "Well, you've been standing there for a while, what do you want?" Will noticed the man kept one hand near his sword, and the other on the coin purse. Not scared but practiced.

"I have a proposition." Will reached out his hand in greeting. He'd never done this before, and he wondered what the protocol was, his doubts increasing as the man glanced at his hand but didn't take it.

"Well, you look strong enough, but you're not armed, and if you're from the Reach, you have no training. I don't take unexperienced Guards." The man took his hand off his sword and pointed at where some other Merchants wagons were at. "Check with a smaller merchant. They sometimes want a strong back to help load and unload the wagon."

Being a caravan guard struck him as amusing. He'd never be able to do it. He was born for a hammer, not a sword. "No, I think you've... misunderstood. I need, well, the Reach itself, needs you. Look around, do you feel the air?"

The Captain's eyebrows went up a bit at that response, before looking around the square, maybe for the first time. "It is far busier than I expected." The Captains voice stopped as Will watched his eyes travel from an armed group to an armed group.

"What's going on here lad? I need to gather my men if trouble is brewing."

"Trouble. That's a mild word for it." Will steeled himself. "The Reach is about to be attacked. By the Valni."

The Captain shook his head and laughed, but the laughter stopped as he looked at Will. "You're serious? But there's the barrier!"

Let the sparks fly Will guessed, he hoped it was the right move. "It's coming down. For a while, but the moment it falls, the Valni will attack. They will make for the Church of the Eight, and the city lies between those two places. The Valni will hunt, kill, and maim, anyone and anything in their path. They hunt me. The city has taken up arms to stop them. My people. My city. But these are miners, smiths, laborers. Strong yes, but we have no mind for strategy. We do not know of how to deploy people for the best defense."

Will pointed at the man's sword. "I come to you. You have experience. Your arms are well cared for, but well used. Your sword carries the pommel of the Army of Palnor. And your helm, the design denotes a rank. So, I come to you. Help us. Organize us."

The Captain stood and looked at Will for a long moment crossing his arms before speaking. "Lad. You almost had me there. I don't get what you're after but…"

Will cursed his luck. He wanted to do this without theatrics, but he wasn't a Forgemaster yet. So, theatrics it was. He hoped Amder was listening. Will pulled out his hammer, the Wight Iron glowing in the light and with a lift Will spoke. "The Valni will attack. They are coming for me, because, tonight, I bring Amder back to the world. Tonight, I work the forge to return a God. Out there, on the other side of the barrier, the High Priest of the Blood God works to stop me, they want my blood. Our actions here, tonight, in this place, will govern how the world works for the next thousand years. Help us. Help me." As he spoke his hammer glowed brighter and brighter still.

The Captain who had the beginning of the speech had rolled his eyes, now stood, mouth agape. "What in the name of Palnor?"

"Help us. My Name is William Reis. Tonight, I not only bring a God back to life, I claim the name, the title of Forgemaster. Help us. Help me and have your name live forever. What do you answer? Help us!" Will poured himself into every word. He needed this man. Time was wasting.

And without a word, the Captain nodded. "By my blade. I will." Will wasn't sure who was more surprised, the Guard Captain, or himself at the words.

"Good. What should we call you then? I'll introduce you to the Town council and leave the defense of this place to you." Will lowered his hammer, and put it away, aware than his little show had drawn the attention of two dozen onlookers.

"My name is Vin. Vin Tolin. But I guess call me Captain Tolin." Captain Tolin motioned for Will to lead the way. "You're serious? The Valni will attack? Crazy man-beast things that show no mercy, and will feast on blood, flesh, all that?"

"Yes. Have you ever seen one of the Valni Captain? Ever fought one?" Will lead the man toward the Chisel which had become the place for meetings tonight. The watching crowd parted as Will led Captain Tolin to speak to the town council. This was their job, not his, something he was happy about.

"Well, I've run into a few, here and there. Sad things they are if you think about it. Poor souls. One whiff of those mists and you become a killer." The Captain shuddered. "How many do you think will attack?"

Will knew the man would ask that question and hated to give the answer. "All. As many as they can summon. It will be a horde." He looked back at Captain Tolin. He could see the man was shaking his head in thought. "I know. There's not enough people in the Reach to stop that. But we don't have to stop them forever. There's two goals. One, stop them from killing everyone in the Reach. Two stop them from getting to the Church of the Eight. Once I've completed my task, Amder will return. At his return the barrier will spring back and, every single Valni on this side of the barrier will be dealt with by Amder."

"How long?" Captain Tolin stopped walking. "William, right? How long will you need? How long do we have to keep the defense up?"

"I don't know. I've never brought a God back to life before." Will tried to crack a smile but didn't feel it inside. "They won't attack until I start the process. The barrier will only fall then, that's got to count for something, right?"

Captain Tolin nodded for a second before grimacing. "Yes, but the longer we wait to shore up a real defense, the more of those creatures they can get ready to storm the Reach, right? We have a question. How long for a decent defense setup, up against waiting too long and the other side gathering a horde so big that no amount of defense will work."

Will hadn't considered that. Taking too long, makes the other side stronger. But if they move too fast, they wouldn't be able to mount a decent defense. At least the Captain had the forethought to consider it. "Come on." Will walked on, and soon they entered the Chisel, with Regin who had waited by the door following them in. Will spotted the council, the six of them sitting around an oval table in the back with a small army of people trying to get their attention.

"Hold!" Will yelled at the crowd as he got closer, and to his surprise, they listened. He didn't think he'd ever get used to this, the way Reachers treated him now. "We need someone who can lead the defense. It can't be me. We need someone who knows at least where the best places to set up a defense would be. So, I present Captain Vin Tolin. Formerly of the Palnor army, and now Caravan Guard. He's offered to help."

"Well, you didn't give me any way to refuse," Captain Tolin said, speaking up. A small laugh went off, defusing tension in the air. "Right. If I will help, I need a map of the city. Now. I need to know what these little groups of people are doing. I'm seeing them run around. If those groups have leaders, I need to speak to them, now." Captain Tolin looked around and pointed at a young man, no older than fourteen. "You, you're my runner. Go get me that map, and every leader you know."

Will smiled. Men like Captain Tolin were used to obedience, and they got it. One of the older merchants on the Council looked red at the usurpation of his power, but he could read the room. Captain Tolin would be obeyed.

"Captain, I leave the defense of the Reach to you." Will reached out a hand in respect. "I assume you will send a runner telling me when I can start? When you're ready?"

"I'm not sure how I ended up here, but I'll do my best. And yes, of course. Expect it to be sooner rather than later. In my mind we can't afford to wait too long." Captain Tolin took his hand and gave it a shake.

Will nodded to Regin and Myriam, who hadn't said a word. Regin was smiling, but Myriam, she eyed him as if she was trying to figure out if he'd cheated at cards. "What?" Will asked them as they exited the Chisel.

"Nothing. You are taking on the Forgemaster mantle far faster than I expected. Well done. But now, where to?" Regin asked as they stood on the porch of the Chisel.

"I'm not sure who you are." Myriam shrugged. "From the last time I saw you till today, something has changed, you're far surer of yourself, but, somehow, dangerous."

"Dangerous?" Will turned to Myriam. "What do you mean?"

"William, you just had that crowd willing to fight to the death against horrible monsters, because you asked them to. That's dangerous." Myriam poked his chest with a finger. "I'm not sure who this person is."

"Myriam…" Will trailed off. She was right, there wasn't time. He wanted to go home. Show her the Reach, show her who he really was, where he was from. But he couldn't. There was only one location to go to. The Church of the Eight. It was time to go. "Let's go get ready. As ready as I can be. To the Church of the Eight." Will, Regin, and Myriam this time returned to the cart, and started down the cobblestone streets, heading due east. It surprised Will at the lack of fear he felt. He raised his hand, and there was no tremble. Maybe because it was a smithing job. An important one, but a smithing job. He could do this, right?

69

The Church of the Eight stood, dark and empty. A few Reachers were sitting out front of the place, all carrying smithing hammers of various sizes. "Halt! Who's that?" One miner stood, smacking his hammer in his hand, the heavy hammer moving without effort.

"Mr. Darrew. If you don't recognize me, you're getting old after all!" Will yelled back, happy to see someone he knew. Falkirk Darrew had been a friend of his Da's and Duncan's Da. He'd lived a few doors down, and after their fathers had both vanished, he'd looked out for them from time to time.

"William Reis! Good to see you lad. Quite a speech you gave back in the Square." An older man, hale but grey looked at the others still loitering around. "Stand up! Show respect to the Forgemaster." The others stood, one grumbling, but still, he stood.

"Not one yet Mr. Darrew. Not one yet. Why are you here?" the cart pulled to a stop, and Will climbed out.

"Well, when we chased that damned fool of a Priest out and his men, we figured a few of us needed to stick around in case the others came back, the ones that had run off into the night. Haven't seen em though. Doubt we will if the Valni are attacking." Mr. Darrew hooked a thumb toward the Church. "It's empty though. I and this lot will stay here, in case."

"Be careful Mr. Darrew. A lone Valni isn't anything to scoff at, and the chances are there will be far more than one." Will liked the man, he didn't want him to die for him.

"William Reis. If you're right, and I see no reason you're not, then stopping the Valni will mean the return of Amder, and the end of the Mistlands. It's worth the risk." Falkirk poked Will in the chest with a thick callused finger. "And stop calling me Mr. Darrew. My name's Falkirk. You're not a child anymore, Will."

"Sorry Falkirk. Habits." Will reached out a hand, which was taken, and a shake exchanged. "I can't think of anyone else I'd rather have guarding my back here. Thanks." Will meant it. Falkirk Darrew was getting up there in years, but still strong and smart. He wasn't a warrior, but Will had once seen him break up a street fight between two drunk men. He'd smacked their heads together hard enough they both went down like rag dolls, ending the fight as it had started.

"Go on. Take a torch and do what you need to do." Falkirk pointed to a lit torch by the main door to the Church.

"And this is where I stay." Master Regin got off the cart and hefted a hammer he'd had in the cart.

"What? Regin, we can use you! You're a full Master." Will was surprised.

"You only need one person to help you return Amder to this world. Myriam is a better choice. I need to do this William. You've forgiven me I know, but I haven't forgiven myself. Jaste is dead because of my actions. Myriam here was in danger because of my actions." Regin swung his hammer a few times, testing its balance.

"And should the worst happen, I have a feeling Myriam Volfar would be damned if anyone was going to attack you, other than herself." Regin winked at the two of them. "Go. Do your job."

"Master Regin, are you sure?" Myriam asked. "I'm just an Apprentice, not even that anymore."

"Yes, I'm sure. If my rank means anything, I'm ordering you to go with William here." Regin waved them to the open Temple. "Go."

Will nodded and led Myriam into the Church of the Eight. The torchlight illuminated the main hall, the glinting metal work appearing like sparks overhead. "Nice church. Don't see many Churches of the Eight like this," Myriam said as he examined the walls. "Fantastic metalwork. Old, but great work."

"That's because this place didn't use to be given over to the Eight. It was dedicated to Amder before the Godsfall. Remember, his Forge is here. My ancestor worked that Forge. This was the center of Amder worship for untold ages. But after the Godsfall, the Priesthood moved things to Ture, closer to the center of power." Will pointed to the reliefs and metal. "But this place stayed around. They rededicated it to the Eight, including the Blood God, which I always found insulting."

"Can't imagine why." Myriam remarked before turning her attention to Will. "So, what's the plan?"

"Well, according to Amder, every door and window in the place needs to be open. Just what I want when the rampaging horde of Valni attack, but it's necessary for the return of Amders blood." Will shrugged. "So, let's open them."

Shortly they had opened every outside door and window they could. Half the windows wouldn't open or couldn't open. Will worried about that, should be break them? A whack of his hammer would do it, though breaking the windows in this place, any church, didn't make him feel good. He decided to risk it and leave it the way it was.

"Doors and windows open. So?" Myriam looked around. "What's next?"

"Well, according to what I was told, the Forge and the Hammer are here, we just have to find them. They are in the chambers under the Church." Will smiled at a memory of being eight or nine, his mother had died, and his father was losing himself to Cloud. But Will had come here, and bored, had tried to sneak down the stairs. Haltim had caught him and hauled him home, only to find Will's Da lost to the world. Haltim had told him to never go down the stairs but had left his punishment at that.

"Myriam, might want to go tell Mr. Darrew we will be under the church. Don't want the runner wasting time looking for us." Will waited while she did so. He watched as she walked back outside, her reddish-brown hair fading into the night. He still couldn't quite believe she was here, now. He'd somewhat resigned himself to the idea that he'd never see her again.

"Why are you smiling like that?" Myriam asked as she reappeared.

"Later. When we talk after all this is over." Will hoped there would be a later, but there wasn't time for it now. "Let's go down the stairs and see what we can find."

The stairs led down in a spiral pattern, the polished stone of the upper church giving way to a rougher older cut. Small signs that this was once dedicated to Amder appeared, an ancient bucket bracket, for putting our forge fires, and even a soot stain.

The stairs ended in a hallway that for all of Alos reminded Will of the Guild. It had the same feeling. "Sparks. This place looks like the Guildhall," Myriam exclaimed examining the walls.

"I was thinking the same thing. But I guess it makes sense, both are the works of Amder, before the Godsfall." Will shrugged. "I guess open doors and see what we find." Myriam nodded as they tried each door they came to. Two were rooms were bunkrooms, occupied it appeared by the Guards that had fled by the gear left behind.

Several storerooms were next, full of food and drink. The fourth door they tried was locked. A door painted red, with a heavy iron padlock. Will drew out his hammer, and without a word struck the lock, hard.

The howl of the Wight Iron echoed down the Hall, making Myriam jump. "Sparks Will. Warn me next time." Will laughed as his blow had cracked the iron as easy as an egg. The door pushed open to show what must be the forge!

It was a huge space. The light from the hallway only illuminating a small fraction of the room, the Forge itself taking up what appeared to be an entire wall. Huge, old, and stone cold. "Well, we found the Forge." Will walked into the room, holding his torch high to get a better look. The forge was plain, but anyone with skill could tell, it was put together without flaws. Each stone, and layout were all done to assist the Smith in creation, not holding him back.

"How do you light such a thing?" Myriam asked as he followed Will into the room. "I've never seen a forge like this."

"Good question. But let's find the Hammer first. We need to hurry; I can't imagine that Captain wanting to wait much longer." Will led the way, the hallway stretching out in front of him, giving him that same uneasy feeling the Guild did. A shiver ran down his spine at the thought, knowing this was a God at work.

The next three doors led to empty rooms, dusty and only some old cobwebs to see. The fourth door led to a storeroom. And sitting in the corner, a large pile of cloth, old robes! "This better be the place Haltim stashed the Hammer!" Will motioned Myriam into the room with him and pulled old robes out of the way. Most of them ripped as he searched, the cloth weak from age.

"Watch your hands, don't want to get bit by a spider." Will yelled as they searched.

Myriam shook her head, poking at the pile with a pair of old rusty tongs she'd grabbed from a shelf nearby. "Hate spiders," Myriam exclaimed before giving a yell.

"What? Get bit?" Will came over to Myriam to find her not bit, but instead digging out a large leather wrapped bundle. "That must be it!" Will handing the torch over to her, taking the package and unwrapping it. His breath caught as he once more beheld the Hammer of a God.

Will could hear Myriam's intake of breath at the sight. This was THE Hammer. A God had made this, used this to craft, and used it to make parts of this church. Will could feel it pull as the Heart quivered as he held the Hammer. The moment stretched out for William. He was a man from the Reach, and yet, here he was, holding the Hammer of a God, carrying the Heart of that same God. How had this come to pass?

"Why leave that here? It's the Hammer of Amder! Almost sacrilegious." Myriam poked at the pile again.

"I don't think Haltim meant to leave it here. He hid it, and after he was evicted, hoped no one would go to the old storerooms and clean them. It payed off, and the Hammer wasn't found. I'm sure he expected to be back here someday." Will could remember the old Priest, trying to interest Will in something other than the Guild. He wondered if Haltim would be proud of him after today. Would his Da? Or even his Mother?

"Will!" Myriam's voice cut into his memories.

"Let's get back to the Forge. I need to find out what to do." Will hoisted the Hammer over his shoulder, its weight noticeable even for him. It was far larger than he used, and he wondered if he could use this thing for an extended period. Amder had been still unclear about the process this was to take. How long would Will need to hammer for? Did he need to quench and harden? Did he use a special oil secreted around the place?

The Forge stood before them and as Myriam used the torch to light wall sconces, came into further relief. It covered one full wall, and was filled with strange blueish black rocks, and if it was coal, it was nothing he'd ever seen before. An Anvil black with carbon stood nearby. Will's eye could tell it hadn't used in more time than he could count. A set of bellows, old as well stood by the forge, an ancient style set of bellows, using a simple chain pull system at that.

"Myriam, keep an eye on the door. I will have a talk with Amder." Will pulled out the Heart as he spoke. The light from it was bright, far brighter than normal. He had the Heart, the Forge, and the Hammer. All were here. The weight of it all hit him. *He was about to return a God to life!* Not that Amder was dead in the mortal sense, but... He, William Reis, was about to do something that no one had even known could be done, outside of the highest orders of the Priesthood.

Myriam who had been examining the tools turned to William. "Do you... do you do that often? Talk to a dead God?"

"No, not often." Will tried to give her a smile. He knew she was here for her own reasons, and those reasons were not all about him. She knew what the stakes were.

"Trust me, if you had told me a year ago that I'd be here, under the Church, about to bring Amder back to life to save Duncan from being sacrificed to the Blood God, I would have thought you'd drank too much or worse." Will shrugged. "But yet, here I am, holding the Heart of Amder, the Hammer and the Forge."

Jaw clenched, he breathed out. He hadn't done it yet, and nerves were never good when you were about to take on a new project. Still, seeing the Hammer, Heart and Forge together, he had to smile, the excitement was more than he could take, until he remembered the Reach.

All those people, willing to die for him. Ready to die to bring Amder back. Ready to face a force that had no remorse, no pity, only raw rage and anger. The Valni would swarm over the Reach, and their killing would be total.

"William." Myriam walked over to him her face unreadable. "I don't know what you are. I don't know who you are. I don't know why I'm even here. You came into my life, led me on a merry chase, with me chasing after you of all things. And then, when finally, things were good, I find out it all was a lie. All of it."

"I know, I am sorry." Will wanted to add that he had wanted to tell her, but was that the truth? He'd thought about it, but he'd been scared. Just scared.

"I know you are; I just haven't decided yet if I accept it. But now you have something larger to do, something greater. You're a different man than I met before. And I believe in this man." Myriam shook her head. "Go, let's do what we have to do."

Raising the Heart, Will closed his eyes, reaching, straining to the faint sound of hammers. There! And as before, he found himself in a smithy, THIS smithy. But this time, he was alone. No indistinct shadow of a God, no sign of the last Forgemaster, nothing.

"Hello?" Will turned in a circle, seeing no one. He wondered for a second if he was in the real smithy, but that idea fled when he realized that wherever he was, there was no door. In fact, the room had no exits or entrances. No way for smoke to leave the smithy either, which didn't reflect the real location.

"Hello? Amder? Forgemaster?" Will's voice fell flat in the space, and to his growing worry, the room grew darker. What was wrong?

"William, this is hard. So many Valni at the barrier, so many to keep out. My strength is thinning, you can only hammer metal so much before it breaks."

Amder's voice was more a whisper than anything else, but the message it carried worried Will. "How do I start this? I need to know!"

"Heart into the forge. Heat the bracer, start to forge the bracer into a helm, or a gauntlet... Doesn't matter. The process will start. Be careful, Heart going into the forge will drop the barrier. At that moment, until I live again, there will be nothing I can do to protect anyone."

The darkness grew more, to the point Will had a hard time seeing the Forge right in front of him. Amder's voice was gone, leaving behind a cold pit. He had no idea how long this would take, but it didn't matter. William had to start soon, or whatever was left of Amder wouldn't last.

He shook himself and pushed the vision away. Blinking as his eyes adjusted, he was in the Forge, Regin watching him his expression unreadable, the forge ready and waiting, the anvil and hammer set up for the working. And the bracer, the bracer on his wrist. He'd tugged at it before and would not move. This time a slight pull and it split open, weighing nothing in his hand. Its colors, shining in the light.

"We can't wait Myriam. Amder is failing. The Valni are growing at the barrier to where it's taking all the strength Amder has." Will shrugged. "We can't wait for the Captain to be ready."

"You know what that means, right Will? Many people might die because of that decision." Myriam grabbed the bellows chain. "I'm with you, either way."

"I know. But if Amder fails, and the barrier falls that way, there might not be enough of Amder to bring back. And all this, all the sacrifice, all the pain and toil, all it would be worthless." Will held up the heart, its normal bright glow faded more than he thought possible. "I hope the Captain is ready. I hope the Reach is ready." Will held the Heart over the Forge. "I hope they forgive me if I fail." His hand opened, and the Heart fell.

70

Zalkiniv felt the pressure vanish as if a bubble had popped. She stumbled forward; her concentration broken at the sudden release. All around her the Valni erupted into howls and screams. The barrier was gone! Which meant they had started the rebirth of their soot stained God.

Hordes of Valni surrounded her. More than even she in all her lives had ever seen on one place together. Her working had touched them all as shown by the lack of blood now on the ground. She had needed every speck. Capture, hurt, but do not kill William Reis. Follow the one who had tasted his blood. Kill any others you see or find. Simple instructions.

Gripping the shaft of Valnijz in one hand, and the Claret stone on her neck in the other, she released her army. No words needed to be spoken, nor would the Valni be able to listen. She had worked the blood to her commands, now she needed to wait. She wished she could watch the Valni horde descend on the Reach, the first to fall to the Blood God. There would be many others yet to watch, she had to stay here, with her prize.

Duncan stood in the same place he had been all the time she'd been working the blood. Face locked into a sneer of rage and hate. The cut on his arm had stopped bleeding long ago, and for all the dust on him, he appeared almost a statue, cruel and dangerous, a monument to some dark power.

Her Underpriests with the Blade should be here soon, and when they did, they would prepare Duncan for sacrifice. The hate and anger he was feeling now would be amplified, too levels no person could take for long. And then, when the other one, the other Reis was brought before her, she would let him see Duncan, so he would know, that he had left his only family in this state. Crush his spirit, and in the final moments of his despair, let Duncan watch her kill his cousin. The memory of the pain Haltim's death had caused in her puppet would be nothing compared to what he would feel when right before Williams death, she released her control. His soul would die as he realized what he had done, what she had done. And that pain, that hurt, that anger would fill his blood with power, enough to fulfill her life's work. The Scaled One would return tonight, and there was nothing anyone could do to stop it.

***

Captain Tolin watched yet another group of Reachers leave the Chisel, orders in hand. It had been a whirlwind of activity since he, somehow, ended up in charge of the defense of this place. He still wasn't sure how that had happened. He was paying his men, and figuring out which ones to fire, when that William Reis person had showed up.

And now, he was to try to defend this place from a rampaging army of Valni. He'd fought off Valni before, and even two or three could tear through a caravan. But to defend a place like the Reach? A city with no walls, no real gates, and a small maze of streets and ways in and out. He'd done his best so far though. The map they had given him did a good job of showing the ways in. True to what they say about Reachers, if he told a group to make a barricade on a street, they did it, right away, and well.

And good barricades. Reachers did good work, and even on these emergency structures, they were well made, strong. The people themselves, he wasn't sure about. They were all loyal, surprisingly so. He'd thanked the first group he'd talk to for defending the city, and they had looked at him as if he had grown an extra head. "We defend our own." Was all the head of that group had said, with nods from the rest. An interesting people.

But even so, he doubted it would be enough. With what was setup, or going to be, they would funnel the Valni toward the town center, the largest open area to fight in. He'd setup every man, woman or older child with a bow or crossbow on the roofs with as many arrows and bolts as could be found with orders to open fire at the points where the Valni would enter the square. Strict orders to not fire into the middle. These weren't trained soldiers, and every fighter counted. He needed no one taking fire from the roof who was fighting melee.

He took a long drink of his weak beer and turned to his men. The ones he had come into the Reach with. They had all agreed to stay and fight. Even the two he'd been about to fire. "I've done all I can here. Come, let's get to the square, and hope it's been enough." Vin led them out, standing on the porch, watching the activity. Most had scrapped together some protection and weapons. Lots of heavy leather aprons and bracers, some metal work. The Reach didn't make a lot of arms or amour.

"We want to help." A voice broke into his thoughts. Two armed men, wearing the garb of the Church of Amder were tied up nearby. "Please."

Captain Vin Tolin knew the story with these men, guards who had been captured when the Reachers took the church. Vin didn't care about the reasons, but these were two armed guards, with training. That was valuable here. "Do you now? Why?" Tolin knelt by the men, his hand on his boot knife.

"We heard them talking. If the barrier really falls, and the Valni attack..." the man speaking shuddered. "We can fight. Better than being tied up and torn apart by those things." The other man spoke up. "We are anointed guards of the Church of Amder. It is your duty to release us from these bonds."

"I don't care if you are Blademasters who have mastered the eight lost styles. What I do care about is that you swing a sword and help me defend this place. I don't give two glasses of piss about the Church of Amder. I care about what will happen here. So, if I release you, you agree for the length of the battle, to obey my orders, not run and flee, and to attack and kill only Valni?" Vin pulled his knife and placed it on the bounds that held the men. "Well?"

"I agree," the first guard said, the other, self-righteous one shrugged and then nodded. "Good enough." Captain Tolin sliced their bonds watching them stand and rub wrists and legs. The ropes had bound them for a while, and they needed to get the blood flowing again.

"Either of you fought Valni before?" Vin pointed at them both. "Or any real fighting?"

Both shook their heads. "Trained, but no, never fought," the less obnoxious one answered.

"Better than nothing." Captain Tolin led the men, now with the guards to the middle of the square. "When I give the word, a runner will travel to the Church, we will have twenty minutes, and then the barrier will fall, from my understanding. Then another ten or fifteen before the Valni get here. Let's talk about the Valni.

"They were once men, but don't ever for a second think they are men now. More animal than man, they run in a loping motion, like a wolf. Dirty, wearing rags. But fast, quick. Strong to, stronger than any of us by far. Once saw a Valni break a sword in half with its bare hands. The edges cut the thing, it didn't even flinch. They won't be organized; it will be a mass charge. Raw rage and anger. Always strike to kill. Wounding a Valni is a fool's choice. One, they don't care if it hurts. Two, they love blood, so strike to kill." Captain Tolin pulled his sword and ordered his men to check gear. Wouldn't be super useful, but he'd been in enough battles to know if you kept them busy, they'd worry less about what was to come.

Captain Tolin was a third of the way done with honing the edge of his blade when a younger man came running to the square at full tilt. "VALNI COMING!" he yelled as he ran toward Captain Tolin.

"What in the blood laced piss are you talking about? I didn't give word!" Tolin didn't get to finish. He heard it then, the howls, and sound of the Valni, loud, and getting louder. If he heard it here though... hundreds, or even more. Vin Tolin wondered what had gone wrong, but there was no time. "READY!" Vin yelled, projecting his voice as far as he could. "THEY COME!"

Whetstone placed back in his belt pouch; he gripped his sword. He hoped it had been enough, he didn't want to die tonight.

71

The Heart fell into the Forge of Amder as Will watched. As it landed, the Heart of Amder, the artifact on which the Priesthood had built its power, shattered. The cracking sound of the crystal was loud and surprised Will to where he dropped the Hammer and Bracer in his hand. Thousands of glittering crystal fragments spread out from the impact each one glowing pink and white, but far dimmer than he'd ever seen the Heart glow.

Will's breath caught in his throat, had he done something wrong? As each crystal fragment landed, its glow went out, a tiny flicker of light, and it was gone. In less than a moment's breath, the Heart was gone. And the Forge lay cold, silent. Will glanced over at Myriam to see her standing, eyes wide.

What had gone wrong? Should he have placed the Heart in the Forge and not dropped it? The crush of doubt fell on him, panic gripped his own heart at the idea that his foolish move had doomed not just the Reach but everyone.

Light.

The Forge erupted in light. Brighter than any other he'd ever seen, Will threw up an arm to block it from blinding him. As his eyes adjusted, he saw Myriam had done the same, but was blinking still at the sudden change. The whole forge was glowing, and heat rose from it. Letting out his held breath, Will pushed out his doubts and fears, this he knew. It was time to remake the world.

The bracer in his free hand he grabbed a pair of tongs from the rack of tools here and placed it in the now glowing forge. He watched the bracer as it heated, first a shimmer, then the edges a light orange, and then the thicker part going red orange. Will pointed his hammer at Myriam who started the bellows, pulling the chain as they moved air into the forge, increasing the heat. Will observed it with the eye of a Smith. The bracer was a mixture of metals, first made by men as a covering for the hammer, and then remade by Amder himself, he had to be right in his estimation of when he could work this.

Finally, he grabbed it again, glowing yellow white from the forge and placed it on the anvil. Myriam dropped the chain and took the tongs from Will without speaking. Both knew their jobs.

Will locked onto the bracer, and taking the Hammer of Amder in both hands, raised the hammer, and struck.

The peal of the Hammer striking the bracer reverberated in his bones. The sound was pure, a tone that didn't taper off, but instead grew in richness and complexity with each hammer blow. Will had no idea how long it would take for the Blood of Amder to get here from the Mistlands, but with each blow, he called to Amder's blood, and the rebirth of a God.

***

Zalkiniv watched the last of the Valni vanish into the night, heading toward her target as sure as an arrow fired by an archer. Thousands had answered her call, each one a man or woman, tormented and changed by the blood of her God. The Mistlands had claimed so many for her Lord.

From the direction of the Mistlands it came. A white glow, dim and glowing brighter. Soon the night was lit up as if someone had plucked a city and placed it here in the wastelands, the night washed with light. A white light. The fool was doing better than she had thought. Why hadn't her Valni got to him yet?

The sound of approaching feet made her whirl around, only to discover twenty Underpriests, and forty slaves. Some were pulling the carts the Priests rode in, and others were carrying a blood-stained chest. The Blade!

Pushing slaves to the side, Zalkiniv opened the chest. There, the Blood blade lay, unpitied or rusted, undamaged by the blood both ancient and far newer that covered most of its surface. She knew that one more of these Underpriests had tried to use the blade. They may have even succeeded. Once her Lord had returned, she'd have to deal with anyone who had managed it.

Lifting the blade, she nearly passed out from the pleasure and pain of holding both the blade and the shaft. In this moment she could bring the Blood God back. Sacrifice Duncan, bring the Scaled One to life once more. It tempted her but dared not.

The God of Rage and Destruction wanted both of the Reis bloodline. He didn't have to have it, but it was his wish, to wipe out any hope of ever returning Amder to this world. And Zalkiniv would see it done. Even if they couldn't sacrifice Duncan yet, it didn't mean they couldn't prepare.

"Make ready! We bring our God back to life today!" Zalkiniv ordered the Underpriests to set up the sacrificial ritual. Every Priest of the Blood God knew it by heart, it was the first one drilled into any Priest. As she watched them prepare with a smile on her face, the occasional glance at the glowing sky brought a tinge of worry and wonder at what was taking so long.

***

Captain Tolin thrust his sword deep into the neck of a Valni who had got past the first layers of the killing ground. The thing howled and screamed as it died, its arms and hands, dirty and covered with half healed sores and wounds tried to grab his body and cloak before falling limp.

Howls and screams continued as the Reachers did far better than he expected. The barricades had done their job, and then there was the Valni themselves. While they attacked anyone in their way, they ran past others who had fallen to the side or moved. Heading straight for the Church of the Eight where, if all was to be believed, William Reis was bringing Amder back to this world.

The archers and crossbowmen on the roofs had done miracles though, piles of Valni lay at the three entrances to the Square, most so covered in arrows and bolts as to resemble nothing more than some strange Wasteland cactus. Captain Tolin watched as one of the Valni even stood, swaying with 4 arrows stuck in parts of its body, and still move forward! Blood damned things.

A Reacher dispatched quickly the creature, a two-handed maul made quick work. He wasn't sure how many had already died, both Reacher and Valni. Still, he was pleased, they had survived so far.

"More coming, MANY MORE!" one of the lookouts from a roof yelled out and Vin Tolin grimaced.

"Damn things, how many are there?" Captain Tolin wiped his sword clean on a scrap of cloth tied to his arm for that purpose. They had survived the first wave, but the second? The third? How many arrows and bolts did the Archers above even have left?

All time for talk and worry ended when a new wave of Valni, far larger than the first broke over the corpses and poured into the square. "Stay together!" Tolin yelled to any within earshot as he thrust his blade out and into the side of what had once been a person. A scream forced him to reorient himself as two of his men were overwhelmed. Both were killed, their bodies ripped apart as the Valni attacked. *How much longer?*

***

Will concentrated on the task at hand, rhythmic strokes with the Hammer of Amder, watching each blow and the metal react. He had changed it from a bracer once yellow white hot, to a more solid rectangle. Holding up his blows, he nodded to Myriam. Flux, then back into the forge.

Myriam placed the formed billet into the fire as the lack of sound from the hammer blows returned the silence of the room. Normal forges made a noise. A crackle or soft noise of the coals, even the sound of the bellows. But not here. The bellows were silent, and whatever the fuel in this forge was, it didn't make a sound as it 'burned' and heated the billet back up.

"How do you think they are doing?" Myriam worked the bellows as she spoke. "I wish there was more we could do for them. I've only been here a week, but I like the place, a lot."

Will knew what she meant. There hadn't been enough time, time to get a good defense organized, time to make weapons, or armor, time to get the weak, old or young out of town. No time to do any of it. "Well, I hope." was all he could say. Fears of what was happening in the Reach tried to creep into his thoughts. All he had was metal and heat, hammer and anvil.

With a nod, Myriam placed the billet back on the anvil, and Will struck. Sparks flew and the sound, the pure sound came again. But, Will cocked an ear, something, something was different. Will struck again, and then, with a sound like wind rushing through the trees, the first crystal appeared.

A smaller one, it flew like an arrow straight *into* the billet, and to Will's unbelieving eyes, melted into the metal without a sound. "What by the sparks ..." Will said before another came, and another. Will watched as each vanished with contact, and the billet grew!

"Will?" Myriam reminded him of his duty, as he lifted the Hammer and struck, again. The metal wasn't cooling, if anything it glowed brighter, and to his surprise, formed an arm. Each blow moved to its own spot, each lift of the hammer and Will could feel it. The passion for creation, the act of making something new. The joy of it engulfed him.

72.

Zalkiniv was satisfied with the work the Underpriests had done. An altar to the God of Blood and Rage now stood here and even sanctified by the blood of over half the slaves they had brought. It smelled right, the tang of iron filled the air, and echoes of sorrow.

The glow remained, and even more bothersome, it had moved. Toward the Reach! She must have both prizes, but if the Valni somehow failed, would she have time to sacrifice her prize? Would the Scaled one forgive that? Could it even work?

"My prize, my Blood blessed hunter." She walked to Duncan still standing as still as the rocks that dusted him. A few of the Underpriests had watched him for a while but had not approached him. Cowards they were. "Soon my prize, soon your cousin will be here before me, before you, and together, your blood will bring back our Lord. And he will raise me up, and I will live forever, leading all in the worship of the Blood God."

She could see it now, they would conquer first Palnor, as each town fell, and even Ture. Blood would run in every street, every farm and stable. They would leave a few to feed the faithful, but the rest would die, or become Valni, but ones controlled by the Scaled One. Valnijz reaching out his arm, spear in hand, directed the Horde in its wanton destruction. And standing next to him, Zalkiniv. In this body, or her prizes. It was a simple matter to take it over after the Scaled one was done with it, and the thought of ruling from the body of a Reis? *Delicious.*

Her dreams ended as pain and blood fountained from her chest. A dagger, black iron, a sacrificial dagger, plunged into her back, between the vertebrae of her back. They had betrayed her!

"You have failed High Priest. We will not serve you for another thousand," the voice of one of the Underpriests whispered to her as she fell, her spinal cord severed, her hands released the shaft and blade. This was not how it was supposed to be! This was her time of victory!

Her eyes fell on her prize, Duncan Reis. She tried to speak, but no sound escaped her lips, only blood. Darkness creeped on the edges of her vision, and she fell forward, her blood covering her prize, and her body falling into the rocky dust at Duncan's feet.

Will struck again, lost to the rhythm of the hammer on the metal. His arms, as strong as he was were burning with the weight of the Hammer of Amder, but still, he struck. *For the Reach, For Amder, For Duncan!* Myriam kept the metal moving, turning it, and flipping it as each blow brought more of Amder's blood into the room. Streams of the glowing crystals entered the room, the larger ones breaking apart mid-flight into pieces no larger than a fist.

William struck; each blow placed where it was needed. He took each breath in time with each blow. An ache crept at the edges flowing from the shoulder he had injured escaping the prison of the High Priest of Amder.

William paused. Sweat covered his face and body. His breath came in gulps, eating the air. He was done. What lay on the anvil was now a somehow a form of a body? Details were missing, but they had done it.

"The forge. Place it on the forge." The barest whisper came to William. Was it the Forgemaster? Amder?

"Place it on the top of the forge, in the middle." Will grabbed another set of tongs helping Myriam take the form and place it on the forge. The metal had grown to the size of a wolf in the hammering. The figure shimmered as the forge fires surrounded it and somehow got sucked into the form.

Will paused, hefting the Hammer of Amder in his hand. There was one last step, every blacksmith needs a hammer. Will threw the Hammer into the forge, it landed half onto the form, and the other half in the fire. And yet, it still wasn't complete. *My hammer.* Will pulled his hammer out. It held a spark of the Blood of Amder. He rubbed the decoration with his thumb. Duncan had given him the metal for this, it was perfect. But it was time, Amder was more important. Will tossed his hammer into the forge, watching it melt away into the form.

"No!" Myriam yelled and tried to grab the hammer. Will grabbed his arm before she got close.

"It's his, not mine." Will watched as both the Form and Hammer glowed in the forge, orange, then red, then yellow. He knew this was the right way, it had to be!

Yellow to white, the heat grew. Will and Myriam were forced back from the forge, too hot, too much! The surrounding air rushed in, the heat and forge sucking in air to grow its heat. Will couldn't even see the forge now, the light was too bright, too hot.

The sound came, a soft hammering, growing larger. Its peals reverberating in his chest, and from there, the surrounding walls. "Can you feel that?" Will pulled Myriam out of the room, their backs to the wall in the hallway watching the room through their fingers, trying not to go blind.

Myriam nodded; her features unable to be seen in the bright light. The sound grew larger still, a hammering that echoed down the hall forcing them to move farther away from the forge. Will could feel it everywhere, each hammering blow sent reverberations up his legs shaking the world.

"Is that a heartbeat?" Myriam yelled next to him, trying to talk over the noise.

She was right, what had once been a hammer blow, was now more organic, a double thump, the beating of a living heart.

The heat continued to grow, to where they moved all the way back to the stairs. The heat blackened the spot they had stood moments before and with a crack several of the stones spilt, unable to deal with the sudden assault.

"Amder returns!" Will couldn't contain his smile. He had done it. All would be better. Duncan would be safe.

***

Captain Tolin knew it was lost. There were too many Valni. How many of the cursed things were there?! His little band of seven, the only real fighters in Ture was down to two. One guard from the Church of the Eight, and one of his guards from the caravan. All the others had died to the Valni.

The archers on the rooftops had long ago run out of ammunition, and had taken to throwing rocks, or whatever else heavy they could find. Most did little damage to the attackers, and those that hit, it didn't stop them. A Valni wouldn't scream for healing, it would keep moving, keep attacking, keep killing.

Vin could see only small pockets of the defenders, the ones that had been closest to walls, which had let them not be surrounded. Any that had gone out into the square proper were gone, torn apart. Bodies, hundreds, were everywhere. They had to retreat, but where could they run to?

The sound of a hammer striking metal echoed through the air, but loud, so loud it overwhelmed the sound of battle. Its echoes down the stone walls and streets of the Reach made the ground tremble.

Silence, shocking in its totality fell. Even the Valni stopped moving, as every face, human or Valni stopped in sudden surprise.

The sound came again, even louder, and the ground shook in its echoes. Another came, and then another, the earth trembled then heaved in constant motion. Light sprung in the air, a pure light, overwhelming whatever torchlight that still burned. And Captain Vin Tolin, a veteran of the Armies of Palnor, wept. Not from the sound, or the light, or the shaking.

Captain Tolin wept because as one, the Valni did something he'd never seen one do, and never thought he would. The Valni fled.

As one the Valni stopped attacking and ran. Ran back toward where the barrier had been, ran away from the Reach, and ran away from the Church of the Eight.

The hammer sound came one last time, a huge sound, and more than a few of the remaining survivors held their ears at the sound. Its echoes grew, and doubled over each other for a rising second, before fading away and silence returned.

And there, on that blood-stained square, where heaps of dead, covered with the bodies of the Valni and Reachers alike, Captain Tolin cried.

***

Duncan blinked. The red fog, the voices, the anger and hate, the dreams of death and killing faded, how long had it been? He hurt. His jaw and back burned with pain as if he had not moved the muscles in days. Where was he? What had happened?

A quick glance and he knew, he wasn't anywhere he wanted to be. A group of men in brown and red robes were all yelling at each other, many of them had long black knives drawn, and several were wet with blood. He was in some dusty ravine, dry rocks everywhere, and he couldn't see anything that resembled home.

A vague memory of Rache, no... Zalkiniv came to him, a cave? But the surge of emotion at the thought of the woman who betrayed him, who had never been the person he thought she was pushed it aside. She had betrayed him! Memories came flooding back. The prison cell, the torture, all the killing she had made him do.

Nausea crept up as he remembered tearing a man's throat out, all for a horse to ride. Anger and sadness warred in his heart, but not the anger of before. This was anger born of being forced to do something he hated, something against his will. There was something about Haltim, his last memory of the old Priest was yelling at him about Rache, something he now regretted. He hoped the old Priest of Amder would forgive him.

Moving his head, a throb of pain pushed up his neck, but he got a better look of what was around him. There was blood, fresh on his clothes and the surrounding ground. Not his though it didn't appear. Too fresh. The sight of it made his mouth water, a feeling he pushed down, with some effort. So that Curse was still very much with him. Why had he been released from the hell that Rache had put him in?

The sky was also strange, it was night, but it was lit up in such a way that made it... pale. And while he could not understand the men nearby, the glances up at the sky and the gestures made him think, they didn't like it, whatever it was. One robed figure gave a yell, and waved a blood-stained knife in the air, breaking through the noise.

He yelled at the others, in whatever language they spoke, and to Duncan's sudden realization, pointed at him with his dagger. He realized his doubts when four of the robed figures left the group and approached him. As they got closer, he forced himself to not react. The four were all men, and four of the roughest looking people Duncan had ever seen. Covered with visible scars, and fresher cuts. Some badly healed. And the smell... Duncan had once come across a merchant's wagon out scaving, it had been attacked by some wild animal, and parts of the horse remained, but had been sitting out in the sun for a week, that was a mild smell compared to these men.

Two grabbed his arms, leading him toward the others. Duncan dragged his feet, not sure what they wanted, but it couldn't be anything he wanted to be a part of. Approaching the group, it parted to a scene that both brought a small sense of satisfaction and a far larger one of terror to his already overwhelmed feelings.

An altar stood in a larger open section of the ravine, an altar covered with blood, and the bodies of multiple men and women were strewn around, necks cut blood soaked. Followers of the blood god then, he was still in the proverbial forge fire. The figure on the actual altar that gave him the only sense of satisfaction he'd had in an untold amount of time. For the person on the altar, not breathing, was Rache. She was dead!

His only regret was that he hadn't seen it as himself as the real Duncan. She deserved whatever had happened to her. The man who had ordered the others to take him stood in front of the altar, raising his hands yelling in the same harsh language. One good look and Duncan knew what was to happen, and whatever happiness, if that was the right word, felt at the end of Rache fled, and despair filled him.

In one hand of the chanting man, a long wooden staff, black in the dim light, and in the other something that brought a chill to his soul. The blade. That thrice cursed blade of the Blood God! One nick, a thin cut, and his life had fallen into madness. There could be no doubt, they would sacrifice him to the Blood God.

Duncan had no intention of letting them do that. They didn't know he was awake, which was the one advantage he had. He closed his eyes and wished he could say goodbye to William. Something William had said to him in the prison circled him, he couldn't remember it all, but he had blamed himself for everything. *Typical Will.* None of it was his fault. Duncan knew, his own greed had been the base cause. If he hadn't gone back to that tomb alone if he hadn't broken into it... none of this would have happened.

The yelling Priests voice grew louder, and Duncan opened his eyes and knew his time was short. One chance then. He'd die, but he wouldn't be a sacrifice, not now. Duncan had always been strong, a wiry strength, the last span of time had only in some ways made him stronger. Without a word he wrenched his arms free of the men holding him.

With all his strength, he launched himself at the man holding the blade and whatever that staff was. The man's voice cut off midway through some dark prayer, as Duncan's head met his midsection full on, knocking the wind out of the man. Retching from the smell of the robes that had gotten half wrapped around his face, he knew he only had one chance. If the Priest was holding the blade up with that staff... it had to be part of the Spear that Haltim had spoken about once, long ago.

As the Priest fell both the blade and staff fell from his grip, just as Duncan had hoped. A noise rose from the other robed figures nearby, a voice of anger. Duncan reached for the blade and staff, his fingers finding both surfaces, cold, but covered with a sticky liquid, blood. His Blood Curse roared to life at the touch of them both, a torrent of anger, and rage.

Kill... Kill them all... use the blade, kill them...

Duncan screamed; this was not who he was!

Kill... watch the blood blow, feel the skin give way... use their deaths, join the blade to the shaft...

His arms trembled, he felt forced himself to bring the two items together, for the glory of the Scaled One! His mind screamed this wasn't who he was, he was Duncan Reis, and he would never serve the Scaled God!

Let them die... fools they were... all. Join the blade and staff, and you will be my vessel on this place. I will lift you above all!

Duncan, the tiny part of who he was, fought the voice. But to fight a God is something a mortal can't do. His control slipped, the force before the words in his head, the words of Valnijz, overwhelmed his tiny scrap of self. He could feel it, his hopes, his self, and draining away under a landslide of hate and anger.

His eyes fell on the robed people around him, he could hear the blood flowing in their bodies, red, powerful, strong. Blood would flow, death would bring forth the Blood God!

A sound came then, the sound of a hammer striking metal, it echoed over the land, a rising crescendo of sound that left only two things in its wake. One was total silence as the voices, both external from the Priests, and internal vanished in its wake. The other was the return of his control. Duncan felt sick, the Blood had claimed him for a moment.

If Valnijz wanted the blade and shaft together too much, Duncan would oblige! *For you William, I love you cousin.* With a burst of effort, Duncan hammered the blade into the middle of the shaft, the metal of the blade meeting the wood with an explosion of its own. The shaft cracked, then broke in half in his hands.

A scream. A scream of hate sounded around him as the Priests screamed in unison. A scream that didn't end. The ground shook with the force, the rock walls shivered, as the ravine collapsed from the force of the sound. Duncan hunched over; ears covered but still even unable to think. But he was happy for the first time in a long time. He had done it. The Scaled God would not be reborn tonight, nor any other. He would be free of the Blood, he would die here, but he would be free. He, Duncan Reis, had stopped a God.

Stumbling, he made his way to the fallen form of Rache. Emotions warred inside him. This person had brought so much pain to his life, so much hate, it had twisted his very soul. Still, he had feelings for who she had pretended to be. For that person he had thought he had known.

It was stupid. It was sad. He would die here, but his thoughts would not be on hate. His nightmare was over. A huge chunk of red stone fell, crushing half a dozen bodies, a few still screaming in tune with the sound that never ended. Another fell, half falling on the altar. And another, and finally, a whole wall collapsed, filling the ravine with rubble.

The sound trailed off, and silence ruled the now filled ravine.

73

The light faded out, and the last echo of the hammering sound that had brought tears to his face faded away with the light. It was over. Will wiped his arm across the tears the feeling of joy fading with the sound. "So, Amder is, what, alive?" Myriam asked peering down the hallway. "How do we know?"

"Well, I don't know. But I know we did it." Will felt his nerves. *Had they succeeded?* "Come on, I guess we need to look." Reaching to his belt, he felt for his hammer before he remembered it was gone.

"Lead the way kind sir." Myriam gave a semi-exaggerated bow as she spoke. Will felt a laugh spring forth, releasing a bit of the tension he carried.

"Fine, stay behind me, fair maiden smith." Will answered back and headed back toward the forge.

The walls they passed the closer they got to the Forge showed the heat that had boiled out into the halls. Black and dirty at first, the closer they got to the place the walls got smooth, and shiny. As if the heat form the forge had melted the rocks themselves. But what was surprising was that all, regardless of appearance were now freezing cold to the touch, no heat came from them.

They went to the door, but it was gone. Destroyed in the heat and reduced to a fine ash on the floor. But again, all was as cold as if the forge hadn't been used in a hundred years. The room looked the same from the hallway if darker and colder.

"Where's the body?" Myriam asked as she looked through the doors arch. "The forge is empty, no form, and no Hammer."

"I don't know. I expected Amder to be here, in front of us. Though that does sound crazy." Will bit his lip in thought. *What was going on?*

Will took a step into the smithy, and all changed.

He was back, back in the dream of Amder. And there, in front of him stood the God.

Shiny metal, swirled and glowing made up the form. The last time he'd been nothing more than a vague outline, a shadow of a God. Now, he was here. His face, both wise and strong watch Will with a smile, one that grew bigger as Will entered the smithy.

"William Reis you have done it!" Amder's voice boomed in the space. "I knew you would, but I live once more!" Amder hefted the hammer that half an hour before Will had used.

"I Amder, God of Creation and Craft, Name you my Forgemaster. Place your hammer on the anvil William and take my sign." Amder pointed the anvil that dominated the room in a way it had not before. In fact, the more Will looked around, he noticed many changes. The forge was smaller by far, the anvil larger. The bellows, gone.

"My lord Amder, I put it in the forge, it had part of your spark. Part of you." Will answered. *I'll miss that hammer.*

"Nonsense. It's right there, on your belt." Amder pointed and as if it had never been gone, it was back. "I wouldn't be much of a God of Craft and Creation if I couldn't remake a hammer, now could I?" Amder asked.

Will looked at his hammer, his creation. He tried to swallow but found his throat dry. As if in a trance, Will put his hammer on the anvil and stood back. He wasn't sure what Amder would do to it now, but he had gotten it back.

Amder approached the Anvil and raised his hammer, the room shifted to accommodate the size of them both. "I Amder, LIVE! Tonight, my fall has been reversed. All know this, my return was brought about by one man, one person. William Reis, I name my Forgemaster. He is the representation of all I hope and wish for all mankind. He will bear my mark, from this day to his last."

Will was numb, how could he do all that? And who was Amder talking to?

"Forgemaster William Reis. You have done everything I could have asked, at great cost. I thank you." And without another word, Amder brought his hammer down on Will's hammer. The peal was almost as loud as the final one that had signaled the Gods' return. And with the blow, his hammer changed.

Where once the hammer had been silvery white that shimmered in the light the head now had a distinct reddish yellow tint. Amder picked up Will's hammer and handed it to Will, who took it, all the while feeling like he was out of his own body, that every move was being controlled by someone else.

The other change was obvious. On one side still was the decoration he had made himself. The other which before had been blank, now bore a crest. A silver hammer and a golden anvil, surrounded by copper flames.

"My lord Amder, I don't know if I'm worthy of this. And who were you talking to?" William fought his urge to try to not be the focus of attention.

"My Priesthood, the Guild. All of them, good and bad now know the truth. We will see how that works out. And no one else could have done this. You have earned it William Reis. Do not doubt yourself. Never again." Amder waved his arms around the Smithy. "To live again, I had almost forgotten how it feels. I hope you like the change to your hammer; a good smith is always partial to his own tools." Amder's smile faded away. "William, I need to tell you something. Your cousin, Duncan."

"Duncan! Where is he? I need to go get him." Will couldn't believe in all this that he'd somehow forgotten Duncan.

"William, Duncan is gone." Amder's voice dropped. "I tried to find him, to save him, but..."

"Duncan can't be dead! If I did this, I was supposed to save him. He can't be dead!" Will yelled at Amder, disbelief giving weight to his words. "He isn't supposed to be dead! You're a GOD, do something!" Duncan had to be alive, he had to be.

Amder shook his head and lowered his head. "I can't. Your cousin did something I can't fix. I don't know the details, the place where it happened is hard to see. But I know the basics. Somehow, your cousin, he stopped my brother, Valnijz from being reborn. He broke the spear. Without that the Blood God will only exist as a dead God, and I can't think of a way he can return. He saved the world from ever having to face the Scaled One ever again." Amder paused and raised his head, eyes wet. "You should know, at the end, he was free. He chose to do it. He could have run, but instead he destroyed the spear."

Will leaned against the wall, sliding to the floor. Duncan was gone. Dead. It would be like him to sacrifice himself. Duncan had always crafted this persona of not caring, of being above it all, but when the time came, he'd be as unselfish as a person could be. His head hurt, his eyes burned, and everything he had done, everything he'd thrown himself into, had been to save Duncan.

And he'd failed in that task. His neck jerked as he tried to stop his sob that wanted to come. *Sparks burn you Duncan! We could have saved you!* But the thought came, Duncan didn't want to be saved, if it meant living with the curse.

"I'm sorry Duncan." William whispered. "I wanted to save you, but in the end, I guess you saved yourself, and a lot more people besides." Will sat for a few minutes, trying to gather his thoughts. "Amder how do we…" but Amder was gone.

Will climbed to his feet, and as he did so the Smithy changed again, back to how it should look, it shimmered and there was Myriam, looking at him with a stunned and terrified expression.

"What's the matter?" Will asked her as she continued to stare at him.

"Amder, he spoke! He spoke to everyone. He named you Forgemaster!" Myriam then, much to Will's surprise threw her arms around him, hugging him tightly for a moment before stepping back.

"Duncan is dead. He died saving us, stopping the Blood God from ever returning. He was the hero, I'm just the smith." Will blinked back tears. "I wish you could have met him; Duncan was quite the man."

Myriam rested a hand on his chest. "It's ok to mourn Will."

Will rubbed his arm across his eyes and face, wiping away the tears that still were on his face. He'd mourn more to be sure, but not now. Not here.

"I don't even know what a Forgemaster does all the time." Will hefted the hammer in his hand, the gold crest shimmering in its own light. "But… let's go figure that out." They ascended the stairs to find the Temple above, the Temple of Amder, changed. The bust of the Blood God was gone, leaving nothing but a pile of broken rock and dust. And Amder's now stood uncovered.

"William!" Regin burst into the Temple followed by Mr. Darrew and the Reachers. One less Reacher than before Will noted sadly. Blood was on each of them, and Regin was limping.

"What happened?" Will walked over to them. "Valni?"

"Yes Forgemaster Reis. This friend of yours Master Regin, was rather useful after all." Falkirk Darrew clasped Reign on the back. "Those blood raged creatures tried hard, but we held them off, even took down three before the sound came, and they took off running towards the Mistlands."

Regin swallowed. "William... Forgemaster Reis sorry, I..."

"Just Will please, at least for you and Myriam." Will held up a hand. "We can discuss the rest later."

"Well then William." Myriam walked towards the exit of the Church. "Let's go figure out what a Forgemaster does."

Will watched her go. She still called him William. Her anger and hurt were there, but maybe, in time, things would change. He wanted them to. *Just be honest lad, things will take their course.* The voice of Amder echoed in his head. *Go, spread the word.*

***

Amder the God of Creation and Craft had returned and named a new Forgemaster. The nightmare of the Blood God, the Scaled one, God of Rage and Destruction was over.

EPILOGUE

Dry wind swirled around fallen rocks and the crushed bodies of men in robes. Here and there, like some strange subterranean animal faint red tendrils would snake out from under cracks in the walls and from in between fallen boulders, only to jerk back and vanish.

Outside the wind everything was quiet. Silent. Not even the faint scurry of insects or buzz of flies to feast on the corpses that littered the area. No living thing would enter, even upon the pain of starvation. In the dawn hours a painfully thin wolf had approached the area, able to see the sprawled dead, but the air of the place had driven it away.

The sun rose, baking the end of the valley, filled with rubble and the dead, until....

Rocks shifted.

If you enjoyed this book, and would like to know when the author has more books coming out in this series and other books, please visit www.joshccook.com and join the newsletter. Giveaways, announcements of free books, and more.

Thank you,

Joshua C. Cook

INDEX

Alos - The world

Amder – God of Craft and Creation. Killed by the Blood God Valnijz at the end of the Kinwar. An event now known as the Godsfall.

Anvil Test – The final test a potential Guild Apprentice must undergo before fully becoming a member of the Guild. The practice piece the applicant has made must be struck against a special anvil in the Guildhall. The tone that is produced shows the level of skill the maker had. If the piece makes no sound, the applicant is rejected because they did not actually make the item.

Axessed – An ancient creature of the Blood God, now all but vanished, supplanted by the Valni. They were more intelligent, scaled men. Clawed, and ruthless.

Berog – A not uncommon predator of the Skyreach Mountains, appears as a large bear/cat hybrid.

Blood of Amder – The crystalized blood of Amder which fell when he died. As it is in the Mistlands, it is forbidden to try and get any because of the Blood mist. Legends say that if the Blood of Amder is added to a forge before crafting anything, the item made will be blessed and considered of the finest make.

Blood Memories – The knowledge of countless followers of the Blood God, kept in vials. Each vial contains thousands of memories and the lives of centuries. Used as a sort of living library of knowledge.

Blood Mist – The blood of Valnijz the God of Rage that also stays in the Mistlands where Valnijz fell. One touch of the mist will turn a human into a Valni. Nonhumans die screaming, in moments.

Bracer of Amder – A bracer made of multiple metals, made by Amder himself from the metal cloth that shrouded his Hammer. Made as a sign and tool for Haltim initially, it later was used at times to loosen the grip of Valnijz on Duncan Reis. It was also used as the 'seed' to start the reforging of Amder.

Bracin Monsteen – The High Priest of Amder, fully corrupt and dedicated to not allowing anyone to bring Amder back to life. He uses the Heart of Amder to enrich himself and cement his power.

Church of the Eight – The ancient temple just outside the Reach. Once dedicated to Amder only, after the Godsfall and the Church move to the capitol, Ture, was rededicated to all Eight Gods.

Claret Stone – Artifacts of the Blood God, the stones are similar in appearance to dark red rubies. They are in fact the crystalized blood of thousands of sacrifices to Valnijz. Once they are bound to the holder, they offer the wielder great power.

Cloud – A drug often used to escape sadness and other feelings. A single dose makes the imbiber unable to feel anything, not just pain, but anger, sadness, happiness, curiosity, etc. Often abused, and if too much is taken the effect is permanent. Those who have taken too much are said to have 'gone to the sky' and wander off to die.

Dernstown – A settlement on the southern end of the Skyreach Mountains. Known for its stone quarries. Dernstown is considered very out of the way, and rural.

Drendel – Unknown ancient race, only known from the rarely found items made of Drendel Steel.

Drendel Steel – Steel found only in old artifacts. Made by a race only known as the Drendel. Who or what the Drendel were is a mystery. Drendel steel is noted for its strength, and blue-green cast it has. It does not rust.

Duncan Reis – The cousin of William Reis, and one of the last two of the Reis family line. Thin and tall, Duncan is more daring and relaxed than William.

First Night – the traditional celebration of the Guild, when the potential Apprentices trade in their orange cloaks for grey ones, signifying acceptance as full Apprentices. Followed by a huge feast.

Forgekeeper – Servants of the Church of Amder and the Smithing Guild.

Forgemaster – An ancient blessed follower of Amder, a Forgemaster was a title given by the God itself. Forgemasters were charged with helping anyone in the land. The final Forgemaster was Justin Reis, who gave up his life so that Amder might be able to stop the Blood God.

Goldflake – Similar to normal Gold, Goldflake is rarer, its prime ability is that if you know how, anything inlaid with Goldflake will never come off.

Gorom – A very rare race that only follows Grimnor. Do not mix with other races except when they must.

Grimnor – God of the Mountains and Stone. Grimnor in the last several hundred years has started to be followed by more and more humans in Palnor, and elsewhere due to the death of Amder.

Guild Cloak – Cloaks worn by the Smithing Guild to denote rank. Potential Apprentices wear orange, full Apprentices wear grey. Journeymen wear Red, and full GuildMaster's wear blue.

Guild test – The testing done across the land for those who want to join the Smithing Guild.

Guildhall – the home of the Smithing Guild in Ture. Built by Amder himself. One of the two most powerful organizations in all Palnor, if not Alos.

Haltim Goin – The Priest assigned to the Church of the Eight in the Reach. Considers himself in his heart to just be a Priest of Amder.

Hammer of Amder – The Hammer used by Amder to craft anything, one of the most holy artifacts of his faith. Hidden after the Godsfall and lost.

Heart of Amder – Recovered after the Godsfall and used by the Priesthood of Amder to enrich themselves and grow in power.

Jaste Naom – Guildmaster in the Smithing Guild, he makes up the plan to get William Reis into the Guild. Known for not being formal and enjoying finding new Apprentices.

Justin Reis – Ancestor to both William and Duncan Reis, he was the final Forgemaster named before the Godsfall. He sacrificed his life to allow Amder to defeat Valnijz

Kilvar – A herding/droving town on the main road to Ture. Known for the huge number of sheep and goats, and the smell that many animals produces.

Klah – A sharp intensely garlicky spread from the Reach and eaten nowhere else. Made from two dozen raw garlic cloves, vinegar, salt, and hot pepper smashed together.

Markin Darto – The assumed name of William Reis when he entered the Guild. Supposedly from Dernstown.

Mistlands – The long rift valley that borders the barrier. Its name derives from the blood red mist from Valnijz's blood from the Godsfall that fills most of the valley.

Myriam VolFar – A potential Apprentice who joins William in Kilvar. Focuses on jewelry and fine skills. Comes from a family that owns a large Inn on the Southern Trader circuit, her paternal Grandfather was a Guild Smith.

Mistress Shal'ton – A Saltmistress Knowledge broker in Ture.

Mucker – Sewer cleaners and treasure seekers in Ture.

Narmack – A small white rodent native to the Skyreach Mountains. Its only use is its bile. Narmack bile is a potent anti-poison and venom.

Narmor – A large predator native to the foothills and mountains of the Skyreach, it usually poses no threat to humans unless hungry or in pain. Known for its very strong bite.

Palnor – A land originally blessed of Amder, ruled from Ture. It's King and nobles are mere figureheads now, subservient to both the Smithing Guild, and above them, the Church of Amder.

Rache Lontree – The fake name given by Zalkiniv, High Priest of Valnijz when she traveled with Haltim and Duncan.

Regin Hamsand – A Guildmaster of the Smithing Guild. As a Journeyman he traveled with Jaste Noam, and suspected Markin Darto of being from the Reach.

Saltmistress – A race of people blessed by the Ocean Goddess. Almost never found outside the Ocean or coasts.

Silverflake – Like Goldflake, Silverflake is identical to normal Silver. It does not tarnish however, and like Goldflake can be inlaid and never come off.

Skyreach Mountains – A long and large mountain range in Palnor. Very rich in metals and gems, the Skyreach is also littered with ruins. The only city in the Skyreach is the Reach.

Spear of Valnijz – The weapon of the Blood God. Broken at the Godsfall, the shaft of the spear was recovered by the Priesthood of Blood God. The blade of the spear was lost, and in fact was recovered by the followers of Amder. Legends, barely whispered in secret circles, say that if the Spear was remade, Valnijz would return.

The Barrier – A line of wardstones, made by the Priesthood of Amder using the Heart in the distant past, soon after the Godsfall. The Barrier makes it impossible for the Valni to pass. It is believed somewhat in error, that there is no way for followers of Valnijz to pass the barrier.

The Blade – The spearhead of the Spear of Valnijz. Lost for ages, it was hidden by the Priesthood of Amder. Its location was kept from being discovered by the fact that it was hidden with the Hammer of Amder, making the followers of the Blood God unable to pinpoint its location.

The Reach – The only city in the Skyreach Mountains, once the seat of Amder on Alos. Even today the city has the highest number of the followers of the dead god. It makes its living from mining and smelting.

The Shaft – The shaft of the Spear of Valnijz, recovered after the Godsfall by the faith of the Blood God. Using the Shaft one can exert control over the Valni, one of the only ways they can be controlled at all.

The Tempered – A sect in the Church of Amder that originally was dedicated to seeking out heresy, has been perverted and changed into a group of murders and torturers. They are fully dedicated to the current High Priest of Amder, and act as his secret guardsmen and police.
Trinil – A race of tall thin people, blessed by the Forrest God. Rare, but seen more often than other races. Trinil are known to have an ability to know when someone is lying.

Ture – Capitol of Palnor, and the largest city in that land. Home to both the Church of Amder, and the Smithing Guild. Also, home to the King of Palnor and his court. Parts of the city were built by Amder and are held still in a form of reverence.

Valni – Humans who exposed to the blood mist, turn into monsters. Anything they had been before was gone. Known to not feel pain, they never flee and attack in a mindless rage. It is known that if a Valni tastes a person's blood, and that person manages to escape somehow, they can be found by that same Valni.

Valnijz – The Blood God, God of Rage and Destruction. The Scaled One. A mad god, and now thankfully dead, defeated by Amder at the Godsfall.

Wight Iron – A near mythical metal, Wight Iron is very valuable. It is impossible to find as an ore, and only is found now as already made items or ingots. Its name comes from the sound the metal makes when it is struck. A long and loud moaning sound.

William Reis – One of the last two of the Reis bloodline, William Reis has for most of his life been after a goal that many in his family has had but failed at, to be a Guild Smith. William is stocky, strong, and somewhat naive.

Zalkiniv – The near immortal High Priest of Valnijz. Able with the use of Blood workings to transfer his/her spirit into new bodies as needed, Zalkiniv has been working for centuries to bring back the return of the Blood God. Having been stymied by the barrier, unable to find the blade of the Spear.

Printed in Poland
by Amazon Fulfillment
Poland Sp. z o.o., Wrocław